BOOK FOURTEEN IN THE RAIDING FORCES SERIES

ALWAYS SO FEW

PHIL WARD

A RAIDING FORCES SERIES NOVEL

Published by Military Publishers LLC Austin, Texas
www.philward.author.com

ISBN 978-1-7327669-3-8

Distributed by Military Publishers LLC
Cover design by Stewart Williams

For ordering information or special discounts for bulk purchases, please contact Military Publishers LLC at 3616 Far West Blvd., Ste 117, Box 215, Austin, TX 78731

DEDICATION

Wayne Decker, a true Texas cowboy, RIP.

COVER COLOR BY LUKE

RANDAL'S RULES FOR RAIDING

RULE 1: The first rule is there ain't no rules.
RULE 2: Keep it short and simple.
RULE 3: It never hurts to cheat.
RULE 4: Right man, right job.
RULE 5: Plan missions backward (know how to get home).
RULE 6: It's good to have a Plan B.
RULE 7: Expect the unexpected.

RAIDING FORCES
ONGOING OPERATIONS

OPERATION AVALANCHE—The invasion of Italy at Salerno.

OPERATION BOARDMAN—An A-Force/OSS deception plan which was designed to mislead the Axis into believing the real invasion would take place on Sardinia. (Cover for **AVALANCHE**—Joint deception operation)

OPERATION FIRE EATER — Small Raids Incorporated/ Strategic Raiding Forces small-scale raids on the hundreds of islands in the Aegean Sea.

OPERATION GOLDEN FLEECE — "Pinch" operations to capture Nazi encoding/ decoding equipment. Lt. Cdr. Fleming's project, aka OPERATION RED INDIAN.

OPERATION HUSKY—The Allied invasion of Sicily.

OPERATION LEAF EATER—Diamond interdiction program. Command and Control team—code name **CARD GAME**, consisting of Col. Randal, Major the Lady Jane Seaborn, Captain "Geronimo" Joe McKoy, Captain Billy Jack Jaxx, Waldo Treywick, Captain Pamala Plum-Martin, Mandy Paige, Beverly Blackwell, and King.

MANHATTAN PROJECT—The most important military undertaking in U.S. history.

OPERATION OVERLORD—The eventual Allied invasion of enemy-occupied France being marshaled in Great Britain.

OPERATION PURPLE—Mission to obtain serial numbers from German tanks

OPERATION RED INDIAN—Mission to STEAL: Strategic Taking and Extracting to an Alternate Location, aka OPERATION GOLDEN FLEECE.

OPERATION TORCH—Largest armada in the history of the United States to ever set sail with the intention of invading of a foreign power; the most ambitious, complex, high-risk amphibious operation at that time.

OPERATION ULTRA SECRET—The penetration of the German Enigma encoding machine.

OPERATION ZEPPELIN—a Top Secret deception plan designed to deceive the German High Command, meaning Hitler, into believing Allied intentions were to invade the Balkans.

SITUATION

Eleven major islands in the Dodecanese form a front facing the Allies on the northern seaboard of the Mediterranean. They are primarily garrisoned by detachments from the German 22nd Air-Landing Division and the Italian 33rd Mountain Division. The German and the Italian regular divisions are supported by the infamous Nazi Division, a penal unit made up of violent convicts released from prison.

Over 276 smaller islands dot the Aegean—not all are inhabited. The Wehrmacht does not have the resources to station sizable units of troops on every one of them. The Germans have resorted to occupying the more populated islands with company-sized garrisons for a few weeks and then rotating them to other big islands on a regular basis.

Raiding Forces is tasked with harrying the German and Italian personnel stationed on the remote smaller islands, in an effort to force the enemy to reinforce them with troops that the Axis can ill afford to tie up guarding isolated outposts of little military value. The mission is classic Economy of Force. A small number of rigorously trained, highly motivated, well-led special operation troops—never numbering more than 400 men scattered over a vast theatre of operations—will attempt to tie down as many as eight enemy divisions.

Colonel John Randal has orders to carry out a clandestine, small-scale, amphibious guerrilla war. Due to exigent circumstances, it will have to be fought mostly at night over long distances from motor gun boats, caiques, or amphibious aircraft by small teams of Raiding Forces. The days of swashbuckling buccaneers, military adventurers, and licensed privateers is back.

**The United States is refusing to provide substantive air or naval support for what it considers to be a peripheral theatre of operations that diverts resources from the campaign in Italy and draws down on the buildup for OPERATION OVERLORD—the eventual invasion of enemy-occupied France being marshaled in Great Britain.*

***Adolf Hitler has no intention of giving up the Aegean without a fight*

RANKS, AWARDS AND NICKNAMES

PROTOCOL FOR RANKS:

The first time a person is named in a chapter or after a chapter break their full rank and name is given. In the military rank is respected. At all levels rank is earned and those who have it from a corporal to a four-star general are proud of it.

DECORATIONS:

In the British military officers are authorized to put the initials of their decorations after their name. In the Raiding Forces Series the protocol is the first time an officer is introduced in a book the initials of his decorations are listed following his name. After that for the rest of the book they are not.

In the U.S. military officers do not have the same privilege.

NICKNAMES:

In the British military nicknames are endemic. Radio operators are called Sparks, red heads are called Ginger, tall people are called Lofty but sometimes short people are called that too etc.

In the U.S. military there are a lot of nicknames but nothing like the British.

THE MISSION

OPERATION FIRE EATER: Small Raids Incorporated/ Strategic Raiding Forces.

PHASE I. Attack Enemy Shipping: The *Kriegsmarine* does not have enough shipping in the Aegean, even though the Nazis have built, brought in coastal craft, and/or chartered boats locally—primarily motorized sailing schooners and caiques. However, with their far-flung garrisons to supply, the Germans will never be able to acquire resupply ships in the numbers needed. Therefore, shipping is where the enemy is most vulnerable.

Nazi shipping and sea lines of communications are to be attacked relentlessly until the enemy is starving and no longer possesses the capability of supplying, reinforcing, or evacuating their troops from the small remote islands they occupy throughout the Aegean Theatre of Operations.

PHASE II. Strike Outlying Enemy-Occupied Islands: Attacks are to be focused on the most remote enemy garrisons. The idea is to pin down the German occupiers and trigger reinforcement of islands of no real military value with troops best employed elsewhere. Having to supply the additional manpower sent to strengthen the far-flung islands will place an even greater burden on *Kriegsmarine* shipping because, after arriving on their remote outposts, the additional troops will have to be supplied.

PHASE III. Piracy, Banditry, and General Hell Raising: Every inhabited island is targeted to be raided by land and sea elements of Small Raids Incorporated/Raiding Forces. Operational tempo shall be nonstop. Isolated, hated by the

Greek islanders, short of food, afraid to sleep because of the constant threat of being attacked under cover of darkness, without mail or willing female companionship, the Axis soldier's morale is bound to deteriorate—making them a softer target for Raiding Forces when they come calling.

*The *Kriegsmarine* has a plan to counter these moves. Throughout the Aegean, it has stationed small coast-watching teams on the most distant islands, usually consisting of a petty officer and three sailors with a long-range radio to maintain a shipping watch.

**These small teams of enemy coast-watchers are the target of choice of Small Raids Incorporated/Raiding Forces.

EXECUTION

Because the need for overland gun jeep raiding has been eliminated by the collapse of Rommel's Panzerarmee Afrika, Raiding Forces is being reorganized to conduct small-scale, long-range amphibious raiding operations in the Aegean Theatre of Operations. Due to a critical shortage of surface ships, the Royal Navy Director of Operations Division (Irregular), Vice Admiral Sir Randolph "Razor" Ransom, has begun raising a fleet of armed caiques (motorized sailboats) —styled the "Levant Schooner Flotilla" (LSF), under the command of Lieutenant Commander Adrian Seligman—to serve as troop transports.

The idea is to develop a striking force for small-scale raids against enemy commerce and isolated garrisons, insert/extract agents for the Inner Services Liaison Department (ISLD)—the cover name for MI-6, the British Secret Intelligence Service (SIS)—MO 4—the cover name for Special Operations Executive (SOE)—and to bring out evaders for MI-9 (Escape) under the direction of Mrs. Veronica Paige. Brigadier Dudley Clarke's A-Force, Political Warfare Executive (PWE), and the Office of Strategic Services (OSS), will also be clients.

Strategic Raiding Forces located at Raiding Forces Headquarters (RFHQ) outside Cairo with an Advanced Base on Castelrozzo Island (ABC) will be the controlling authority. However, a battle is brewing for control of raiding operations in the Aegean Sea, with Middle East Command Headquarters (MEHQ) setting up its own Director of Combined Operations (DCO).

Due to the inter-service character of the missions, a small joint executive known as Small Raids Incorporated (SRI) is also to be located at RFHQ, with offices in Alexandria and on Castelrozzo, chaired by VAdm. Ransom. SRI will select targets, coordinate organization and training, serve as liaison between the various services, allocate troops, boats, and aircraft for the operations, and assist the subordinate commanders with the detailed planning and mission preparation necessary for their individual raids

Colonel John Randal has the dual role of Commander of Raiding Forces and Deputy Commander of Small Raids Incorporated. His command will now consist of an expanded Sea Squadron, the Special Air Service, the Long Range Desert Group (LRDG) recently retrained as parachute/amphibious/mountain-qualified reconnaissance operators, the Special Boat Section (SBS), and the Greek Sacred Squadron (GSS).

By any measure, this is one of the most eclectic groups of cutthroats to ever set sail.

1

PLAY HIGH, IMPROVISE, AND DARE

THE TWO SLEEK 55-FOOT SEA SQUADRON MAS BOATS (*motoscafo armato silurante*), captured at Massawa on the Red Sea following the Abyssinian Campaign in East Africa and pressed into service by Raiding Forces, were pounding across the midnight waters of the Aegean at top speed—in excess of 50 mph. While they were called "torpedo-armed motorboats" there were no torpedoes on these boats. They had been replaced by U.S. Navy NH9605 Elco Thunderbolt gun mounts.

The Thunderbolt mounts came in several configurations. On these boats, the armament, which could be operated by a single gunner, consisted of a pair of 20mm cannons with an additional six .50 caliber machine guns all firing in unison. Four pairs of

.50 Browning M-2 machine guns manned by other sailors were bolted along the length of each craft wherever there was space available. While this was not heavy firepower by naval gunnery standards, any small enemy vessel—E-Boat or F-Lighter—that was engaged was going to be in for a nasty surprise.

The hope tonight was that none would be encountered.

Twenty of Captain Billy Jack Jaxx's Small Operations Group operators were on one boat crammed in like sardines. The 1st Platoon (-), B

Company, 10th Ranger Battalion, under the command of Captain Roy Kidd, was on the other. The 10th Rangers should not have been there tonight, but they were.

When the 575th Parachute Infantry Regiment (-) (Separate) (Special) was being withdrawn from Sicily after capturing a strategic bridge on the night prior to D-Day during OPERATION HUSKY, Colonel John Randal and SOG were flown back to Raiding Forces Headquarters outside of Cairo. The remainder of his troops, which should have consisted of the 1st Battalion 575th PIR, were put on board a fast troop transport to return by sea. However, Major Jack Dance, the commander of the 10th Ranger Battalion (Airborne), had loaded his troops as well.

The 10th Ranger Battalion had not been assigned to Raiding Forces. He did not have orders to make the movement. So why go absent without leave? Maj. Dance had overheard Colonel James "Jumping Jim" Gavin, the commander of the 505th Parachute Infantry Regiment (PIR), 82nd Airborne Division, telling his boss, Major General Matthew B. Ridgway, that he wanted to have the Rangers broken up and used as replacements for the losses the 505th PIR had incurred during the drop on Sicily.

The 10th Ranger Battalion was what was known in the military as a "bastard" outfit because it did not have a parent organization—it was an independent. Like all the Ranger Battalions, it was "provisional," meaning not a formal part of the military establishment. There was always the risk of being disbanded at the whim of a theatre commander due to exigent circumstances.

Maj. Dance was not about to let that happen if he could help it. So, he set sail for Egypt on his own initiative. What was the worst the army could do—send him to WWII?

To say that Col. Randal was surprised to see the 10th Ranger Battalion disembark when he went to the dock to greet his returning troops would be an understatement. Captain "Geronimo" Joe McKoy, standing next to him when Maj. Dance and his Rangers landed, said, "Never look a gift horse in the mouth, John."

Col. Randal said, "I don't intend to."

The funny thing was, no one ever seemed to miss the 10th Ranger Battalion—all 245 of them. Actually, what arrived at RFHQ was the 10th Ranger Battalion (-) because fifty-two Rangers had been misdropped on the night of HUSKY and were still classified MIA; eleven Rangers had been killed either assembling or during the fight at the bridge; and the company that did not make the jump had been left behind to guard Lieutenant General Dwight D. Eisenhower's Allied Force Headquarters.

Col. Randal wasted no time integrating the 10th Rangers into Raiding Forces. Nothing had come of a previous request to Brigadier General William "Wild Bill" Donovan for 100 ordnance men to replace the paratroopers from the 1/575th PIR, who were currently detailed to OPERATION PURPLE to collect the serial numbers off the gearboxes of shot-out German panzers in order for the Office of Strategic Services to determine the monthly production rate of enemy tanks. The hundred troops were lost to Raiding Forces.

Raiding Forces had a new mission, and it was undergoing a complete reorganization. Col. Randal could not get his men back from PURPLE. He needed Maj. Dance's Rangers.

So, he kept them.

Tonight, the men of the 1st Plt., B Co., 10th Rngr. Bn.—the same platoon that had sailed up the Sebou River on the USS *Dallas* with Col. Randal to capture the Port Lyautey Airfield and had jumped on Sicily with the 575th PIR—were about to get their initiation into small-scale amphibious raiding.

Only this mission might not turn out to be so small.

Porcupine, a sixty-ton brigantine belonging to the LSF (not to be confused with the HMS *Porcupine,* a damaged destroyer being towed back to England) had experienced engine trouble and put in at Vatrachos on Serifos Island to effect repairs, believing incorrectly that there were no enemy troops present. It was promptly captured. Major the Earl George Jellicoe, DSO, MC, Commander of the Special Boat Section, had dispatched an eight-man team to rescue the *Porcupine* in the belief there was only a small Italian garrison on the island.

Unknown to Lord Jellicoe, a company-strength contingent of Germans from the 999th Light Afrika Division had recently arrived on Vatrachos. It captured the SBS operators. An ominous development. Hitler's infamous Commando Order of 1942 required all special operations troops to be executed immediately or turned over to the *Sicherheitsdienst*, SD–Security Police, for harsh interrogation prior to being shot.

Word of the *Porcupine* reached Vice Admiral Sir Randolph "Razor" Ransom, VC, KCB, DSO, OBE, DSC, RN, the Royal Navy Director of Operations Divisions (Irregular) and Chairman of SRI. He ordered Col. Randal to proceed to Vatrachos with all due speed "to put things right."

When VAdm. Ransom wanted a thing done, he wanted it done—and do it now. Col. Randal said, "Yes, sir." Then swung into action.

Capt. Jaxx was ordered to assemble Small Operations Group (SOG). Maj. Dance was directed to provide Lieutenant Chase Starrett's platoon of Rangers. Brandy Seaborn was instructed to make her MAS boat ready for sea. Her son, Lieutenant Randy "Hornblower" Seaborn, DSO, OBE, DSC, RN, the commander of Raiding Forces' tiny fleet of Patrol Torpedo (PT) boats, MAS boats, and the Motor Gun Boat (MGB) 345, was to take personal command of the second MAS Boat.

It had been dumb good luck Hornblower was at RFHQ when the orders for the mission came down. Lt. Seaborn may no longer have been the youngest officer in his grade in the Royal Navy, but he was arguably the most battle-experienced small boat skipper.

Mandy Paige and Beverly Blackwell were dispatched to call on all of the intelligence gathering organizations with offices in Cairo to obtain current information about Vatrachos.

The girls drew a blank.

With nothing to go on, Col. Randal issued a Warning Order that was basically, "We have a mission. Get your gear. Prepare to move out—I'll get back to you with details."

The two captured Regia Marina MAS boats were primarily used by SRI for clandestine missions for MI-6 (Secret Intelligence Service), Special Operations Executive and MI-9 (Escape). The 50-foot "fast motor torpedo boats" were paired up for the mission to maximize their blazing speed. Since the Italian boats were not as large as either a PT boat or a Motor Gun boat, both were needed to transport Col. Randal's party tonight.

Capt. Jaxx, Lieutenant Clint Hays, Ensign Theodore Hamilton, OBE, aka "The Great Teddy" and SOG were on Lt. Seaborn's boat. Col. Randal, Capt. Kidd, Capt. McKoy, Lt. Starrett and Lieutenant Dan Bonham were on Brandy's. A four-man team of the Long Range Desert Group, recently extensively retrained as parachute/mountain/ amphibious/reconnaissance operators, were also aboard. There was little chance the LRDG would ever see another desert in this war, but they stubbornly insisted on retaining "Desert."

The LRDG had been alerted that it was to be attached to Raiding Forces permanently.

The small, two-boat element of Sea Squadron was headed into the great unknown—Vatrachos Island. What was to be found there was a complete mystery. What *was* known was that the enemy held Rhodes—which was en route. There was an enemy airfield on the island. Aircraft flying off of it posed a serious threat should the MAS boats not reach their objective before sunrise.

At one point, the channel between Rhodes and the coast of Turkey narrowed to some seven miles. The two boats, with Brandy Seaborn's leading the way and Captain Penelope "Legs" Honeycutt-Parker, OBE, GM, RM, serving as the navigation officer, entered the restricted waters at high speed and made ready to run the gauntlet.

If the Kriegsmarine or the Regia Marina were on their game, they would have picket boats patrolling the channel to prevent Raiding Forces or any other Royal Navy surface craft from infiltrating the Aegean.

None were spotted—the two MAS boats continued their mission.

The next checkpoint was Cape Krio—jutting out westward from the Turkish coast. A Turkish lighthouse on the point was lit. And while the sight was comforting in that it confirmed Capt. Honeycutt-Parker's navigation, the light also illuminated the MAS boats.

Nothing happened.

The two boats powered on in the direction of the large Italian-occupied island of Kos, which also had an airfield near the village of Antimachia. Passing through the strait between Kos and the mainland, the Turkish peninsula jutting out from Bodrum posed a hazard, so Capt. Honeycutt-Parker set a course for Leros where there was another narrow channel between the island and Kalymnos to the south. The strait was shallow and possibly mined.

Standing on "nevertheless," the two Royal Navy-flagged MAS boats arrived before dawn off Serifos Island without incident.

The LRDG reconnaissance patrol, augmented by a member of Major Zargo's GSS acting as their interpreter and the mercenary soldier King, was rowed ashore by a Lifeboat Serviceman. Their mission was to slip in, make contact with one of the local population to ascertain how many enemy personnel were on the island, where the crew from the *Porcupine* and the SBS operators were being held, and any other pertinent information Col. Randal could use to develop a rescue plan.

It was a high-risk assignment—the team had to remain on Vatrachos all day.

As soon as the Lifeboat Servicemen returned, the MAS boats immediately made a mad dash to an uninhibited island twenty miles away. The plan was to lay up under camouflage during the day and then return to pick up the LRDG team the following night. Ens. Hamilton was along to supervise concealing the boats.

Working with a sense of life-and-death urgency while using the young officer's custom-tailored netting and bamboo poles, in less than half an hour the MAS boats could not be distinguished from the rugged cliff face from ten yards away. Like The Great Teddy was quick to explain, the idea was not to make whatever he intended to hide invisible—it was to make it look like something else. All that any aircraft or passing boat was going to spot were jagged rocks.

The illusion was amazing.

Col. Randal, Lt. Seaborn, Brandy, and Ens. Hamilton had one of the Lifeboat Servicemen row them in an assault raft to inspect the finished work from seaside.

Col. Randal said, "Outstanding, Ensign." Brandy said, "You *are* 'The Great Teddy.'"

Ens. Hamilton said, "Not that difficult, actually."

Col. Randal asked, "Can you teach this level of camouflage skill to all our crews?"

"Absolutely, sir."

Col. Randal ordered, "When we get back to Castelrozzo, commence training for all hands immediately. No boat or caique sails until you certify the crew capable of meeting your standards. Be a hard grader, stud."

"Sir!"

CAPTAIN BILLY JACK JAXX'S SMALL OPERATIONS GROUP and Captain Roy Kidd's 1st Platoon, B Company, 10th Ranger Battalion, took turns coming up on the deck of their boats for a rotation of fresh air. Unfortunately for the men, there was no swimming allowed in the inviting turquoise blue water. An enemy E-Boat might appear at any moment.

The two MAS Boats might be invisible. A group of swimmers—no way to hide.

Colonel John Randal debated stationing a lookout at the top of the cliff. He eventually elected against the idea, which may not have been the best decision. Raiding Forces still had a lot to learn about small boat operations in the Aegean. What they were doing was completely different from the early days of small-scale pinprick raiding across the English Channel out of Seaborn House against targets on the Enemy-Occupied French Coast.

Two things were immediately clear to Col. Randal. Axis airpower controlled the Aegean by day. Raiding Forces owned the night. They could pick their targets, strike at will, and be gone. And there was nothing the Germans or Italians could do about it.

Because of a total lack of intelligence—no maps of the interior of Serifos Island and no local expert along to provide information—Col. Randal left his junior officers and the troops to relax prior to the night's mission. Most spent the time sleeping, reading paperbacks or working on their gear, though no weapons were to be disassembled at this point in the mission because they could not be test-fired after being reassembled.

SOG invested a lot of energy in sharpening their Fairbairn Fighting Knives. Col. Randal observed their effort with amusement. Except for King, not one man present had ever eliminated a sentry with a knife.

However, the enthusiasm the Raiders put into honing their blades to perfection did give him something to think about. Raiding Forces had gone through the Special Warfare School at the Commando Depot located in Achnacarry, Scotland. Upon graduation, the Raiders had been awarded the stilettos they carried with pride. The 10th Ranger Battalion, the Long Range Desert Group, Special Air Service, Special Boat Section, and Greek Sacred Squadron now made up the larger part of his command, and not having the benefit of attending the Commando Training Center, they did not have Fairbairn Fighting Knives.

There was no way all of them were going to be able to attend training at the Commando Depot. A large shipment of the highly coveted Fairbairn Knives was never going to be shipped to troops who had not successfully completed the Special Warfare School. They were an item of equipment only issued to Achnacarry graduates.

Col. Randal did not much care for the term elite. Every soldier wanted to be thought of as elite. If everyone was elite, then no one was elite. One thing that was not going to happen on his watch was for there to be an elite within an elite.

Raiding Forces needed its own unique symbol of excellence. What might that be?

He had no idea but intended to give the subject thought.

It was not unpleasant spending the day on Brandy's MAS boat. Time idled by. Lying up for sundown on what was basically a motor yacht in the Aegean was considerably more enjoyable than sitting in a laager under camouflage netting on a gun jeep patrol in the Great Sand Sea. Whether it was at a departure airfield prior to a jump, a patrol base in the desert, or rocking gently at anchor on a speed boat standing by to execute the next mission, one thing was exactly the same—hurry up and wait.

The waiting to launch was the hard part.

At long last, the sun plopped into the sea. Unlike sunset in the desert, where dark was almost instantaneous, the spectacular colors in the Aegean took their time fading away—becoming even more beautiful as they mellowed. As dark settled in, anticipation spiked on the MAS boats.

Camouflage netting was taken down and stowed. Troops broke out rations and ate their evening meal. Tonight's plan called for them to be standing off the beach where the rendezvous with King and the LRDG recon patrol was waiting to take place at 2100 hrs. The two boats eased away from their cliffside hideaway, cruising at a sedate 10 mph.

Everyone was glad to be underway at last, even if the speed was mind-numbingly slow.

It was dark. The moon had not yet come up when the boats hove to off the beach.

Almost immediately a red, filtered light flashed two shorts, one long—the correct authentication signal.

The boats idled in almost to shore, running on their virtually silent electric auxiliary engines. Col. Randal, Captain "Geronimo" Joe McKoy, and Capt. Jaxx slipped off the side of the MAS boat and waded to the beach. King and the LRDG patrol leader, Corporal Leslie Cooper, were waiting.

Col. Randal said, "Give me a report, Corporal."

Cpl. Cooper said, "The Greek Sacred Squadron lad and your man, King, made contact with a local from the town. A company of the 999th Light Afrika Division was on the island when the SBS came to rescue the *Porcupine,* sir. The Nazis executed the entire eight-man patrol in accordance with Hitler's Commando Order—shot them publicly in the town square.

"The crew of the *Porcupine* are being held under guard on the ship, sir." Col. Randal said, "How many German troops in the company?"

Cpl. Cooper said, "Believed to be approximately one hundred men, sir. The Nazis use a warehouse near the pier as their troop barracks.

"According to our Greek contact, the 999th Light Afrika Division troops have unleashed a reign of terror against the islanders, sir. No woman is safe from being molested—even during broad daylight. The local asserts that the Germans treat rape like a spectator sport.

"The company commander, one Oberleutnant Wurst, is described as mad. Our contact claims the captain walks down the street roaring drunk with a Luger in his hand, randomly shooting people in the head. He enjoys sleeping quarters at the mayor's residence where it is said he molests the mayor's thirteen-year-old daughter.

"Not like the desert—we fought a clean war, sir."

Col. Randal asked, "Do the Germans have patrols out?"

"Negative, sir. The soldiers maintain a self-imposed lockdown in their barracks after sundown. If you post guards out, someone has to go check on them—that is not about to happen on Vatrachos. The Germans may be brave bullies by day, but they are afraid to venture out in the dark, knowing the townspeople hate them with a passion."

King said, "The 999th Light Afrika Division is a penal unit made up of murderers, rapists, and pedophiles released from prison to join the Wehrmacht, Chief. Only violent offenders need apply—the worst of the worst. The idea behind the Nazis raising a penal division was to weaponize criminals.

"I do not believe our contact is exaggerating."

Capt. McKoy said, "Pack a' rabid dogs shootin' our SBS boys." Capt. Jaxx said, "I'm all about payback, sir."

Col. Randal said, "We'll see if we can arrange to make that happen."

BACK ON BOARD BRANDY SEABORN'S MAS BOAT, COLONEL John Randal assembled all his officers and Master Sergeant Mack Beckwith to issue a Raid Order below deck. Brandy and her son, Lieutenant Randy "Hornblower" Seaborn, attended. Brandy's legendary gunner, Guns, was present as was Gunnery Sergeant Frank Polanski, the Thunderbolt gunner on Lt. Seaborn's MAS boat.

On the deck in the sailor's billets, King had laid out—with whatever he could find—a hastily improvised and highly creative mockup of the dock area of Vatrachos. Everyone gathered around, paying close attention as Col. Randal used a cleaning rod from one of the Lovat Scouts' .30 M1 Garand rifles as a pointer. This was serious business. Following this Raid Order, they would give their own to their individual teams.

"Situation: An estimated one hundred-man company of the 999th Light Afrika Division occupies Vatrachos. The Germans are holding the Levant Schooner Flotilla's ship *Porcupine* at the dock located here, with its crew locked below deck."

With the M1's cleaning rod, Col. Randal tapped the leather rifle sling laying on the floor that represented the pier. The *Porcupine* was represented by a magazine from King's 1911 Colt .38 Super.

"The Germans are located in a warehouse on the east side of the dock."

Col. Randal tapped a .30 caliber ammo can of belted machine gun ammunition for Captain "Geronimo" Joe McKoy's highly modified U.S. Para-Marine "Stinger" LMG to indicate the barracks.

"Mission: Rescue the sailors on board the *Porcupine*, then kill or capture the Nazi 999th personnel located in the warehouse/barracks.

"Execution: The Concept of the Operation is to drop Captain Jaxx and his SOG personnel a half mile offshore in four rubber assault rafts. They will paddle to the dock, board the *Porcupine*, eliminate any guards they encounter with silenced .22 High Standard pistols and effect the rescue of the LSF sailors.

"While SOG is taking down the *Porcupine*, Captain Kidd will go ashore with his party of Rangers and set up an assault line approximately here."

Col. Randal pointed with the tip of the cleaning rod to a place seaside of the warehouse/barracks.

"My command party, the GSS operator with the local islander, and the LRDG team will land ashore at this point."

Col. Randal tapped a spot near the ammo can.

"After dropping off SOG, the Rangers, my command party, and the LRDG team, Brandy and Lt. Seaborn will reposition the MAS boats to the closest distance offshore that provides them unobstructed line of sight to the warehouse/barracks.

"While this is taking place, King, our GSS interpreter, the local islander, the LRDG patrol, and my command party will move overland from here to the dock area approximately here."

Col. Randal tapped the porcelain coffee cups representing the houses.

"King, the GSS interpreter, and the LRDG team will quietly evacuate the residents from these private residences located here, here, and here and move them to a position of safety out of the line of fire from the MAS boats.

"Once the civilians are safe, the LRDG will set up a blocking position behind the warehouse, making sure they are out of the line of fire from the MAS boats."

For a second time, Col. Randal tapped the coffee cups representing the houses. "My command party will travel with King, the GSS operator, and the LRDG team to the release point where they will peel off to carry out their civilian evacuation assignment and then set up their blocking force.

Lovat Scouts Ferguson and Fenwick will accompany me to approximately here."

Col. Randal tapped the tip of the leather rifle sling, which represented the land side end of the pier.

"Captain Jaxx will signal me with three flashes of his red filtered flashlight when the rescue of the crew on the *Porcupine* has been effected. I will then fire a green flare, followed by a white for illumination. That's the signal for the MAS boats to commence fire on the enemy troop barracks/warehouse with all organic weapons.

"Once the building has been reduced to my satisfaction, I'll put up three red flares to signal check fire. As soon as the firing has stopped, I'll put up a green flare. Captain Kidd and the Rangers will immediately assault the barracks. Once it is secured, all personnel ashore will consolidate on the objective.

"At that point, the crew of the *Porcupine* will sail for home. The MAS boats will pull up to the pier to re-embark SOG, the LRDG, the Rangers, and my command party.

"We'll call it a night. "Questions?"

Captain Roy Kidd asked, "What am I supposed to do with the 999th troops we capture, sir?"

Col. Randal said, "The plan is to turn over the enemy weapons seized to the town's police force. Hand off your prisoners at that time. The local Greek officials can determine their disposition—it's their island.

"Any more questions? OK then, rejoin your troops—let's do this."

As the mission brief was breaking up, Col. Randal pulled Capt. McKoy aside, "Travel with me tonight, Captain. I want to see your Para-Marine light machine gun in action."

Capt. McKoy said, "Sounds like a plan."

Col. Randal said, "The Scouts can serve as your ammo bearers."

Ensign Theodore Hamilton, aka "The Great Teddy" said, "Sir, where do you want me?"

Col. Randal hesitated. He did not have an assignment for him tonight. The Great

Teddy had been brought along solely because of his camouflage skills. "You're on me—stay close, Ensign."

"Yes, sir!"

THINGS BEGAN HAPPENING FAST AFTER COLONEL JOHN Randal issued his order. Upon landing back ashore, Col. Randal, Captain "Geronimo" Joe McKoy, the two Lovat Scouts, and Corporal Leslie Cooper linked back up with the three other LRDG operators. Led by King, the GSS Greek interpreter, and the local islander, the group moved out. They had a little over a mile to cover.

The two MAS boats crash-started their electric auxiliary engines and glided silently into the night. Captain Billy Jack Jaxx aka Jack Cool on Brandy's boat, and Captain Roy Kidd on Lieutenant Randy "Hornblower" Seaborn's boat, issued their own Raid Orders to their troops. The men paid close attention. Once they were released, they checked their weapons and equipment for what must have been the hundredth time each.

The moon was up now and it was bright—a beautiful Mediterranean night. Col. Randal's party went ashore. The ground was flat with no volcanic rock, making for easy going. The order of march was King on point with the GSS man and the local islander, Col. Randal behind the point element, followed by Capt. McKoy and the Lovat Scouts, with the LRDG team bringing up the rear.

Out at sea, Lt. Seaborn hove to when he reached the point where he was going to offload the Rangers into their assault rafts. His mother continued silently on. When Brandy could see the pier through her night glasses, she cut the engine.

Capt. Jaxx, Master Sergeant Mack Beckwith, and the SOG operators, assisted by the MAS boat sailors, lowered their rubber assault rafts over the side and climbed in for the paddle to the pier. Disembarking from a boat into a bobbing assault raft is not a simple task even if the water is calm. Due to its unusually cool temperature, the Aegean was seldom still.

SOG was highly skilled in the procedure. They made it look easy.

The four assault rafts began paddling silently toward the pier. The wooden catwalk came into sight in short order. It was a beautiful night, but Capt. Jaxx would have been happier if the big, rat cheese yellow moon was not so bright.

Lt. Seaborn maintained station until Brandy rejoined. Then the two MAS boats silently eased their way toward shore. They were not concerned about being seen. If anyone did notice, they would see two Italian patrol boats.

So what?

The Rangers went over the side, waded ashore, and moved inland. Capt. Kidd had Lieutenant Chase Starrett out front leading the way. In minutes the column came to a halt.

Capt. Kidd moved forward to confer with Lt. Starrett. "Warehouse dead ahead, sir."

Word was passed back down the column for Capt. Kidd's other Ranger officer, Lieutenant Dan Bonham, to move forward to confer. On a training exercise, this would be the time to conduct a Leader's Recon—meaning the officers and possibly the NCOs would advance to physically observe the objective.

Whoever dreamed up the tactic had to have been drinking at the time. Certainly he had never led a patrol in enemy territory. On paper, a Leader's Recon was a wise and prudent thing for a commander to do—lay eyes on the target to confirm the best tactical deployment of his troops and to personally point out to his subordinates what was expected of them in order to prevent confusion during the attack.

Worked swell on graded field training exercises during peacetime maneuvers. Almost like cheating—which was probably where the idea came from. For training exercises, the typical thinking of most Special Operations/Ranger/Commando types was, "If you ain't cheating, you ain't trying, and if you get caught, you weren't trying hard enough."

Col. Randal was a leading advocate of that line of thinking.

However, on an actual raid, having all the leaders travel in one small group to closely observe an enemy position prior to attacking it was at best high-risk and at worst criminally stupid. If the members of the Leader's Recon were killed or captured—which happens from time to time to patrols infiltrating no-man's land between the lines—who would take command of the troops left behind and continue the mission?

No commander in his right mind ever conducted a Leader's Recon except by doing a group map study, from extreme long range—like from a mountain top—or on the extremely rare occasion when there was an opportunity to go forward and take a look with little or no risk.

Tonight, conditions were perfect for a Leader's Recon done by the book. The enemy was known not to be out and about after dark for fear of reprisal from the local population. There was a hard point-type target to observe. And visibility was adequate.

Capt. Kidd whispered to his platoon sergeant, "Lt. Starrett, Lt. Bonham, and I are going to move forward to conduct a leader's reconnaissance. You remain here in command of the platoon. We'll be back in twenty minutes or less."

Technical Sergeant Ronnie Allred said, "Yes, sir." He did not sound enthusiastic.

Capt. Kidd said, "Don't worry. It's so bright you'll probably be able to observe us the entire time we're gone. Consider yourself in an overwatch position. If we don't make it back, you're in charge—continue the mission."

"Thanks a lot, sir."

Capt. Kidd made one last check of his weapons before moving out. He loved exotic firearms and was constantly experimenting with different makes and models, enemy and friendly. Tonight, in addition to the silenced .22 High Standard Military Model D Col. Randal had issued him during the siege at RAF Habbaniya, he was carrying the 9mm Lathi L-35 King had procured for him on a trip to Switzerland. The Finnish pistol was his absolute, all-time, most-favorite handgun ever—for the moment. It looked like a P-08 Luger but mechanically it was completely different.

Unlike a Luger, the Lathi was 100 percent reliable—it locked up like a steel vault. Capt. Kidd's primary weapon tonight was a chopped 13.2 pound, .30cal Browning Automatic Rifle with an oversized Cutts Compensator on its 18-inch barrel. Originally a standard issue BAR, it had been modified for Raiding Forces by Sergeant Roy Dunlop at the U.S. 27th Ordnance Company. As his model, Sgt. Dunlop used the extremely rare .30 Colt Monitor that Colt Manufacturing Company had presented

Capt. McKoy for his part in tracking down and killing the outlaws Bonnie and Clyde.

No one liked the name "Monitor"—Jack Cool called the one he carried a "Baby BAR." The name stuck. The cut-down Baby BAR weighed only 4 pounds more than a standard issue M1 Garand rifle.

Capt. Kidd wished a Baby BAR had been available when he had been assigned to eradicate man-eating leopards and tigers when he was stationed in India. An American serving in the British Army, Capt. Kidd had been loaned by his commander of the 1st Battalion King's Own Royal Regiment to the Colonial Department to eradicate man- eating leopards and tigers preying on the native population. Some of those tigers were over twelve feet and weighed close to 700 pounds. All he had to use was his service issue .303 Mark III Enfield Rifle.

He could have used the extra firepower.

The three-man officers' patrol moved out silently. Capt. Kidd, being a highly experienced hunter of big cats that would eat you, was one of the most talented practitioners of the art of fieldcraft. He moved like a phantom and seemingly had the ability to become invisible.

The Ranger lieutenants were suitably impressed.

On their line of march, the warehouse swam into sight almost immediately. Capt. Kidd halted and knelt down. Lt. Starrett and Lt. Bonham closed up and went down on one knee with him. The three were so close together they were physically touching.

They observed the objective for some time, but there was nothing happening— zero movement. Warehouses are built to store things. They are big, simple structures. This one did not have any windows. It did have one large sliding door located on the seaside of the building.

There may have been other entrances in back, but it was not worth the risk of exposure to move around behind to find out. If there were back doors, the LRDG blocking force would cover them with fire. That was the purpose of having a blocking force—to meet and greet the bad guys who ran out the back.

Satisfied he had seen everything worth seeing and having selected the best route to move his Rangers into position, Capt. Kidd whispered, "Pull back."

The three returned to the platoon. Lt. Starrett and Lt. Bonham rejoined their troops. Capt. Kidd said to T/Sgt. Allred, "No surprises—perfect setup."

Fifteen minutes later, 1st Platoon, B Company, 10th Ranger Battalion was in position with no one the wiser, standing by ready.

What might be described as a "bayonet charge" was in their future, except that there was not one bayonet or a single rifle in the platoon tonight—only 9mm Beretta MAB-38 submachine guns and .30 caliber Baby BARs. The Rangers were packing heavy with automatic weapons.

CAPTAIN BILLY JACK JAXX'S SMALL OPERATIONS GROUP was silently paddling their rubber assault rafts toward the pier. In the bright moonlight they could see the *Porcupine* tied off near the middle of the long, narrow dock on the port side. Six other caiques of varying sizes were moored at the wharf.

Capt. Jaxx's plan was as basic as he could make the task of capturing an enemy- held ship, which is not a simple tactical exercise. His raft, which was leading the way, would break off and land at the end of the pier while the other three continued on to the *Porcupine.* The man they called Jack Cool would lead five SOG operators down the quay, board the ship, and silently eliminate any guards above deck.

Simultaneously, the rest of his SOG operators, led by Lieutenant Clint Hays, would arrive and board the *Porcupine* utilizing scaling ropes held in place by grappling hooks tossed up from their rafts. On paper it was a good plan. However, in practice a lot could go wrong. The trick was to get on board quickly, eliminate the guards, and liberate the prisoners before the Nazis could kill them.

There was not going to be a second-place winner.

Small Operations Group consisted of handpicked men from an organization made up of handpicked men. It was the go-anywhere, do-anything-on-short-notice, ready reaction team that carried out Raiding Forces' most classified missions. Colonel John Randal was usually along to lead them—and he would have been tonight too, except the mission dictated that he be located ashore in a central location to best carry out command and control of the overall operation.

No reduction in performance was anticipated because of his absence. The SOG operators were Capt. Jaxx's boys—that's what they called themselves. They would follow him anywhere.

Tonight, SOG was going to have to put every bit of training, skill, and experience acquired over the past two years into a takedown that would require split-second timing, precise execution, stealth, speed, surprise, and violence of action.

Some advanced intelligence about the target would have been helpful, but there was none except for a hand-drawn schematic diagramming the below decks compartments, provided by Lieutenant Commander Adrian Seligman, the Commanding Officer of the Levant Schooner Flotilla. It was better than nothing.

Capt. Jaxx's raft nosed into the dock. He leapt out and tied off the rope. The five SOG operators on his team followed close behind. The night was almost too quiet for comfort.

Holding his silenced .22 High Standard Military Model D in both hands at the ready, Capt. Jaxx moved down the pier toward the *Porcupine.* He could see the ship in the moonlight. No one was visible above deck.

That did not mean there was no one from the 999th on board watching their every move right this minute. For all Capt. Jaxx knew, at this critical juncture the rafts had been spotted on the way in. The Nazis might be lying in wait.

Something to think about.

The immediate problem Capt. Jaxx faced was advancing up a fairly steep gangplank, because the *Porcupine's* deck was higher than the pier.

And that channelized them. His troops would be like ducks in a shooting gallery going up that plank if they were walking into an ambush.

As he neared the ship, Capt. Jaxx heard the chinks the grappling hooks made metal against metal as they started flying up and over the rail on the far side. The split- second timing part of the operation was working out as planned. In short order, there would be twenty-four hard-as-nails SOG operators swarming up those ropes with evil intent, a desire to commit mayhem, and a perfectly clear conscience.

Capt. Jaxx mentally reminded himself to look into taping the metal grappling hooks to silence them on future raids. He could have kicked himself for not thinking of that detail before.

When it came to his tactics, Jack Cool was a perfectionist.

SOG's canvas-topped, rubber soled raiding boots did not make a sound as they crept up the gangplank. Then Capt. Jaxx was stepping on board, moving like a big hunting cat. He saw Master Sergeant Mack Beckwith come over the rail amidships with his .22 High Standard in one hand and murder in his heart. The rest of his team was right behind.

They made eye contact and carried on with their appointed tasks.

No enemy personnel were found topside. Capt. Jaxx moved up the short flight of steps to the wheelhouse with two of his men right behind him. A German soldier was sleeping in a chair inside the door.

WHIIIIICH, WHIIIIICH, WHIIIIICH.

Three .22 rounds to the head—fast. The Nazi never made a sound. Capt. Jaxx was a wizard with a pistol.

While he was clearing the wheelhouse, Lt. Hays and M/Sgt. Beckwith led their teams below deck to attempt to locate the British sailors being held on board. Out of the moonlight, it was jet black. Flashlights were broken out.

Lt. Hays peeled off with his team to clear the engine room.

M/Sgt. Beckwith continued on to the berthing compartment where they encountered four Germans asleep in their hammocks.

The two SOG operators behind M/Sgt. Beckwith closed up, moving as if their action was a choreographed ballet. Slow is smooth. Smooth is fast.

On M/Sgt. Beckwith's whispered command, "Now," they all fired three rounds of silenced .22 rounds at the same time. No one missed. Four more members of the Master Race belonging to the 999th Light Afrika Division would not be doing any more murder, rape, or pedophilia—the price paid for failing to post an alert guard on deck.

Still, no sign of the British sailors.

Capt. Jaxx caught up to M/Sgt. Beckwith. A short set of steps led down to a door to the cargo hold. There was a heavy chain and a padlock securing it.

Having foreseen this contingency, a pair of bolt cutters was produced, and the lock was quickly cut. Staring into the sudden glare of flashlights, the British sailors on the far side took a couple of minutes to realize they had been rescued.

After the Nazis had forced them to witness the execution of the eight SBS men, the crew had been expecting to be shot. They thought this might be the night. Once they realized they were actually safe, the sailors were delirious with joy.

Capt. Jaxx ordered the *Porcupine's* skipper, Lieutenant Tremaine Burnet, RNVR, to make the ship ready to sail immediately. Then he returned to the deck to signal the successful completion of his mission.

The raid was off to a good start.

COLONEL JOHN RANDAL WAS STANDING IN THE OPEN, FIFTY yards up the road from the end of the pier with Captain "Geronimo" Joe McKoy, Ensign Theodore Hamilton, and the two Lovat Scouts—his command party. He could see the warehouse the 999th Light Afrika Division troops used as their barracks in one direction and the *Porcupine* docked in the other. Tonight he was acting in the capacity of mission commander as opposed to being an element leader. His primary job was to be in a central location where his subordinate officers knew how to find him.

The idea was for him to be available to make decisions and influence the action as circumstances dictated. His preference would have been leading SOG to rescue the sailors. However, being out of the action was not as bad as expected.

Col. Randal had brought Raiding Forces on a daring operation with almost no intelligence to act on, made an on-scene estimate of the situation based on personal reconnaissance, formulated a simple tactically-sound scheme of maneuver, and put the plan in motion. Now he had to stand back and allow his junior officers to execute their assignments free of his interference, while remaining in over-operational control.

Col. Randal had to accept that island raiding in the Aegean was going to be different than commanding a mule cavalry guerrilla army in Abyssinia or nipping out of the Great Sand Sea desert on a raid in highly mobile gun jeeps. Small-scale amphibious operations to far-flung islands dictated that now he needed to be more of a commander than a leader. He was going to have to adjust to the role.

King came strolling down the road from town.

"All friendlies have been moved out of the line of fire. The LRDG have set up their blocking position. Our GSS interpreter and the local Greek islander have been dispatched to find the chief of police and bring him to . . ."

Three flashes of a blue filtered light came from the direction of the *Porcupine*— Captain Billy Jack Jaxx signaling success. Col. Randal flashed three yellow filtered lights back to acknowledge.

"Ready, Captain?"

"I's born ready, John."

Capt. McKoy had his highly modified, armory purpose built, prototype .30 caliber AN/M2 Browning Light Machine gun (meaning like all Stingers, it was one of a kind, no two exactly alike) resting on one shoulder with a 100-round trailer of .30 caliber ammunitions in the box holder mounted on the receiver. He was holding it by the flash suppressor on the end of its short, chopped barrel. Originally, the weapon had been the tail gun in a U.S. Navy *SDB Dauntless* that crashed on landing. The salvaged Light Machine Gun (LMG) had been rebuilt by Sergeant Roy Dunlop of the US Army 27th Ordnance Company to specs mailed from Pearl Harbor by one of Geronimo Joe's old Para-Marine buddies from his South American Banana War days.

The Para-Marines of the 1st Marine Parachute Battalion were experimenting with modifying AN/M2 Browning air-to-air machine guns retrieved from out of service or crashed aircraft. Before any modifications, the AN/M2's were one third lighter than the standard issue M-1919 .30 caliber air-cooled Browning LMG. What the Devil Dogs wanted was a man-operable, belt-fed LMG that could be fired on the move, capable of putting out a high volume of sustained suppressive fire at close range during the final assault phase of an attack on a Jap position in heavy jungle terrain.

In short, the Para-Marines needed a man portable assault weapon, not a crew- served machine gun that fired from a tripod like their standard issue air cooled M1919 Browning .30 caliber LMG.

The Para-Marine armorers removed the carrying handle. They chopped the barrel and installed a flash suppressor, which is different than a silencer. They fitted a cargo- sized over-the-shoulder strap, removed the spade grip and added a buttstock from an M1 Garand or whatever was in their arms locker—anything they could scrounge.

And then the armorers sat around holding a bull session, trying to think of what else they could cut down or take off to make the gun lighter that would not interfere with functioning or that might be an improvement. Acting out of necessity, good old American ingenuity, and "can do" spirit, the Para-Marine armorers at Pearl revolutionized light machine gun development by creative improvisation.

They called the LMGs "Stingers."

Sgt. Dunlop modified this one for Capt. McKoy and agreed to build others for Raiding Forces if the prototype worked as advertised.

Tonight was a live fire field test, conducted under actual battle conditions.

Capt. Jaxx came jogging up from the pier, "We got 'em, sir. Crew's safe. The *Porcupine* is preparing to get underway, per your orders."

"Good job, stud."

Col. Randal aimed his flare pistol in the air, fired a green flare and then followed it with an illumination round. Night turned into day. What happened next was a volcanic eruption of gunfire. It was hard to say who engaged first.

Capt. McKoy opened, firing short, crisp bursts of six from the shoulder with his Stinger. Guns on Brandy's MAS boat and Gunnery Sergeant Frank Polanski on Lieutenant Randy "Hornblower" Seaborn's commenced simultaneously. Which meant two 20mm automatic cannons and six .50 cal. machine guns firing from each of the Thunderbolt mounts. Plus, an additional eight .50 cal. Browning M2 machine guns mounted on each of the patrol boats were blazing away at the warehouse/barracks.

Putting out what the military calls concentrated firepower.

The sound of the massed automatic weapons did not seem like anything from this earth. In fact, it did not resemble gunfire. The glowing red tracers concentrated in one tight vector were being swallowed up by the warehouse. Loaded with one tracer for every six ball, incendiary, or armor piecing round, they appeared to be a solid beam of red light—difficult to believe there were five other types of rounds between each tracer.

The tracers were almost as bright as the magnesium illumination flare. It was slowly drifting down, swinging under its tiny parachute, casting shadows as it swung back and forth, to finally lay burning in front of the barracks.

Col. Randal put up another one.

He had his field-expedient 45mm Brixia shoulder-fired mortar and a pack containing forty of the little mortar rounds with him but did not see any reason to use it. The blizzard of machine gun fire from the MAS boats was tearing the building to shreds without his help.

Col. Randal indicated the Brixia leaning against the pack of 45mm mortar rounds to Ens. Hamilton. "Light 'em up, Ensign."

"Sir!"

Bullets travel faster than the speed of sound. They make an extremely loud ringing snap like the sound of a bullwhip when they go by, normally described by those who have heard it as a "crack." The higher the caliber, the bigger the crack. The constant sound of thousands of rounds the size of cigars cracking past Col. Randal's command party was impressive, exhilarating, and frightening—all at the same time.

Col. Randal put up still another illumination round.

Then the LRDG blocking force could be heard engaging on the far side of the target. There must have been at least one back way out of the warehouse. Not a problem. No one from the 999th Light Afrika Division was getting away.

Not tonight.

Col. Randal allowed the firing to continue for what seemed like a long time before handing his flare pistol to Ens. Hamilton.

"Check fire—four reds. Then on my command put up a green. That's the signal for Captain Kidd to go in."

"Wilco, sir. Those Thunderbolts are scary impressive." Col. Randal said, "Impressed me."

Capt. McKoy said, "Bet it got the attention a' those murderin' Nazis."

When the red flares went up, the firing from the MAS boats ceased, but not as uniformly as it had commenced, with the gunners wanting to get in a last burst or two.

Col. Randal ordered, "Green."

The flare arched into the sky, and Captain Roy Kidd's Rangers went in, screaming blood-curdling yells, with guns blazing. The lead element of the 1st Platoon, B Company, 10th Ranger Battalion made entry into the building through the big sliding door. Individual shots popping could be heard. It was all one way. The stunned Nazis inside were not capable of resistance.

Shouts of "Clear" rang out, indicating the warehouse was secure. Col. Randal said, "Let's go take a look."

Capt. Kidd met his party at the front of the warehouse. The outside of the building did not seem to have one square inch not riddled by bullets. "We have twenty-three unwounded POWs, sir, meaning ambulatory but suffering shock. I'll have a headcount of the KIAs and WIAs shortly.

"You may not want to go inside, Colonel. It's carnage in there." Col. Randal said, "I think we can handle it."

He might have spoken too soon. Carnage was a major understatement—blood bath was more like it. There probably had been a hundred Nazis sleeping inside. It was hard to tell from the slaughter.

There could have been more.

Capt. Jaxx said, "Overkill never gets enough credit." Capt. McKoy said, "You got that right, Jack."

The MAS boat gunners had directed their fire at the point where the outer wall of the warehouse met the ground. That way any round fired low ricocheted inside. This aiming point also helped reduce the chance of shooting too high. Once the attack started, there was no safe place inside for the criminals of the Nazi 999th Division inside.

Virtually all personnel had been caught asleep in their bunks.

Capt. McKoy said, "Bet these boys wished they'd stayed in prison."

Col. Randal ordered, "Round up the weapons and pile 'em outside."

Capt. Kidd said, "Yes, sir."

King said, "The chief of police has arrived."

Glad of an excuse to exit the barracks, Col. Randal walked out to find the GSS interpreter with a disheveled, middle-aged man wearing pajamas, slippers, and his police hat. Tufts of white hair sticking out gave him the appearance of a confused rooster.

The chief had clearly not been aware anything unusual was taking place in his town until the attack started. He was talking rapid-fire, sounding like a runaway gun. First thing, the exuberant Greek policeman tried to kiss Col. Randal.

King said, "He's saying the Germans are animals gone insane and need to be put down like mad dogs."

Capt. McKoy said, "Told you."

Col. Randal said, "Ask him how long it's going to take to get his men here to take charge of the prisoners."

The police chief responded with a highly melodramatic answer, arms waving. King said, "Five minutes."

Which was less time than it seemed his answer had taken. "Tell him to do it now."

Capt. Kidd's men were bringing out armloads of bolt action Karabiner 7.92x57 98K rifles and a high number of 9mm Bergmann MP-18 submachine guns—nonstandard SMGs the Nazis issued to their static, police, or paramilitary units. Everything was piled on the ground, along with pistols, grenades, bayonets—anything that might serve as a weapon.

Col. Randal informed Capt. Kidd, "Tell your Rangers to help themselves if they see something they like."

Capt. Kidd said, "The men will appreciate it, sir."

Col. Randal said, "We're pulling out as soon as we turn over the prisoners. Get your people ready. I want to be as far away as possible before first light."

The police chief returned with a half dozen of his officers.

Using the GSS interpreter to translate, Col. Randal ordered, "Secure the weapons.

Take charge of the prisoners. Then, go arrest the German company commander. "He's your responsibility now."

On hearing the translation, the police chief threw his arms around Col. Randal and kissed him on both cheeks, again. Then saluted him. He began issuing rapid-fire orders to his policemen. The Greek islanders eagerly armed themselves with submachine guns from the pile. The chief and his force may have looked like something out of a comic opera, but they handled the MP-18s with a skill level that could have only come from experience.

The GSS operator said, "Veterans of our war with Italy. These men know what they are about. We made friends here tonight, Colonel."

As the command party was walking down the pier to board Brandy's MAS boat for the trip back to Castelrozzo, Capt. McKoy said, "You do know what those Greeks are fixin' to do to the prisoners just as soon as we're gone, John."

Col. Randal said, "Why do you think I gave 'em the weapons?" Capt. McKoy said, "Sure they got enough ammo?"

Col. Randal said, "Let's get the hell out of Dodge before I get kissed to death."

2

LESBOS

VICE ADMIRAL SIR RANDOLPH "RAZOR" RANSOM WAS standing in front of a large map of the Aegean Sea in the map room located on the third floor in the private suite of Colonel John Randal and Major the Lady Jane Seaborn, LG, OBE, RM. He was briefing the senior officers of Small Raids Incorporated, to include the Strategic Raiding Forces.

Present were Col. Randal; Lady Jane; Lieutenant Colonel Sir Terry "Zorro" Stone, KBE, DSO, MC; James "Baldie" Taylor, wearing the uniform of a major general; Major Taylor Corrigan, DSO, MC; Major Jeb Pelham-Davies, DSO, MC; Major "Pyro" Percy Stirling, DSO, MC; Major Duke Slater; Major Travis McCloud; Major Baltimore "Mongo" Farquhar, MC; Major Clive Adair; Major Zargo; Major Jack Dance; Wing Commander Paddy Wilcox, DSO, OBE, MC, DFC; Veronica Paige, OBE; Captain "Geronimo" Joe McKoy, OBE; Captain Butch "Headhunter" Hoolihan, DSO, MC, MM, RM; Captain Pamala Plum-Martin, DSO, OBE, DFC, RM; Lieutenant Randy "Hornblower" Seaborn; Captain Billy Jack Jaxx; Captain Roy Kidd; Captain "Dynamite" Dick Coogan; Captain Roy "Mad Dog" Reupart; Captain Stephanie Fawcett-Tatum, RM; Captain Hawthorne Merryweather; Lieutenant Douglas Fairbanks Jr., USNR, Beach Jumper Unit 1 (BJU-1); and Waldo Treywick. Brandy Seaborn had been invited to attend, but she did not care for briefings unless it was a Warning Order for an imminent mission.

There were five new faces in the group: Captain M. H. S. McDonald, RN, aka "Snow White," the Naval Officer in Command Cyprus (NOIC); Lieutenant Colonel Guy Prendergast, Commanding Officer of the Long Range Desert Group (LRDG); Major the Earl George Jellicoe, Commanding Officer of the Special Boat Section (SBS); Lieutenant Colonel H. J. "Kid" Cator, 1st Special Air Service Regiment (SAS); and Lieutenant Commander Adrian Seligman, commanding officer of the Levant Schooner Flotilla (LSF).

As the briefing was about to get underway, Brigadier Raymond J. (R. J.) Maunsell, Brigadier Dudley Clarke, Brigadier General William "Wild Bill" Donovan, who had flown in from the U.S. for this briefing, and Captain Cuthbert Bowlby, RN, aka "Curly", arrived, running late. Mandy Paige was downstairs waiting to escort them to the third-floor suite.

This was the largest assemblage ever convened in the relatively small briefing area off Lady Jane's living room. If the Nazis had chosen that moment to bomb the building, the Middle East Command General Headquarters would have been devoid of naval special warfare officers, senior intelligence officials, and special operations troop commanders.

Mandy Paige and Beverly Blackwell would be introducing the speakers. In a unit cram- packed with larger-than-life characters, very few had done more than these two girls to carve out a place for themselves by sheer force of personality. Mandy and Beverly were involved in everything. Today they were wearing six-inch stiletto heels and skintight, silk sheath dresses to denote their civilian status. A woman needed to be in top-notch physical condition to fit into what were described as pencil or "wiggle" dresses—Mandy and Beverly wore them well. Col. Randal, sitting front and center next to Lady Jane, felt a tinge of déjà vu—thinking back on Mandy coordinating the nightly briefings at RAF Habbaniya during the siege.

Beverly said, "OK, Admiral Ransom will make the opening remarks Admiral."

VAdm. Ransom said, "The war's center of gravity has shifted from Middle East Command in Cairo to General Eisenhower's Allied Forces Headquarters in Algiers. The German Army has been driven from North Africa, the siege of Malta has been lifted, and the Allies are in the process of bringing the Sicilian Campaign to a successful conclusion. Our side will be in a position to invade Italy in the near future, should we so choose.

"For the first time since the war started, the odds have started to turn in our favor. The U.S. Army is building up divisions as fast as they can be shipped overseas. However, the Allied Navy is stretched thin fighting the Battle of the Atlantic—which is not going as well as one would like. The U-boat threat is a constant worry. We do not have a satisfactory countermeasure for it yet.

"Overall in the Mediterranean Theatre, we have approximately 4,000 planes versus the enemies' 850—of which only 500 are serviceable according to the latest intelligence reports. Unfortunately, here in our slice of the war in the Aegean, the Axis powers continue to maintain total air supremacy. Which means most surface travel can only be conducted under cover of darkness.

"At this point in time, the war has grown far too large for all its complexities to be grasped by a single individual. One who has to try is the British Prime Minister. Someday, when total victory has been achieved, Mr. Churchill shall deserve the lion's share of the credit. In no small part due to his bulldog tenacity and unwillingness to quit when lesser men would have bowed to what seemed inevitable defeat.

"That stipulated, there shall also be those who claim the Allies prevailed *in spite of* the PM. The man is constantly dreaming up quixotic undertakings that do not conform to accepted modern military doctrine. Not that anyone in this room cares a fig about conventional thinking.

"What will have an impact on all of us here today is the fact that Mr. Churchill has developed an obsession with the Aegean Theatre of Operations. He is convinced that Allied domination in the region is vital to a war-winning strategy. The PM dreams of tying down a large a number of Axis divisions in the Balkans and inducing neutral Turkey to enter the war on our side.

"In his opinion, to accomplish those things, an aggressive war in the islands is a must. Almost no one agrees with him except Adolf Hitler. Intelligence has confirmed the *Führer* holds the belief that the Aegean is a strategic zone to be defended at all costs—to the last man, last bullet. Any ground conceded must be immediately recaptured on penalty of death for the commander who fails to launch an immediate counterattack.

"Hitler is convinced the Allies will invade the Balkans."

In the crowded room, only Brig. Gen. Donovan, Brig. Maunsell, Capt. Bowlby, and James Taylor were aware that Brig. Clarke's A-Force was surreptitiously carrying out OPERATION ZEPPELIN—a Top Secret deception plan designed to deceive the German High Command, meaning Hitler, into believing the Allies' intentions were to do exactly that.

It was working.

VAdm. Ransom said, "Prime Minister Churchill has proposed an attack through the Aegean into Romania, to seize the Ploesti oil fields and gain control of other strategic minerals produced in the region, such as the copper, bauxite, and chrome vital to the Nazi war machine. Not a bad idea, actually. The problem is virtually all responsible senior military commanders believe such a campaign is impossible without capturing Rhodes—and to do that we first have to take Kos and Leros, and possibly Samos as well.

"And that is where the United States balks.

"The U.S. Military establishment has its own idea how to win the war. Attack straight across the English Channel. Right now, today, launch an invasion of France. Drive on Germany, put a stake in the vampire's heart, kill the Nazi monster, and go home.

"This plan is even more unrealistic that the Prime Minister's.

"When it was being developed, apparently the U.S. Navy was not consulted. If it had been, the Chief of Naval Operations would have certainly pointed out the tremendous amount of sealift necessary to transport our Allied army across the Channel to force a lodgment ashore and keep it supplied for the duration—meaning the rest of the war.

"The shipping does not exist and will have to be built. Bottoms have to be laid in American shipyards, then convoyed across the Atlantic to Great Britain to be finished out. In addition, a great fleet of warships will have to be assembled to shepherd the invading Allied army across to France. All that takes time.

"So, here we are. The British PM wants a war in the Aegean. The President of the United States and General Eisenhower will not support the operation on the grounds that it is a 'tangential adventure.' Prime Minister Churchill has decided to proceed without the U.S. and go it alone. Even without air cover—we all know that is a mistake."

VAdm. Ransom paused and looked around the room before continuing. "What are we to do?

"For one thing, Small Raids Incorporated is not going to pay any attention to the national-level political bickering. We are a combined force of American, British, and Greek units with one goal—kill Nazis. Raiding Forces, which now falls under the umbrella of SRI that I chair with Colonel Randal as my deputy, is preparing to fight a small-scale, hit-and-run amphibious raiding campaign across vast distances against great odds—code name FIRE EATER.

"Our task is to raid every single populated Aegean island at least once. Working with Special Operations Executive, Inter-Allied Services Liaison Department—also known as MI-6, the Office of Strategic Services and Political Warfare Executive, we will be tying down enemy units and paving the way for future guerrilla campaigns on the mainland by establishing contact with patriot leaders. We will lay the foundation for uprisings by planting secret arms and supply dumps on select islands for the patriot forces to draw from. And we will undermine enemy morale with an intensive propaganda campaign.

"We are going to do so with little to no air cover, little or no outside army or navy support, and only token backing from the United States—a handful of General Donovan's OSS operatives are all we can expect. Every German soldier we tie down is one less our troops will have to face on the big day Allied Forces ultimately cross the English Channel to launch the invasion of France."

"While you men and women will be the primary players in this campaign, no one will ever know the details of your activities. FIRE EATER is classified. All record of it will be sealed for seventy-five years."

BEVERLY WALKED TO THE FRONT OF THE ROOM. THE SLIM blonde with the wild mop of hair and sparkling smile said, "OK, next up is Dr. Layton Winthrop of the Cairo Museum. Prior to the war, Dr. Winthrop was a professor of Egyptology at University College London. He is an expert on the geo-political profile of the Aegean Sea from antiquity to present day—specifically, the Dodecanese Islands. Lady Jane thought you might benefit from hearing the historical perspective of our area of operations."

Mandy went to the door and brought in Dr. Winthrop, who had been waiting outside with King. The professor was a slight man with silver, wire-rim glasses. While he had long experience as a lecturer, he had never spoken to any group quite like the people gathered in this room. If the scholar was the least bit intimidated by his audience, it did not show.

Dr. Winthrop said, "The Dodecanese, also known as the Southern Sporades, is a group of twelve principal islands and a host of smaller ones—some inhabited, some not—lying off the southwest coast of Anatolia. Originally it was believed they were a part of the Anatolian mainland. However, today more modern opinion holds the islands to be the peaks of underwater mountains.

"The first European civilization occurred in the insular and peninsular territory between the Ionian and Aegean seas. Our earliest picture derives from the Homeric catalogue between 1,500 and 1,000 BC when the islands were first colonized by the Greeks . . ."

Colonel John Randal noted the room had grown still.

" . . . toward the end of the seventh century, it was ceded to the Saracens. However, during the thirteenth century, the Venetians seized all the islands. The Knights of St. John occupied them from the early fourteenth century until 1522 when Suleiman the Magnificent evicted the knights after a protracted and bloody siege. The Dodecanese then fell under Turkish rule for the next four hundred years—until the Italo/Turkish War when the islands were ceded to Italy."

If Dr. Winthrop interpreted the quiet of his audience for rapt attention, he was making a mistake. At this point, most people present were practically comatose by his presentation. For Col. Randal's part, not one historical person or event Dr. Winthrop had mentioned had even been covered in any class he had taken in high school or college—except for Homer.

" . . . the French occupied Castelrozzo from 1815 to 1921. The First Treaty of Lausanne in 1923, marking the end of the Libyan War, placed the islands in the hands of the Italians, as I mentioned."

Col. Randal wondered, "How did the Libyans get involved?"

" . . . during the Italian occupation, the islanders suffered from economic as well as political disadvantages. While of Greek ancestry, the people were Italian citizens, though they were not accorded the privilege to vote.

"During this period, the Greek Orthodox Church was the driving force of an underground movement for reunification with Greece. Aware of the strategic importance of the islands, the Italians were having none of it. Between 1935 to 1940 the Regia Aeronautica developed a military air base on Rhodes, a landing ground on Kos, and a seaplane port at Leros.

"Throughout the Italian Occupation, the Turks exerted pressure on the Italians with respect to the hegemony of the islands. Turkey has always wanted the Dodecanese returned to what they believe to be their rightful control. Which brings us up to the present day. German and Italian military forces currently hold the islands, and you people, as I understand, are planning to take it away from them. History marches on.

"Questions?"

Col. Randal saw Captain Billy Jack Jaxx's hand shoot up. "Doctor, is it true Castelrozzo has a topless beach?"

Jack Cool.

MANDY ESCORTED DR. LAYTON WINTHROP OUT OF THE ROOM. As the professor walked past Captain Billy Jack Jaxx, he stopped and leaned down for a word. Colonel John Randal wondered what that was about.

In front of the room, Beverly said, "OK, next up is Brigadier Clarke. Even the name of his organization, A-Force, is classified. Those of you who believe you know what he does, well you probably don't. And if you're not sure, don't ask. For those who would like a hint, in the words of the famous Chinese military strategist Sun Tzu, 'All war is based on deception.'

"There will not be any questions taken when the Brigadier concludes his comments." Col. Randal thought, "Where did Beverly pick up quotes from *The Art of War*?" Brigadier Dudley Clarke took center stage, looking, as usual, like a mischievous cherub.

He was in charge of Allied "Deception" worldwide, a fact concealed by his operating out of Cairo, which was now a military backwater—in itself a deception. A-Force had its fingers in a lot of pies not strictly limited to deceiving the enemy. Most likely no one besides the Brigadier knew about all of them.

Not all his projects were sanctioned by higher authority.

In an off-the-record conversation they were "not having," the chief of A-Force had privately advised Col. Randal that everyone in the Aegean Theatre of Operations—no matter how senior—was working for him directly or indirectly. Whether they knew or not.

Most had no idea.

Brig. Clarke said, "Those of you people new to Raiding Forces, allow me to preface my remarks by saying that I have been associated with Colonel Randal and Lieutenant Colonel Stone since they were both lieutenants, back in the dark days when we were dreaming up the idea of commando raiding. I would like to think I helped them on their way, militarily speaking. But that would not be strictly true—talent will out.

"Admiral Ransom—a true living legend—is unquestionably the best man in the Royal Navy to head Small Raids Incorporated. You could not serve with better officers. They enjoy my full confidence. You should unabashedly extend them yours.

"Now we, meaning all of us in this room, are embarking on a bold new endeavor. One that is essential to final victory in Europe. The fact that we shall have to conduct our operations on a shoestring basis in no way diminishes their importance. Do your part to the best of your ability, and for the rest of your time on earth you can rest assured, not only did you play a significant role in winning the war, you helped save the lives of thousands of Allied soldiers.

"Now hear this—everything Raiding Forces does from this point forward is classified. Never discuss our operations with anyone. Our mission is 100 percent clandestine. Trust no one. 'Loose Lips Sink Ships.' You would not want to sink the one you happen to be sailing on. Having had the pleasure of being torpedoed, I speak from experience.

"Here is what I am at liberty to tell you: Our mission is to conduct a piratical war on the enemy's naval lines of communications in the Aegean, to induce Turkey to enter the war on the Allied side, to arm and equip partisan movements in enemy-occupied Yugoslavia and Greece, to weaken the Nazi hold over the Balkans, and to cause the Axis to divert troops the Nazis can ill afford to commit to locations where they will rot in place doing nothing of military significance.

"Recently I have been working with the Turks behind the scene to persuade them to turn a blind eye to Raiding Forces stationing sailing schooners in remote coves and inlets along the length of Turkey's southwestern coastline. Some of you will be living on board these floating barracks, which you will use as mobile bases from which to launch raids by MGB, PT, and/or motorized caique. Under no circumstances are you or the troops under your command to ever discuss our berthing arrangement with neutral Turkey. Ever—consider the subject *above* Top Secret.

"Your mission is enormous in scope. The Aegean Sea is approximately 83,000 square miles—three times the size of the Great Sand Sea. There shall most likely never be more than 400 to 500 of you operating at any one time—a modern day David versus Goliath scenario.

"Expect to fight a dirty war. You shall not be able to count on the Geneva Accords being recognized. What goes on will be out of sight of the rest of the world. Unfortunate, but there it is—war to the knife. Anyone who for personal, moral, or ethical reasons feels they cannot engage in such a campaign may leave the room now with no prejudice."

The statement was met by steely silence. Brig. Clarke studied those present. Only, he did not much remind anyone of a cherub now.

"Let me close by saying that if from time to time you find yourself asked to perform a task that does not make sense—it does."

MANDY SAID, "NEXT WE SHALL BE HEARING FROM ONE OF the new members of Raiding Forces, Lieutenant Commander Adrian Seligman, founder and commander of the Levant Schooner Flotilla. The LSF's motto is 'Stand Boldly On.' One of Colonel Randal's often quoted Rules for Raiding is 'Right Man, Right Job.' With a slogan like the Commander's, he certainly fits our mold. Let us give him a welcoming hand."

After the applause died down, Lt. Cdr. Seligman said, "If I were you, I would not be in any rush to draw conclusions about my qualifications for clandestine work from that introduction. Only got the LSF job because the corvette *Erica* I commanded was sunk when she struck a mine. Then I botched a disastrous interview with a certain senior intelligence service officer from a cloak and dagger organization which shall remain nameless. This spymaster had the nerve to suggest I sail into the Aegean in an HDML on secret service, sink any caique flying the German flag, and machine gun the survivors in the water.

"I refused and was immediately threatened with being arrested and then sent to a private mental institution where I would be incarcerated for the duration. Why? Because I 'knew too much and could be an embarrassment.'

"Fortunately for me, I only just managed to avoid being taken into custody by jumping out of a second-story window. Drove straight to Admiral Ransom's Headquarters in Alexandria to seek sanctuary. Straightaway, the Razor placed me in command of what we elected to call the Levant Schooner Flotilla. Still have the requirement to capture or sink German-flagged caiques—no mention of machine gunning survivors.

"Admiral Ransom assigned me the immediate task of fitting out all suitable single-masted caiques I could lay hands on in Beirut and Famagusta to use as armed caique transports. He also required larger two-masted schooner-rigged ships to act as mobile headquarters, supply, and/or floating troop vessels for Raiding Forces personnel to live on and launch raids from. Once the flotilla is assembled, my orders are to station the boats in secluded anchorages in the fjords along the southwest coast of Turkey as Brigadier Clarke mentioned.

"Since the Mediterranean Fleet—now reduced to a mere four cruisers and a handful of destroyers—has been pinned down by the vastly superior Axis naval forces in the sea lanes off Italy, Small Raids Incorporated is the only naval offensive operation being contemplated in this part of the world. Which means the LSF can count on more than ordinary support in naval stores, equipment, and dockyard services now sitting idle.

"The opportunity to serve under Admiral Ransom made the assignment extraordinarily attractive, with the added benefit of not having to spend the rest of the war in a mental institution," Lt. Cdr. Seligman said.

"Several fairly tricky problems remained to be resolved. First, the caiques—LSF has to operate primarily under cover of darkness, utilizing stealth to achieve the element of surprise to survive. That meant the 20 hp Bolinger diesels that powered most of the caiques to a maximum speed of 5 to 6 knots going *BOM, BOM, BOM*—audible for miles on a quiet night, would have to be replaced.

"What to do?

"Admiral Ransom introduced me to Raiding Forces' chief of maintenance, Mr. Rawlston. He brought the problem to the attention of Lady Seaborn. By some amazing feat of telepathy, crystal ball gazing, or possibly a magic séance orchestrated by Colonel Randal's Zār Priestess slave girls, she discovered the Australians had recently retired their Matilda tanks from service and also learned there were brand-new 90 hp—to 2,000 rpm replacement diesel tank engines for them, wasting away in storage in Haifa.

"We found that when Mr. Rawlston fitted the Matilda engines to our caiques, the boats were able to cruise at 6 to 7 knots, a modest improvement. But the most marvelous thing is that at half throttle or less, the new diesels run silent. We were in business—thank you, Lady Seaborn."

She rewarded him with one of her nearly lethal heart attack smiles. Someone in the crowd went "Yeeeeehaaaa!" It was either a Rebel or Comanche yell, depending on who gave it.

Lt. Cdr. Seligman continued, although he was having trouble looking away from Lady Jane. "As for engine maintenance, a large pool of unemployed tank mechanics was available to draw from. All they had to do was volunteer to go to sea on secret service in leaky motorized sailboats and carry out high-risk missions deep behind enemy lines. More than we anticipated stepped forward.

"Crews to man the caiques were our next problem to tackle. Regular officers and ratings, highly trained on modern equipment, could not be spared for service in what amounts to a backwater guerrilla navy. The only officers available to us are reservists aged nineteen to twenty- three with a bent for adventure. We also accept self-declared yachtsmen from the other services as skippers.

"Although some have proven a trifle guilty of overstating the extent of their seamanship, who am I to deny them their chance?

"Admiral Ransom specified all LSF ratings be volunteers. The men special service appeals to are individuals looking for a less regimented service, habitual defaulters, and others who were, shall we say, *encouraged* to apply.

"Men with that sort of background do not conform to Raiding Forces' rigorous selection standards. However, the navy, with its long tradition of press gangs in times past, operates differently. We are used to taking who we can get and training them rigorously. Nevertheless, without reservation I can say up to this point no naval unit I have ever served in has been more trouble-free than the LSF. Men settle in, quickly establish their place, or find themselves returned to the replacement pool. No appeal, no second chances—gone.

"Next, there was the matter of communications. That one stumped me. LSF needed a radio that was lightweight and simple to operate, with long-range capability, and, well, nothing like that exists—or so we thought. I was riding with Admiral Ransom in his staff car, being driven by one of his WRENs—Bentley, I believe. She suggested we talk to Captain Pamala Plum-Martin. I could not imagine whatever for, until Pamala informed me there were quite a lot of unserviceable P-40 Tomahawks—and they had radios that fit the bill perfectly."

Colonel John Randal had not heard the story about the radios. He turned, looked over his shoulder, and made eye contact with the Vargas Girl look-alike Royal Marine pilot. She gave him a wink.

"Last but definitely not least, there was the problem of navigation we had to overcome. LSF has the requirement to make passages of up to 100 miles over open water at night to arrive at an exact spot on a shadowy coast during the hours of darkness with very junior officers navigating. Survival depends on not risking so much as a lighted binnacle. The only tools available are small RAF steering compasses with phosphorescent dial markings, handheld lensatic compasses, and lead lines.

"Happily, there are so many islands in our AO that it is possible to keep one in sight at almost all times—either the island you are leaving or the one you are going to. The RAF compasses have turned out to be simple and easy to use. All that is necessary is to set the two parallel lines on the cursor to the course you want to steer. Then the helmsman only has to keep the needle pointed between the two lines until he arrives at where he wants to go—works like a charm.

"Well, except for the time when one of the steersmen managed to get the pointer upside down and the caique found itself going 180 degrees in the opposite direction.

"Stand Boldly On . . . hope for the best."

BEVERLY INTRODUCED THE NEXT SPEAKER. "ANOTHER NEW member of the Raiding Forces family, though he has already participated on a raid with Colonel Randal, is Lieutenant Douglas Fairbanks, Jr. I'm sure he needs no introduction. We've all seen his movies.

"Lt. Fairbanks recently organized a group of specialist commandos for the United States Navy called Beach Jumpers. The unit is the result of a request from Brigadier Clarke. Today he is here to brief you on their capabilities.

"Let's hear it for Douglas . . ."

Mandy came over and whispered to Colonel John Randal, "King needs you outside."

Col. Randal stood up as the movie star was beginning his talk. He followed Mandy out to the landing. King was there with Captain Lionel Chatterhorn, commander of the Raiding Forces Field Security Police detachment of the Vulnerable Points Wing. Capt. Chatterhorn had been one of the premier gun jeep patrol leaders for eighteen months before being brought back to RFHQ with his policemen to resume security duties.

Jim followed Col. Randal out of the suite. King said, "We have a problem, Chief."

Capt. Chatterhorn said, "My orders are to refuse entrance to anyone not on the list Stephanie prepared for me, sir."

Col. Randal said, "Roger that. I issued those instructions. What's going on?"

Capt. Chatterhorn said, "There is one unhappy officer—a Colonel Turnbull—demanding to be admitted to your briefing, sir."

Col. Randal said, "I don't know a Colonel Turnbull . . ."

Jim said, "There has been a development at MEHQ while you were away. We should have a conversation later, Colonel. I shall take care of our uninvited guest."

He and Capt. Chatterhorn thundered down the stairs. Col. Randal said, "Wonder who Colonel Turnbull is?"

King said, "Claims to be the new commander of Raiding Forces."

BY THE TIME COLONEL JOHN RANDAL RETURNED TO HIS seat, Ensign Theodore Hamilton aka "The Great Teddy" was in front of the room performing magic tricks. He was very good. Everyone in the audience was enjoying the performance and they were paying attention, which was the point.

Ens. Hamilton said, "Brigadier Clarke says the purpose of deception is to get the enemy commander to *do* something. Captain Merryweather will explain that the purpose of Political Warfare is to get the enemy to *think* something. What I want everyone to take away when they leave today is that the purpose of camouflage is to make an object *appear* to be something it is not.

Mandy walked to the wooden easel in the front of the room. She turned over a large blow-up of an aerial photo of Brandy's MAS boat taken from a Walrus by Ens. Hamilton and Captain Pamala Plum-Martin. It was clearly exactly what it was, an Italian motor torpedo boat tied off next to a cliff.

Then Mandy went over to a second easel and turned over another photo as The Great Teddy said, "Abracadabra."

The only thing visible was the cliff.

Ens. Hamilton said, "It took less than twenty minutes to make the MAS boat in the second photo appear to be part of the rock face."

Mandy went back to the first easel and turned over another photo. This one was of a caique anchored next to the same cliff. The sail had been struck but the mast was sticking up fifteen feet high.

The Great Teddy said, "Abracadabra," as Mandy turned over the next photo. The audience gasped. The boat was nowhere to be seen—completely vanished!

Ens. Hamilton said, "Under camouflage is how Raiding Forces will live to fight another day once the sun comes up on the Aegean Sea. No different than a gun jeep patrol laagering in the Great Sand Sea. Hey, presto—it's not magic, gentlemen."

Then he sat down.

Everyone was on their feet clapping and cheering. The teenager had solved the problem on the mind of every officer in the room. How to survive during the day with the Nazis having air supremacy.

The Great Teddy was the man of the hour. No one would have believed what he demonstrated was possible. And Ens. Hamilton said it was easy.

Abracadabra.

MANDY PAIGE ESCORTED KING INTO THE SUITE. AS SHE WAS introducing the merc, Vice Admiral Sir Randolph "Razor" Ransom, sitting next to Colonel John Randal, said under his breath, "We should promote Ensign Hamilton or have the lad knighted—possibly both."

Col. Randal said, "I'm not sure Teddy's old enough to be serving in a combat zone, Admiral, much less be promoted."

VAdm. Ransom said, "Makes no difference to me. Never bothered you in the past." Col. Randal said, "See what I can do, Admiral."

King said, "Colonel Randal asked me to brief enemy forces. The German 22nd Air- Landing Division is known to us from Crete. While the bulk of the 22nd is stationed on the island, expect to find elements of the division throughout the Aegean. Air-Landing denotes the division is a well-trained, highly mobile, light infantry unit trained for rapid deployment by glider or air landed by JU-52 troop transport.

"Consider the 22nd a formidable opponent.

"The Italian 33rd Mountain Division is also scattered throughout the Aegean. In theory, an elite outfit—in practice, the division is a paper tiger. Morale of the 33rd's homesick troops is low, to the point they are almost combat ineffective.

"The German troops occupying the small islands you will encounter most often are from the 999th Light Afrika Division. The division is an auxiliary paramilitary penal unit composed of violent criminals, murderers, and rapists offered a way out of prison if they volunteered for front line duty. The division commander is a degenerate alcoholic convicted of child molestation whose sentence was overturned because of his fanatical support of the Nazi Party. Atrocities committed against civilians by the criminals in the 999th are so widespread that even SS units complain of their brutality.

"Do not expect quarter if you surrender to any of the three Axis division troops. Prisoners not executed immediately will be turned over to the SD-Security Police for harsh interrogation. Meaning tortured, and then shot.

"My advice is fight it out to the end and save a bullet for yourself.

LIEUTENANT COLONEL SIR TERRY "ZORRO" STONE WAS THE next speaker. "Admiral Ransom and I have been studying the problem of reorganizing Sea Squadron. We have gone through three or four iterations of various Tables of Organization. As soon as we work out what we believe is a reasonable solution, some new, unforeseen development comes along and scuttles it.

"As of today, the Razor and I are essentially back to where we started—no firm plan. The success Eighth Army achieved in driving the Desert Fox out of Libya freed up all our Raiding Forces personnel running gun jeep patrols for service in Sea Squadron. One decision we have made is to drop the Sea Squadron title and simply operate as Raiding Forces.

"The recent infusion of Major Dance's Rangers and Major Zargo's Greek Sacred Squadron has been a welcome addition to our ranks. Prior to their arrival, we simply did not have the manpower to carry out any meaningful number of raids. Now, we have progressed from being able to deliver a flea bite to inflicting a bee sting—always darkest before pitch-black.

"It is not clear at this time if Major the Earl Jellicoe's Special Boat Section and Colonel Prendergast's Long Range Desert Group will be assigned to Raiding Forces permanently or merely attached for administrative purposes. Hopefully they will become full-fledged members, because even with the addition of the SBS and LRDG, we will be hard-pressed to dedicate the numbers of troops previously mentioned to raiding operations.

"Raiding Forces has always had to make do with hand-me-downs and castoffs. Back in our early days, running cross-channel pinprick raids, we operated off Brandy Seaborn's private yacht and were armed primarily with Browning sporting shotguns. In Abyssinia, Colonel Randal's Force N rode mules. And when we started patrolling the desert, the Colonel was forced to employ the services of a car thief to steal civilian trucks off the streets of Cairo to use. This was before Lady Jane requisitioned Lend Lease jeeps, which no one at MEHQ had ever heard of, had any use for, and were delighted to have someone take off their hands.

"The art of making do is second nature in Raiding Forces. That said, Commander Seligman's Levant Schooner Flotilla has taken the concept to a new level of ingenuity. Sailing boats powered by tank engines, manned by press ganged brig birds who may or may not have volunteered, commanded by teenage reserve officers—and he claims it's the best outfit he has ever served with. One could not make that up.

"Admiral Ransom and I started out to develop a Table of Organization for Sea Squadron. That transformed into planning a TO&E for a complete reorganization of Raiding Forces. Unfortunately for us, Colonel Randal has been away on other assignments and unavailable to consult. As we know, he is not an officer inclined to allow other people to trifle with his command without his input.

"Now, with the Colonel back, at last we can restructure, and designate officer assignments and troop allocations. Once we commence full-scale operations, the seagoing elements will be acting independently. You troop leaders will be pirate kings. Perhaps Fairbanks will play one of you in a movie someday."

Lieutenant Douglas Fairbanks, Jr. called out, "Won't be you—Errol Flynn already has dibs on that role."

Lt. Col. Stone said, "And what a fine job he shall do, old stick. To wrap . . . here is where we currently are in our thinking: Raiding Forces will be organized into squadrons, flotillas, armadas, or some such blood-curdling title normally assigned to a much larger unit. And that, ladies and gents, is as far as we have progressed with our planning.

"Say tuned for further developments."

COLONEL JOHN RANDAL WENT LAST. "OUR   MISSION IN THE Aegean is a classic Economy of Force operation. A small number of Raiding Forces personnel are to tie down a large number of enemy troops by carrying out a lightning campaign of small-scale raids— hitting and running. That's what Raiding Forces was originally raised to do when Brigadier Clarke organized the unit shortly after Dunkirk.

"The thing to keep in mind is that the actual number of enemy killed and amount of equipment we destroy will not be as important as the impact of our arriving in the dark of night, unannounced and unexpected—as

Admiral Ransom said, 'at a time and place of our own choosing,' utilizing surprise, speed, and violence of action.

"The purpose of the exercise is to attack the enemy's morale. To do that, it'll be necessary to meld deception and psychological warfare with nonstop, small-scale raiding. Success will rest on the leadership exhibited by junior officers commanding small teams of highly skilled troops operating at long range from base, with little or no supervision and no hope of support.

"Teamwork will be essential.

"One last thing. You should be aware that upon learning of our raid on Vatrachos, the 999th Light Afrika Division immediately dispatched replacements to retaliate for the local's cooperation with us. The Nazis massacred every male over the age of twelve on the island.

"That is all."

MANDY SAID, "THIS CONCLUDES OUR BRIEFING. NOW, WE shall all move downstairs. Stations are set up in the ballroom. You have an opportunity to stroll around and stop by to visit with the key people manning them to ask questions of the different elements assigned to or working with Small Raids Incorporated. Stephanie—Captain Fawcett-Tatum—is the ringmaster. If you have a question, check with her.

"Colonel Randal will be available for private, one-on-one discussions. See Beverly downstairs in the Operations Room to schedule.

"Lady Jane has arranged for the Gezira restaurant to cater our noon meal. During lunch, the popular dancers from the Kit-Kat Club, Rita Hayworth and Lana Turner, have agreed to perform. Captain McKoy plans to put on a demonstration of pistol twirling and knife throwing. And The Great Teddy shall do a few more magic tricks—enjoy."

As the suite was clearing out, Colonel John Randal took Major the Lady Jane Seaborn into the master suite. She was on light duty, still recovering from being wounded in an assassination attempt outside the

Gezira Club restaurant on orders from one or more members of the Big Four—who may have been harboring a grudge against Col. Randal for making them sell their illicit diamonds to Waldo Treywick, aka Mr. Big, as a part of OPERATION LEAF EATER.

Lady Jane said, "I thought that went well."

Col. Randal said, "Lie down and get some rest. I'll be back for you at noon." Lady Jane said, "You are being overly protective, as usual."

Col. Randal said, "Dr. Milam ordered me to make sure you don't overdo. Officially, you're still on light duty. Rest—that's an order, Marine."

"Aye, aye, sir."

When he came back out into the living room, he saw Mandy standing with Captain Billy Jack Jaxx in the briefing alcove, studying the large wall map of the Aegean AO. The SOG commander appeared to be trying to locate something.

Col. Randal said, "What did the professor have to say as he was walking out, Jack?"

Capt. Jaxx said, "He told me it was the French girls who swam topless at Castelrozzo, but most of them departed the island after France lost control back in the twenties, sir."

Mandy said, "Dr. Winthrop informed our hero there was another island he should check out where the girls swim nude."

Col. Randal said, "Really, which one?"

Capt. Jaxx said, "Lesbos—I'm looking for it, sir."

Mandy laughed. "Billy Jack, you idiot. The professor was having you on. According to legend, the Isle of Lesbos is where the word *lesbian* originated. The women may swim naked, but what would they need you for?"

Col. Randal said, "Tough luck, Captain."

3
IT'LL BE FUN

COLONEL JOHN RANDAL WAS IN VICE ADMIRAL SIR "RAZOR" Ransom's office off the Operations Room on the ground floor of Raiding Forces Headquarters. Col. Randal had given his own office to Captain Stephanie Fawcett-Tatum because he seldom used it, preferring the third-floor suite for meeting with people. The office was immaculate—the Razor almost never used his either.

Brigadier General William "Wild Bill" Donovan was sitting across the desk. He had flown to Egypt, he claimed, for the Small Raids Incorporated briefing. His new Chief of Station, Valerian Lada Mocarski, had traveled with him to take up residence in the recently opened Secret Intelligence office in Cairo. The walled compound had formerly been the residence of one of the Middle East's Big Five crime lords, recently deceased.

Mr. Mocarski was not present today at Raiding Forces Headquarters. In order to avoid a future turf war, Brig. Gen. Donovan had the foresight to build a firewall between OSS/SI and OSS/SO—SI meaning secret intelligence (Mocarski) and SO meaning special operations (Randal).

James "Baldie" Taylor was tapped to serve as go-between.

When Captain "Geronimo" Joe McKoy heard the name of the OSS officer who would be heading up the OSS/SI Cairo office, he said to Col. Randal, "Donovan has the idea anybody with an exotic foreign name ought to make a good intelligence man."

The observation was not unfounded.

Col. Randal intended to deal with OSS/SI the same as he did with SOE: as little contact as possible. Raiding Forces would cooperate on SI-generated missions when the tasks proposed were militarily doable. He would insert or extract agents, transport arms to locations behind enemy lines, and carry out direct action missions on request.

But he would not allow OSS/SI to plan the execution phase of any operation.

Unknown to Brig. Donovan, Col. Randal, or Mr. Mocarski was that the British Secret Intelligence Service (SIS) had no intention of allowing OSS/SI to become involved to any extent in what they regarded as their private dominion—the acquisition and dissemination of secret intelligence.

A business best conducted by gentlemen . . . according to MI-6.

On the other hand, SIS was delighted to allow OSS to carry out Special Operations to its heart's content. In fact, Brigadier Stewart Menzies DSO, Chief of MI-6, had instructed Captain Cuthbert Bowlby, his Chief of Station Cairo, to overload OSS with actionable intelligence for SO on the premise that "any thug can arrive by dark of night, kick open a door, and shoot everyone inside." SIS's intent was to keep the Americans busy carrying out assignations, raids, reconnaissance missions, etc., to distract them from the fact that they were not being welcomed into the rarified world of Secret Intelligence.

MI-6 planned to play OSS the same way it had played its sister British organization SOE from inception.

Even though he had commanded the "Fighting Sixty Ninth" Regiment, New York National Guard, in the last war and was the recipient of the Medal of Honor, Brig. Gen. Donovan was essentially a politician in uniform. He had run unsuccessfully for governor of New York.

Politicians are always looking ahead to their next office, elected or appointed.

Wild Bill was angling to become the director of the first civilian national intelligence agency in U.S. history after the war. To that end, he was primarily interested in building up his Secret Intelligence credentials because Special Operations have a limited role during peacetime.

Unfortunately for Wild Bill, OSS did not have much in the way of SI to boast about.

To offset the deficiency, Brig. Gen. Donovan regularly brought Col. Randal's after-action reports to the Oval Office for his daily meetings with the President—using SO to cloak his lack of SI credentials.

In the murky world of politics and intelligence, nothing is ever what it seems.

Raiding Forces missions were real-life action adventures the director of the Office of Strategic Services used to entertain his boss and make OSS (meaning him) look good. Not that Brig. Gen. Donovan needed to do much to improve his standing with the President.

The two men had gone to college together. Donovan had been Roosevelt's football hero. The President told him so. One of Wild Bill's most closely guarded secrets was he had no memory of *ever* meeting FDR during their college days—none.

Then there was OPERATION LEAF EATER, the code name Raiding Forces had given the assignment to stop diamond smuggling from Africa to the Third Reich. It was OSS's highest priority mission. Even higher than ULTRA aka GOLDEN FLEECE/RED INDIAN—except it wasn't.

Not exactly.

Unknown to Col. Randal, what made LEAF EATER so critical was that OSS was using it to cloak the super-secret MANHATTAN PROJECT— *the most important military undertaking in U.S. history*. The complete details of LEAF EATER, as it related to the MANHATTAN PROJECT, were so highly classified and compartmentalized that the entire story was known only to Brig. Gen. Donovan, Prime Minister Churchill, and President Roosevelt, and had almost nothing to do with diamonds.

The Allies' master of deception, Brigadier Dudley Clarke, who was cleared for virtually every military secret on the books, had been tasked with developing a cover story to mask the acquisition of a certain strategic material required by MANHATTAN PROJECT that could only be obtained in the Belgian Congo.

For once, the A-Force commander did not have a "Need to Know" what secret he was concealing, its code name, what strategic material the U.S. needed, why, or what it was to be used for once acquired.

Like all good cover stories, the premise of LEAF EATER was *almost* completely true.

The situation, as explained to Col. Randal and others:

1. The Nazis needed industrial-grade diamonds to build precision weapons. Germany had no territory of its own where diamonds could be mined. The only option available to the Germans was to clandestinely purchase stones from illegal traffickers.

2. If the flow of diamonds being smuggled to Germany could be cut off, the Third Reich's war machine would grind to a halt in six months—maybe less.

3. The only places Nazi Germany could purchase diamonds in the necessary volume were the Belgian Congo or the diamond markets in Cairo and Tangier.

Numbers one and two were true. Number three was not. There were other places the Nazis could obtain diamonds. Any number of mining companies in South America were willing to export them. DeBeers Diamond Company, a British mining conglomerate based out of South Africa, was alleged to be secretly selling stones to Germany through cutouts in neutral Switzerland. There were also diamonds making their way to the Third Reich from Palestine, the Netherlands, and as far away as India.

Stopping the flow of diamonds to the Nazi war machine was impossible.

The LEAF EATER Command and Control team—code name CARD GAME, consisting of Col. Randal, Major the Lady Jane Seaborn, Capt. McKoy, Captain Billy Jack Jaxx, Waldo Treywick, Captain Pamala Plum-Martin, Mandy Paige, Beverly Blackwell, and King, smelled a rat.

CARD GAME's suspicion was raised when Brig. Gen. Donovan failed to exhibit the requisite amount of interest expected for shutting down diamond smuggling out of Tangier and only half-hearted enthusiasm in taking control of the Cairo diamond bazaars, other than to "liquidate the traffickers." Wild Bill was insistent on that point.

However, he was 100 percent locked in on stopping the flow of industrial diamonds out of the Belgian Congo—a red flag to CARD GAME.

On a trip to the States, Waldo Treywick discovered there was a diamond mine in Arkansas not being commercially developed. If there actually was a shortage of industrial diamonds in the U.S., as had been claimed, CARD GAME knew the President had the authority to nationalize the mine by simply signing an executive order—problem solved.

Then it was learned that the volume of industrial diamonds needed by the Nazis could be easily smuggled to Germany from around the world concealed in Red Cross packages or diplomatic pouches—the poundage was not all that great.

Finally, after Capt. McKoy's team of ex-law enforcement officers got boots on the ground in the Belgian Congo, they reported that completely stopping the flow of diamonds from the colony was a physical impossibility. The stones were too easy to conceal. And once the diamonds got into the hands of skilled traffickers, there were many, many ways to move them out of the colony. One was discovered sewn in the craw of a freighter captain's parrot.

CARD GAME came to the conclusion that Raiding Forces had been intentionally assigned a mission it could not accomplish. Why? No idea. OSS would surely have developed the same intelligence as Capt. McKoy's team of ex-law enforcement officers. The Outfit, as OSS was called by the men and women serving in it, had an SI team in the Congo.

If the Office of Strategic Services had the same information as Raiding Forces, why was stopping the diamond smugglers from the Congo such a high priority? And why was Brig. Gen. Donovan so adamant about liquidating anyone involved in trafficking the stones?

CARD GAME came to the conclusion that the traffickers must be capable of smuggling something else *even more* critical to the war effort than industrial diamonds. That was the reason they had to be eliminated. Which raised another question—what could possibly be more important than cutting off the flow of diamonds to Germany if the Nazis' industrial military complex would grind to a halt in six months or less without them?

CARD GAME had no idea.

Col. Randal realized there was more to LEAF EATER than he was being let in on. And he suspected part of what he had been briefed on was not true—or at least misleading. He was OK with that in principle. In the event of capture, you can't reveal what you don't know.

Raiding Forces had its orders to go after diamond smuggling and target the traffickers. That was exactly what his Raiders were going to do. "Damn the torpedoes." Who cared about the inconsistencies?

Not him.

Nevertheless, there were undercurrents of suspicion between Raiding Forces and the Office of Strategic Services that did not quite rise to the level of mistrust. Brig. Gen. Donovan was not satisfied with the progress LEAF EATER had made thus far. He wanted results *yesterday*.

Col. Randal had no intention of taking action until he understood the situation as best he could, had developed a plan, and ensured all the players were in place. There are times when a commander has to initially sacrifice speed at the start of an operation in order to have a strong finish.

He would not be rushed.

Brig. Gen. Donovan said, "Raiding Forces has made substantial progress in a remarkably short period of time."

That was a little vague—Col. Randal wondered if he was being rebuked for the progress of LEAF EATER in the Congo.

"A lot of moving parts, sir."

Switching gears, Brig. Gen. Donovan said, "I would like to visit Castelrozzo before flying back to the States. Funny, my staff found three different spellings by last count and no one, not even the people who live there, seem to know what the name means. Dr. Winthrop shed light on the island's history but not enough to tell us how to spell it correctly."

Col. Randal said, "Best get there before all the generals and admirals show up to inspect the enemy defenses and risk the hazards of the wine cellars, sir."

Brig. Gen. Donovan laughed. "Truer words . . . I'll talk to Admiral Ransom. We should declare the island a secure site. No unauthorized visitors.

"On another subject, I plan to send you a thirty-man Operational Group—what's your preference—Greek speakers or Italian?"

Col. Randal had never been impressed with the idea of concentrating men with one particular language skill in an Operational Group (OG). He had served in four different countries so far—not counting the Congo. What were the linguists going to do when they were needed someplace where a different language was spoken? "I'd prefer the thirty best people you have, General—regardless of language capability."

Brig. Gen. Donovan said, "That does not conform to our OG's table of organization. We will have to rob from the Groups in training. I can arrange it if that's what you want."

"Any operators you provide will be welcome, sir."

Col. Randal did not point out that this was the second time Wild Bill had promised an Operational Group—the first one had never shown up. One had shipped out for Raiding Forces but been diverted to North Africa prior to TORCH.

Brig. Gen. Donovan said, "You rotate a team of Raiding Forces personnel restricted to light duty through Camp X in Canada to train OSS field agents. We can arrange for a couple of your people to travel to Washington to interview potential OG candidates.

"Take the thirty your men say they want."

"I'd like that, sir."

"When I get back to Washington, I shall make it a priority."

Col. Randal said, "My guess is you'd like a briefing on the status of LEAF EATER, General."

Brig. Gen. Donovan said, "Read my mind. I have to report to the President upon my return. The old man is following LEAF EATER personally. It has that high of a priority."

Col. Randal said, "Stopping diamond smuggling is a complex assignment, General." Brig. Gen. Donovan said, "If the mission was easy, anyone could do it."

Col. Randal said, "Understood, sir. I'll run it down for you from the top. Here in Cairo, Mr. Treywick, masquerading as 'Mr. Big'—a gangster from Chicago—recently cornered the diamond market after one of the Big Five Middle Eastern crime lords was shot due to his lack of enthusiasm for our offer to sell his diamonds exclusively to the Chicago mob, meaning us. After that, the surviving four crime bosses became noticeably more interested in selling their stones to Mr. Big.

"The concept of the operation is small black marketeers have to sell their diamonds to the Big Four. They have to sell to us.

"One of my officers, Captain Butterfield, worked for Cartier in Paris before the war, sir. He grades the diamonds and sets the price we'll pay. The crime lords have no say, there's no negotiation. They can accept his number or the Big Four will become the Big Three on the spot."

Brig. Gen. Donovan laughed. "A business model not taught at Harvard."

Col. Randal said, "Gets better, sir. Mr. Treywick sells the diamonds purchased from the Big Four to traffickers at an inflated price. The smugglers spirit the stones across the desert by camel caravan to Turkey to be sold to Nazi purchasing agents.

"Only they never make it.

"Captain Butterfield is a highly decorated ex-Foreign Legion officer and one of our best gun jeep patrol leaders. He's put together a team of former Legionnaires to intercept the caravans, recover the diamonds, and execute the smugglers as per your orders, sir."

Brig. Gen. Donovan said, "Any chance that would be Preston Butterfield? I know the family. Own a large chain of high-end retail stores. My law firm represents the firm in New York.

"Preston's the family black sheep."

Col. Randal said, "That would be him."

Brig. Gen. Donovan said, "I will have a quiet word with his father when I return, to let the family know the captain is working for the Outfit."

Col. Randal said, "On another front, sir—Tangier is not encouraging. It's an international city. The Spanish seized control when the war started. Makes it hard to corner the diamond market with a Nazi-leaning neutral country's police force patrolling the streets."

Brig. Gen. Donovan said, "I would not waste much energy on Tangier, Colonel. What's the status of the Congo?"

Col. Randal said, "Captain McKoy recruited retired law enforcement officers to investigate diamond trafficking in the colony. They identified three ways diamonds are making their way out of the Congo, sir.

"Miners working in the Belgian mines routinely steal stones. They sell to middlemen who in turn broker to traffickers. The diamonds are moved to the coast to be shipped to Cairo or Tangier, concealed aboard tramp freighters. From there, the stones are smuggled to Turkey or Spain, then on to Germany.

"Then, there's the potholers—local natives who eke out a living digging up stones along the banks of the Sebou River. The potholers sell what they find to middlemen who travel up and down the river searching for product. The middlemen then broker to the traffickers.

"Last but not least, corrupt government officials extort kickbacks from the mining companies. The way it works, when a mine needs a license renewed, the company has to pay a bribe. Payoffs also have to be made to pass quarterly safety inspections or for police protection.

"Diamonds are the currency of choice.

"The government officials sell their stones to Nazi agents claiming to be Swiss mining engineers who fly in and out of Léopoldville."

Brig. Gen. Donovan said, "Have you been able to discern the identity of the treasonous officials?"

"Chief of Police of Léopoldville's the front man, but the corruption goes all the way to the governor, sir."

Brig. Gen. Donovan said, "The Congo's trade in diamonds—is it pervasive or limited to a handful of war profiteers?"

Col. Randal said, "Widespread, sir—it's going to be virtually impossible to bring under control. The Congo consists of a handful of towns surrounded by millions of miles of teeming triple canopy jungle, much of which is primal swamp. Darkest Africa, unexplored, lawless and dangerous.

"A handful of remote trading posts serve the interior. Merchants who supply goods to the trading posts limit travel. And when they do venture out, they take riverboats to their destination. No roads penetrate the interior. We're going have to operate deep in the jungle where the potholers, middlemen, and traffickers do their business.

"What's your plan, Colonel?"

"It's a work in progress, General. Our thought is to capture the diamond market by outbidding the middlemen. A slightly different twist on what we're doing in Cairo. If that doesn't work, we'll take out our competitors—bang . . . you're dead, right there."

Brig. Gen. Donovan said, "Exactly what I want—my recommendation is to go with Plan B from the start."

Col. Randal said, "Captain Butterfield is recruiting a team of diamond buyers to work the Congo. If you know any men classified 4F, or who are over the age to be drafted, with a background working in the jewelry industry that would like to serve their country, Preston can put 'em to use, sir."

Brig. Gen. Donovan said, "I will message my staff in Washington to start recruiting immediately."

Col. Randal said, "Our buyers, acting as middlemen, will sell their stones to the traffickers, which provides us their identity. We'll take them out. Then, when new people turn up to take their place we'll repeat as needed.

"We're not going to bother the potholers. They're poor natives eking out a living. They'll be glad to sell to us once we 'disappear' the Nazi buyers or pay more for their stones."

Brig. Gen. Donovan said, "Your description of LEAF EATER as it relates to the Congo is more complicated than my staff would have me believe. The illegal buying and selling is not concentrated in one central location like you have in Cairo. Sounds like a problem. Are you confident you can handle it?"

Col. Randal said, "We're getting ready to find out, sir. One of my people, Frank Polanski, was a Marine in the Banana Wars, sir. Left the Corps, went to Abyssinia to be a soldier of fortune—worked for me in Force N. I intend to finance a mercenary army and leave the rest to him. He'll take out the traffickers."

Brig. Gen. Donovan said, "I like it. Full deniability. Mercenaries are nonaligned, freelance shadow warriors. OSS can't be held responsible for their actions—don't work for us."

"Unless they do, General."

"A fact not in our best interest to advertise." Col. Randal said, "Exactly, sir."

"How do you intend to resolve the issue of the corrupt public officials in Léopoldville? We have to consider anyone in the diamond trafficking pipeline a direct threat to the national security of the United States. Even when they happen to be officers of the federal government of Belgium—one of our allies . . . except apparently when it comes to making money."

Col. Randal said, "I'll get back to you on that, sir."

BEVERLY'S SIX-INCH HEELS CLICKED ON THE TILE FLOOR as she ushered Brigadier Dudley Clarke in to see Colonel John Randal next. She was always careful around the Brigadier. He was relentless in his effort to recruit her away to A-Force where she would become one of "Dudley's Duchesses." That was never going to happen.

Brig. Clarke said, "Only a few items, Colonel. Naturally, nothing we discuss shall leave this room since this meeting never happened."

"Wilco."

"General Donovan wants to visit Castelrozzo. I shall travel with him.

He is interested in seeing Raiding Forces' new version of Oasis X. I intend to use the visit as an opportunity to visit Kas, the Turkish town in Antalya Province on the Turquoise Coast opposite the island. I want to introduce him to General Kamel Bakkal, the Province Chief.

"The Turks have mixed emotions about the British since they fought on the German side against us in the last war, but they feel differently about Americans. General Bakkal will be impressed that a senior U.S. Army officer has paid him the honor of a courtesy call. General Donovan will be glad of the opportunity to do Prime Minister Churchill a service in the Aegean in hopes that 'Winnie the Pooh' will repay the favor by helping OSS get up and running in Europe."

Col. Randal said, "Maybe you'd like to take Major Adair with you since he's going to be serving in the dual capacity of Phantom commander and Mayor of Castelrozzo like he did at Oasis X.

"I shall make a point of it—Clive's a good man. I intend to introduce Lady Jane to General Bakkal. I understand she is going to be redecorating the buildings Raiding Forces Advanced HQ intends to occupy. It would be in everyone's best interest if she were to do as much of her shopping in Antalya Province as possible.

"General Bakkal receives a 'komisyon' from the merchants in his province." Col. Randal said, "I'm sure Jane will be happy to cooperate, sir."

Brig. Clarke said, "One hand washes the other. The more we do for the General, the more willing he will be to turn a blind eye to our LSF activities. Do enough, the man will be totally sightless."

"I hear you, sir—loud and clear."

"You shall need to have The Great Teddy perform one of his magic tricks on the island. Have him set up a decoy headquarters complex as far away from your real HQ as possible in the event the Axis decide to bomb Castelrozzo again. There is always the possibility of a raid as long as the enemy maintain air superiority."

Col. Randal said, "Ted did exactly that at RAF Habbaniya when the Golden Square rebels were plastering the base with artillery—I'll have him make it a priority."

Brig. Clarke said, "Until I tell you differently, Raiding Forces occupying Castelrozzo is classified. After that, there is no need to hide the fact. In fact, I shall *want* you to advertise it."

"Yes, sir."

One glance at the map had made it clear to Col. Randal that Castelrozzo was never going to suffice as a base to launch raids as far west as Raiding Forces would need to operate. Now he realized Brig. Clarke intended to use the island as a deception to cover the LSF schooners being moored in the inlets along Turkey's rugged coastline.

A good plan.

With Dudley Clarke, nothing was ever what it seemed—lies, half-truths, disinformation, misdirection, smoke and mirrors—deception with just enough real truth to make it all seem plausible.

Col. Randal said, "Can you plant a story in a newspaper if I ask, sir?"

Brig. Clarke said, "Why yes, absolutely most any of them worldwide—including papers in Berlin if you need."

Col. Randal said, "Good."

NEXT, BEVERLY BROUGHT IN CAPTAIN CUTHBERT BOWLBY, the MI-6 Chief of Station, Cairo. Like Brigadier Raymond J. (R. J.) Maunsell, the head of Security Intelligence Middle East (SIME), who liked to be addressed by his initials, Capt. Bowlby never used his rank and always dressed in civilian clothes. Unlike with R. J., Colonel John Randal could never quite bring himself to call the SIS spymaster by his nickname—Curly.

There had been bad blood between MI-6 and Raiding Forces over the DeBeers Diamond Company, Major the Lady Jane Seaborn, and OPERATION LEAF EATER. It had been resolved. As is often the case when both sides are acting in good faith to cross purposes, conflict turned into consensus and then close-knit teamwork.

Cuthbert said, "Wanted to remind you of our conversation about MI-6 establishing a listening post on Castelrozzo."

Col. Randal said, "No problem. Captain Fawcett-Tatum will be your point of contact on the island. As we also agreed, you can count on Raiding Forces honoring our commitment to insert or extract agents throughout the Aegean for you on request. Your people will get VIP treatment, but it may not be luxurious. Most likely have to rely on LSF caiques unless you have a time-sensitive mission."

Cuthbert said, "The LSF will suffice nicely for the majority of MI-6 requirements. One less thing for me to worry about. Transportation has always been a major headache. Thanks for taking it off my hands."

Col. Randal said, "Coordinate with Lady Jane. Tell her what you need in the way of quarters. She'll be traveling to Castelrozzo in the near future. Ask her to scout out a location or send one of your people with her. The island was extensively bombed a couple of years ago. A lot of the structures are abandoned or in disrepair. There's a good chance any place that suits your needs will need repairs. We'll make that happen for you."

Cuthbert said, "Outstanding. My intent is to use the island as a listening post and as a waystation for SIS operatives en route to their target areas. We shall have need of a small HQ and transit quarters for the people passing through.

"My primary interest is signals intelligence. Castelrozzo is the perfect location to set up to eavesdrop on the Turks, the Nazis on Crete, Rhodes, Kos and Leros, and the Italians scattered throughout the Dodecanese."

Col. Randal said, "In that case, touch base with Major Adair. Phantom is in the process of relocating Raiding Forces' long-range signals station from Oasis X to Castelrozzo. Possibly your people can set up at the same time."

Cuthbert said, "I shall."

He did not mention that MI-6 and Phantom had a history of mutual cooperation.

Intelligence officers like to keep their secrets. Even little ones.

Col. Randal was well aware of the relationship—he chose not to point that out.

BEVERLY ENTERED WITH THE NAVAL OFFICER IN CHARGE (NOIC), Cyprus.

"Captain McDonald to see you."

Captain M. H. S. McDonald aka "Snow White" for the simple reason he had a full shock of thick, snow-white hair. The NOIC Cyprus was something of a legend among sailors. When a Levant Schooner Flotilla caique was scheduled to arrive, he routinely waited on the dock in a 1908 Rolls-Royce with his companion, a female acrobat called Peter Pan.

No one knew her real name.

Snow White had a dry sense of humor, which he did his best to conceal, though some felt Capt. McDonald did not work at that hard enough. He enjoyed running up clever signals to the skippers arriving—pointing out weaknesses in their seamanship—which naturally could be read by all the other sailors in the harbor. When one of the LSF caiques, commanded by an eager young army subaltern long on enterprise but short on actual sailing experience, crashed into the side of a Motor Gunboat, Capt. McDonald put up flags announcing, "Anti-demolition training to commence in one hour."

If anyone fit the Raiding Forces mold, it was Snow White.

Capt. McDonald said, "I shan't be long. Simply wanted to introduce myself."

Colonel John Randal said, "Your reputation has preceded you, Captain."

"Yes, well, the lads do gossip, what!"

Col. Randal said, "Admiral Ransom informs me you've taken a special interest in the Levant Schooner Flotilla."

"Bold lads sailing in harm's way aboard dilapidated ships. Count on my full support to keep them in repair with a speedy turnaround. When an

LSF caique or any of your other FIRE EATER small boats arrive in Cyprus, they shall go to the head of the queue for dockyard service."

Col. Randal said, "Given any thought to stationing your people on Castelrozzo?"

"Yes, actually I have. If you agree to supply living quarters and victualing, we can keep a team of naval workmen on the island. Maintenance following a voyage will go a long way toward keeping your little fleet at sea. Save time not having to sail all the way to Cyprus."

"Have one of your officers speak to Captain Fawcett-Tatum. She'll be the point of contact on Castelrozzo. Stephanie will make sure your people are taken care of. If there's ever a problem, contact me immediately."

"Looking forward to a bountiful relationship, Colonel."

Col. Randal said, "One other thing. Captain Jaxx—commands my Small Operations Group—he'll probably turn up on Cyprus from time to time."

"The youngster who asked the professor about topless swimming?"

"Keep an eye on Peter Pan when he does."

COLONEL JOHN RANDAL'S NEXT VISITOR WAS ONE OF THE most colorful characters in the British Army, which is saying something— Lieutenant Colonel H. J. "Kid" Cator. He was at RFHQ today as the new commander of the Special Air Service. Lt. Col. Cator had been commissioned in the Royal Scots Greys one year into the last war and served with distinction on the Western front. After the Armistice, he left the army to help manage the family "farm" which bordered on the Royal Estate at Sandringham in Norfolk. He was personal friends with the Royal Family, frequently being invited over to shoot with the King. When WWII began, he rejoined his regiment as an overage subaltern.

It sailed for the Middle East to join the 1st Cavalry Division.

However, Kid soon tired of chasing Arab dissidents, so he volunteered as soon as he learned the Palestinians were forming pioneer companies and needed British officers. His command, 401 Company, Auxiliary Military Pioneer Corps (AMPC) consisted of Jews, Arabs (Sudanese, Egyptians, Iraqis, Somalis, and Palestinians), Poles, Czechs, Russians, Bulgarians, Romanians, Austrians, Germans, Spaniards, Portuguese, and Latvians. His company sailed back to England, then over to France in time to turn around and be evacuated from Dunkirk.

Lt. Col. Cator was forced to navigate the Brixham trawler transporting his troops across the Channel because the captain was so drunk he had to be carried aboard ship on a stretcher and locked in his cabin.

Back in England, Commandos were being raised. Kid was selected to command one of the new units. However, 401 Company was alerted to return to Egypt, and he was not about to leave it no matter how glamorous the command of a Commando might be. Lt. Col. Cator was an example of the finest type of officer the British Empire could produce. He put his men before himself, even though his troops had once been described as the "scrapings of the worst slums in the Middle East."

Many officers claimed they put their men first—few did.

Through a series of military adventures back in Egypt, 401 Company was transformed into 51 Middle East Commando. Eventually the unit found itself invading Abyssinia. That was where Lt. Col. Cator had first met Col. Randal.

Back in Egypt, 51 Middle East Commando had been ordered to carry out one poorly designed raid after another by the Plans Division, MEHQ—which failed.

"After David Stirling managed to get himself captured, the 1st SAS was broken up. Major Mayne formed the Special Raiding Service out of parts, other members went to the Raiding Support Regiment, the Special Boat Section was split off, and a handful of people remained as SAS under my command.

"Unfortunately, I have been ordered to return to England immediately to take up a position on Boy Browning's staff in his 1 Allied Airborne Corp.

I can provide a list of suitable candidates for transfer to Raiding Forces if you wish."

Col. Randal said, "That's too bad. I was looking forward to us working together. Lady Jane was hoping to have you as a dinner companion. She'll be disappointed."

Lt. Col. Cator said, "Duty calls—possibly you would care to nominate one of your officers to take my place."

Col. Randal said, "Do you happen to know Major Baltimore Farquhar of the Lancelot Lancers?"

"Mongo—excellent choice, first-class fellow, what!"

THE NEXT VISITOR BEVERLY BROUGHT TO SEE COLONEL John Randal was the noted desert explorer Lieutenant Colonel Guy Prendergast, commanding officer of the Long Range Desert Group. He had been one of the three original founders of the LRDG. Lt. Col. Prendergast had been in command of the unit since 1941. He had learned to fly while serving with the Western Arab Desert Force in the Sudan before the war. He was a through and through professional desert operator and a brilliant commander of special forces.

Unfortunately, there was no longer a need for desert warriors.

Lt. Col. Prendergast was not enthusiastic about being at Raiding Forces Headquarters today. The Long Range Desert Group had been the premiere long-range reconnaissance unit in Middle East Command. When Panzerarmee Afrika was pushed out of Libya into the hills of North Africa, maps had been broken out and the LRDG officers searched the world for another desert to conduct operations in.

No joy.

While there was no longer any requirement for such a highly specialized unit, there was always a demand for long-range reconnaissance and no one in authority wanted to disband an outfit with such a stellar record. The decision was made to retrain it. However, because of the way the LRDG worked, most of its patrols were on loan from their regiments for rotating tours of temporary duty.

Most of those troops had already been returned to their parent organization.

The remaining men were subjected to medical examinations, which some of them failed as a result of living for years in a harsh environment under primitive conditions with Spartan creature comforts. Those who passed were shipped off for mountain warfare training, parachute training, and amphibious/small boat training. Tough courses. More men failed.

At this point, the LRDG had been reduced to approximately the size of an infantry rifle platoon—a mere shadow of itself. The LRDG had always been an independent command. Now Lt. Col. Prendergast had to suffer the indignity of having his unit assigned or attached to Raiding Forces. And the idea of being commanded by an officer considerably younger—who outranked him—did not sit well.

Who would blame him? Certainly not Col. Randal.

The LRDG had flown high, but now had been brought down to earth.

Lt. Col. Prendergast said, "Checking by to see if you have any information on our status—assigned or attached?"

"Not yet."

"What role do you see the LRDG playing in FIRE EATER, Colonel?"

"My thought is to use your people for reconnaissance. That's what you're good at. Gather intelligence on islands we intend to raid and/or as Beach Watchers."

"Beach Watchers?"

"Something the Australians pioneered in the Pacific. Small teams . . . or even individuals. . . with a long-range radio stationed on islands to report the movement of Jap shipping. That should work in the Aegean—a small clandestine LRDG team on an island with a powerful telescope and a radio."

Lt. Col. Prendergast said, "Might offer possibilities—worth exploring. LRDG are not Commandos. My worry is my lads will be misused the way the SAS was."

Col. Randal said, "Raiding Forces has a rule. 'Right Man, Right Job.' We try to put round pegs in round holes."

Lt. Col. Prendergast said, "So I have been told."

Col. Randal knew this relationship was never going to work well.

COLONEL JOHN RANDAL COULD TELL BEVERLY LIKED THE next visitor — Major the Earl George Jellicoe, a stocky young playboy with a mischievous smile and a reputation for the ladies. The son of the Commander of the Fleet during the Battle of Jutland in the last war, he was the commanding officer of the army's Special Boat Section.

Col. Randal had been briefed on his military record. Commissioned out of Sandhurst into the Grenadier Guards Regiment, Lord Jellicoe had volunteered for No. 8 Commando that came out to Egypt as part of Layforce. After having been thoroughly misused by incompetent staff planners in the Operations Division of Middle East Command, Layforce was disbanded.

Lord Jellicoe found himself assigned to the Special Air Service in command of the Special Boat Section, an assignment he had no previous experience or training for—other than his father having been an admiral. Not to worry, the SBS was employed as jeep raiders and never went anywhere near the water.

Then the SAS commander, Lieutenant Colonel David Stirling, aka Big Sloth, managed to get himself captured because of lax signals security on a patrol. The 1st SAS Regiment was broken up. SBS was assigned or attached to Raiding Forces. The distinction had yet to be resolved.

Unlike Lieutenant Colonel Guy Prendergast, Lord Jellicoe was delighted to have the opportunity to work with Raiding Forces. Lieutenant Colonel Sir Terry "Zorro" Stone, his wingman chasing refugee Greek girls in Alexandria, had given Col. Randal a five-star recommendation. Besides, he knew Major the Lady Jane Seaborn.

Anyone she would fall for had to have the right stuff.

Col. Randal said, "Terry speaks highly of you, Lord Jellicoe."

"Please, sir, address me as Major, Jellicoe, or George as you see fit—no titles."

Col. Randal said, "Not going to happen. In Raiding Forces, we take advantage of every opportunity that presents itself. Having a pet Earl might come in handy."

Lord Jellicoe laughed, "Fair enough. Feel free to use my title any way you see fit. I am here to do my bit. No special treatment."

"Good. My thought is to deploy the Special Boat Section as one of Raiding Forces' new amphibious maneuver elements. You'll be stationed on board LSF barracks sloops. Meaning SBS will pretty much be operating independently."

"Like the sound of that, sir."

"There may be certain political aspects to FIRE EATER that develop from time to time. If that turns out to be the case, with your experience in the House of Lords, you'll be my go-to political advisor. Make sure to keep a capable second in command in place ready to take over in your absence."

"I have the best, sir—Captain Alistair McLean."

"Questions, George?"

"Is Beverly dating anyone?"

COLONEL JOHN RANDAL ASKED, "WHO'S NEXT?"

Beverly said, "Lady Jane and Sergeant Major Beckwith are waiting for you, Johnny." The golden-haired beauty with the smile as big as Texas was the only member of Raiding Forces brave enough to call him by that name. Beverly only did it when the two were alone or when Major the Lady Jane Seaborn was present.

Lady Jane had started doing it in private when she was teasing him. Col. Randal said, "I told Jane to rest upstairs . . ."

"Well, she didn't pay attention."

"Right."

When Col. Randal walked out, Lady Jane was sitting with Master Sergeant Mack Beckwith, waiting for him to finish.

In the U.S. Army, Master Sergeant was the highest enlisted grade. However, the senior NCO in a battalion or larger-sized unit was called "Sergeant Major." Unlike the British Army, where a Sergeant Major was a warrant officer, accorded the privileges of an officer and called "sir."

The protocols could be confusing.

Col. Randal had no idea how the rank worked in the Greek Sacred Squadron—he made a note to check into it because he believed military courtesy to be an important aspect of respect and exercised it at all times. Rank was earned and a matter of pride. In Raiding Forces, officers and NCOs were addressed by their rank at all times. The officers were permitted to use first names only when not in front of troops.

They almost never did it with him. "Ready."

The four of them walked to the main ballroom. RFHQ was located in a compound owned by one of King Farouk's family members and leased to the British Army for the duration. Rumor had it the King used it to stage his orgies—though that had never been confirmed.

By the time they arrived, the Small Raids Incorporated trade-show style convention was in full swing, with display tables set up around the room under crystal chandeliers. Captain "Geronimo" Joe McKoy was demonstrating the features of his chopped M1919 .30 caliber Browning light machine gun called "The Stinger." It was built to specifications and sent to him by a Para Marine buddy at Pearl Harbor. Ensign Theodore Hamilton had tripods set up with photos of camouflaged caiques and examples of the three colors of camouflage netting—brown, green and chalk white they would be using.

Lieutenant Randy "Hornblower" Seaborn was displaying photos and diagrams describing the Motor Gunboats and PT boats that would be used—emphasis placed on various gun packages. His mother Brandy and Captain Penelope Honeycutt-Parker were at another table, giving an orientation about the specifications of high-speed MAS boats. Lieutenant Commander Adrian Seligman was at a table discussing the Levant Schooner Flotilla.

Captain Roy Kidd was using a couple of tables to exhibit the nonconventional weapons used by Raiding Forces—not all the 10th Rangers, LRDG, SBS, GSS, and LSF personnel were familiar with some of the more exotic models. Captain Billy Jack Jaxx was briefing the four island raids he participated in to give an idea of what to expect in the way of future targets.

There were a lot of stations. Much to see and much information to be disseminated. Every officer and noncommissioned officer in any unit assigned or attached to Small Raids Incorporated was in attendance. It was an impressive assemblage of Special Operations professionals from all branches of service from four different countries, counting the Australian Matilda tank mechanics. U.S. Army Rangers mingled with LRDG reconnaissance specialists, LSF skippers, Greek Sacred Squadron Commandos, Lady Jane's Royal Marines, etc.

The idea was to bring all those in leadership positions up to speed on the shift from desert patrolling to remote island raiding. Also, Col. Randal wanted to give the operational officers, NCOs, and the people who supported them an opportunity to meet each other—some for the first time. It was a chance to put a face with a name previously only seen on an after-action report, known by reputation or heard over a radio.

It was a gathering of eagles—the first and last time all those present would be in the same room.

After two hours, James "Baldie" Taylor took Col. Randal into a side room for an impromptu meeting with Vice Admiral Sir Randolph "Razor" Ransom, Brigadier Raymond J. Maunsell, Brigadier Dudley Clarke, Brigadier General William "Wild Bill" Donovan, and Captain Cuthbert Bowlby.

King stood at the door to make sure they were not interrupted.

Jim said, "Colonel, while you were away campaigning in Sicily, a power play to take over control of Raiding Forces was initiated by the Operations Division of Middle East Command."

R. J. said, "MEHQ has become a military backwater now that the

Eighth Army has moved on. There are no longer any major maneuver units stationed in Egypt or Libya. All that's left are a handful of RAF and U.S. Army Air Force squadrons, a few—as in a very few—Royal Navy ships berthed in Alexandria, and some second-rate British Army battalions who were detailed for security duties."

Jim said, "General "Jumbo" Wilson, who replaced Field Marshal Alexander when he left to take over Fifteenth Army Group, has found himself the master of acres and acres of military warehouses, a vast conglomerate of rear echelon support units, and an army of clerk typists doing who knows what.

"Shall be a challenge for Jumbo to have himself promoted to Field Marshal if he does not fight anything but paper battles. His desire for advancement, combined with the Operations Plans Division not having anything of substance to plan, have sown the seeds of a disaster."

Brig. Clarke said, "The Plans Division staff have always had their knives out for you, Colonel, because of your refusal to allow them to plan Raiding Forces missions."

R. J. said, "And rightly so."

Cuthbert said, "The bloody fools."

Jim said, "General Wilson received the Prime Minister's missive, 'now is the time to aim high and dare' in the Aegean—the General thought he saw an opportunity."

VAdm. Ransom said, "Jumbo ordered preparations be put in motion on an out-of-date plan to occupy Rhodes, Leros, Kos, and Samos—the only offensive that can be attempted due to the acute shortage of shipping. Total Royal Navy assets consist of one mixed destroyer flotilla at Alexandria and six submarines. Coastal Forces has four MTB and ML flotillas, which I contend fall under my command."

Jim said, "A gunner officer, Colonel Douglas Turnbull, was designated 'Commander of Raiding Forces, Middle East.' He was ordered to occupy the four named islands with the 234th Infantry Brigade. It is arriving piecemeal after having spent the last three years on garrison duty at Malta being bombed night and day—not razor-sharp fighting troops.

"The plan was for the 234th to be augmented by Raiding Forces, LRDG, SAS, SBS, and the GSS."

VAdm. Ransom said, "Turnbull intends to go after Leros first, then Kos, and then the rest. He and Plans Division staff are mainly concerned about which island to occupy next and how soon can it be done without taking into consideration what the other side might have to say about it.

Jim said, "Always a mistake holding your enemy in contempt."

R. J. said, "Turnbull is in the process of building a house of cards."

Jim said, "Try pointing that out to the armchair Commandos at Plans Division—I did."

Cuthbert said, "Intelligence indicates that the senior German Field Marshal whose responsibilities include the Aegean Islands, "Smiling Al" Kesselring, has standing orders from Berlin to immediately retake any territory given up in the islands. A parachute regiment of the Brandenburg Special Operations Division has been dispatched to the Aegean AO on alert for a drop. The Nazis can be expected to hit back hard and fast."

VAdm. Ransom said, "The Luftwaffe's *Fliegerkorps X* with an airfield on Kos gives the Germans the advantage of total air supremacy. That checkmates our side being able to fly missions in support of 234th Infantry Brigade during the day. It also keeps our surface ships in dock during daylight hours."

Cuthbert said, "The Royal Navy is not willing to risk any more losses in an ancillary theatre of operations, no matter the Prime Minister's obsessions about the Aegean."

VAdm. Ransom said, "That's when we stepped in. Turnbull is putting FIRE EATER in jeopardy. His intentions will set in motion a series of moves and counter moves that ultimately will result in Raiding Forces becoming embroiled in a defensive land battle someplace, sometime. That is a fight that cannot be won due to our lack of friendly air, which MEHQ steadfastly chooses to ignore."

Jim said, "Like R. J. so astutely pointed out, Turnbull is building 'a house of cards.'" VAdm. Ransom said, "General Wilson was informed in writing by Combined Operations

Headquarters, London, that Small Raids Incorporated was the controlling authority for Strategic Raiding Forces. Admiral Cunningham wrote a memo confirming the chain of command. It bypasses MEHQ and ends up at the Admiralty where it will be referred to the Director of Operations, Irregular—me."

Cuthbert said, "MI-6 and SOE's London headquarters have both registered protests with the Chief of the Imperial General Staff's office over the misuse of what they consider an irreplaceable intelligence asset. And Commander Fleming hand-carried a note from his boss, the Chief of Naval Intelligence, to the Prime Minister warning the ability to quickly respond to GOLDEN FLEECE missions would be compromised if Raiding Forces was wasted as infantry."

Brig. Gen. Donovan said, "I will have my OSS London Office contact the Prime Minister as well—this will not stand!"

Brig. Clarke said, "Turnbull has been ordered by MEHQ to cease using the name Raiding Forces. He was signing documents, 'Commanding, Raiding Forces *Regiment,*' which completely defeats the deceptive purpose of the name. The enemy has no idea how large a unit Raiding Forces is.

"It could be anything."

R. J. said, "I believe the new name the Plans Division has come up with for Turnbull is 'Middle East Combined Operations.'"

VAdm. Ransom said, "It was explained to Turnbull that he was not to meddle in Small Raids Incorporated projects. If he does, I have made it abundantly clear he will not be provided so much as a canoe to transport his troops or supplies for the rest of the war. Admiral Cunningham has agreed to back me up on the threat."

Col. Randal said, "Doesn't sound like the Colonel got the word, sir— showed up here to crash our briefing."

Jim said, "I had a conversation with him. He does now."

VAdm. Ransom said, "Here is where things stand. The good news: Turnbull has no say in anything related to Raiding Forces. The bad news: the LRDG and the SBS will temporarily remain under his command. GSS was initially penciled in as well, but Major Zargo blew his stack, and the idea was scrapped."

Brig. Gen. Donovan said, "I've already stuck my neck out by getting involved in the Aegean Campaign with the President, the Army Chief of Staff, and General Eisenhower not on board with the mission. So, feel free to quote me that I'll pull out the only U.S. support the British have in the theatre if MEHQ interferes with Raiding Forces operations.

"Keep me fully informed.

Col. Randal said, "Brandenburgers are the best troops the German Army has—Colonel Turnbull's in for a fight."

AFTER LUNCH EVERYONE WAS INVITED OUTSIDE RFHQ TO observe what was billed as Colonel John Randal making a demonstration parachute drop. Some attendees, most notably from the Levant Schooner Flotilla, had never seen one. Captain Billy Jack Jaxx was acting as static Pathfinder for the drop, standing by with smoke grenades and a radio operator. When Beverly Blackwell radioed him the jump aircraft was on its final approach, he would pop smoke to mark the drop zone (DZ).

Lawn chairs had been set out for Major the Lady Jane Seaborn and the senior officers. Everyone else stood around, waiting, watching the sky. No matter how much experience they had with airborne operations, everyone loved to watch a jump. Word went around the group that the Big Four would be on board enjoying a VIP hop.

Some people knew who the Big Four were. Some did not.

The passengers were already seated in the twin engine Airspeed Envoy when Col. Randal's jeep arrived at the departure airfield. The aircraft was obsolete as an operational model before the war started. This one had been used to transport VIP senior officers, then as a trainer. The plane looked good but was barely airworthy.

The door had been removed to facilitate the jump.

Col. Randal climbed aboard and walked up the aisle to the cockpit. He waved at the four crime lords buckled into their seats. They waved back happily. It was good to be an important person.

As soon as Col. Randal was strapped in the co-pilot's seat, Beverly began to taxi.

"OK, I hope we can get this rattletrap off the ground. Glad we're wearing parachutes. The RAF has already DX'ed this aircraft off their books. The pilot who delivered it told me not to bother bringing it back."

"I've got confidence in you, kid."

"It's a death trap."

"Yes, it is."

The plane clawed its way into the air. With a top speed of only 170 mph the day it was built (a long time ago), the Airspeed Envoy slowly struggled to gain 3,000 feet. Beverly brought the ship around and leveled out. In the distance, the Mediterranean sparkled turquoise in the sunlight. They were headed out to sea.

It was a beautiful Egyptian day.

Col. Randal spotted RFHQ. Beverly spoke into her mike. Violet smoke appeared drifting gently along the ground, blown by a wind speed of three to five knots. Conditions were perfect— "copacetic" in paratrooper speak, on the drop zone.

Which is what Jack Cool radioed, "DZ is cope-ah-cetic." They were good to go.

Beverly said, "Any time, Johnny."

Col. Randal said, "Let's do this."

The two unbuckled their seatbelts, stood up, and with Col. Randal leading the way, they strolled down the aisle of the plane past the Big Four.

Col. Randal said, "Feel free to get out of your seats. Move around the cabin—go check out the cockpit. It'll be fun."

Beverly laughed, "Y'all are going to be *sooo* popular in hell."

Continuing on to the tail of the plane, they hooked their snap links to an improvised steel cable beside the open door and, with Beverly leading the way, exited the aircraft. The drop was what is classified as a "Hollywood

Jump," meaning no equipment, not counting sidearms. The two parachutes cracked open and it was an enjoyable ride to the ground—absolutely fantastic. Col. Randal and Beverly came down together reasonably close to where Capt. Jaxx was positioned. He appeared out of the violet smoke drifting 'round—a color U.S. Army Paratroopers referred to as, "Goofy Grape."

Capt. Jaxx said, "Nice jump, sir?"

"It was."

Captain Karen Montgomery, Raiding Forces' chief rigger, and King recovered the X-type parachutes.

Lady Jane and Happy drove out to meet them in a jeep. "Who's flying the plane?"

Beverly said, "It's on autopilot."

Lady Jane said, "Autopilots are not capable of landing an aircraft."

Col. Randal said, "You sure about that?"

4
GOTTA LOVE HISTORY

COLONEL JOHN RANDAL, CAPTAIN "GERONIMO" JOE MCKOY, Captain Billy Jack Jaxx, Waldo Treywick. and Lieutenant Mandy Paige, OBE, were sitting in the briefing area of the third-floor suite. They were waiting for Beverly Blackwell to arrive with Gunnery Sergeant Frank Polanski. Waldo passed out his long, thin custom-rolled cigars—Mandy declined.

No one lit up, as Major the Lady Jane Seaborn did not allow cigars to be smoked in her apartment.

Capt. McKoy said, "You and Beverly just waltzed down the aisle and bailed outta that airplane?"

Col. Randal said, "We did."

"Nobody said nothin'?"

"That's the beauty of the element of surprise, Captain."

Capt. Jaxx said, "We know all four conspired to have Lady Jane assassinated, or at least knew it was going to happen and failed to warn us. What'd they expect you'd do—sooner or later?"

Waldo said, "I'd-a' liked to have murdered 'em myself. We've all been wonderin' what was takin' you so long to get around to doin' it, Colonel, but now what? You done eliminated all my contacts in the illegal diamond trade."

Mandy said, "Major Sansom is carrying out raids on the Big Four's private compounds as we speak, Mr. Treywick. I phoned him the moment I realized what happened. When we talked, Sammy asked for me to inform you that he is confident he knows who the new crop of successors will be."

"Dog eat dog in the criminal underworld," Capt. McKoy said. "One boss goes down, two or three second-tier crooks step up. Sansom plays his cards right, he'll get to pick the winners. Deal with who comes out on top, Waldo—you ain't gonna miss a step."

Capt. Jaxx said, "I wish I could have seen the expression on those gangster's faces when they realized no one was in the cockpit."

Waldo said, "You reckon it's up there still flyin'?"

Mandy said, "Hope so—serves them right."

"You done a good thing, John, Capt. McKoy said, "sending a message that you're not a man to cross. Gonna pay off dividends with the lowlifes we got to work with down the road."

Col. Randal said, "I gave fair warning that Raiding Forces female personnel were under my protection."

"Yes, you did, John," Mandy said. "Those criminals got exactly what they deserved. I feel like a bullseye has been removed from my back.

"Thank you."

Waldo said, "One thing's for sure, Colonel. After today, you ain't never gonna have to worry none about nobody tryin' to beat your time with Lady Jane."

Capt. Jaxx said, "That's a definite Rodge!"

Beverly walked in with King and Gunnery Sergeant Frank Polanski. Col. Randal said, "Frank, I have a mission for you."

The Marine immediately perked up. "Sir?"

Col. Randal said, "You have to volunteer before I can give you the details."

GySgt. Polanski was a tough-as-nails United States Marine Corps Gunnery Sergeant with a break in service during the time when he became a freelance soldier in Abyssinia. Volunteering had rendered mixed results for him in the past.

However, he had enormous respect for Col. Randal.

Capt. McKoy said, "This assignment's right up your alley, Frank, 'Right Man Right Job' with the hair on."

GySgt. Polanski said, "If you say so—count me in, Colonel."

Col. Randal said, "You'll still be a Marine. You're also going to be a member of the Office of Strategic Services. Your assignment is to recruit a band of mercenaries for an independent operation in the Belgian Congo."

"I run the show?"

"Captain McKoy's in command from here in Cairo. You report to him. In the field, you'll be in charge with a free hand, but my guess is, knowing the Captain he'll fly in to check on you from time to time. Your mission is to track down traffickers who smuggle diamonds out of the Congo to Germany.

"United States' national security is at stake. OSS has issued orders to eliminate the traffickers with extreme prejudice — that's your mission."

"Extreme prejudice mean what I think it does, sir?"

"Abyssinian Rules are in full force and effect."

"Got it, can do, sir. Affirmative."

"Give yourself any rank you feel appropriate. Impress the locals like we did in Force N. This is a big job, Frank."

"Commander General sound about right, sir?"

"Perfect."

Beverly laughed, "Commander General Devil Dog—excellent."

Capt. McKoy said, "Do a good job and we'll put you in for a bonus. Give a whole new meaning to 'soldier of fortune.'"

Waldo said, "Joe ain't kiddin' . . . we pay top dollar. Get the job done, and you ain't ever goin' to have to work another day in your life. I kid you not."

Commander General Frank Polanski said, "I knew back then that signing on with Force N was a smart move, Colonel. Especially after you shot my employer. When do we get started?"

"Just as soon as Captain McKoy and Mr. Treywick finish your briefing and we can arrange transport to the Congo."

MAJOR THE LADY JANE SEABORN ARRIVED WITH BRANDY
Seaborn and Captain Penelope Honeycutt-Parker. Brandy and Parker were
now dressed in their trademark rolled up khaki shorts, canvas-topped raiding
boots and sidearms. Before going in the bedroom to change, Lady Jane said,
"Beverly, you and Mandy—work clothes. R. J. is standing by downstairs to
take us to the Big Four's compounds."

Colonel John Randal said, "Wait a . . ."

Lady Jane said, "We have to conduct an immediate search of the
premises of all the Big Four's properties. No time to waste. We cannot risk
the Egyptian Police looting them."

Captain Billy Jack Jaxx said, "Am I on deck, sir?"

Col. Randal said, "Get Roy Kidd . . . we'll need him in on this too."

Captain "Geronimo" Joe McKoy said, "Searching crime scenes for
stuff people don't want anybody to find is my stock in trade, John."

Col. Randal said, "I need you and Mr. Treywick to remain here and
start briefing Frank on our plans for the Congo. We want him operational as
soon as possible. When you're finished come on over—I'd like your help."

"Will do, John."

Col. Randal said, "Mr. Treywick—hook Commander General Polanski
up with Captain Butterfield. Some of his ex-French Foreign Legion people
he's not using for LEAF EATER may want to sign up for Frank's Army."

Commander General Polanski said, "I'm gonna need a few reliable
men I can trust, Colonel. With mercs, you got to sleep with one eye open at
least until the bad apples are weeded out. Even then, it pays to be careful."

Col. Randal said, "Sergeant Major Mikkalis did a tour in the Legion
before the war. I'll assign him to help you with your recruiting. Take him
with you to the Congo and keep him as long as you need until you're set up."

Captain Stephanie Fawcett-Tatum and Veronica Paige arrived with
Sub/Lt. Bentley St. Ledger.

Captain Pamala Plum-Martin walked in right behind them.

Col. Randal said, "Pam, I need a responsible adult to make sure Jane
doesn't overexert herself. She's not listening to me."

Lady Jane's green eyes flashed. "I am perfectly fine."

The Vargas Girl look-alike Royal Marine said, "Leave me out of this one, love." Brandy laughed. "Sounds like an insurrection."

Ignoring her, Col. Randal said, "Jack, go bring me the first four 10th Ranger platoon leaders you can find."

"Wilco."

"Stephanie, arrange truck transport for four platoons of Rangers. I want Lady Jane's search teams to have additional security. Advise Captain Chatterhorn he's in charge."

"Yes, sir."

"While you're at it, have Terry report to me."

Lady Jane came out of the bedroom wearing a faded pair of blue jeans tucked into yellow alligator peewee cowgirl boots. Her ivory handled Colt .38 Super was buckled around her waist.

The pistol grips had originally belonged to Col. Randal before she appropriated them. Happy was on a leash. The ex-Nazi German shepherd used to be his dog, too, but Lady Jane had taken him as well.

Lady Jane said, "We shall have a search party for each property. I shall have one. Brandy—you and Parker lead one. Veronica—you take one, and Stephanie—you have one as well. Bentley, go inform the Royal Marines and WRENs that we require their services out front of RFHQ immediately."

"Roger."

"Stephanie, as soon as you get off of the phone, go downstairs and organize the girls into four groups."

Capt. Fawcett-Tatum put her hand over the speaker. "Only be a minute."

Lieutenant Colonel Sir Terry "Zorro" Stone came charging up the stairs. While Lady Jane continued to brief her women, Col. Randal took his officers off to the side of the room.

"Terry, you team up with Stephanie; Jack, you're on Brandy and Parker; Roy, you've got Veronica. I'll go with Jane. Secure the perimeter of your individual compounds while the interior search of the main building is underway. Have your Ranger platoon leader set up security inside the compound and have them perform a search of the outbuildings. I want the

Egyptian Police to set up outside the compound's walls unless escorted in.

"Post guards on the gates and at the doorway to every structure inside the compound. Don't let anyone enter unless you personally know they are associated with Raiding Forces.

"Make sure everyone in residence on the premises at the time of the raid is searched. Major Sansom will perform the searches. Keep the detainees under close observation until he arrives.

"Do not, I say again, *do not* allow the Egyptian Police inside the compounds. We need live people to interrogate. They'll slit the prisoner's throats, given the opportunity. Questions?"

No one had any.

Beverly and Mandy came back in dressed in the uniform of the day—jeans tucked into alligator boots, wearing sidearms.

Col. Randal ordered, "Pam, Mandy, Beverly—on me." They moved to a corner for additional privacy.

"I want each of you to take a different location. Stay on site until the search is completed. You're my CARD GAME officers. Take physical control of all contraband such as diamonds, gold, or cash—any liquid asset that can be used to fund LEAF EATER."

Capt. Plum-Martin asked, "What should we do with the valuables once we locate them?"

"Radio me. I'll send Captain Chatterhorn over with his Field Security Police to pick 'em up. Don't make a big deal out of it. The first rule of safeguarding a clandestine operation like CARD GAME is that you can't tell your friends without alerting your enemies what you're doing."

Mandy said, "One of the finer points of intelligence. Very good, John."

Col. Randal said, "You're the one who taught me."

"Never occurred to me you were actually paying attention," Mandy said.

As everyone was clearing the room, Col. Randal held Mandy back. "I'm placing you in charge of total asset recovery—not just the searches of the residences. I don't believe we did such a great job of uncovering the hidden assets belonging to the first couple of mobsters we took down.

"Get with Major Sansom. See if he has any thoughts on the subject."

"Why me?"

"Because you're the smartest person in the room."

"There are only the two of us in here."

"Just do it, Mandy."

Capt. Jaxx and King returned with the 10th Ranger lieutenants in tow.

Col. Randal said, "Gentlemen, have your platoons assembled fully armed and equipped in front of RFHQ any time in the next five minutes. Each of you will be assigned to secure a private residence in Cairo which Lady Jane's Royal Marines will be searching. Do not let anyone in or out without permission from the senior Raiding Forces officer present at your location.

"Is that clear?"

The Ranger officers responded in unison, "Clear, sir!"

"Move out."

As they were headed for the door, Capt. Jaxx ordered, "Lieutenant Starrett, your platoon's on me."

Col. Randal knew Capt. Jaxx was interested in the Ranger officer for his Small Operations Group. Probably already would have brought him in if the jump on Sicily had not intervened. He was always striving to improve SOG.

Jack Cool had an eye for talent.

As they were going down the stairs, Col. Randal said, "King, find Colonel Prendergast and Major Jellicoe. Have them report to me before we move out."

"Can do, Chief."

OUTSIDE OF RAIDING FORCES HEADQUARTERS, A FLURRY OF activity was taking place. Captain Lionel Chatterhorn had assembled his Field Security Police, Vulnerable Points Wing gun jeeps with their red lights flashing. Orders were ringing out. Rangers were climbing on U.S. Army two-and-a-half-ton GMC trucks called "deuce and a halves" being driven by Chief Warrant Officer Hank Rawlston's men.

Brigadier General William "Wild Bill" Donovan, Brigadier Raymond J. (R.J.) Maunsell, Captain Cuthbert Bowlby, and James "Baldie" Taylor were getting into Major the Lady Jane Seaborn's white Rolls-Royce with Flanigan at the wheel. King pulled up in a jeep, ready to pick up Colonel John Randal, Master Sergeant Mack Beckwith, Rita, and Lana. Captain Stephanie Fawcett-Tatum was making sure the Royal Marines were all boarding the right trucks. Lady Jane was pacing back and forth with Happy on his leash.

Word had spread among the attendees of the conference at RFHQ about the Big Four taking a flight of no return. A crowd of people gathered to see what was taking place now. Was all the activity related?

No one was saying.

King walked up with Lieutenant Colonel Guy Prendergast and Major the Earl George Jellicoe.

Col. Randal said, "I have just been informed your two units won't be coming to Raiding Forces at this time."

Lt. Col. Prendergast could not help looking relieved.

Lord Jellicoe exhibited the exact opposite reaction. "Colonel, I intend to do everything in my power to have the SBS transferred to Raiding Forces straightaway. Plans originating at MEHQ are not my cup of tea. Called it 'Muddle' East Headquarters, staffed by 'Gabardine Swine', when I was with the Special Air Service.

"Consider the SBS men you have attached now to be my advance party—they shall be staying with Raiding Forces until the rest of us arrive."

"Good, we need you, George."

Lady Jane and Happy hopped in her Rolls.

Col. Randal made eye contact with Captain "Geronimo" Joe McKoy. He walked over.

The two had a brief conversation.

No one could hear the exchange.

Capt. McKoy said, "I'll set 'er up, John."

Col. Randal climbed in his jeep. "Let's roll."

Capt. Chatterhorn turned on the siren as he led out. King pulled in after him. Flanigan fell in behind Col. Randal's jeep. The rest of the Field Security Police turned on their sirens as the trucks rolled out.

The convoy raced toward Cairo.

The road, which had always been packed with military vehicles when Eighth Army was in Egypt, was now almost completely deserted. The few cars and trucks using it immediately pulled over to let them scream pass. On the outskirts of Cairo, Major A. W. "Sammy" Sansom had his policemen waiting to escort the different search parties to their respective compounds.

The column split into four elements.

Maj. Sansom personally led Capt. Chatterhorn to the compound Lady Jane's team was to search. His men had the walls surrounded by the time they arrived. Maj. Sansom's Cairo Security Police—not to be confused with the Cairo Police Department or any Egyptian Military Police, had already breached the gate and taken down the criminals inside. The crime lord's family was in custody, being held in the detached six-car garage.

The body of one of the gangster's security guards was lying in the circular drive in a pool of blood when Col. Randal's jeep rolled in, just ahead of Lady Jane's Rolls.

King and Flanigan—who was armed with the sawed off 12-gauge Browning A-5 shotgun he always kept next to him in the front seat when he drove—led the way inside. The house had already been secured by Maj. Sansom's men, but no one was in a mood to take any chances.

Not with Lady Jane present.

The mansion was like something out of a Hollywood movie—standard operating procedure for Middle Eastern crime bosses. They flaunted their wealth as a means of demonstrating their power. However, this mansion proved that money did not translate into good taste.

Almost immediately, Happy began straining on his leash. Lady Jane followed him to a closet off the main room downstairs. The dog was on the prowl for trouble.

King pushed her aside and carefully opened the door. Nothing. The closet was packed with racks of clothes and stacks of boxes piled up. Happy began barking furiously and tugging on his leash, almost jerking Lady Jane down.

The dog wanted in. Maj. Sansom shouted a command in Arabic. No response. Lady Jane released Happy. The animal rushed in, growling viciously. His attack was followed by terrified screams. King moved in, pistol in hand. Happy had someone by the leg and was doing his best to gnaw it off. The man had been concealing himself in a tiny space behind the boxes,

King grabbed the leash to pull off the dog. Happy was not having any of it. He was out for blood.

Lady Jane gave a command in German. The dog immediately stopped his attack. She had put him through English language obedience school, but he still responded to certain things better in the language learned as a pup when he had been trained by the Nazis.

King dragged a screaming man out of the closet. Maj. Sansom handcuffed him, then turned him over to one of his policemen to be taken out to the garage to be searched.

Scratching Happy between the ears, Col. Randal said, "Nice going, dog—you traitor."

Lady Jane reached inside her shoulder bag, retrieved a treat and gave it to Happy. "Good boy!"

Happy looked — happy.

The search was on. Lady Jane and Col. Randal first went to the coat closet next to the front door. From previous experience, they had learned the criminals usually kept bail out bags full of cash, diamonds, or other lightweight, easily convertible valuables ready and waiting in the event they had to make a run for it.

They found suitcases that were packed and ready to go. Unfortunately, the bags only contained a small amount of money in bills and a few jewels. Apparently, the Big Four had slacked off in their personal security preparations once they made a deal with British and U.S. Intelligence.

The heads of the four major crime families had thought themselves untouchable.

Upstairs in the bedrooms, it was not going much better. Tens of thousands, possibly hundreds of thousands, of dollars' worth of jewelry was found. Monster diamond rings—both men's and women's—and garish necklaces so big the stones did not look real. There was a large collection of gaudy diamond-encrusted men's watches. But nothing like the treasure trove expected.

The stash had to be somewhere.

No respectable gangster would put his money in a bank. There was no way to get to a safety deposit box with the police on your heels in the middle of the night. Besides, funds in banks could be seized by the authorities.

Lady Jane's Royal Marines searched behind every painting, every armoire, every mirror. Rita and Lana wiggled down every crawl space. Rangers were tapping on walls. The Lovat Scouts had done this twice before and knew the drill. They were all over the house—nothing. They found several safes containing valuables of one kind or another but none containing the wealth of treasure to be expected.

That did not mean there was not a lot of value inside the mansion. The Oriental rugs alone were worth a king's ransom. The mobster's sporting firearms were best grade bespoke weapons from the finest European gunmakers. There were rare stamps and coins. Even a butterfly collection. But the total in value was nowhere equal to what was to be expected of one of the four top Middle Eastern crime lords.

They were fabulously wealthy.

Brig. Gen. Donovan, R. J., Cuthbert, and Jim were poking around checking out the lifestyle of Cairo's criminal elite, amazed at the tawdriness of it all—almost overwhelming.

Col. Randal said, "Finding anything you like?"

Cuthbert said, "R. J. and I have been admiring the men's suits."

"They're yours."

Brig. Gen. Donovan said, "There is one oil painting that would work in my office."

"Show Jane. She'll have it professionally removed from the frame and packed in a tube so you can take it back on the plane."

"Extremely valuable."

"It's yours, General."

Brandy arrived, having left Captain Penelope Honeycutt-Parker in charge of the search at the mansion the two of them were responsible for.

"See what I have, handsome."

She took Col. Randal and Lady Jane into a side room where they were alone and produced a black velvet bag out of her purse. Brandy poured a handful of sparkling diamonds into her palm. "Thought you might like to see these before I call Captain Chatterhorn to secure them."

"Nice work, Brandy."

Lady Jane said, "No joy here."

Brandy said, "Have you interrogated the prisoners?"

Col. Randal said, "Not talking."

"Possibly not being asked the right way—take me to them."

"Follow me."

Col. Randal led her out of the house, around back to the six-car garage where Maj. Sansom's men were holding the mobster's family members and others who had been present when they raided the property. They had been stripped, handcuffed, and gagged to keep them from conversing with each other. Everyone had already been searched by Maj. Sansom's Security Police, but the invasive full body searches had not turned up much of value.

Brandy ordered one of the Rangers, "Bring me a water hose."

"Yes, ma'am!"

"Any idea who the top gangster present might be?"

Ranger Corporal Matt Jefferson, the NCO in charge of the detail, pointed to one of the detainees. "I believe that would be the man you're looking for, Mrs. Seaborn."

"Drag him over here, put him on his back. Take off the gag. Have your men ready to restrain him."

The water hose arrived. Brandy picked up one of the women's cotton blouses laying on the floor. She folded it into a square and laid it over the naked prisoner's face. Without warning she soaked the cloth with water.

The man choked, writhed, fought wildly, straining at his handcuffs until blood ran.

In a calm tone barely above a whisper, Brandy said, "I am going to ask you a question and you are going to answer it for me."

Then, without a saying a word, she soaked the cloth covering his face again. The man went berserk. He appeared to be having a convulsive seizure. The Rangers holding him down struggled to keep him under control.

The prisoner was sobbing.

Col. Randal said, "You forgot to ask him the question."

Brandy said, "Where are the valuables hidden?"

Before there was a chance to answer, she soaked the folded blouse again.

The man began blabbering incoherently, or trying to, begging. He was crying. Brandy took the cloth off his face. He started screaming, retching, and trying to recover his breath all at the same time, which is impossible.

"Stop! You are killing me! I will show you!"

Brandy said, "Corporal, have one of your people escort this man to the house."

"Yes, ma'am."

Brandy said, "Now, which one is the recently deceased Big Four gangster's widow?"

The nude woman was led over, her eyes wide in horror. The sight of one of her husband's professional killers crying like a baby and having been stripped and publicly cavity searched had its intended effect. When the gag was removed, she screamed like a panther.

Brandy ordered, "Stretch her out."

The cloth was placed over the woman's face. She was fighting and kicking, insane with terror. Brandy soaked the rag.

This time Brandy showed mercy, of a sort, by asking the question before applying the water. The mobster's wife went wild—bucking, writing, straining—having totally lost all control of her bodily reflexes. When the wet rag was pulled off, she began babbling hysterically.

Begging to be given the privilege of showing them where her late husband's treasure was hidden.

As a Ranger was leading her to the house, Col. Randal said, "Remind me not to get on your bad side. Where did you learn that water trick?"

Brandy said, "You did notice both of them walked out of here on their own power?"

"Yes, they did."

Brandy said, "Thirty seconds after the wet rag was pulled off, both were perfectly all right, no permanent damage, and we have our information."

Col. Randal said, "True, better than getting worked over by the Egyptian police with rubber hoses. Still . . ."

Brandy said, "Go see what they find in the house, handsome."

Col. Randal said, "What are you planning to do?"

"Chat with the rest of these people. One never knows. The first two might be holding something back."

Col. Randal said, "Yeah."

It was not lost on him that Brandy had not answered his question about where she had learned her interrogation technique. Not an accident. And there was one other thing he had noticed.

Brandy did not seem to mind putting her skills to use—possibly enjoyed it.

VERONICA PAIGE FOUND COLONEL JOHN RANDAL SITTING ON a green velvet half-moon couch in the rotunda next to a circular staircase that looked like something out of *Gone With the Wind*—only bigger. He and Major the Lady Jane Seaborn were examining the contents of three safes that had been concealed beneath the tile flooring in various parts of the house.

The haul was truly impressive: diamonds and other rare jewels worth millions at the going rate in Cairo, which was thirty times their prewar value. riches.

Lady Jane excused herself to contact Captain Lionel Chatterhorn to come collect the riches.

Veronica said, "Colonel, I have received an urgent, time-sensitive request from the Royal Air Force. Two pilots whose plane went down were captured and are being held on Arkoi Island in the Dodecanese. The RAF has asked MI-9 to retrieve them."

"Any intel on the island?"

"Only that it's a minor islet even for the Dodecanese. A detachment of Italians, likely 33rd Mountain Division troops, is known to be garrisoned in its only town located by what is described as a 'harbor.' Reports indicate the pilots are being held in the local jail."

"I'll take care of it."

"May I come?"

"Negative."

"Are you still angry at me because of what happened on our last mission together?"

"No, I'm not."

"Then why not allow me to travel along to observe?"

"The RAF called on MI-9 to rescue two of its pilots. You came to me. I accepted the mission, which means now it belongs to Raiding Forces. We're working for you, but I command the operation—which means I say who goes and who stays."

Which was not exactly accurate—Col. Randal owned Escape in Middle East Command, so technically Veronica worked for him.

Col. Randal said, "We'll attempt to recover the RAF people. If successful, they'll be turned over to MI-9. You get the credit, but I don't want a straphanger along to distract my people."

"I shall stay out of the way."

"Negative—your job is to develop Escape missions, not swim ashore with a knife in your teeth to rescue the evaders yourself. Maybe you've lost sight of the fact the MI in MI-9 stands for Military Intelligence.

"Get captured and you'll be lucky if the only thing the bad guys do is stand you in front of a firing squad."

Veronica said, "No wonder Mandy stays so frustrated with you, Colonel. You can be quite maddening at times."

"Your daughter has the idea she's my parent."

"There *is* the possibility you could use one."

"You're not going."

Col. Randal walked outside and spoke to 10th Ranger Lieutenant Paul Duncan. "Radio Captain Jaxx, have him report to me here immediately. Tell him to bring Lieutenant Starrett with him."

"Yes, sir."

"After that, contact RFHQ and ask Admiral Ransom, Commander Seligman, and Lieutenant Seaborn to stand by there until I can send someone to speak to them about a breaking MI-9 mission."

"Wilco."

Col. Randal went back inside to look for Jim. He found him on the third floor in the gun room admiring the trophy heads lining the walls. The late owner had been an enthusiastic big game hunter.

"Have you ever heard of Arkoi Island?"

"No—why do you ask?"

"The RAF has asked Veronica to rescue a couple of pilots held there."

"I shall start working the phones to see what I can find out."

"That would be helpful."

Col. Randal went back downstairs to find King.

"Veronica has tasked us to rescue a pair of RAF pilots on Arkoi Island. No one seems to know anything about the place. I need you to drive back to RFHQ and talk to Admiral Ransom and Commander Seligman. See if they have any useful information. Find out if Lieutenant Seaborn has a boat at Castelrozzo he can use to transport a rescue party."

"On the way."

"I intend to send Captain Jaxx with a SOG team to liberate the pilots. Jack Cool and Hornblower tearing off into the wild blue . . . how would you feel about going along?"

"My pleasure."

"SOG will fly out to Castelrozzo this evening. Sail for Arkoi tonight. Effect the rescue and be back no later than tomorrow night."

"What's the urgency?"

"I have other need of your services."

"Consider it done, Chief."

Col. Randal produced a strange-looking knife from one of the bellows pockets on his faded khaki BDU jacket, "Colonel Cator gave me this. It's a locally made knuckle duster knife adopted by 51 Middle East Commando. You're my fighting knife expert. Evaluate this one and give me a report."

"Wilco."

King did like blades.

Col. Randal went back outside to see Lt. Duncan again. "Radio Captain Plum-Martin and Beverly—have them report here to me immediately."

"Yes, sir."

Col. Randal went in search of Lady Jane. She and the WREN, Sub/Lt. Bentley St. Ledger, were sprawled on the super-king-sized bed in the master bedroom with a gigantic mirror on the ceiling. They were poking through an impressive pile of women's fine jewelry spread out on the comforter.

And occasionally glancing up at the mirror and laughing.

Since Lady Jane never wore any ornaments except her diamond ear studs and the Sheba diamond ring Col. Randal had given her, she was only playing. From a tender age, Bentley had inherited or been given enough jewelry to open a modest-sized shop and was almost as sparing in what she chose to wear. However, that did not mean the two did not like to look and try on.

Col. Randal said, "It's occurred to me that adjustments need to be made to our intelligence gathering procedures once we set up on Castelrozzo."

Lady Jane said, "In what way, John?"

"We'll be sending out raiding parties. Most likely several will be at sea at any given time. There's nine to fifteen of what are described as 'major' islands in the Dodecanese chain, depending on who you talk to, and at least a hundred fifty smaller ones. Our operational tempo's going to be intense."

Lady Jane said, "Eighty-six thousand square miles is a big area for Raiding Forces to cover."

Col. Randal said, "I'm thinking it would be a good idea to debrief the team leader of every mission. That way we can disseminate information about the islands they raid to the other teams. Didn't always do that as well as I'd have liked when jeep patrols returned to Oasis X."

"What is it you wish from me, John?"

"I'd like you to organize a mobile team of your Royal Marines to be the debriefers— when a raiding party returns from a mission. MI-6 or one of the other agencies should be able to provide a syllabus for the interview techniques they'll need to master. Jim or Cuthbert can supply trainers to get them up to speed."

Lady Jane said, "What is your take, Bentley?"

"Love to be one of the debriefers if you allow me to badge over to your Royal Marines."

Lady Jane laughed, "The Razor will be annoyed with me for poaching one of his favorite WRENs."

Bentley said, "Mother as well. Detests Marines. May have something to do with marrying two of them."

Lady Jane said, "Raquel shall simply have to get over it—she always does."

A jeep arrived, delivering Beverly. Captain Billy Jack Jaxx drove in with Lieutenant Chase Starrett, and Captain Pamala Plum-Martin pulled up a few minutes later.

Col. Randal took them into one of the side rooms off the rotunda, "MI-9 has sprung a hasty mission on us."

In military terms, a "hasty mission" is exactly what its name implies. Veronica's request to rescue two pilots from an island no one had ever heard of and do it right now before the POWs could be moved to another location was about as hasty as a mission could get.

Col. Randal preferred to have the benefit of actionable intelligence developed by a reliable source with time for detailed planning in order to draft and issue a Warning Order, then an Operations Order, conduct rehearsals, test fire weapons, etc. Unfortunately, most of Raiding Forces operations now either had short fuses or did not have the intelligence necessary to do any significant planning or rehearsing.

If there was one capability that set Raiding Forces apart, it was the ability to put a small team in the field, armed and equipped to carry out a complex mission on short notice, with a high probability of success.

The troops called it "high speed low drag."

Col. Randal said, "Are you prepared to accept a mission?"

He was not asking a question, merely giving the standard Raiding Forces preamble to an assignment. Anyone *not* prepared to accept when asked had better have a good reason or needed to find some other place to serve. There were some who did from time to time, unable to stand the tempo.

No one said a word—an acceptable response.

"Captain Jaxx, you are to organize a six-man SOG team. Proceed to Castelrozzo immediately by air and then to Arkoi Island in the Dodecanese by sea where you will effect the rescue of two RAF pilots being held prisoner somewhere on the island. King is en route to RFHQ to see if Admiral Ransom or Commander Seligman have any information on Arkoi."

"Roger, sir!"

"Lieutenant Starrett, you are to accompany Captain Jaxx. We'll see how you like small- scale raiding."

"Yes, sir!"

"Move out, gentlemen. Link up with King and Lieutenant Seaborn—Hornblower will be providing your sea transport."

As the two hard-charging young officers were rushing out of the room, Col. Randal said, "Pam, I need you and Beverly to fly the SOG team to Castelrozzo."

The snow blonde Vargas Girl look-alike pilot said, "Beverly, let's give Billy Jack something to think about—show up wearing parachutes."

Col. Randal said, "That'll get his attention."

Beverly laughed, "Seriously."

Col. Randal said, "I issued instructions to King to make sure SOG returns to Castelrozzo by tomorrow night. Fly back to RFHQ as soon as they arrive. I need you and Beverly available for a PBY flight to the Belgian Congo."

Capt. Plum-Martin said, "In that case, I shall order the ground crew to perform pre-flight maintenance on the Catalina and have it ready."

Col. Randal said, "Don't mention the Congo to anyone."

Capt. Plum-Martin and Beverly glanced at each other. They were fairly certain he meant Lady Jane. Why?

Col. Randal stuck one of Waldo's thin, custom-rolled cigars between his teeth, "How did your searches go—find anything?"

Beverly laughed, "We did, Johnny—jackpot."

Capt. Plum-Martin said, "LEAF EATER is well-funded, love."

COLONEL JOHN RANDAL WENT UPSTAIRS TO TELL MAJOR the Lady Jane Seaborn he was returning to RFHQ. The search was still underway; however, at this point most of the real valuables on the premises had been discovered. Now, items were being inventoried. Soon the Royal Marines would host the mother of all garage sales. Everything would go.

Except for the more expensive or collectible items, which would be sold at auction. There was a lot of work to be done.

Lady Jane said, "I know you want to fly out to Castelrozzo with Billy Jack to see his team off. That would be a negative, Johnny. You and I have plans tonight, Stud."

"Really?"

Col. Randal noted Lady Jane had been picking up some of his—or maybe it was Beverly's—slang. It came off sounding tantalizingly erotic in her cut glass accent . . . which was an absence of accent . . . only precise pronunciation delivered in a poised, husky voice you had to strain to hear at times.

"Jack's a big boy. He does not require handholding."

Col. Randal said, "If a jeep patrol ran into trouble, we could send someone to get them. There might even be another patrol in the area that could be diverted to go to their aid. In a serious emergency, we had the capability of dropping a rescue team by parachute.

"With these sea-going missions, once a raiding party sails, they're on their own—takes getting used . . ."

Lady Jane said, "Always looking out for your people. One of the traits that makes you such a superb commander, John. Taking care of your troops."

"I won't fly to Castelrozzo."

"Perfect. Meet me at Mena House after you see SOG off."

Col. Randal went back outside. Master Sergeant Mack Beckwith was waiting for him. Jim and Brigadier General William Donovan were there. Since King had driven off in the jeep they had come in, Lieutenant Paul Duncan provided two other jeeps for the trip to RFHQ.

Immediately upon arrival, the group went to the Operations Room. Mandy was already there conducting an intelligence briefing for Captain Billy Jack Jaxx, Lieutenant Randy "Hornblower" Seaborn, and the SOG operators. It might have been better termed a *lack* of intelligence briefing.

The mission was a "go to the target area and wing it" type operation. Col. Randal slid into a seat next to Veronica.

Mandy said, "The distance from Castelrozzo to Arkoi is 180 miles. The island is a volcanic formation of approximately two-point-five square miles with what is optimistically described as a 'harbor' located on the south shore where the town of Arki is located, also on the south shore. Most people live in town with a few herders scattered up in the hills. The population of the island is fifty-four adults as of the last census count taken before the war. The inhabitants are Greek. However, the island has long been claimed by Italy.

Italian sovereignty is a source of friction between the Italians and the Turks since Arkoi is about as close to mainland Turkey as is Castelrozzo—meaning approximately a mile, maybe less.

"The terrain is mountainous with pastureland in the valleys. Main occupations are goat herding, fishing, or working in one of the four taverns in Arkoi."

The room erupted in laughter.

"That's right, boys—four taverns for fifty-four people. Bar hopping is definitely the local sport."

The SOG operators cheered. Arkoi was their kind of place.

Pointing to the eastern tip of the island on the map, Mandy said, "Pay particular attention to this location. Here is where you will find what the locals call the 'Italian Jail.' Most likely the jail will be the place the two RAF pilots—Flying Officers William Lansdale and Peter Sturgis— are being held.

"There is a large cave in the immediate vicinity of the jail known for its colorful stalactites and stalagmites, though it may be difficult to locate the entrance due to the mouth reportedly being covered by olive trees and underbrush. In the event any of the Italians guarding the jail attempt to flee when you attack, you may find them hiding in the cave.

"That concludes my briefing. What are your questions?"

With so little information, there was nothing to ask.

Capt. Jaxx went next.

"Situation: We're here. Arkoi is 180 miles that-a-way. No one knows how many Italian troops are on the island. There are six of us.

"Mission: Rescue two RAF pilots being held on Arkoi.

"Execution: A six-man team consisting of myself, Lieutenant Starrett, King, a GSS interpreter, and two SOG operators—Hale and Martagree, will depart for Castelrozzo by air within the hour. Upon arrival, the team will board a PT boat commanded by Lieutenant Seaborn and set sail for enemy shores. We'll arrive off Arkoi before sunrise, carry out the rescue, lay up under camouflage during the rest of the day, then sail for home under cover of darkness.

"Concept of the operation: We'll land on Arkoi, shoot everyone not wearing the same uniform we are, rescue Willie and Pete, and come home—maybe hit a bar or two prior to departure.

"Command & Signal: "I say frog—jump.

"Administration & Logistics: Get your gear and prepare to move out."

Even for Jack Cool, this was an abbreviated Frag Order. The brevity did nothing to make Col. Randal feel any better. However, he could not complain.

Col. Randal taught his officers that the best plan is the simplest one, provided it is executed boldly without hesitation. While he believed that to be true, in a case where there was almost a total blackout on intelligence, when you said it out loud, the concept did not sound quite as convincing as he would have liked.

Lt. Seaborn went next, "See you on the boat when we get to Castelrozzo."

Captain Pamala Plum-Martin spoke last. "Wheels up in ten."

So much for detailed mission planning.

BRIGADIER GENERAL WILLIAM "WILD BILL" DONOVAN appeared at the seaplane departure dock where Captain Pamala Plum-Martin and Beverly Blackwell were preparing their amphibious Supermarine Walrus to fly to Castelrozzo. How the general knew about the when and where of departure was anybody's guess. The exact details had not been mentioned in the Operations Order.

However, Brig. Gen. Donovan was Director of the Office of Strategic Services. Knowing things was his business.

"Have room for one more?"

Capt. Plum-Martin said, "We do, General. Unfortunately, our flight plan calls for Beverly and me to drop off Captain Jaxx, refuel, do a fast turnaround, and fly straight back here."

"I'll ride along anyway."

"Yes, sir—enjoy your flight."

Veronica Paige arrived to see off the SOG team. Colonel John Randal pulled up in a jeep driven by her daughter, Mandy, with Master Sergeant Mack Beckwith in the back seat. Captain Billy Jack Jaxx and his men were following right behind in a deuce and a half.

Mandy went on board to talk to Capt. Plum-Martin and Beverly. Col. Randal and Veronica huddled with Brig. Gen. Donovan. The SOG operators dismounted the truck nonchalantly. Small scale raids, "dirty deeds done quick," were their stock in trade. Travel nearly 500 miles to rescue a couple of pilots from an island no one had ever heard of without any actionable intelligence, specific knowledge of enemy forces, no backup, etc.—not a problem.

The Raiders were armed to the teeth—very casual.

Brig. Gen. Donovan wanted to make the flight because he wanted to have an opportunity to confer with Veronica. In Middle East Command, she was in charge of Escape for both MI-9 and X-2 Counter Espionage for OSS.

When MI-9 was initially being organized in Middle East Command, no one wanted the job, so it was delegated to A-Force. Brigadier Dudley Clarke gave it to Raiding Forces. Col. Randal could not spare one of his officers for a noncombat assignment so he asked Veronica—a woman he respected enormously after their siege at RAF Habbaniya—to take it on.

In the U.S. Army Table of Organization, the Office of Strategic Services had responsibility for Escape. However, it also had Secret Intelligence, Special Operations, and X-2 Counterintelligence overseas—except for South America, which was a domain of the FBI since OSS was being organized from scratch, and Brig. Gen. Donovan did not have the manpower or skill sets to tackle everything at once. After discussing the matter with Brig. Clarke, he too had assigned Escape to Raiding Forces, with Beverly being the Action Officer on paper.

However, Beverly's other However, Beverly's other duties kept her from being able to devote the requisite time to the assignment.

Again, Col. Randal handed it off to Veronica. A precedent had already been established for a British intelligence officer to hold an American intelligence post when Mandy was recruited by Brig. Gen. Donovan to be the OSS X-2 counterintelligence officer, even though she was a British citizen working for MI-5.

Brig. Gen. Donovan said, "Ready for the flight, Mrs. Paige?"

"No, afraid this is as far as Colonel Randal will permit me today, General."

"That's unfortunate. I was looking forward to hearing your plans for Escape in the future. The Colonel has been telling me what a magnificent job you're doing. Possibly he might reconsider?"

Realizing he had been outmaneuvered, Col. Randal said, "You have permission to fly to Castelrozzo, Veronica. That's as far as you go."

"Thank you, Colonel."

Col. Randal excused himself and walked over to where Capt. Jaxx and Lieutenant Randy "Hornblower" Seaborn were standing, "I'm giving you two a direct order—don't let General Donovan or Mrs. Paige talk their way into tagging along to observe tonight."

Since neither officer could remember the last time Col. Randal had phrased his instructions as a "direct order," the two were more than a little surprised.

"Yes sir."

The big pusher prop on the Walrus wheezed, backfired, and turned over. Mandy came off the plane. "Boarding call."

Col. Randal said to his young officers, "Make it happen, gentlemen—everyone who goes in, comes out."

The SOG operators filed up to the door and disappeared inside. When Capt. Jaxx went by, Mandy impulsively kissed him on the cheek. "No need to be a hero tonight, Jack."

The SOG commander repeated something he had picked up from the 10th Rangers, "Danger's no stranger to a U.S. Army Ranger."

Which was true.

Mandy said, not for the first time, "You are such an idiot."

The Walrus taxied out into open water. The engine revved up to a high-pitched scream. Capt. Plum-Martin began her take-off run. The amphibian slowly lifted into the air. The key word being slowly. The plane had a top speed of 130 mph; however, its cruising speed was less than 100 mph.

It was approximately 450 miles to Castelrozzo.

MENA HOUSE HOTEL 2200 HOURS.

ONE OF THE BIGGEST FULL MOONS COLONEL JOHN RANDAL had ever seen was hanging over the Great Pyramid, approximately 600 yards line of sight from the private pool at Major the Lady Jane Seaborn's Mena House Hotel suite. The icy silver globe looked like something out of a Jules Verne science fiction movie. He and Lady Jane had been sitting on the steps in the shallow end enjoying the view and each other's company.

Ever since she'd been shot, Lady Jane seemed to need to be close to him.

Considering they spent every possible moment together that the war allowed, they were already close. Col. Randal had never had any woman trust him the way she did. The thing was, he trusted her back.

So, how had that happened? Col. Randal had no idea. It just did.

Now he was in a terrycloth robe reclining on a double wide lounge while Lady Jane went inside to retrieve the "surprise" she had promised. Col. Randal did not much like surprises— unless he was delivering one to some unsuspecting enemy in the dark of night, unannounced and unexpected.

However, he did not tell Lady Jane that. Besides, she gave great presents. He wondered what it might be.

Lady Jane returned carrying a jar. She was wrapped in a towel that did not cover up very much. He liked the way things were shaping up so far.

"You killed four men for me today—well-played, John."

Col. Randal said, "Technically, Beverly killed 'em."

Lady Jane said, "I was short with you earlier. You were only showing concern for my health, not wanting me to overexert myself. Hopefully, tonight you shall let me make amends.

"Will you forgive me?"

"Let me hear my surprise first."

"Dr. Winthrop gifted me a decanter of ancient honey recently recovered from a dig. A wedding present for when we finally do become married. Still edible after 3,000 years."

"Really?"

"During what is known as the 'Old Period of Egypt,' the Egyptians traditionally presented a flask of honey to high caste newlyweds on their wedding night. The professor said he would like us to celebrate like Egyptian royalty.

"The problem is, with Mallory marooned in the subarctic Shetland Islands, my divorce may take years. I thought . . . why wait? Let's sample ours tonight."

"Fine by me. You forgot the rolls, Jane."

"Tradition called for the couple to spread the honey on their partner's body to 'tastefully get to know each other.'"

"You're making that up."

"Why do you think it's called a honeymoon?"

Col. Randal said, "Gotta love history."

5

STAND BOLDLY ON

LIEUTENANT RANDY "HORNBLOWER" SEABORN'S 76-FOOT Higgins built PT-70, originally a prototype built for U.S. Navy trials before being transferred to the Office of Strategic Services, was blazing across the Aegean Sea powered by a trio of Packard 4M-2500 marine engines at fairly close to its top speed of 47 mph. Lt. Seaborn was trying to make up for lost time. Captain Billy Jack Jaxx was on board with a SOG raiding party.

The destination was Arkoi Island, specifically the port town of Arki. The names of the islands in the Dodecanese and the towns located on them did not always make a lot of sense. Arkoi Island had a "harbor" town named Arki—why drop the "o"?

Did not make much sense.

No one on Capt. Jaxx's six-man team was thinking about spelling tonight. All they were interested in was getting to the island before daylight, rescuing the two Royal Air Force POWs held there, laying up in Arki or on a nearby island with the PT boat under camouflage during the following day, then making a high-speed run back to Castelrozzo under cover of darkness to avoid enemy air.

After that, the plan was on to the fleshpots of Cairo. Unfortunately, the mission was not following the script.

The Aegean is a beautiful turquoise sea—except for when it is an ugly black sea. In his briefing, Professor Winthrop said the ancient Greek poet

Homer described it as a "wine dark sea." No one knew what that meant exactly since there was no known sea on the planet the color of wine. However, from antiquity the Aegean's waters had a deadly reputation for going from perfectly calm to semi-hurricane force winds in a heartbeat.

Tonight Lt. Hornblower's PT boat had run into a violent squall that sprang up out of nowhere and raged for two hours. The storm was so fierce at one point that Lt. Seaborn had concerns his little fighting vessel might actually sink.

He kept those thoughts to himself, there being no reason to alarm the army contingent on board. The ship and crew fought their way through in the best tradition of the Royal Navy. In the process they were also living up to the Levant Schooner Flotilla's new motto: "Stand Boldly On."

The problem was that time had been lost. That was why Lt. Seaborn was pounding full speed ahead . . . or as near to it as possible. Even so, the PT boat was not going to arrive off Arkoi until well after sunrise. Not good, as the small team of Small Operations Group operators needed to utilize the element of surprise to compensate for their lack of numbers.

That was going to be difficult, if not impossible, to achieve during broad daylight.

Capt. Jaxx and Lieutenant Chase Starrett came up on the bridge. Lt. Hornblower broke the bad news.

Capt. Jaxx said, "Take us straight in to the harbor. We'll offload at the dock. That ought to surprise 'em."

Lt. Seaborn said, "We got away with that once before, Jack. You believe the direct approach will work a second time?"

"You have a better idea?"

Holding your enemy in contempt is never a good idea. It could result in the element of surprise being reversed if SOG encountered Italian soldiers willing to fight. Capt. Jaxx was a bold and daring commander but never one to take a chance that was not necessary. In this case, there was little choice. Because of the time lost, a simple plan vigorously executed was about all he had left in his bag of tricks.

It was a risky move.

Lt. Seaborn pressed on, wringing every ounce of speed he could out of the Packard engines. PT-70 powered straight to Arki. To no one's great surprise, the tiny island's "harbor" turned out to be more of an inlet. Not that it mattered.

Capt. Jaxx had his team assembled on the deck. SOG was keyed up, ready to storm the town. Six men against the unknown.

The first sight to meet their eyes as they motored into Arki Harbor were three large caiques under German charter. It was easy to tell by the red Nazi flags with the swastikas superimposed over a white circle flying from their masts. Greek ship owners who contracted to transport cargo for the Germans were collaborating with the enemy. The Greek government in exile considered them traitors.

The Nazi-flagged caiques were legitimate targets.

Lt. Seaborn ordered, "Hoist the battle ensign"—a flag the size of a bed sheet the Royal Navy runs up prior to battle to give the opposition something to shoot at. Normally the practice was reserved for ships-of-the-line, but PT-70's skipper was not called "Hornblower" for nothing.

"Commence fire!"

PT-70's armament consisted of two pair of twin Browning M2 .50 caliber machine guns. One pair was mounted forward on the bow and the other at the stern. Originally the 70 boat had a 37mm cannon; however, it had been removed because the gun had proved to be wildly inaccurate. Four M2s put out a lot of firepower: .50 caliber bullets are the size of cigars.

Lt. Seaborn's gunners opened on the nearest caique.

A blizzard of intense tracer, armor-piercing, and incendiary rounds converged on the motorized sailboat so concentrated the air blurred. No wooden craft, regardless of size, could sustain that kind of punishment for long. In less than a minute, the caique blew up and went down burning, leaving its main mast sticking out above the shallow water with the Nazi flag still flying.

SOG operators and PT-70's sailors were cheering at the top of their lungs.

Realizing there was an opportunity to be had, pointing to the second caique in the queue at the pier, Capt. Jaxx said, "Let's capture her."

Lt. Seaborn ordered, "Boarding party, stand by."

As PT-70 warbled up to the starboard side of the nearest caique, SOG leaped across, landing on the motorized sailboat's deck. No one was aboard. The third caique berthed next to it was deserted as well.

The crews were all ashore investigating the island's four taverns.

While the GSS interpreter hauled down the Nazi flag on the second caique, Capt. Jaxx, Lt. Starrett and King went below to lay an explosive charge. When the fuse lighter was pulled, there was a snap and the pungent smell of burning. The three came back up on deck moving slow in a hurry—the technique taught in demolitions school.

It was considered bad form for demo men who have placed a charge to trip and fall with the fuse burning—especially if they immobilize themselves.

"Fire in the hole!"

While PT-70 rumbled off to a safe distance, SOG retired down the pier to the beach to observe the results. There was a muffled crack that was not particularly loud, however, the damage had been done. The caique began taking on water, going down with her back broken.

The mayor and a sizable number of the island's population arrived, along with the crews of the three caiques. The sailors were ordered to assemble on the quay in a rough semblance of a military formation. Through the Greek Sacred Squadron interpreter, Capt. Jaxx read off a lecture on the inadvisability, economic risk, and physical perils of collaborating with the enemy.

He ordered the men's names recorded so they could be turned over to the Greek government in exile for future recourse.

Then the caiques' crews were released on their own recognizance—poorer but wiser men. The skippers had owned the caiques. Now they were destitute. No way to pay off the sailors.

The crew could consider themselves lucky the GSS translator did not shoot them on the spot. He wanted to. That did not mean the Greek government in exile—sometimes called the "Cairo Government" because it was located in Cairo—would not do so at a later date.

Greek exiles took a dim view of collaboration.

Capt. Jaxx ordered the GSS translator to find out the whereabouts of the Italian soldiers on the island from the man identifying himself as the town mayor.

Before answering the question, the mayor spat on the ground in contempt.

"He says four men total—an NCO and three privates, Captain. The mayor says they ran away to the hills when the firing started. He says they are cowards."

"Ask him where the RAF pilots are being held."

After another exchange, the GSS man said, "Both of them are in town, sir. The Italians did not view them as a potential threat. The 33rd Mountain Division soldiers were lazy and did not wish to guard them at the jail. When our attack began, unsure of what was taking place, the RAF pilots went into hiding.

Capt. Jaxx was in his element—in charge, situation under control. He ordered, "Lieutenant Starrett, take Hale and one of the townspeople, go retrieve the pilots."

"Yes, sir."

"Tell the mayor I want to conduct an inspection of all enemy installations on the island."

After a brief exchange, the GSS interpreter said, "The only position the Italians manned was an observation post in the bell tower of the church. The jail is unoccupied."

Capt. Jaxx said, "King, take Martagree and go check out the OP."

"On the way."

"Then stop by the telegraph office and blow the undersea cable system."

"My pleasure."

Capt. Jaxx ordered the GSS translator, "Now, ask the mayor the best place in town to have breakfast."

A crowd, which was nearly the entire population of Arki, had gathered. Lt. Starrett returned in a few minutes with Flying Officers Peter Sturgis and William Lansdale. The pilots looked none the worse for wear after having their Bristol Beaufighter Benheim night fighter shot down two weeks previously.

Their captivity had been more like a bad vacation than being prisoners of war. Nevertheless, the RAF officers were relieved to be rescued. They did not welcome the possibility of being shipped off to a POW camp on the Italian mainland.

The pilots were taken on board PT-70.

After invading and conquering Arkoi Island, driving off the enemy occupation force, sinking two vessels flying the Nazi flag, capturing another, and rescuing the RAF personnel he had been ordered to retrieve, Capt. Jaxx was sitting down to a well-earned meal when a cry went up from the people out in the street.

Upon inquiry he was informed that a large, Nazi-flagged caique was entering the harbor. The ship was known to the mayor. She was the *Eugenia* out of Piraeus, most likely bound for the German-held island Leros.

At that moment, King walked into the tavern. He handed over a pair of 8X30 San Giorgio binoculars to Capt. Jaxx. Pvt. Martagree was lugging a heavy Stazione R-1 manpack Model 1935 long-range radio he had brought back from the Italian OP.

"We placed a delayed fuse on the explosives at the telegraph office."

BOOOOOM!

"Good job, King." Capt. Jaxx passed the binoculars to Lt. Starrett. "Use these until we can capture you a pair of German Zeiss glasses."

Then, less than pleased that his meal was being interrupted, Capt. Jaxx led a procession of SOG operators and townspeople down to the pier where the *Eugenia* was docking. He went on board, followed by Lt. Starrett, King, and the GSS translator. The Greek skipper was dumbfounded to find himself confronted by an unhappy U.S. Army officer.

Capt. Jaxx said through the GSS translator, "You and all your crew are under arrest. I'm confiscating your boat."

Upon hearing the translation, the caique's skipper began wailing, begging, and wringing his hands in despair. He was about to lose a ship acquired after a lifetime of work, scrimping and saving. The captain was well aware his fellow Greeks dealt harshly with those they viewed as Nazi collaborators.

His life was ruined in an instant.

Capt. Jaxx was reminded of something Captain "Geronimo" Joe McKoy said from time to time that seemed to apply in this case: "Greed kills." In this case, the *Eugenia's* skipper was looking at a firing squad.

The Greek crew went wild with joy at the prospect of being arrested. The sailors wanted to join the refugees living in exile in Egypt. Most wanted to volunteer for one or another of the Hellenic military units fighting the Nazis—or so they claimed.

The crewmen led the way below to show Capt. Jaxx the cargo of "officer's comforts" bound for German-occupied Leros: six cases of *Moet et Chandon* champagne, ten cases of genuine Pilsner beer, thirty kegs of Samos wine, twenty-five long-range Stazione R1 radios, eleven typewriters and fifty boxes of stationery.

After the inspection, Capt. Jaxx walked back down the pier to the camouflaged PT-70 to confer with Lt. Seaborn. It was decided to send a message back to RFHQ. Being responsible for all that champagne, wine, and beer was a heavy burden.

```
AKOI SECURED STOP POWS RECOVERED STOP TWO
CAIQUES DESTROYED STOP TWO CAIQUES WITH CARGO
CAPTURED STOP PT-70 WITH KING AND PILOTS TO
RETURN TO RFHQ TONIGHT STOP REQUEST PERMISSION
TO CONTINUE THE MISSION STOP JAXX
```

COLONEL JOHN RANDAL ARRIVED AT RAIDING FORCES Headquarters at 0800 hrs. He had driven in from Mena House Hotel. Captain Stephanie Fawcett-Tatum said, "You are looking chipper this morning, John."

Col. Randal said, "Find out what Dr. Winthrop drinks and send him a case of it."

"Yes, sir."

"Any sentiment?"

"Not necessary."

"This message arrived a few moments ago from Captain Jaxx."

Col. Randal scanned the flimsy. "Jack wants to go hunting — permission granted."

Capt. Fawcett-Tatum said, "You are speaking to the officer volunteers this morning."

"Roger."

Captain "Geronimo" Joe McKoy and Waldo Treywick were waiting. Col. Randal said, "Frank briefed and ready to go?"

Capt. McKoy said, "Commander General Polanski is plannin' to make things hot for those traffickers."

"Good—what are you two doing here?"

Waldo said, "Me and Joe wanted to hear your talk."

Bentley St. Ledger walked in the Operations Room wearing a Royal Marine uniform with the insignia of a lieutenant.

Col. Randal said, "Lieutenant St. Ledger—that was quick."

"Lady Jane is capable of miracles. I prefer the Marine uniform. What is your opinion?"

"I'm with you, Bentley."

Capt. McKoy said, "What kinda project's Lady Jane got goin', Bentley'?"

Lt. St. Ledger said, "The colonel wants Royal Marines to debrief our raiding parties. I hoped to play a role. Doubt that shall happen now."

Col. Randal said, "Why not?"

Lt. St. Ledger said, "Cuthbert Bowlby and Dudley Clarke are of the opinion that debriefers need to be at least thirty years old."

Waldo said, "Leaves you out."

Col. Randal said, "Jane will find something interesting—welcome to Raiding Forces."

"I cannot wait to learn how to parachute. Mandy says it is better…"

"Don't believe everything Mandy tells you."

"Sounded too good to be true—now, if you will follow me, Colonel, the candidates for direct commissions are assembled."

When Col. Randal arrived, he found Major the Lady Jane Seaborn, Major Duke Slater, and Master Sergeant Mack Beckwith sitting with seven self-conscious volunteers ranging in rank from private to master sergeant—three British, four Americans. He had been hoping for a larger turnout.

Some of the men he had expected to volunteer were not present.

The candidates were more than a little uneasy to have publicly stated their ambition to become officers. Would their friends consider them to be taking on airs? What if they were not accepted?

None of the prospective officers seemed concerned about shouldering the weighty mantle of responsibility associated with troop command. What they desired was to have their own teams. Which was exactly what Col. Randal wanted of men aspiring to command his troops—the desire to lead.

The British Army believed social status to be the determining factor in the quality of leader an officer will be. U.S. Army doctrine postulated that leadership can be taught. Col. Randal believed they were both wrong—at least in part.

Leadership has little to do with a man's family tree, though it does not hurt for an officer to come from a long line of military service. He did not agree that leadership could be taught— except for the basic principles. Command authority is granted, but leadership is an intangible that has to come from within.

All men are created equal, but they do not all make good combat officers. Someone called, "ATTENTION!"

The volunteers jumped to their feet.

Col. Randal ordered, "As you were—the smoking lamp is lit."

As the men returned to their seats, fumbling for their cigarettes, Col. Randal brought out his old battered Zippo with the gold U.S. 26th Cavalry Regiment crossed sabers embossed on the front and lit one of his own. He wanted the group to feel like contemporaries right from the start.

These men were going to be his "studs"—maybe.

"Thank you for taking the initiative to be here today. The first step in becoming an officer is to say you want to be one. Your presence here speaks well of you. Raiding Forces needs small unit leaders. While I've always thought it healthy to bring in fresh talent, this is my opportunity to promote from within, reward good service—part of my job I enjoy the most.

"As you are aware, we're reorganizing and going back to our Commando roots. On most missions, we'll be operating in elements of less than ten men. Long range, small-scale amphibious raiding is not for the faint of heart. It will demand small unit leaders with confidence, fortitude, tactical ability, and the desire to win.

"At this moment, Captain Jaxx is approximately two hundred miles deep inside the enemy-occupied Dodecanese Islands, leading a five-man team. Jack has invaded Arkoi, rescued two POWs, destroyed a pair of Nazi chartered caiques and captured two more. Now he's continuing the mission at his own request, utilizing one of the captured caiques as transport, to carry out additional raids on neighboring islands because the PT boat he arrived in has to return to base.

"That could be you.

"Raiding Forces has a policy. Officers lead. Not because our NCOs are not capable, but to demonstrate the importance of each and every mission. Also to show our commitment to success.

"Major Slater is here to explain the commissioning process—Duke."

Col. Randal turned to leave, then stopped himself, "You men will *not* let me down."

Someone called, "ATTENTION."

The volunteers in the room jumped up and snapped to a ramrod position so hard there was an audible *CRAAACK.*

As they were strolling down the hall, Lady Jane said, "Nicely done, John. Do you believe all of them will become officers?"

"They'll all be commissioned. Then they'll be tested. Those who don't measure up will be returned to their unit in the rank of lieutenant. They'll all make good officers—but not all will be good Raiding Forces officers."

Lady Jane said, "Hopefully everyone will qualify."

Col. Randal said, "I won't have any but the best of the best for my troops."

Lady Jane said, "Nor should you."

ON ARKOI ISLAND, AFTER SETTING ASIDE A CASE OF PILSNER for consumption on his subsequent operations, Captain Billy Jack Jaxx ordered the rest of the liquid refreshments transferred from the *Eugenia* to PT-70. Then the caique set sail for Castelrozzo— minus the Greek skipper who would be staying behind to await his fate for collaboration with the enemy. On board was a prize crew made up of the original complement of Greek sailors plus one Royal Navy swabbie, Able Seaman Damian Smith, purloined from Lieutenant Randy "Hornblower" Seaborn's PT boat to command the prize crew.

AB Smith was instructed to sink the caique with explosives rather than allow it to be recaptured by the enemy.

Despite the fact that it was broad daylight, Capt. Jaxx and his four remaining men bade farewell to Lieutenant Randy "Hornblower" Seaborn's PT-70, boarded the other caique, and sailed for Patmos, which could be seen in the distance eleven miles away. The Greek Sacred Squadron interpreter said, "The people in Arki claim many bad things take place on that island."

Capt. Jaxx said, "There's a good chance they will when we get there."

The SOG operators went below to avoid being spotted in the event any enemy aircraft over flew the caique. Once again, rough weather blew up. The motor dory from PT-70 being towed for use on subsidiary expeditions took on water, swamped, and was lost.

As they approached Patmos, the dominant feature was the massive Greek Orthodox monastery complex located on the highest point of the island.

Lieutenant Chase Starrett said, "This is a tiny island, so where did the labor come from to haul all those giant blocks of stone up to the crest of such a sheer hill?"

Capt. Jaxx said, "Beats me. I've been wondering that ever since we jumped on the castle at Castelrozzo. Massive cut stones stacked up on the highest terrain feature with no trail wide enough or straight enough to haul 'em up there—pretty strange."

The GSS translator said, "Patmos is famous for its cats. There are more of them than people. No rats."

The caique dropped anchor inside the bay at the capital city, Chora. However, it was not able to hold due to the weather. With no other option available, Capt. Jaxx ordered the boat to sail around the thirteen-square-mile island like a hobby horse on a merry-go-round. One Raider had to stay on board to prevent the crew from having a change of heart about traveling to Egypt. Now the team invading Patmos was down to four operators.

While these dispositions were being decided, two *carabinieri* appeared and hailed the caique from shore. GG, the sole Italian speaker on the team, was below. Capt. Jaxx responded with the only word he knew in this "Romance" language: "pepperoni."

Worth a try, but since it was not the correct countersign or even the answer to the question and had been delivered in a Texas accent, the Italians ran away, realizing something was not right. Not wanting the two soldiers to spread the alarm, Capt. Jaxx jumped off the caique. He landed waist deep in the water, fought his way ashore, and gave chase with his team storming after him, trying to catch up.

The foot chase through town ended at the police station.

A sloppy, overweight German *feldwebel* from the 999th Light Afrika Division came to the door in his sweat-stained undershirt to inquire what all the commotion was about. Capt. Jaxx blasted him on full auto at virtual contact distance with his chopped .30 Colt Baby BAR.

As the rest of SOG came up, a gunfight ensued.

A second Nazi ran out with a Luger in hand and was shot dead in a hail of fire. As quickly as it began, the fight ended. Inside the building six Italian soldiers were discovered hiding under their bunks.

The town mayor came to investigate the gunfire. When he realized Americans were responsible—not the Nazis shooting his constituents—the local big wig launched into a highly impassioned dialogue with the GSS interpreter. The Greek was beside himself with joy.

Capt. Jaxx said, "What's he telling you?"

"The mayor says welcome to Patmos. His people are without food, their crops have been confiscated and they have not been allowed to fish. On average, three people a day are dying of starvation out of a population of less than 2,500. The Italians and Germans have been very bad sir, very bad."

Capt. Jaxx said, "Tell him we can help."

The abbot of the Greek Orthodox Monastery of St. John, founded in 1088, arrived on the scene, having ridden a donkey down from the mountain to the village. He was a wizened little white-haired fellow. He and the mayor were the two top men on the island.

The abbot was the senior man for ecclesiastical politics and theological dogma. The mayor was a garden-variety elected official. One ministered to his flock and the other had an island to run, with an eye to being reelected.

They hated each other's guts.

If there was one thing Capt. Jaxx had zero interest in, it was politics. He had come to the island to blow things up and kill bad guys—not become embroiled in local political bickering.

"Mr. Mayor, I have twenty tons of foodstuffs on my boat—all yours, compliments of Raiding Forces."

When the GSS translator explained what Capt. Jaxx said, the mayor was ecstatic. The abbot was not. The man of the cloth immediately launched into a highly animated diatribe.

"What's he saying?"

"All foodstuffs donated to the island have to be distributed through the office of the Red Cross."

"OK."

"There is no Red Cross on Patmos, Captain."

The mayor started screaming at the abbot. The priest stood his ground, shaking his head back and forth, eyes blazing. He shrieked back furiously. A crowd was gathering. The mood was turning ugly.

Capt. Jaxx said, "How long's it going to take to get a Red Cross representative here?"

The GSS interpreter said, "Weeks—possibly a month. Response to communications between the islands is primitive, sir."

"Why's the priest demanding our food not be given out until the Red Cross arrives— doesn't make sense with people starving to death?"

"He does not want the mayor to receive the credit, sir."

Capt. Jaxx said, "You're kidding—order the abbot to return to his monastery immediately or I'll arrest him for interfering with an Allied military operation."

"Sir, you will upset the religious faction . . ."

"Do it now!"

"Yes, Captain."

Capt. Jaxx said, "Lieutenant Starrett, dispatch a man to the beach. Have him signal the caique to land ashore next time it sails by."

"Roger."

"Order the mayor to organize a party of stevedores to unload the rations—just the food, not the booze. You're in charge. Make sure nothing gets looted."

The Reverend Mother of the Convent of Evangelismos arrived with four of her nuns. The woman was as charming as the abbot was obstinate. Upon learning about the supplies, she offered to ensure the food was distributed fairly.

The ugly mood among the islanders de-escalated rapidly after the Reverend Mother took charge.

As he stood watching the locals forming a human chain to pass the crates of rations up from the beach, Capt. Jaxx said to the GSS interpreter, "Where's all those cats you were telling me about?"

"People ate them, sir—they really have been starving."

"Remind me not to order a hamburger."

Lt. Starrett returned from the beach, "The mayor has taken charge of the unloading. The Reverend Mother is down there now monitoring the work party to make sure none of the foodstuffs are siphoned off. Our SOG operator is guarding the booze."

Capt. Jaxx said, "Go locate the telegraph station and blow up the undersea cable system."

Lt. Starrett said, "Yes, sir."

A man came out of the crowd and identified himself as the chief of police.

By now, Capt. Jaxx was beginning to feel like he was getting a handle on dealing with what the military calls Civil Affairs. Nothing to it. Take charge. Delegate everything.

Threaten to arrest anyone who disagrees with anything.

"I'm turning the captured weapons and the prisoners over to you, Chief."

The policeman said, "A mob will form, storm the jail, and murder the Italians if you do, Captain. Those scum behaved badly during their time on our island—very badly."

"Not my problem, Chief."

VICE ADMIRAL RANDOLPH "RAZOR" RANSOM, BRIGADIER General William "Wild Bill" Donovan, Colonel John Randal, Captain M. H. S. McDonald aka "Snow White," Lieutenant Commander Adrian Seligman, Captain "Geronimo" Joe McKoy, Waldo Treywick, Mandy Paige, Sergeant Major Mack Beckwith, and Sergeant Major Mike "March or Die" Mikkalis,

MC, DCM, MM, were on board a Walrus en route to Paphos, Cyprus. They were en route to visit the fitting out base for the armed caiques of the Levant Schooner Flotilla that Snow White had under his command. The location was ideal for clandestine operations because in nearby Cove, LSF vessels were able to work up in secret under conditions similar to those they could expect to find in the islands.

Capt. McKoy and Waldo had come along to "see the show." MSgt. Beckwith went wherever Col. Randal went. No one was sure why Sgt. Maj. Mikkalis was on the plane. He pretty much came and went as he pleased.

Mandy was on board because—like Capt. McKoy and Waldo—she did not want to miss out on anything. The beautiful British spy catcher did have a reason for making the trip. She was OSS's Counter Espionage (X-2) officer in Egypt on loan from SIME. In fact, Mandy was the only X-2 officer the Outfit had in Middle East Command—a one-woman shop.

Counter Espionage (X-2)—as the Office of Strategic Services called counterintelligence (Britain's much larger independent counterintelligence organization MI-5 was officially named the Security Service or "Security" for short)—had a low priority. The Outfit was still struggling to get the Secret Intelligence (SI) up and running. However, LEAF EATER was a counterintelligence mission, at least in principle, and it was the single most important operation OSS was responsible for anywhere worldwide.

The last part was known only to Wild Bill.

Brig. Gen. Donovan was delighted to see Mandy on the plane. He was interested in hearing his X-2 officer's thoughts on the state of plans to interdict diamond smuggling. The Director of the Office of Strategic Services did not know she was CARD GAME.

He did not have a "Need to Know", which would be a surprise to him if he found out. Shortly after takeoff, Brig. Gen. Donovan, Col. Randal, Capt. McKoy, Waldo, and Mandy moved to the rear of the aircraft where they could hold a private LEAF EATER bull session.

Up in the front, VAdm. Ransom held a FIRE EATER conference with Capt. McDonald aka Snow White, Lt. Cdr. Seligman, and Sgt. Maj. Mikkalis. How two codenames totally unrelated to each other could both have the word

"EATER" tacked on the end was one of those flukes that seem to have an ulterior motive but did not. One was named after a dinosaur rumored to be living in the Congo, and the other had been issued randomly by the admiralty because it had a bloodthirsty ring to it.

Nevertheless, to avoid confusion Col. Randal was considering coming up with another codename for Raiding Forces operations in the Aegean.

While no new information came out of the LEAF EATER discussion, Brig. Gen. Donovan gained valuable insight into the depth of the planning that had gone into Col. Randal's response to his orders to shut down diamond trafficking. He was pleased to hear the diamond cartel in Egypt was firmly under Raiding Forces' control and satisfied that steps were about to be undertaken to implement a similar plan in the Belgian Congo.

Three things in particular impressed Wild Bill:

1. Col. Randal understood his orders and he was making efforts to carry them out.
2. LEAF EATER was going to be accomplished without leaving OSS's fingerprints.
3. Raiding Forces had not asked for much assistance once they had been given their marching orders.

One other item worth noting: Col. Randal was a dangerous man to cross.

Brig. Gen. Donovan could not wait to tell President Roosevelt the story about the Big Four's one-way airplane ride when he returned to Washington. FDR had been following the exploits of Raiding Forces ever since his son, Jimmy—now serving in the Pacific as the XO of the 2nd U.S. Marine Raider Battalion—had fought in several engagements as a "neutral observer" with Col. Randal during the siege of RAF Habbaniya.

In the front of the plane, VAdm. Ransom said, "Originally SOE had a fleet of caiques procured by the Principal Sea Transport Officer, Middle East supporting Force 133. They were tasked with running guns and inserting intelligence operatives throughout the islands. Initially it was thought we would simply expand their mission to include transporting Raiding Forces teams." That idea flamed out, when, acting on Jim's advice, Randal refused to subordinate Raiding Forces to SOE.

"At that point, I stepped in and divided the naval assets into the Levant Schooner Flotilla and the Levant Fishing Patrol.

"Small Raids Incorporated has the exclusive use of LSF while SOE's Force 133 keeps the LFP. An intensive course of boat handling, using a variety of small craft, has been initiated for both Raiding Forces and the Levant Schooner Flotilla personnel. The syllabus includes—but is not limited to—caique motorized sailboats, folding infantry assault boats, rigid and collapsible canoes, rubber dinghies, U.S.-type dinghies, and captured enemy rubber assault rafts.

"In addition to boat handling and seamanship, all crew members are required to have a working knowledge of navigation, signaling, demolitions, gunnery, and camouflage.

"The most suitable armament for a caique has been found to be the 20mm Swiss S- 18/100 Solothurn anti-tank rifle, with a ten round magazine mounted forward and two M-2 Browning .50 caliber machine guns aft, on collapsible stands in order for them to be concealed. As added firepower, any number of .303 Vickers K machine guns can be fired from improvised gun ports bored through the gunwales in various places—exactly like pirate ships of other days. Mortars will be carried on board as needed to support landing parties ashore or engage fixed enemy positions. Each boat will also carry a supply of limpet mines, demolitions, and smoke canisters.

"The plan is for a rapid expansion of the LSF. The PSTO has been tasked with procuring additional caiques and motorized sailing schooners. A patrol out now being led by Captain Jaxx has captured two more caiques. So, it has been established that we can count on seizures to increase our fleet.

"A typical caique crew will consist of a skipper, a leading seaman, coxswain, stoker, and a wireless operator—men twenty-one years of age on average. Recruiting is underway to find volunteers to fill the slots. As it stands now, some of the Greek civilian crews will have to be retained in service until a sufficient number of our men can become qualified in the necessary skills."

Capt. McDonald asked, "How is the training program progressing?"

Lt. Cdr. Seligman said, "We have a fairly steep learning curve to overcome, sir—Stand Boldly On."

Waldo said, "The Problem's the Solution."

2200 HOURS.

COLONEL JOHN RANDAL ARRIVED AT THE THIRD-FLOOR SUITE he and Major the Lady Jane Seaborn shared at Raiding Forces Headquarters after a whirlwind tour inspecting the Levant Schooner Flotilla facilities on Cyprus. He put in a call to Lady Jane at Mena House. Flanigan came on the line and informed him she was dining in Cairo with Commander Ian Fleming.

King tapped on the door.

Col. Randal said, "Give me a report."

"We encountered a storm on the way to Arkoi. Cost enough time to make us arrive after daylight. Three German flagged caiques were tied up at the pier. Lieutenant Seaborn sank one with his organic weapons, Captain Jaxx boarded one and sank it with demolitions, then captured the third. He is having it sailed back to Castelrozzo.

"Our two RAF pilots were located and brought out by Lieutenant Seaborn." Col. Randal said, "What did you learn from the mission?"

"Chief, my takeaway is that these small island raids appear to fall into two categories. On some, we encounter enemy installations and there is some semblance of military order and discipline. On others, we find a handful of 'beach watchers' who have been dropped off under the command of an NCO and left to fend for themselves. In both cases, when we arrive, the Germans resist but the Italians either flee or surrender with little or no resistance.

"When we operate against the principal islands like Rhodes, Leros, or Kos we should not expect to have the same easy success."

Col. Randal said, "What time are we flying out to the Congo?"

"Pam told me to have you at the dock at 0500 hrs."

"Any idea why Fleming is in town? This would not be a good time for him to spring a GOLDEN FLEECE on us."

"Negative."

"Good report—see you in the morning."

Moments after King departed James "Baldie" Taylor arrived. "How were things on Cyprus, Colonel?"

"Don't know much about naval maintenance facilities but I'm favorably impressed with Captain McDonald and Commander Seligman."

Jim said, "I know I promised not to become involved with LEAF EATER unless you asked, but we have worked together for a long time."

"That is a fact."

"You are flying out tomorrow on a recruiting trip to enlist mercenaries for Frank Polanski's anti-diamond trafficking guerrilla army in the Congo. On my own volition, I asked Cuthbert Bowlby to discreetly inquire if Sir Ernest Oppenheimer might assist in locating men with military backgrounds available for freelance work."

"Good idea, Jim—should have thought of it myself."

"Sir Ernest leapt at the chance. Offered to have DeBeers agents in Kenya and Rhodesia conduct the recruiting. He will supervise the effort to find mercenaries in South Africa."

Col. Randal said, "Oppenheimer have any idea what our plans are?"

Jim said, "Negative. But you can count on him to find out. For once in this whole sordid diamond affair, Raiding Forces, The Diamond Company, the Office of Strategic Services, and the Secret Intelligence Service all have the same goal—if for different reasons—stop diamond trafficking out of the Congo."

Col. Randal said, "I'll take all the help we can get.

Jim said, "While DeBeers has no desire to be publicly connected to LEAF EATER, not only will the Diamond Company assist in raising your mercenary army, but Oppenheimer has also offered to fund the project through one of his shell corporations."

Col. Randal said, "Offer accepted."

"Sir Ernest has also volunteered to provide intelligence on the illicit diamond trade.

DeBeers has its own private industrial espionage organization. It is a good-faith offer."

"I like it, Jim."

"Hope I am finally back in your good graces."

Col. Randal said, "We both serve our own country's best interests. Nothing was ever personal except for the part Jane took as a slight. She's over it."

Jim said, "Good to hear—answering to our masters is what we do, who we are." Col. Randal said, "I always knew where you stood."

COLONEL JOHN RANDAL ROLLED UP TO THE CATALINA AT the seaport in a jeep driven by King, with Master Sergeant Mack Beckwith in the back. The PBY was what was known in the United States Navy as a Patrol Bomber—that's what the PB stood for. The Y indicated the manufacturer—Consolidated Aircraft Corporation. This particular PBY had been modified by the Naval Aircraft Factory (NAF) located in Philadelphia, Pennsylvania. Now it was designated as a PBN-1 Nomad—the N replacing the Y standing for Naval Aircraft Factory. There were other names for the plane used by different countries who flew it, but almost no one ever called the amphibian anything except a Catalina or PBY and sometimes both.

The most important modification the NAF made was to increase the size of the fuel tanks, which added 50 percent more range—over 3,000 miles, depending on cargo, bomb load, or number of passengers. All weapons and corresponding crew had been removed from the Raiding Forces Catalina because it was primarily used as a troop transport.

Admiral of the Fleet Sir Andrew Cunningham had loaned his personal PBY/PBN-1 to Raiding Forces for an operation. Then, desiring to have it replaced with a Short Sunderland, the Admiral had written the plane off as a combat loss, knowing full well the aircraft had not suffered so much as a scratch to its paint on the mission.

Now it belonged to Raiding Forces.

Sergeant Tim Authury and Sergeant Frank Hawkins were waiting when Col. Randal stepped out of the jeep. The two were a couple of his longest serving soldiers. Sgt. Authury had been in Swamp Fox Force from day one when he arrived at Calais. Sgt. Hawkins was in the first intake of the Life Guards polo squad. And he had been on Col. Randal's personal five-man team during OPERATION TOMCAT—the first parachute raid on Enemy-Occupied France.

Both NCOs had served on his Ranger Patrol.

Returning their salutes, Col. Randal said, "What can I do for you two men?"

Sgt. Hawkins said, "Tim and I have been talking it over, sir. If it is not too late to apply, we would be interested in volunteering for your direct commission program."

The sergeants were exactly what he was looking for in officers. Col. Randal said, "Took you long enough."

Sgt. Authury said, "Not sure if you would be open to the idea, Colonel—know the pair of us too well."

Col. Randal said, "You'll have to sit through the orientation and pass the leadership test—mostly how to issue orders. The hard part's going to be getting past Lady Jane's etiquette class.

"Better bone up on your forks and spoons, boys."

The sergeants laughed, relieved after taking the plunge. They chorused, "Thank you, sir."

"Report to Colonel Stone."

"Sir!"

Red, the stunning Clipper Girl/MI-6/OSS agent—and Lieutenant Colonel Sir Terry "Zorro" Stone's semi-permanent girlfriend (Sir Terry would never admit to being committed to any one woman exclusively, even though he had dated her for over three years)—was supervising the loading of cold cuts delivered from the Gezira Club restaurant for the flight.

Col. Randal said, "What are you doing here?"

Red flashed one of her highly polished, best grade Clipper Girl smiles, "Flying, John."

She was a past master in the art of projecting sex appeal, coupled with total nonavailability, while exuding the fabled Clipper Girl charm. Red tended to make rich, famous and/or powerful men crazy.

She and Col. Randal were good friends.

"This is a military flight. We don't have hostesses."

"Now you do."

Col. Randal said, "I see." But of course he did not.

Mandy Paige arrived with her luggage. Since she was a member of CARD GAME, there was a razor-thin excuse for her tagging along on the trip. The real reason was because she wanted to go.

"Morning, Mandy."

"Good morning, John."

Captain Roy Kidd rode up in a jeep. He was coming along to help Commander General Frank Polanski organize his band of mercenaries. Capt. Kidd had jungle experience gained as an American expatriate serving in the King's Own Royal Regiment in India before the war.

Having him along fell into the 'Right Man, Right Job' category. The downside to leaving him in the Congo for an extended period of time was losing one of the two most experienced commanders of Duck Patrol. And that made him ideally suited to help with the reorganization of Raiding Forces.

Col. Randal said, "Got something for you, Roy."

"Sir?"

"General Donovan brought a pistol he'd like evaluated. OSS is considering placing an order. You and Capt. McKoy are my go-to experts on all things firearms-related. Check it out when you have a chance and give me a report."

Capt. Kidd said, "Looks pretty much like a standard issue 1911 Government Model .45, sir."

Col. Randal said, "Ballester-Molina made in Argentina. Completely sterile. Having Colt stamped on the frame's a dead giveaway for an undercover agent."

Capt. Kidd racked the slide three times to ensure the weapon was clear. "Beautiful craftsmanship. Locks up like a steel vault. I'll wring it out for you, sir."

James "Baldie" Taylor and Captain Cuthbert Bowlby stepped out of a car. They were carrying bags. Neither man was on the manifest.

Jim said, "I informed Cuthbert of your acceptance of Sir Ernest's offer. We decided it would be beneficial for us to fly down to his private estate in South Africa and coordinate with him directly."

"Roger—good idea."

Captain "Geronimo" Joe McKoy, Waldo Treywick, and Commander General Frank Polanski arrived and immediately boarded.

Sergeant Major Mike "March or Die" Mikkalis showed up next. He had served a tour in the French Foreign Legion, which made him an excellent choice to help with the recruitment and organization of Frank's soldiers of fortune. The downside was that he was the *other* experienced leader of Duck Patrol.

Sgt. Maj. Mikkalis traveling to the Congo, like Capt. Kidd, was a matter of priorities— LEAF EATER first.

"Good morning, sir."

"Good morning, Sergeant Major."

A jeep pulled in, driven by Ensign Theodore Hamilton, aka "The Great Teddy." Col. Randal said, "What are you doing here, Ensign?"

"I came to see you off, sir."

"Good, I've been wanting to talk to you. I read after-action reports from the Pacific in hopes of finding something that might be of use for us. The U.S. Navy converted some of their PBY squadrons to gunships. Painted black for night operations against Japanese troop transports and barges. Called 'Black Cats.'"

"Interesting, sir."

"You think it might be a good idea to paint our planes black?"

"Maybe we should experiment with painting the Walruses a green and brown earth tone pattern since they are going to be hiding concealed under netting during the day. Maybe paint the bottom black. I shall try out different camouflage variations—always a smart idea to experiment, sir."

Col. Randal said, "I'll leave it to you, stud."

Ens. Hamilton said, "As for the Catalina, let's do it, Colonel—our own Black Cat."

Beverly walked off the PBY. She and Captain Pamala Plum-Martin had completed their preflight checklist and were ready for departure. The University of Texas beauty queen came over to speak to Col. Randal.

At that moment a car drove up with Brandy Seaborn and Captain Penelope "Legs" Honeycutt-Parker. The two women had no known reason to be there. Both were carrying luggage.

They boarded the PBY.

Col. Randal said, "Beverly, what the hell?"

"OK, I know you told me to keep this flight quiet, but somehow things spiraled out of control."

Major the Lady Jane Seaborn's white Rolls-Royce cruised in and glided to a stop. Flanigan stepped out, went around, and opened the door for her. Then he went to the back of the car, removed her bags from the boot, and carried them to the Catalina.

Beverly said, "Not my fault."

Lady Jane walked up.

Col. Randal said, "It's a sixteen-hour flight, one way . . ."

Lady Jane said, "Perfect. I love to travel."

Realizing he was on a slippery slope and wanting to avoid saying anything sounding even remotely protective, Col. Randal said, "So, how was your evening with Commander Fleming?"

Lady Jane said, "Conversation was what one would expect but the sex was fantastic!" Then she breezed by and proceeded to board.

Col. Randal said, "Not funny."

6
WHEN IN DOUBT, LIGHT 'EM UP

CATALINA PBYS ARE ELEGANT AMPHIBIANS. BEFORE THE WAR they were usually depicted on billboards or magazine advertisements winging their way to some exotic destination with a palm tree or hula girl in a grass skirt in the foreground. Flying boats were developed because there were not enough airfields in the more remote regions of the world to support commercial travel. The longest distance flown by a PBY was 3,433 miles, and the longest time airborne without refueling was thirty-two hours. The normal complement of crew on the military model adopted by the U.S. Navy consisted of command pilot, co-pilot, flight engineer, navigator, radio operator, and five gunners. For the trip today, the air gunners were not on board because the flight plan was nowhere near enemy territory.

The Catalina's long range was attributable to its "wet" wing." What that meant was the wings also served as the fuel tanks—a novel, highly effective marvel of aeronautical engineering. However, the airplane was slow, cruising at a mere 124 mph. Because of the long duration of PBY flights, the engineer was also a qualified pilot. There were bunks near the tail so the three flying officers could rotate, sleeping between four-hour shifts on duty in the cockpit.

Since the Raiding Forces plane had more or less been a gift from Admiral of the Fleet Sir Andrew Cunningham, it was configured as a passenger transport for VIPs. An aisle ran down the center between two rows of padded leather bench-type seats that backed up to the bulkhead on each side of the cabin. The result was a friendly seating arrangement. Carrying on a conversation across the aisle was easy. Also, passengers could stand up, stretch their legs, and move around to talk to different people at their leisure.

For combat missions, the plush VIP seats were removed and up to twenty-eight heavily- armed Raiding Forces Commandos could be carried.

Colonel John Randal was last on. He took a seat next to Major the Lady Jane Seaborn on the port side next to the bulkhead separating the cockpit from the cabin. She snuggled up close to him. The drop-dead gorgeous Royal Marine was excited to be traveling, not really caring where they were going — Lady Jane just wanted to have fun.

She said, "I understand why everyone else is on this flight, John, but you never explained to me why your presence is required in the Congo?"

Which was true.

Captain Pamala Plum-Martin came on the intercom. "Prepare for takeoff."

0545 HRS. LIPSI ISLAND, DODECANESE CHAIN, AEGEAN SEA.

CAPTAIN BILLY JACK JAXX, LIEUTENANT CHASE STARRETT, A Greek sacred Squadron interpreter, GG, and two SOG operators were aboard the caique captured the previous day. It was beginning to be daylight as they cruised into the anchorage of Lipsi. The town and the island had the same name—Lipsi. The caique's Bolinger diesel engine was going *BOM, BOM, BOM.*

Capt. Jaxx said, "Be a lot better when this boat gets it motor changed out for one of those tank engines Commander Seligman briefed us about."

Lt. Starrett said, "Roger that, sir. We're not very stealthy."

They had almost no information about Lipsi—the village or the island—other than the names and the island's land mass, six square miles.

The GSS translator claimed it had a reputation for being a "mysterious" place. That may have been because in the last century pirates had used it as a secret hideout—or possibly there was something about the place they did not know about yet.

Capt. Jaxx said, "I like mysteries."

Lt. Starrett said, "Yeah, but not when our objective's one, sir."

"That's a good point, Lieutenant."

No one was around at the pier when the caique docked. The GSS interpreter was dispatched to slip into town surreptitiously and spy out the lay of the land. Specifically, he was tasked with finding out how many enemy personnel were on the island and where they might be found.

Capt. Jaxx and his men spent the time while he was gone inspecting their weapons and equipment—not that it was needed. SOG operators routinely made a habit of checking their gear at every possible opportunity.

On a small-scale raid, there was no such thing as being too sure.

The GSS interpreter returned in less than twenty minutes. He had Lipsi's mayor with him. This mission was shaping up like the last few. Land, locate the local civic authority, have him lead the way to the enemy.

Capt. Jaxx said, "What's the opposition look like?"

"Five Italian Blackshirt Fascists, under the command of a German corporal from the 999th Light Afrika Division—a beach watching party, sir."

"Where can we find 'em?"

"At the police station. They've appropriated it as their barracks, Captain."

Capt. Jaxx said, "Lock and load, boys. Let's go pay a wakeup call on the bad guys. Mr. Mayor, lead the way.

"Move out smartly, sir."

Leaving PFC Bronson behind to secure the caique, following a very reluctant town mayor whose martial ardor had noticeably cooled, they strolled along the dock and proceeded into the quaint little village. The place seemed abandoned. No one was moving about this early.

When the patrol reached the police station, it found broken ouzo bottles littering the cobblestones in front of the building. The enemy forces on Lipsi were a hard-drinking crew and they drank appropriated Greek brew. When they finished a bottle, it was tossed out in the street. The Axis troops took pleasure in showing their disdain for the Greek islanders.

PFC Hale was dispatched around back to cover the rear of the station with his Stinger light machine gun.

The .30 caliber M-1919 LMG was a Browning design produced by Colt's Manufacturing Company and modified by Sergeant Roy Dunlop of the U.S. 27th Ordnance Company to U.S. Marine 1st Para-Marine Battalion specifications—sort of. Being hand-built from scrounged parts meant no two weapons were exactly alike, but it was proving to be an outstanding weapon for Raiding Forces.

The belt-fed LMG's barrel, chopped to within three inches of the front sight—the length Raiding Forces preferred—made it easy to carry aboard and jump out of aircraft or maneuver in tight quarters below deck on small boats.

The Stinger provided a Raiding Forces team with belt-fed walking fire, turning a primarily defensive tripod mounted weapon into one that could be used to travel with the assault element in an attack—it was a beast.

Raiding Forces had a history of modifying existing weapons to meet their needs, dating back to the early days at Seaborn House when Captain "Geronimo" Joe McKoy remedied their lack of submachine guns by adding extension magazines to 12-gauge Browning A-5 semi- automatic shotguns, then sawing off their long, bird hunting barrels. Now, with modern arms readily available, Raiding Forces still engaged in altering standard issue line infantry weapons to improve their performance or increase lethality.

Capt. Jaxx pounded on the door of the police station with the steel butt plate of his big .30 caliber Browning Automatic Rifle that he called a Baby BAR. It was also custom built by Sgt. Dunlop to the prewar Colt R-80 Monitor configuration developed by the FBI: barrel shortened to eighteen inches and the weapon dramatically lightened by the removal of unnecessary wood and steel parts.

The addition of a pistol grip and an oversized Cutts Compensator made the weapon extremely controllable to fire on full automatic from the shoulder and deadly accurate when switched to semiautomatic. Arguably the best full power automatic rifle ever fielded, the Baby BARs were an overnight smash hit with Raiding Forces. From the time they arrived, the .30 M1941 Johnson LMGs were left in the arms locker.

Except by the Greek Sacred Squadron. The Greeks loved their Johnson light machine guns. There is no explaining taste in weaponry. Everyone has their own opinion about which is best.

Inside the police station, the sound of someone stirring could be heard. Instead of opening up, an irate voice on the other side of the door shouted something in a guttural accent. Sounded like a sleepy Italian soldier suffering from the mother of all hangovers.

GG, along on the mission for contingencies such as this, translated, "Told us to go away, sir."

Capt. Jaxx said to Lt. Starrett, "I only have one rule for enemy contact: When in doubt, light 'em up."

He reversed the Baby BAR then, shooting from the hip, emptied half of a 20-round magazine of .30 caliber full metal jacket slugs through the wooden door at waist level. A guaranteed cure for hangovers and bad manners. Then he kicked open the door.

Lt. Starrett tossed in an M-2 fragmentation grenade.

WHOOMPH.

In the confined space of the tiny one-room police station, men were screaming and choking on the smell of the acidic Grenite explosive from the frag grenade. Capt. Jaxx entered with the big automatic rifle at his shoulder, firing short bursts at the mangled forms curled up in their bunks and on the floor. When the magazine ran dry, Lt. Starrett stepped around him and took up the slack, emptying his .30 M-1 Carbine as fast as he could pull the trigger.

By then, Capt. Jaxx had changed magazines. He retook the lead, sweeping the room with the barrel of his Baby BAR for targets. No one was moving. The enemy had all been killed, wounded, or stunned into unconsciousness.

The engagement, if you could call it that, was over. Capt. Jaxx had crafted a tactical plan, put it into action on the move, and not a single friendly casualty was incurred. The brief firefight was characterized by surprise, speed, and violence of action with a healthy dose of audacity.

Also, superior firepower.

It was a classic small unit action of the type Capt. Jaxx was known for and one of the reasons men followed him so readily. He made good tactical decisions. It was not lost on his troops that he was first through the door.

It was widely understood that Jack Cool led from the front.

The result was one German and one Italian KIA with the four remaining Blackshirts WIA, nonambulatory. All enemy personnel stationed on Lipsi had become casualties in less than ten seconds.

A search was initiated. Nothing of significant intelligence value was found. There was a .380 Walther PP and five .380 Beretta M-1934 pistols recovered that would come in handy as trading material with the rear echelon armchair commandos at MEHQ in Cairo.

A pair of Zeiss binoculars in a leather case was hanging from a nail on the wall.

Capt. Jaxx tossed them to Lt. Starrett, "Didn't take long for you to trade up. These are good glass."

Lt. Starrett said, "Thanks, sir. Check this out . . . I found a code book on the desk."

Capt. Jaxx said, "Tag it and bag it. Probably for encrypting sighting reports. Low-level stuff but you never can tell."

"What do you want to do with the rifles, sir?"

"Donate 'em to the Lipsi Police Department, compliments of Raiding Forces."

GG pulled a wool blanket off what at first glance had appeared to be a small table standing in one corner of the room.

Capt. Jaxx said, "Oh, yeah—that's what I'm talking about." Under the blanket was a cast-iron safe.

"Ask the mayor if he knows the combination."

The GSS translator said, "Claims to have no idea, Captain."

"Tell him to send someone to locate the chief of police. Bring him here. Maybe he has the numbers."

After a brief conversation, the GSS translator said, "The mayor *is* the police chief."

Lt. Starrett said, "Know much about demolitions, sir?"

"Only what I learned from observing Percy Stirling in action, and he's a bad influence when it comes to blowing things up. If you're ever around when "Pyro" lights off a charge, my advice is to relocate as far away as physically possible. Then try to get a little further out if you can."

Lt. Starrett said, "What do you think's inside, sir?"

At that moment there was a disturbance out in the street. Capt. Jaxx and Lt. Starrett went out to see what was happening. One of the Greek sailors from the caique was running toward the police station shouting.

The GSS interpreter said, "A motorboat has been sighted approaching."

Worst-case scenario for a small raiding party was to be ashore when a superior force of enemy troops from some other island arrived unexpectedly.

Capt. Jaxx ordered, "Follow me—let's go, boys. Down to the pier on the double. Bring the mayor along."

Leaving the enemy dead and wounded where they lay, SOG took to a narrow back alley to avoid being seen running down the main street. They raced the three blocks to the jetty. In the distance, a 25-foot watercraft was entering the bay.

At first glance, it appeared to be packed with people. Upon further study through binoculars, it was determined there were actually only four passengers. They were wearing field grey German uniforms.

The mayor babbled something.

The GSS interpreter said, "He says day trippers. Nazi tourists taking photographs. He hides the women when they come."

At a single glance, Capt. Jaxx made an estimate of the situation. "They'll tie off at the dock. Let 'em get out of the boat and then on my command, open up with everything you have.

"Hale, take up a position of your own choosing providing the best field of fire for your Stinger."

"Yes, sir."

"When I open, that's the signal to commence. No one fires until I do. Keep blasting, boys, until they're all down."

It was fashionable in the British Army to blow a whistle to initiate an ambush. A lot of U.S. Army officers had adopted the practice. Not Capt. Jaxx. When a party of the enemy entered the killing zone of one of his ambushes, he liked the first sound they heard to inflict casualties.

He did not believe in giving the enemy any opportunity to react—no matter how small.

Moving with drill team-like precision acquired from hard training, repetitive practice, and a lot of practical experience, the SOG team moved into position. The operators were concealed behind large nets that Lipsi fishermen had hung up on poles to dry. The setup was configured exactly like a gun range, which is what makes the linear ambush so effective.

Distance to the kill zone was approximately twenty-five yards. There was a slight downhill slope that would prevent them from being able to achieve grazing fire. But no ambush is ever perfect.

As the Germans were climbing out of their boat, the mayor poked his head up to see what was taking place. Capt. Jaxx shoved him back down. "Tell this man to stay under cover."

Ambushes seldom go as planned. Something always goes wrong. Capt. Jaxx had set enough of them to know to never count on developments working out according to plan. However, on a tiny island nearly two hundred miles from the nearest known Allied base, the last thing any of these Nazi sightseers would be thinking about today was being ambushed.

The enemy soldiers made their way along the pier toward the shore. Like the mayor predicted, all four storm troopers had cameras hanging around their necks in brown leather cases. The Germans were equipped only with sidearms.

They did not believe they had anything to fear from the Greek islanders.

As the group approached the land end of the dock, Capt. Jaxx pulled the steel butt plate of his Baby BAR tight against his shoulder. He took a deep breath. Looking through the ghost ring rear sight, he placed the front post center of mass on the first Nazi and let out half his breath.

Then he squeezed the trigger.

At his first shot, the rest of the team opened as one. The roar of the sudden explosion of fire came like the clap of a violent thunderstorm. Every SOG operator was a professional. They were putting out short, crisp, disciplined bursts. A withering cone of steel jacketed bullets converged on the enemy soldiers.

Splinters flew up from the wooden planks of the dock as rounds danced around in the killing zone.

The Nazis never stood a chance. Three went down in the initial burst. One turned to run. PFC Bronson, who was laying low in the caique tied off at the dock calmly observing developments, shot him with his 9mm Beretta M-38 submachine gun as he came back past.

"CHECK FIRE!"

PFC Hale let off an extra burst from his belt-fed Stinger, his fighting spirit running hot.

Then, all was quiet—deadly still.

It was always like that at the end of an ambush. Extreme violence followed by calm. The silence never seemed natural.

Capt. Jaxx said, "You boys conduct a search for anything of intelligence value the Nazis might have on 'em—secure their sidearms. Lt. Starrett and I are going to go blow that safe. Be ready to pull out as soon as we return.

"We're done here." Jack Cool.

ON BOARD THE CATALINA WINGING ITS WAY SOUTH toward the jungled parts of Africa, Captain "Geronimo" Joe McKoy was entertaining the people around him with a tale about a trial he had attended during his law enforcement days in the U.S. Marshals Service. Everyone was laughing. Capt. McKoy was a master storyteller.

"I'm sittin' in the courtroom waitin' to testify. Man was bein' tried for first-degree murder. We'd caught him red-handed. Dead body, murder weapon, fingerprints, eyewitnesses, didn't stand a Chinaman's chance. Nonetheless, his court-appointed public defender gave it a shot, tryin' to examine the coroner—a cantankerous old codger who did not suffer fools lightly, hated lawyers. 'Doctor, how many autopsies have you performed on dead people?'

"'All of 'em, the live ones squirm around too much.'"

Major the Lady Jane Seaborn had her arm draped across Colonel John Randal's shoulders, "What are you reading, John?"

"A U.S. Navy report on PT boat operations in the Solomon Islands. Our mosquito boat sailors out there have made major in-theatre upgrades to the gun packages on their PT boats. One Elco 80-footer was retrofitted with a 40 mm Bofors, a belt-fed 37 mm M-4 auto cannon, a pair of 20 mms, three M-2 Browning .50 caliber machine guns, and four Mark XIII torpedoes."

Lady Jane said, "The array of guns on Brandy's MAS boat are more impressive."

Col. Randal said, "That's a fact. I've requested that General Donovan requisition half a dozen additional Thunderbolts."

Across the aisle, Capt. McKoy said, "Not discouraged by a shaky start, the defense attorney takes another crack at it. 'Now doctor, do you recall what time you performed your autopsy?'

"'It was 8:30 AM.'

"'And was the victim dead at that time?'

"'If not, he was when I got finished.'"

Capt. McKoy said, "At this point, the poor lawyer decided to go all in attemptin' to establish the exact time a' death to prove it couldn't a' been his man who done the deed. 'Doctor, isn't it true that when someone dies in their sleep they don't know about it until the next day?'

"The coroner says, 'Are you sure you passed the bar exam?'

"Now the defendant was sittin' there listenin' to all this and he shouts, 'Judge, I demand new counsel!'

"'On what grounds?'

"'With this fool, I'll be lucky if you don't give me thirty days in the electric chair.'"

Lady Jane said, "Ian wanted to speak to you but he could only be in town for the one night."

"What about?"

"The Royal Navy is cleaning house at the top after the Dieppe disaster."

"Really? That was a year ago."

"The Navy waited a discreet amount of time before taking action so that the changes look like routine transfers. Now Mountbatten is out as the Chief of Combined Operations. Instead of firing him, the Prime Minister promoted him up and away, a long way. Dickie is to be the new Supreme Allied Commander Southeast Asia Command.

"We shall not be hearing from him anytime soon."

Col. Randal said, "I've noticed when a senior officer needs to be fired, instead they're shipped out to the China-Burma-India Theatre."

Lady Jane said, "Exactly, happened to Ian's boss at the Naval Intelligence Division. Admiral Godfrey has been held accountable for Dieppe too. He has been transferred to command the Royal Indian Navy."

Col. Randal said, "I always thought he was a good intelligence officer."

Lady Jane said, "Ian served as the Admiral's personal assistant. He handled NID's most sensitive projects. Over cocktails, he claims he dreamed up quite a lot of missions someone else was going to have to go carry out."

Col. Randal said, "Yeah, like Raiding Forces."

Lady Jane said, "GOLDEN FLEECE/RED INDIAN has always been Ian's responsibility. The Nazis have made a new modification to their signals encoding device that our boffins have not been able to penetrate. Ian's new boss wants him to devote his efforts entirely to capturing one of the machines so our side can back-engineer it.

Col. Randal said, "What's that have to do with us?"

Lady Jane said, "Ian knows you have been tasked with small-scale raiding throughout the Aegean, which shall spread Raiding Forces thin. He is also aware the U.S. Army has called on us for short-term strategic missions and expects that practice to continue. The Commander's resigned to the fact he cannot always count on our being readily available when a target pops up."

Col. Randal said, "True."

Lady Jane said, "Ian saw no other option than to form his own team 30 Assault Unit—he calls them his 'Red Indians.'"

Col. Randal said, "I heard he'd gone into the raiding business for himself."

Lady Jane said, "We poke fun at Ian and he makes light of himself. However, I have it on good authority he is much higher up on the intelligence totem pole than most people are cleared to know."

Col. Randal said, "I like Fleming."

Lady Jane said, "Ian's Red Indians carried out their first attempt at making a pinch in Sicily during OPERATION HUSKY—actually their second, if you count the fiasco at Dieppe when they never even made it ashore."

"How did that work out?"

"Not well, apparently—Ian asked us to retrain 30 Assault Unit for him." Col. Randal said,

"We can do that."

Across the aisle, Captain Cuthbert Bowlby was saying, " . . . colonists in the Belgian Congo trafficking illicit diamonds to the Nazis at a time their homeland is occupied by the German Army is something our masters have chosen to turn a blind eye to. A sacred cow politically."

Capt. McKoy said, "Sacred cows make the best hamburger." Waldo said, "I like a good burger."

Col. Randal stared across at Capt. McKoy. Capt. McKoy stared back. Both men were on the same page.

Captain Pamala Plum-Martin and Beverly Blackwell walked out of the cockpit, leaving the flight engineer/third pilot to fly the plane. The

Vargas Girl look-alike Royal Marine walked past and took a seat toward the rear with King. Beverly squeezed in on the end so that now Col. Randal was sandwiched between the Texas beauty queen and Lady Jane.

Which was not a bad thing.

Across the aisle, Capt. McKoy was saying, "When me and Frank Hamer was tracking Bonnie and Clyde, we tried to learn everything we could about their tendencies. Now Bonnie, she smoked Camels. Clyde was a Bull Durham man . . ."

Col. Randal said, "Beverly, I thought we had a special relationship." Beverly said, "We dooo!"

"You're supposed to have my back."

Beverly said, "Seriously, if you think I'm *ever* getting between you and Lady Jane when you two are teasing each other, that is so wrong. You have to save yourself. Sink or swim, cowboy."

Lady Jane said, "What makes you think I was teasing about Commander Fleming?"

Mandy made her way forward from where she and Captain Roy Kidd were sitting. She leaned up against the bulkhead to the cockpit. "I talked to Sammy about your concerns."

Col. Randal said, "And they were?"

"Not recovering all the hidden assets from the first crime lords we took down. Sammy asked if we checked behind the paintings."

"Well, did you?"

"Absolutely, we were searching for hidden safes. That was not what Sammy was inquiring about. Criminals need to be financially liquid. The bulk of their capital is almost always in diamonds or other precious gems because a fortune's worth is lightweight enough to be transported by a single individual on the run."

Col. Randal said, "Not new information."

Mandy said, "Fine art minus the frame is lighter than diamonds and can be even more valuable if painted by one of the Old Masters."

Beverly said, "I was an art and drama major at UT. The Big Four's paintings that I saw were basically pornography. None were by famous artists."

Lady Jane said, "Agreed. Kama Sutra in black velvet."

Beverly said, "Daddy would probably like to have one or two for his gun room, though."

Mandy said, "The mistake we made is not investigating the possibility that a second, more valuable painting was concealed *behind* the erotica."

Lady Jane said, "Uh-oh!"

Col. Randal said, "Did you go back and check the art in the four houses we're preparing for sale?"

Mandy said, "A second canvas was hidden behind nearly every single one. They may be extremely valuable. I am having them appraised."

Lady Jane said, "Wonder how many masterpieces we auctioned off for next to nothing?"

Mandy said, "Not to worry. Sammy secured a list of buyers from the auction house. His Security Police are in the process of recovering the art. After we remove the secret paintings, the original purchases will be returned, with the buyers none the wiser."

Col. Randal said, "Good report, Mandy. What else do you think we might have missed?"

Mandy said, "Working on it, John."

Across the aisle, Capt. Kidd was showing Capt. McKoy the Ballester Molina .45. "The Colonel asked me to evaluate this pistol for General Donovan."

Capt. McKoy said, "I know this handgun. Argentina-made— outstanding craftsmanship. Legend has it the steel comes from the German pocket battleship the *Graf Spee*. The merchant raider was sunk in 1940 in the River Plate estuary off Argentina and Uruguay. When you release the slide and it slams into battery, the pistol chimes like a bell."

Cuthbert said, "May not be a legend, Captain. The German pocket battleship *Graf Spee*— actually the ship was a cruiser but we called her a 'pocket battleship'—took refuge in Montevideo to effect repairs after a series of running sea battles with the Royal Navy. Warships of belligerent nations are only allowed to remain in a neutral port for twenty-four hours. The German captain managed to persuade Uruguay to extend his deadline to seventy-two hours. That may have helped him, but it gave the Royal Navy additional time to assemble reinforcing units off Montevideo, lying in wait in international waters for the Kriegsmarine ship to sail.

"The Nazis decided to avoid the optics of a defeat at the hands of the Royal Navy—every news organization with an office in South America was on hand filming events. So, when the time finally expired, the *Graf Spee* sailed, only to be intentionally scuttled without giving battle.

"Fortunately for us, the *Graf Spee's* skipper made two mistakes. He was not outside the Argentinian three-mile territorial limit when he gave the order to explode the ship's torpedo heads. And the depth was only four fathoms—the superstructure was still above the water after the ship settled.

Capt. McKoy said, "Man got in a hurry, huh."

Cuthbert said, "MI-6 photo interpreters noticed an array of antennas sticking up where normally there were supposed to be none. The *Graf Spee* had been noted for her incredibly accurate fire, which some Royal Navy analysts attributed to luck. SIS was not so sure.

"Since I had been Navy before joining The Firm, Brigadier Menzies dispatched me, along with a team of technicians, to make an appraisal of the situation. Working with the British Ambassador, I was able to purchase the wreck of the *Graf Spee* through a front company for the equivalent of sixty-seven-thousand U.S. dollars. Part of the arrangement was that after we finished with the ship, the government could reclaim it for salvage—Argentina suffers an acute shortage of steel."

Capt. McKoy said, "Sounds like you got yourself a pretty good deal there, Cuthbert."

"Yes, it was. Our technicians were able to remove the electronic warfare equipment. Turned out to be a state-of-the-art secret radar fire control system we immediately reverse- engineered and now have installed on all Royal Navy warships.

"I would not be able to reveal this story except when the Nazis realized what was taking place, they chartered a fleet of small boats and circled the *Graf Spee* for days watching our workmen—helpless to stop them. The press turned the event into a media circus, hiring boats of their own. They even chartered an airplane to fly overhead with a camera crew. Newsreels of my teams working were shown in theaters around the world.

"Arguably, the recovery turned out to be the most highly-publicized— *as it was taking place*—in history. All the news coverage pushed the *Graf Spee's* captain over the edge. He committed suicide in his hotel room in Buenos Aires."

Waldo said, "You think Roy's gun really is made outta that Nazi battleship?"

Cuthbert said, "There is no reason not to believe it, Mr. Treywick. Shortly after the sinking, Argentina received an unsolicited order for 10,000 handguns from an undisclosed buyer—Special Operations Executive. You are looking at one of them."

From across the aisle, Lady Jane said, "Love the chime."

Jim said, "SOE agents are shooting Nazis with pistols made out of steel from one of their own battleships."

Capt. McKoy said, "Yeah, that's a nice touch."

These were serious men—tops in their fields—professionals. It was good for them to be able to spend time together, talk, swap stories, and laugh. Normally when they interacted, it was in a high-stress environment with a dangerous mission imminent, and at times working at cross purposes.

Mandy stayed up front for a while to chat. Beverly reluctantly drifted away to one of the bunks for her mandatory sleeping period before her next stint of flying. Lady Jane and Brandy broke out a deck of cards. Col. Randal stood up and wandered to the rear of the plane to stretch his legs.

King joined him, as did Capt. McKoy, Waldo, and Capt. Kidd. Naturally, Mandy tagged along, suspecting correctly that something of interest would be discussed. Sergeant Major Mike "March or Die" Mikkalis was already in the tail with Master Sergeant Mack Beckwith, talking to soldier of fortune Commander General Frank Polanski.

Waldo passed out his custom-rolled cigars, which everyone stuck in their teeth but no one lit. Cigarette smoking was permitted, but Lady Jane banned cigars on the flight.

Everyone listened intently as Capt. McKoy laid out the plan.

"We're gonna drop Sergeant Major Mikkalis off in Nairobi. He'll meet up with the local DeBeers representative, who'll put him in touch with mercenary types in Kenya available to sign on for Frank's army. After he gets done traveling in civilian clothes, Mike'll make his way independently to the Congo with his recruits.

"Waldo's goin' to catch a flight from Nairobi to Cape Town. He'll hook up with the DeBeers man down there to do his recruitin' of some tough South Africans the Diamond Company's got lined up down there. Once he's got his people hired, he'll move 'em to a location somewhere in the Congo he'll coordinate with Frank.

"Jim and Cuthbert are flyin' out to Johannesburg. They're headed to Sir Ernest Oppenheimer's private estate, Brenthurst. They'll confer with him to see how DeBeers can assist us in closin' down the smugglin', then fly back to Cairo commercial.

"For once, the Diamond Corporation and Raiding Forces have a common interest. Those bad actors in the Congo are not only a bunch a' traitorous SOBs, but they're cuttin' into DeBeers' profits and the Company don't like it one little bit.

"Colonel Randal, Roy, King, Mack, Frank, and me will continue on to Léopoldville in the Catalina. The Colonel and King have a meetin' to go to in town. I'm gonna link up with my ex-law enforcement boys workin' undercover to get a first-hand read on what's happenin'.

"Frank and Roy'll board a riverboat and head upstream to check out the Kasai River jungle country Frank'll be operatin' in. Take a little look-see, recon, boots on the ground—that sorta' thing."

Waldo said, "Time spent on reconnaissance is rarely wasted —ain't no substitute for it."

Cdr. Gen. Polanski said, "Affirmative."

Mandy asked, "What about the rest of us?"

Capt. McKoy said, "You'll be stayin' at a resort hotel in Nairobi. Lay out by the pool. Do a little sightseein'. Sir Ernest invited you ladies to visit his estate with Jim and Cuthbert, but we'll be comin' back through Nairobi pretty quick on the Catalina. You wouldn't have time to make the trip and get back to fly home with us."

The group broke up.

Waldo pulled Cdr. Gen. Polanski aside, "Frank, the bonus we promised is gonna be performance-based, tied directly to how many diamonds you recover. Mercenaries ain't choir boys. They've been known to have sticky fingers. Your main job is gonna be to kill traffickers, get the stones they bought back, and make sure the rocks don't get hijacked by your own men— that last part ain't gonna be easy."

Cdr. Gen. Polanski said, "You'll get your sparklers, Waldo."

Waldo said, "You run into any trouble on that front, Joe and me'll come down and help take care of it—might bring King."

"I ain't running into trouble."

"Positive thinking—that's good, Frank."

Col. Randal had a word with Sgt. Maj. Mikkalis. "Any thoughts on what you want to do after Raiding Forces completes its reorganization? I could use you taking your captain's commission back."

Sgt. Maj. Mikkalis said, "With permission, Colonel, I would prefer to work with Mrs. Paige—skipper a caique. She has one pegged for me we named *Santa Claus*. In addition to rescuing people for MI-9, I will be delivering bags of SOE toys that go 'bang' to bad little girls and boys."

Col. Randal said, "Never saw that one coming."

THE CATALINA SPLASHED DOWN AT THE ROYAL AIR FORCE seaplane base in the Nairobi River outside of the capital of Kenya. Nairobi was located at an elevation of over 5,000 feet above sea level. The high altitude is what the European expatriates blamed for the rampant promiscuity sometimes described as "white mischief" in the colony among the prewar Happy Valley Set.

No outside parties were buying the explanation.

The five-star Stanley Hotel had limousines waiting at the dock to whisk the passengers to their quarters in luxury and anonymity. There was a need to be discreet. Most everyone in the party had been in Nairobi carrying out a clandestine mission at one time or another.

At least one murder was still unsolved.

On a dark night three years earlier, Colonel John Randal and Major the Lady Jane Seaborn had lain in wait on a dirt road outside of Nairobi for Lord Josslyn Hay, 22nd Earl of Erroll, the philanderer-in-chief of the hedonistic Happy Valley Set. Lord Hay was also the Italian's master spy in Kenya.

Col. Randal shot him dead, on orders from the British Secret Intelligence Service.

For reasons unknown, the individual wrongly accused of the crime confessed. At trial, the defendant was found innocent by a jury of his peers, even with his confession being entered as evidence against him. Possibly he got off because he did not commit the offense . . . or it may have been because the Earl had slept with several of the jury member's wives, their daughters, or both—in at least one case both at the same time—and bragged about it.

With no one convicted, the case was still open, officially. For that reason, Col. Randal was traveling incognito as Major Jones. Why take a chance? Lady Jane was too well-known in Kenya Colony to use a cover name. However, no one would have suspected her of playing a role in the assassination.

In actual fact, she had orchestrated it for MI-6.

It was after sundown when the party arrived at the hotel. They were immediately escorted to their rooms by the manager without the inconvenience of having to register. The Stanley had a reciprocal agreement with Lady Jane's hotel in London, the Bradford, making check-in/check- out easy.

Alone in their suite after Col. Randal finished ordering room service, Lady Jane said, "Explain again why I am not being allowed to fly on to Léopoldville with you."

Col. Randal said, "It's 1,500 miles at 125 miles per hour. We probably won't be on the ground over an hour. Long flight round trip. All work, no play."

Lady Jane said, "What shall you be doing?"

"Pam and Beverly will see to refueling the Catalina. Captain McKoy is going to meet with his ex-law enforcement people. The Commander General will disembark a crate of 9mm Erma submachine guns for his mercenary army—German weapons—so it won't look like he's running a U.S. or British-backed operation. Roy and the Commander General are traveling upriver, and I have a meeting in town.

"Those of us returning will fly straight back here."

"I want to travel with you."

Col. Randal said, "How about this? Stay here, pamper yourself, rest, go to the spa—make yourself pretty. Then we'll see if the Professor can round up another jar of that honey when we get back to RFHQ."

Lady Jane laughed, "Why not phone room service and order some right now? We can pretend it came from a pyramid. Who needs 3,000-year-old honey?"

Col. Randal said, "It wouldn't be me."

THE CATALINA HAD BEEN FLYING OVER THE JUNGLE FOR hours. Colonel John Randal stared out the window. This was what he had always thought Africa was supposed to look like, but it never did. Giant triple canopy trees with snakes hanging down and Tarzan swinging on a vine. The vastness of the Congo was incredible, and the few times he could see through the trees the ground appeared to be everglades, sunlight reflected off water. Waldo might be right—there could be a leaf-eating dinosaur down there. Who would know? Clearly, Europeans had never explored all the green vastness that stretched from horizon to horizon.

If the plane went down, no one was going to come and rescue them.

Captain "Geronimo" Joe McKoy said, "*The Heart a' Darkness.*"

"You read Joseph Conrad?"

"You know the book, John?"

"My English literature student teacher, Miss UCLA, assigned it to me in high school."

Capt. McKoy said, "She had you pegged. That book was written about the Congo over forty years ago, but my boys tell me conditions ain't changed much since then. They say it's an evil place—a green hell. We're gonna have to be real careful down here and watch our backs.

"The Belgian colonists don't think the rules apply."

"What rules?"

"Any of 'em—legal, international military, Bible . . ."

"Sounds like Abyssinia."

"Worse, maybe—I'm just sayin'."

"I'll keep that in mind."

"The good news is, white men almost never venture outside the big towns. When they do, it is usually by riverboat to a handful of remote trading posts scattered along the banks of the major rivers. As far as travel into the interior, that doesn't happen except for the occasional big game hunter. Even they rarely go in very deep. Some who do never come back out.

"Like I said, the Congo is a dangerous place."

Col. Randal said, "Frank's primary concern is the Kasai River. That's where the potholers find diamonds buried in the sandbanks. I looked at the map—it's a big river."

Capt. McKoy said, "I'm thinkin' maybe I'll put some a' my people in those trading posts. Work out some kind a' concession deal to buy gems."

Col. Randal said, "The Nazis aren't going to like that idea."

Capt. McKoy said, "Probably not."

The PBY splashed down and taxied to the Congo River Flying Boat Port. It was steaming hot with humidity nearing 100 percent. The amphibious airport was located three miles outside of Léopoldville.

Col. Randal did not like the look of things. It was just a feeling. He sensed the Congo was going to live up to its reputation as a bad place. He made an immediate change of plans.

"Captain, I want you to keep Pam and Mandy with you at all times while we're on the ground—don't let 'em out of your sight."

"Can do, John."

He went into the cockpit and told the pilots a lie. "You girls go with Captain McKoy. I want you wired in on what his men have going. Give me a private report when King and I get back from town.

"Let the flight engineer handle refueling."

Pam and Mandy perked up. This was better than staying with the plane. They liked being included and given a mission.

Col. Randal and King disembarked. They were incognito, wearing standard colonist attire of khaki bush jackets with no rank or insignia, Australian slouch hats, and U.S. Army Air Force issue teardrop Ray-Ban flying sunglasses. While the smoked glasses were not of the type worn by the Belgians, they did make it virtually impossible for anyone to ever identify them later.

Capt. McKoy introduced one of his operatives. "This is Buck Meredith, an old Border Patrol agent buddy a' mine. He'll run you into town, then bring you right back when you're done. Buck's a good man."

The ex-Border Patrol agent was a tall leather-faced individual with wrinkles around his eyes from a lifetime of squinting into the burning sun on the Mexican border. He looked like someone who had stepped right out of the old West. Law enforcement along the border was dangerous work without a lot of backup—billy club and handgun, not necessarily in that order. No questions were asked when a prisoner was brought in shot repeatedly or beaten to a pulp.

Border Patrol agents were not paid to engage in fair fights.

Col. Randal climbed in the front seat of Buck's battered automobile of a European make and model he did not recognize. He noticed the ex-Border Patrol agent had a .45 cal. Thompson submachine gun lying next to his leg with its Cutts compensator resting on the floorboard. No one said much on the ride.

Most of the trip was through one of the worst slums on the planet. There was an unusually large number of natives with arms or legs missing. The ride was depressing.

Buck said, "Back in the day, cuttin' off a hand or two, maybe a foot, was the misdemeanor punishment for natives—still do it, just not as much. Saves from having to feed 'em in jail.

"When a colonist accidently hits an African with his car, first thing he makes a U-turn, goes back and runs him over again because if a European kills a local nothing much happens. If the native survives, there's got to be money changing hands.

"Make no mistake, gentlemen, this is a tough crowd."

Col. Randal said, "Lovely."

As they drove into the colonists' section of Léopoldville, the houses were all freshly painted, yards manicured and there were no people missing hands or feet along the street. It seemed like a pleasant place to live.

Buck said, "With the Nazis occupying Belgium, more European refugees show up out here every day. A white man can live like a king in the Congo on a few pennies a day unless he don't have a few pennies. What I can't understand is why the locals don't rise up and kill every European in the country—they outnumber 'em ten thousand to one."

Col. Randal said, "What about the military?"

Buck said, "The Force Publique has a hard time raisin' and lowerin' the colors, Colonel. They're a combined military and police outfit. Spend most a' the day in their barracks sleeping off hangovers from the night before."

The car pulled up to a colonial style police station with a sign in the three languages of Belgium. English was not one, so Col. Randal had no idea what they said.

There were four primary native languages spoken in the Congo, but there were no signs in any of those languages.

Col. Randal said, "We won't be long—keep the motor running, Buck."

He and King walked into the police station. Inside, nothing much was going on. There was a sleepy desk sergeant sweltering under an exhausted ceiling fan rotating so slowly it seemed it was going to grind to a halt at any second. No one else was visibly present.

King said in French, "The chief is expecting us."

The sergeant pointed listlessly to a flight of stairs that went up to a single office that looked down on the room.

The chief of police was the front man of illegal diamond trafficking in the Congo. All off-the-books diamond payoffs from the diamond producers in the colony funneled through him. However, he had a problem.

There was only one buyer—Nazis.

They set the price the Third Reich would pay, which was the standard international prewar price as set by DeBeers Diamond Company in 1938.

Prior to Col. Randal's trip, it had been stage managed by MI-6 for the chief of police to learn that illicit diamonds in Cairo were selling for thirty times the prewar price. He was shocked. Not only were the Nazis occupying his motherland, but they were also cheating him on the diamonds he sold them.

Col. Randal had been described as being a purchasing agent of the Chicago mob—it was known the chief was a great fan of American gangster movies. The chief of police was also led to believe that he had extensive business dealings with the major crime lords in Cairo, being the liaison between the mob in Chicago and the mob in Cairo. And that he was interested in establishing a pipeline of illicit diamonds from the Congo to the United States and would pay the current Cairo rate of thirty times prewar price.

This sounded good.

When King and Col. Randal reached the office at the top of the stairs, they went straight in without knocking and closed the door. They had an appointment. The chief of police was eagerly anticipating their arrival.

He stood up from his desk as they walked in. King went to the venetian blinds on the picture window overlooking the floor of the station below and closed them. This was a private meeting—strictly business. No one was interested in making new friends.

With the Merc interpreting, Col. Randal said, "I understand you have something to show me."

The police chief was more than happy to comply. These people did not waste time, a sign he took to mean they were serious men. He was not wrong about that. The chief opened a safe, extracted a quart-size glass candy jar with a little green crocodile on top and placed it on his desk. The jar was full of sparkling cut diamonds from the *Société Internationale* . . . the mining conglomerate with a semi-monopoly in the Congo.

Col. Randal shot the chief three times in the heart with his silenced .22 High Standard Military Model D. *WHIIIIIICH, WHIIIIIICH, WHIIIIIICH.*

A quarter could have covered all three bullet holes. The police chief was dead before he hit the floor.

Placing the jar with the little green crocodile on the lid in his briefcase, King said, "Not enough money in the world to pay thirty times prewar price for this cache of diamonds. How did the fool think we could come to terms?"

Col. Randal said, "That's the art of the deal." King said, "You are a tough negotiator."

THE NEXT DAY WHEN ROOM SERVICE BROUGHT BREAKFAST to Colonel John Randal and Major the Lady Jane Seaborn's suite at the Stanley Hotel in Nairobi, a complimentary newspaper was on the tray. Col. Randal was in the bathroom shaving when the paper arrived.

While Col. Randal slept, Brigadier Dudley Clarke had been in Cairo doing what he did best— disseminating information that was not completely true.

In this case he fed the media an accurate account geared to target a specific audience.

```
CHIEF OF LÉOPOLDVILLE POLICE
ASSASSINATED BY ALLIED AGENTS ALLEGED TO
BE SELLING DIAMONDS TO NAZI GERMANY
```

Lady Jane called, "How did your meeting go?"

"Fine."

He walked out wiping shaving cream off his face with a towel. Lady Jane held up the front page of the newspaper. "This why you left me here in Nairobi?"

Col. Randal said, "It's not as bad as it looks."

"Seriously, the Léopoldville chief of police . . ."

Col. Randal reached in his parachute bag and brought out the jar of diamonds. "Brought you a trinket."

Lady Jane laughed, "You are a charmer."

7

EARTHWORM

COLONEL JOHN RANDAL AND LIEUTENANT COLONEL SIR Terry "Zorro" Stone were in the small briefing/map area of the third-floor suite at Raiding Forces Headquarters that Col. Randal shared with Major the Lady Jane Seaborn. Lt. Col. Stone was laying out plans for the reorganization of Raiding Forces. Big change was in the works.

Lt. Col. Stone pointed to a map of the Turkish coastline, "As you are aware, the Levant Schooner Flotilla plans to position a minimum of ten schooners along the coast moored in small, out-of-the-way inlets. Each schooner will house approximately thirty Raiders—a captain and three teams led by lieutenants—stationed on board. Each team—or perhaps we shall continue to call them patrols—will be a self-contained raiding unit supported by an LSF caique for transport to and from their targets.

"PT boats, MAS boats, or 10th Motor Gun Boat Flotilla MGBs will be available on call to provide fast transport when time is of the essence. For some missions, a team will be inserted by amphibian aircraft."

Col. Randal said, "So, in effect, the schooners will be floating patrol bases with the troops living aboard between missions?"

"Affirmative."

"Do you have the ten schooners?"

"No, only three at the moment—not as easy to organize as it sounds, old stick."

Col. Randal said, "And the Turks have agreed? They're going to allow us to use their waters as a launch site for military operations?"

Lt. Col. Stone said, "Dudley Clarke concluded a Top Secret off-the-books unwritten agreement with President Ismet Inonu to do exactly that. Do not take it to infer that everyone in their military is entirely in agreement with the idea. A number of Turkey's more senior officers fought against us in the last war and are decidedly anti-British. Also, there are more than a few Nazi sympathizers in the country.

"Expect problems from time to time."

Col. Randal said, "Why would Dudley Clarke be negotiating with the Turkish president?

Wouldn't that be a job for diplomats?"

Lt. Col. Stone said, "One wonders why Dudley does any number of things."

Col. Randal said, "Well, the plan should work. It's more complex than running gun jeep patrols out of Oasis X. We've got a diverse group of people from different branches of the service working together for the first time, challenging logistics, and non-stop coordination all focused on putting a small team on a distant objective and bringing it back."

Lt. Col. Stone said, "Not a walk in the park—militarily." Col. Randal said, "Detailed planning, flawless execution . . ."

Lt. Col. Stone said, "What you have me for, old stick. I shall be setting up a joint Army/Navy operations staff with offices here at RFHQ, at Small Raids Incorporated HQ in Alexandria and at RFHQ Advanced Base on Castelrozzo—ABC.

"Try to envision the Aegean Theatre of Operations as desert raiding minus the desert and the gun jeeps."

Col. Randal said, "Not the same. If something goes wrong on a raid, there's no hiking back to base."

"True; however, we shall not be going up against the Desert Fox and Afrika Korps either."

Col. Randal said, "Point taken—I understand Veronica is trying to assemble her own MI- 9 caique fleet. You involved?"

"Meaning are *we* involved? Yes, we are."

King walked in from his desk on the landing outside the door. "Admiral Ransom requests the presence of both you and Colonel Stone downstairs in his office at your earliest convenience, Chief."

Since Vice Admiral Sir Randolph "Razor" Ransom seldom used his office at RFHQ and almost never held meetings in it, this request did not fall into the category of business as usual. Not to be taken lightly. Col. Randal and Lt. Col. Stone immediately stopped what they were doing and headed downstairs to the Operations Room.

On the way, Lt. Col. Stone said, "Newspaper is reporting the chief of police in Léopoldville was shot and killed three days ago. Apparently in retribution for being engaged in trafficking diamonds to the enemy. Enjoy your visit to the capital of the Heart of Darkness, old stick?"

Col. Randal said, "Must have your days mixed up, Terry."

"You forget, old stick, my new assignment requires me to know your whereabouts. I have your contact information readily at hand at all times. May become necessary to consult with you at a moment's notice, anytime, anywhere.

"Besides, Red was on the plane. I knew her schedule."

When they arrived in the Operations Room, Beverly was standing by. She escorted them straight to VAdm Ransom's office. Already present in the room besides the Admiral were Brigadier General William "Wild Bill" Donovan, Lieutenant Junior Grade Jackson Taylor, USNR—an orthodontist turned Frogman, now the commander of the OSS Maritime Unit (MU) detachment assigned to Raiding Forces—and Brandy Seaborn, the Admiral's daughter.

Beverly stayed for the meeting.

Col. Randal immediately clicked q2.

VAdm. Ransom passed a stack of 8x10 aerial photos across the desk. "Naval air reconnaissance took these at dawn this morning."

Col. Randal picked up the stack. Three ships were visible in the black and white glossy photographs. A destroyer and two supply ships. They were resting at anchor.

VAdm Ransom said, "What you are looking at is a Regia Marina Folgore-class destroyer and two cargo transports berthed in the harbor at Portologo, Leros. There are three primary islands in the Dodecanese Chain. Kos, which has the only airfield; Rhodes has a port but it's not large enough to support major Axis naval operations; and Leros, which has Portologo—a deep- water Regia Marina base the Italians constructed prior to the war.

"Colonel Randal, are you prepared to accept a mission?" Couched like that, it was not a question.

"Yes, sir."

"Tonight, elements of Raiding Forces will enter the Port of Portologo under cover of darkness utilizing the cockleshells of Lieutenant Taylor's OSS Maritime Unit and place limpet mines on the three enemy ships anchored in the harbor—with priority to the Italian destroyer.

"The MU teams are to be flown to within a mile and a half of the objective by a Seagull piloted by Captain Plum-Martin and OSS Operative Blackwell. The raiding party shall disembark with their folboats, paddle to the objective, place their limpet mines on the targets, and extract by paddling an additional twelve miles to a rendezvous point on Kalymnos Island where they will link up with a MAS boat for the return trip—your boat, Brandy.

"Questions?"

Col. Randal was angry and he did not try to hide it. The operation, while small in the number of personnel and assets involved, was extraordinarily complex. On such short notice and with no time to prepare, the raid was bordering on suicidal.

LtJG Taylor said, "The mission you have outlined requires a minimum of two Mark II boats, Admiral—four operators. My MU currently consists of Corporal Jenkins and myself. The remainder of the team is still in the U.S. completing mandatory OSS agent training."

Col. Randal felt better immediately. Paddling a two-man canoe into an enemy harbor at night and attaching limpet mines to enemy warships was a mission that called for highly skilled specialists. He tended to dislike using the word "elite," but it most certainly applied in this case. The MU training was incredibly rigorous. LtJG Taylor had the only qualified canoeists assigned to Raiding Forces, and he did not have enough men in-country to accomplish the mission—good.

Lt. Col. Stone said, "The advanced party of the obsessively secret Earthworm Section of the Royal Marine Boom Patrol Detachment, a cover name to cover another cover name, under Lieutenant William Pritchard-Gordon, has recently arrived in theatre and been attached to Raiding Forces for administrative purposes.

"The RMBPD does not patrol booms and Earthworm Section does not burrow in the earth. It consists of sixteen handpicked Royal Marines extensively trained in the gentle art of canoe raiding."

This was news to Col. Randal. He had never heard of the Royal Marine Boom Patrol Detachment, much less Earthworm Section. He could have cheerfully throttled Sir Terry. The last thing he wanted was to discover a way to carry out a high-risk, hastily thrown together mission, utilizing men who did not know each other and had never worked together previously.

Brig. Gen. Donovan said, "I want Lieutenant Taylor to command."

VAdm. Ransom said, "Colonel Stone, place Lieutenant Pritchard-Gordon on alert for the mission immediately. Instruct him to provide one of his boat teams to be attached to the OSS MU. Have the Earthworm people link up with Lieutenant Taylor here as soon as this briefing is concluded."

Lt. Col. Stone said, "Sir!"

VAdm. Ransom said, "Lieutenant Taylor, take charge. You will command the raid team. I shall be in overall command from here at RFHQ. Work out the concept of the operation and scheme of maneuver for the canoeists, then brief me on your plan. In the event you need additional support or equipment, I need to know as soon as possible. Bring problems to me immediately."

"Yes, sir!"

Beverly said, "Pam's in Kabrit. She flew Bentley St. Ledger to Mad Dog's No. 4 Parachute Training School, Admiral."

VAdm. Ransom said, "Does that pose a problem, Miss Blackwell?"

"No, sir. I don't really need a co-pilot as long as I have my navigator, Corporal Murphy."

VAdm. Ransom said, "Brandy, you have remained unnaturally quiet."

"My boat is at Castelrozzo, Father. I can radio ahead to have it serviced, but someone will need to fly Parker and me there straightaway. Kalymnos Island is an eight-hour voyage. We can be at the RVP by 2400 hours tonight, provided our departure takes place no later than 1600 hours."

Lt. Col. Stone said, "That can be arranged."

Brandy said, "Also, I want The Great Teddy on my boat. We shall have to remain on station undercover all day tomorrow. He can camouflage the MAS boat from what will surely be an intensive air/sea search."

Col. Randal said, "I'll make it happen."

In his opinion, the MU and RMBPD boat teams were a write-off. Nothing to be done about it—not his call. However, he was not going to leave any stone unturned to protect the MAS boat and crew. Brandy was absolutely right to stack the deck in her favor as much as possible.

VAdm. Ransom said, "Questions?"

Everyone in the room was a professional. No one said a word. That did not mean they did not have questions. It only meant everyone present realized there were no ready answers or they would have been covered. The downside to being a Quick Reaction Strike Force—an assignment Raiding Forces was transitioning into more and more—was that when intelligence turned up on a priority target, the operation had to be launched immediately and with only the personnel readily at hand.

More and more often, Col. Randal's raid team leaders had no time for detailed planning, no time to conduct rehearsals, and on occasion not even a chance to test fire weapons. It was a hasty frag order issued by a harried mission commander, then "get your gear, prepare to move out—move out."

Being in Raiding Forces was not for the faint of heart, or an inflexible mindset— conventional thinking had no place in their world.

Col. Randal ordered, "Make your phone calls now. Be in my suite in fifteen minutes for a briefing. Move out, people."

As everyone was rushing to leave, Brig. Gen. Donovan said, "Colonel, I would like to attend the mission brief—possibly hitch a ride with Mrs. Seaborn tonight to observe."

Col. Randal said, "Sir, you are welcome to sit in on the briefing. Any input you have will be welcome. There's no chance I'm going to authorize you to go on the mission."

VAdm. Ransom came to his rescue, "I have express orders from the Prime Minister not to allow the chief of the Office of Strategic Services to be killed on my watch. He knows you have a penchant for traveling in harm's way, as does your President, who specifically requested the PM issue those instructions.

"For what it is worth, the same applies to me—Colonel Randal barely allows me out of sight of dry land."

Brig. Gen. Donovan said, "I hear you loud and clear, Sir Randolph, and I bow to your orders. Do not confuse my acquiescence as a desire not to participate. I would dearly love to ride along on the MAS boat tonight."

"As would I."

Both men were national heroes, each the recipient of their nation's highest decoration for valor. They represented the best the United States and Great Britain had to offer. Neither liked ordering troops out on dangerous missions they could not participate in. In earlier days, the Razor and Wild Bill had been aggressive, take-charge, lead from the front commanders. In their hearts, they still were.

VAdm. Ransom said, "Colonel—a word."

Col. Randal said, "Yes, sir."

When everyone had cleared the room, VAdm. Ransom said, "I have known you almost from the time you arrived in England. My having the experience of being around you socially and working on operations together, it should come as no surprise that I realize you are less than thrilled to be handed this assignment with no time to adequately prepare."

Col. Randal said, "Roger that, sir."

VAdm. Ransom said, "You probably feel this is a hare-brained, suicidal mission and that the lives of the men participating are being needlessly thrown away—I disagree. We are going after a worthy target. An enemy destroyer in Aegean waters is equal to a battleship anywhere else.

"Attacking enemy shipping berthed in a harbor is precisely the type of target our national war planners had in mind when they ordered the forming of the RMBPD and MU. Both units consist of picked men, extensively trained and highly skilled in the performance of their mission. "Do your duty, Colonel. Make sure the two folboat teams are delivered to their release point armed, equipped, and ready to fight. Have Brandy standing by to bring them home. I shall be responsible for the lives of the people involved."

Col. Randal said, "Shared responsibility, Admiral."

VAdm. Ransom said, "We make a team that complements each other—extraordinarily satisfactory, Colonel."

When Col. Randal walked out of VAdm. Ransom's office, people were frantically placing phone calls in the bay area of the Operations Room. He spotted Captain Stephanie Fawcett-Tatum and made eye contact. The tall brunette Royal Marine was the picture of calm in the eye of the storm.

She came straight to his side.

Col. Randal said, "Any idea where I can find Veronica?"

"In her office."

"Instruct Mrs. Paige to be in Lady Jane's suite in ten minutes."

"On the way, John."

Col. Randal made eye contact with Lt. Col. Stone. The Deputy Commander of Raiding Forces walked over. Sir Terry was clearly troubled about the mission.

Lt. Col. Stone said, "The problem with raiding airfields or harbors, old stick, is the planes can fly away and the ships sail before we arrive to blow them up. When a target is identified, we have to strike fast. And that means no proper prior planning."

Col. Randal said, "I don't want you wasting your time on this one, Terry. Stay focused on Raiding Forces' reorganization. I'll take the Leros raid from here."

Lt. Col. Stone said, "With pleasure. The beauty of Oasis X was not having staff types around to look over our shoulder. Here at RFHQ, half-baked missions can come at us from all directions."

Col. Randal said, "The quicker you can get ABC operational so we can get out of here, the better."

Lt. Col. Stone said, "All right with you if I tap Lady Jane to supervise the restoration and remodeling on the island? The place suffered heavy bomb damage and a large swath of the built- up area on the waterfront was burned out. Dudley Clarke has requested we turn it into a bustling military base—or at least give it the appearance of one."

Col. Randal said, "Affirmative, she'll enjoy the assignment—I'll feel better with Jane on ABC."

Lt. Stone said, "A-Force is footing the bill."

Col. Randal said, "Any idea why Brigadier Clarke is suddenly so interested in Castelrozzo?"

"Not a clue. Dudley never does anything without an ulterior motive. He has been virtually living at Small Raids Inc. lately. The Razor is providing him full access to all our organizational plans. One wonders what it portends."

Captain Butch "Headhunter" Hoolihan arrived in the Operations Room. He had been summoned to report to Col. Randal. The Royal Marine officer had no idea why.

Col. Randal said, "Butch, I have a mission for you."

Capt. Hoolihan perked up. "Sir!"

"Commander Fleming has raised a group of Royal Marines to conduct RED INDIAN/GOLDEN FLEECE operations. Seems they did not perform as well as expected on their first attempt. He's requested Raiding Forces train them for what he calls STEAL missions.

"I want you to run 'em through a four-week course. Get Fleming's Marines up to speed so that we don't have him turning up with missions for us any time it suits him."

"What does STEAL stand for, sir?"

"Strategic Taking and Extracting to an Alternate Location."

"Are you having me on, sir?"

"Negative, that's what the Commander calls his RED INDIAN raids nowadays."

"Why me, sir? I need to be taking part in the reorganization Raiding Forces is undergoing."

"I have you penciled in to command one of the sloops that will serve as floating patrol bases. Only we don't have a sloop for you just yet. Train Fleming's RED INDIANS and then come back here ready for an intensive small-scale raiding campaign."

"Sir!"

"I'm expecting big things from you, Headhunter."

"Under protest, Colonel."

"Noted."

Col. Randal walked upstairs to the third-floor suite. When he arrived, everyone from the earlier briefing—with the exception of VAdm. Ransom—was already present. Lady Jane, Captain Penelope Honeycutt-Parker, Veronica Paige, Ensign Theodore Hamilton aka "The Great Teddy," Master Sergeant Mack Beckwith, and King were new arrivals sitting in.

Col. Randal took the briefing. "Lieutenant Taylor, give us a rundown on your boats."

The popular prewar dentist to the Hollywood stars, now OSS Frogman/MU raider, came up to the front of the briefing area. "MU and the RMBPD utilize the Mark II Cockle, a fifteen- foot double-ended, collapsible, two-man canvas craft built by the Folboat Company that most Americans would describe as an Eskimo kayak. The British call 'em a cockleshell or cockle.

"The cockpit is arranged midships. The deck and bottom are made of one-half-inch plywood with the deck beams of laminated material. The forward and aft breakwaters, paddle blades, cockpit forward, aft, sides, and beadings are all of three-sixteenth-inch three-ply. The compass chocks, bow struts, mast step, cockpit cover, and beam chocks…"

Col. Randal said, "Just tell us how you intend to stow the boats on board a Walrus, Lieutenant."

LtJG Taylor said, "Collapse the Mark IIs and slide them on, sir. Two can easily be transported. My people have run rehearsals to be prepared for this contingency. When we reach the release point, all we have to do is slide the two boats to the door, pop 'em open one at a time, and plop them into the water."

Col. Randal asked, "Have you been able to contact the RMBPD to provide a second crew?"

"Yes, sir. Lieutenant Pritchard-Gordon has two of his Royal Marines and their boat en route at this time. They should arrive within the next hour."

Col. Randal said, "Beverly, give me a report on the flight plan to the release point."

Beverly said, "We have to fly to a location a mile and a half off the entrance to the harbor at Portologo, drop off Jackson's two boat teams, then fly home. It's a simple flight plan."

Col. Randal said, "Any problems reaching Kalymnos in the time allotted, Brandy?"

"None."

"Lieutenant Jackson, once you've carried out your raid on Portologo, are you going to be able to paddle twelve miles to the rendezvous before BMNT?"

"We should be able to, sir. The hard part will be finding the MAS boat once we arrive.

I've observed The Great Teddy demonstrate his proficiency at camouflage."

Col. Randal said, "Veronica, I want a contingency plan that covers how we intend to extract MU or RMBPD operators in the event any of them wind up ashore on Leros escaping and evading."

"Yes, John."

Col. Randal said, "Anything anyone wants to say? No?—Lieutenant Taylor, be prepared to issue your operations order here in this room in two hours' time. Beverly, make arrangements to have one of our Special Duty pilots standing by ready to fly the MAS boat crew to Castelrozzo immediately upon conclusion of Jackson's Op Order.

"Anyone who has anything they need to talk to me about, see me now.

"Let's do this."

As the group scattered, Col. Randal pulled Beverly aside, "Tell the truth. Can you fly this mission—is it doable?"

"Are you worried about me, Johnny?"

"Damn right I am."

"I can fly the mission."

"We're talking about navigation at night behind the Axis lines in close proximity to a major enemy-occupied island, an open-sea landing—you'd tell me if it wasn't feasible?"

Beverly said, "OK, the flight's not all that complicated technically. I've talked to Jackson. The idea is to put his team down outside the entrance to the harbor—far enough away that the sound of the Walrus won't be heard on shore but close enough that the paddlers will be fresh when they arrive at their targets. We don't have to land on a precise grid point—just get close."

"Understood."

"Please quit worrying."

Col. Randal said, "We recruited you to be Lady Jane's personal assistant. No one knew you could even fly an airplane, much less turn out to be Amelia Earhart. I don't want anything happening to you."

Beverly said, "OK, Amelia Earhart's dead. I'm not. We'll fly in low, skimming the waves in the unlikely event the bad guys have radar. The flight plan is to travel to the release point by the most direct route, land, launch the kayaks, take off, and fly back to ABC.

"Piece of cake."

Anytime he heard the phrase "piece of cake" used in conjunction with an impending military operation, Col. Randal winced. In his experience, no such thing ever happened.

However, he did not press the point.

Captain "Geronimo" Joe McKoy and Mandy strolled in, curious about the flurry of activity they had been left out of. Waldo was right behind. Since the three were there and the group remaining in the suite constituted a quorum of CARD GAME, Col. Randal said to MSgt. Beckwith, "Ask King to step inside. You take the desk, close the door, and don't let anyone through without announcing first."

"Yes, sir."

He went into the bedroom and retrieved the alligator jar taken from the police chief in the Congo. When he came back out, the CARD GAME team was sitting on couches around the coffee table in the living area. Col. Randal placed the quart-sized glass container full of diamonds in the middle of the table.

"Compliments of the Léopoldville PD."

Mandy gasped.

Beverly said, "Amazing!"

Capt. McKoy said, "You hit the mother lode."

Waldo said, "Better than finding the elephants' graveyard."

Col. Randal said, "Captain McKoy, take charge of these stones. Secure 'em in a safe place. I'll be trusting you not to be passing out sparklers to the dancers at the Kit-Kat Club."

"Lot a' rocks, John."

Col. Randal said, "These came from the large mining conglomerates who were extorted by the police chief. Payoff for licenses, protection, and for the companies to maintain their monopoly status. As you can see, these are brilliant cut diamonds, not the industrial grade stones being dug up by potholers along the Kasai River."

Lady Jane said, "We have been advised not to be left with a large inventory of diamonds when the war ends."

Capt. McKoy said, "Yeah, that would not be *bueno* for business."

King said, "Flooding the market with this much product all at once could drive down the price, Chief."

Col. Randal said, "Jane, see if your financial advisors can recommend a liquidation plan that won't crater the price."

"Love to."

Capt. McKoy said, "Have to be careful not to overload Captain Butterfield with too many smugglers running our goods all at once, too. We need to kinda trickle 'em out. It's in our best interest for Preston to be able to track down all the traffickers one at a time."

Mandy said, "Pretty sure I can convince Sammy to detail additional SIME operatives to assist us with surveilling the traffickers until their caravans depart Cairo."

Capt. McKoy said, "Do it—our Special Duties pilots can keep 'em under aerial observation once they hit the desert."

Lady Jane said, "As you are all aware, the law firm that represents my interests in the Middle East opened a CARD GAME bank account in Cairo. The proceeds from the sale of our diamonds are deposited in it minus what money is retained to purchase additional stones. Since we are always paid in cash or gold, that makes it possible for a simultaneous wire transfer of our money to a corresponding bank in the States without having to wait for a check to clear.

"We have a fortune on deposit in New York."

Beverly laughed, "OK, I'm totally amazed. The rocks in John's jar alone are worth crazy money. CARD GAME is big-rich."

Mandy said, "We actually pulled this off—as difficult as that is to believe?"

Capt. McKoy said, "We took control of the Cairo Cartel by bein' bigger crooks than they were, wasn't real hard, exceptin' Lady Jane got shot."

Lady Jane flashed one of her deadliest heart attack class smiles. "We also serve who stand and wait."

Col. Randal said, "Try 'standing' out of the line of fire."

"Roger and Wilco, sir."

Capt. McKoy said, "While we done real good capturing the market here in Cairo, it's a different story down in the Congo. Did you know in 1940 *after* the Nazis had invaded their country and occupied the whole place, those colonial low-lifes had the audacity to ask Germany to declare the Congo a neutral state? Don't anybody be expectin' help from our so-called Allies down there.

"John got the easy money."

Beverly said, "You'll come up with a plan, Captain, you always do."

Capt. McKoy said, "Maybe not this time. I thought I'd seen it all. Tijuana, Shanghai, Singapore, you name it. They ain't nothin' compared to

Léopoldville. The Congo's the world's largest slave plantation—forced labor, genocide, mutilation.

"The thing is, my boys say they don't believe the colonists even realize they're doin' anythin' wrong."

Mandy said, "Institutional corruption, a state-sanctioned system so debased that its officials peddle strategic war material for personal gain to the enemy regime occupying their homeland. How do we deal with such an immoral colonial government?"

Col. Randal said, "Our job is to hunt down and kill the diamond smugglers. That's it.

Everything else is not our problem."

Waldo said, "Don't forget the part about us recovering all the diamonds."

Lady Jane said, "Collaborators who traffic with the Nazis are traitors—period. Quislings deserve to be shot. They enjoy no protection under the Geneva Accords.

"Our conscience is clear."

Capt. McKoy said, "Anybody want to hear the part that's bug-eyed crazy?" Col. Randal said, "Now would be the time, Captain."

Capt. McKoy said, "My men have reason to believe the Belgians are selling their diamonds to the Nazis on credit."

Beverly laughed. "Insane!"

Mandy said, "No one can be that dumb."

Capt. McKoy said, "Just reportin' what my boys told me. I didn't hire 'em for their looks or pleasin' dispositions. They're lawmen—good ones . . . they ain't shootin' from the hip about the credit."

King said, "If that is true, there is no way for the Belgians to collect regardless of who wins the war."

Waldo said, "Can't cure stupid."

As CARD GAME was breaking up, Col. Randal walked Beverly to the door.

"I asked General Donovan if he could requisition a faster seaplane for the commute between RFHQ and ABC. No joy. General Eisenhower has issued standing orders forbidding air support for operations in the Aegean."

Beverly said, "Politics—don't you hate 'em, Johnny?"

Col. Randal said, "Send a teletype to your father. Ask him if there's a way to mount floats on our Lockheed Hudson. If anyone knows, Bronc will."

Beverly said, "Perfect, the Hudson cruises almost twice as fast as a Walrus or Catalina."

After the suite emptied, Col. Randal said, "Sounded pretty bloodthirsty about shooting traffickers, Lady Jane. And I thought you were mad at me for capping the chief of police in Léopoldville.

"Did I miss something?"

Lady Jane said, "Only that I was annoyed you did not take me along when you did it."

LIEUTENANT JUNIOR GRADE JACKSON TAYLOR ISSUED HIS Operations Order in the briefing area in RFHQ's third-floor suite. The mission was classified "Need to Know." Everyone present did.

It was a small group.

The mood was businesslike. It was also tense. The raid on Portologo was a serious enterprise requiring highly skilled, specialist small-boat handlers and supporting elements to deliver them to the target area and return them home.

Complicating matters was the fact that Raiding Forces did not have previous experience with missions of this type.

LtJG Taylor said, "Situation: A Regia Marina Folgore-class destroyer is berthed in the harbor at Portologo, Leros. Two Italian merchantmen are also anchored nearby. Possibly other minor ships may or may not be docked there as well.

"Mission: Tonight, OSS Maritime Unit and Royal Marine Boom Patrol Detachment will conduct a joint military operation to enter the harbor at Portologo by stealth, utilizing a pair of 2- man Mark II folboats, and place limpet mines on the enemy destroyer and two merchant steamers berthed nearby.

"Execution: Two MU and RMBPD teams will be inserted by a Supermarine Walrus amphibian aircraft a mile and a half off Portologo. The boat teams will row to the mouth of the harbor. Then it's another mile and a half to the location where the enemy ships are anchored. Once each unit's limpet mines have been affixed to the targets, both kayaks will exfiltrate the harbor independently, placing additional explosives on targets of opportunity if they present themselves, then paddle approximately twelve miles to Kalymnos Island. A MAS boat will be waiting there to return both teams to Castelrozzo Island.

"Concept of the Operation: MU and RMBPD will be inserted into the target area by an aircraft piloted by Miss Beverly Blackwell. She will now brief the air movement plan."

Beverly walked to the front of the room, "Departure time is 1630 hours. Have your two boats loaded on board one hour prior to takeoff. We'll fly from here to Castelrozzo. The aircraft will be refueled, then we depart for Leros at 2330 hours. Flight time from ABC to your release point is a little over an hour and a half. As briefed by Admiral Ransom, I'll put you down approximately one and a half miles off Portologo. Offload your canoes and the raid will commence from there.

"Good luck, boys—anchors away."

LtJG Taylor returned to the front, "The team will be broken down into two elements— MU boat 1 and RMPD boat 2. Boat 1 will consist of myself and Corporal Jenkins. Boat 2 will be manned by Royal Marine Corporals Brockhurst and Stilkins. Once we launch from the Walrus, the two boat teams will proceed independently to Portologo.

"Boat 1 will attack our primary target—the Regia Marina destroyer. Boat 2 will attack the two merchant ships. After placing their limpet mines, each boat will exfiltrate the harbor independently. We will then paddle the twelve-odd miles to an RVP on Kalymnos Island, where we are to link up with a MAS boat commanded by Mrs. Seaborn for the exfil home.

"Mrs. Seaborn . . ."

Brandy stepped forward, tanned and glamorous, "The MAS boat shall be in position under netting at the RVP on Kalymnos when you arrive following your raid. Our camouflage has been designed by Ensign Hamilton and it will be extremely difficult, meaning virtually impossible, to detect. Kalymnos is a large island. You will find us somewhere along this uninhabited five-mile stretch of coastline.

"Odds are you shall not be able to spot our boat. What I recommend is for you to hug the shoreline close in and paddle along it until you bump into us. Expect to find us at some place where there is a steep cliff face sliding into the water. We shall be nestled in a nook on one side or the other of the slide.

"Ensign Hamilton, do you have anything to add?"

"Only that we shall place an observation post on a high point ashore prior to beginning morning nautical twilight. We should spot you long before you reach the MAS boat. When our OP observes your approach, he will signal you in by waving a white towel—see a white towel, you are home free.

"Abracadabra, hey, presto!"

LtJG Taylor said, "Mrs. Paige, our MI-9 officer, will now brief the Escape & Evasion plan in the event any of us find ourselves ashore on Leros—a contingency plan let's hope we never have to use."

Veronica said, "Better to have and not need than to need and not..."

BRANDY, CAPTAIN PENELOPE "LEGS" HONEYCUTT-PARKER and Ensign Theodore Hamilton aka "The Great Teddy" flew out for ABC immediately following the Operations Order. Major the Lady Jane Seaborn and Happy were also on board.

Lieutenant Junior Grade Jackson Taylor and his boat teams repaired to the dock to load their Mark II folboats aboard the Walrus. For a raid as important as sinking a capital enemy warship, there was not a lot of equipment involved—and it could all be collapsed, disassembled for transport, or worn on the body. There were two 15-foot canvas Mark II folboats, four double-ended kayak-type paddles, and two 5 1/2 foot long limpet placing rods that could be broken down and folded, then reassembled by shaking it like a fly fishing pole.

As the day progressed, Col. Randal grew increasingly uneasy about LtJG Taylor's mission. Despite the fact that Vice Admiral Sir Randolph "Razor" Ransom had assured him the cockleshell raiders were eager to conduct the operation and that LtJG Taylor was "salivating at the prospect," past experience with pinprick raiding against the French Coast out of Seaborn House gave him perspective.

He knew that if anything could go wrong it always did, and that was for coastal raids only twenty miles or so across the English Channel.

Tonight would involve a fairly long flight, an amphibious water landing behind enemy lines, a surreptitious infiltration of a defended enemy harbor, the placing of mines by hand on enemy ships, an open sea paddle to a rendezvous on an island likely to have an enemy garrison stationed on it, and a dangerous return to base through enemy-infested waters. It was not lost on Col. Randal that the word "enemy" appeared five times in his personal private estimate of the situation.

Col. Randal picked up the phone in the third-floor suite, "Stephanie, have a jeep brought 'round for me."

"The duty vehicle is parked outside, John."

"That'll work, find Sergeant Major Beckwith. Tell him we'll be flying out with Lieutenant Taylor and his men and we'll remain on ABC until they return. Have him meet me downstairs in fifteen minutes."

"Wilco."

Col. Randal went to the door. "King, I've decided to travel with Beverly as far as Castelrozzo. I may hang out with Jane on the island for a few days. She's going to be restoring the buildings along the waterfront."

"Want me to come with you?"

"Negative, I have a mission for you. Pam's supposed to be back tomorrow. You two take a commercial flight to Tangier. Spend a few days and see what you can find out about diamond trafficking in Morocco."

"Sending us on leave?"

"Yes I am, but that doesn't mean you two can't conduct a LEAF EATER evaluation while you're taking it. Check with Wild Bill—there's an OSS operative named Ortiz you'll want to interview.

"Give me a report when you get back."

"With pleasure—thanks, Chief."

VAdm. Ransom and Brigadier General William "Wild Bill" Donovan were at the dock talking to LtJG Taylor when Col. Randal and Master Sergeant Mack Beckwith arrived. The Mark II Cockles were already loaded aboard the plane, as was all the rest of the equipment for the raid.

When he saw that Col. Randal and MSgt. Beckwith were carrying the parachute bags they used as overnight luggage, VAdm. Ransom said, "Where do you think you are going, Colonel?"

"I'm escorting Lieutenant Taylor as far as ABC, sir."

"Do not let me hear you squeezed yourself into one of those canoes, Colonel—if I cannot go, you cannot go."

"Not going to happen, sir. This is a job for specialists. I don't have the skill sets."

Brig. Gen. Donovan said, "I'm delaying my departure to await results of the raid. The RAF has agreed to fly a reconnaissance plane over Portologo tomorrow morning. I'd like to evaluate their report firsthand before flying out.

"This mission is of vital importance to the Outfit—if for no other reason than to demonstrate to our detractors what OSS is capable of."

Col. Randal said, "Understood, General. By the way, sir, Capt. McKoy wanted me to tell you the Ballista Molina handgun is an excellent weapon. Capt. Kidd will provide his written evaluation when he returns from the Congo."

Brig. Gen. Donovan said, "I'll go ahead and have my staff place the order—if Joe McKoy says it's a suitable weapon for OSS, it's a suitable weapon."

Col. Randal said, "The Captain says legend has it the Ballista Molinas are made out of steel from the *Graf Spee.* Cuthbert Bowlby was involved in recovering Nazi electronics from the ship. Ask him to tell you about the operation—pretty good story, sir."

It was the kind of tale Brig. Gen. Donovan loved to tell the President at their early morning intelligence briefings. "I will."

The Walrus backfired, the pusher engine wheezed, and the prop began to turn over in slow motion before kicking into a full-throated roar.

VAdm. Ransom saluted LtJG Taylor. "Fair winds and following seas, Lieutenant."

"Thank you, Admiral."

Brig. Gen. Donovan said, "Godspeed, Jackson."

Col. Randal, LtJG Taylor, and MSgt. Beckwith boarded last. Beverly taxied out into open waters, began her takeoff run, and the ugliest aircraft ever built struggled into the sky. The mission with no name was officially underway.

Settling into a seat next to LtJG Jackson, Col. Randal said, "Tell me about how MU came to be."

LtJG Taylor said, "There was a British big game hunter named Roger "Jumbo" Courtney.

He liked to float down African rivers in a canoe and surprise elephants coming to water. When the war started, he tried to sell the concept of "kayak Commando raiding" to the Admiralty—no joy. Combined Operations was not interested. SOE said negative.

"So, Roger joined the King's Royal Rifle Corps as a private. Then he volunteered for the Commandos. He tried to get Colonel Vaughn interested when he went through Achnacarry, but even an original thinker like Vaughn wasn't buying in.

"At that point, highly frustrated and never a man inclined to take no for an answer, late one night Jumbo climbed in a canoe and paddled out to the HMS *Glengyle* at anchor in the Clyde River. He climbed up the anchor chain, slipped on board, chalked his initials on the door of the captain's cabin, stole a canvas gun cover with the ship's name stenciled on it, and then departed with no one the wiser.

"Next morning at breakfast, he appeared at the Inveraray Hotel and presented his trophy to a startled group of senior Royal Navy officers—one of whom was the *Glengyle's* skipper. Jumbo was immediately commissioned and authorized to raise a unit of twelve canoeists from 8 Commando. Jumbo's unit came to be called the Special Boat Section.

"When Wild Bill decided he wanted to form the OSS Maritime Unit, he dispatched us to Scotland to train under Captain Courtney. He was a tough taskmaster. It was brutal training, sir."

Col. Randal said, "I was in the KRRC—Rangers Regiment."

"Did you ever meet Jumbo, Colonel?"

"Don't think so."

The Walrus was traveling at close to its top cruising speed of 94 mph. Col. Randal signaled MSgt. Beckwith to follow him. They moved to the front of the plane. Beverly was flying with her ex-LRDG navigator Corporal Tom Murphy sitting in the co-pilot's chair.

Col. Randal said, "Corporal, could you give us the cockpit." It was not a request.

"Sir!"

When Cpl. Murphy left, Col. Randal slipped into the co-pilot's chair next to Beverly, and MSgt. Beckwith took the small fold-down jump seat behind them.

"Close the curtains," Col. Randal said.

When the three had privacy, he said, "Sergeant Major, if I advise you about an ongoing clandestine operation within Raiding Forces known only to a handful of people, will you give me your word to never reveal its existence to anyone?"

"Yes, sir."

"As you know, Raiding Forces is conducting OPERATION LEAF EATER. The general scope of the mission is to stop the flow of diamonds to

Nazi Germany with a follow-on assignment to liquidate the smugglers who arrange their transportation.

"What you are not aware of is that there's a subsidiary operation within LEAF EATER called CARD GAME. Classified above Top Secret, it consists of Lady Jane, Captain McKoy, Captain Plum-Martin, Captain Jaxx, Captain Kidd, Captain Butterfield, Mr. Treywick, King, Mandy, and Beverly. No one other than the people named possess a 'Need to Know' it even exists.

"Is that clear?"

"It is, Colonel."

"CARD GAME serves as the command-and-control element of LEAF EATER. It is also a registered New York Subchapter S Corporation—Card Game Inc. The people I named are the shareholders.

"Each time LEAF EATER interdicts a diamond trafficker, the stones being transported for sale to the Nazis are recovered. They are then resold to other smugglers, who in turn will be intercepted, those diamonds recovered and so on. Proceeds from the sale and resale of the jewels are placed in the CARD GAME Inc. bank account. The amount currently on deposit is enormous—over eight figures.

"CARD GAME is a black operation. It doesn't officially exist. OSS will disavow any knowledge of its activities, even though they are sanctioned by the director. After the war, CARD GAME Inc. will be dissolved. The bank account will be closed and the corporation's shareholders will take possession of the money and go their own way.

"You following me to this point?"

"Perfectly, sir."

"Welcome to CARD GAME, Sergeant Major."

MSgt. Beckwith said, "Sir, I could use a drink."

Beverly laughed. "Buy your own distillery, Mack—you'll be able to afford it."

Col. Randal froze. He had never heard anyone call the Sergeant Major by his first name. The tough-as-nails paratroop NCO appeared to take no offense at Beverly's familiarity. He may have liked it.

The sky was awash in a golden sunset as the Walrus splashed down at Castelrozzo. Having flown in with Brandy and Parker earlier, Lady Jane was standing by on the dock with Mandy and Happy. She had arranged soft drinks and sandwiches for everyone while the Walrus was being refueled for the next leg of the flight.

Col. Randal immediately noticed an elevation in Lady Jane's normal everyday happy girl persona. Not her normal deportment. Women of her class were raised from birth to never show emotion in public.

As soon as Col. Randal had the chance, he pulled her aside. "What are you so revved up about?"

"Being allowed to restore Castelrozzo. I love this island. The architecture of these burned-out Greek structures with the narrow streets and hidden alleyways is fabulous. Being able to bring them back to life—fun."

Col. Randal said, "Make it pretty."

Lady Jane laughed. "Your most endearing quality, John."

"What?"

"You allow me to be me."

"Who else would I want you to be?"

"My point, exactly."

"I brought Sergeant Major Beckwith into CARD GAME."

"Quite a good idea actually, John. Not that you had much choice. The Sergeant Major was never going to permit you to travel without coming along. He would have found out sooner or later."

"Roger that."

Beverly caught Col. Randal's eye, pointed one finger in the air and made a series of small circles.

Col. Randal ordered, "Saddle up."

Beverly and her ex-LRDG navigator, Cpl. Murphy, whom she called "Murph the Surf," boarded the Walrus first, followed by LtJG Taylor, Corporal Ralph Jenkins, and the two RMBPD Earthworm Section Royal Marines.

Col. Randal said, "I'm going to ride along with Beverly. Keep her company. We'll be back in about three hours."

8

MURPH THE SURF

THE WALRUS WAS SCREAMING ALONG, WHAT SEEMED LIKE inches above the tops of the waves. For a slow-flying aircraft at this low altitude, it felt like they were strapped onto the tip of a speeding bullet. The ride was exhilarating. A *real* thrill as opposed to a cheap thrill like being on a roller coaster. They *were* nearly 170 miles deep into enemy waters just off Leros Island. Colonel John Randal was glad he had made the decision to ride along tonight.

He always liked spending time with the Texas cowgirl.

Beverly said, "Having fun yet, Johnny?"

"Affirmative."

Corporal Tom Murphy said, "Anytime, Miss Blackwell."

Beverly picked up the handset to the intercom, "Prepare for landing."

In the cabin behind them, the Maritime Unit and Royal Marine Boom Patrol Detachment personnel were more than prepared. Anticipation to get the mission started was sky-high. Both teams had been training for this type of raid for over a year.

The men were encased in their rubber "Frogman" suits, with a skintight outer shell made of supple leather to keep them warm and dry while rowing their Mark II folboats. The MUs were equipped with .22 Colt Woodsman civilian purchase handguns, their barrels threaded by OSS armorers to allow a suppressor to be installed. The RMBPD operators were not as well-armed, carrying standard issue British Armed Forces .38 Enfield No.2 Mark I revolvers—no silencers. Both teams had 7-inch Fairbairn Fighting Knives obtained during their time spent training in Scotland at the Commando Basic Training Center (CBTC). Other than wrist watches, compasses, and a few minor personal items such as a favorite pocketknife, that was all their equipment— other small items were pre-positioned aboard their kayaks.

Beverly put the Walrus down in a silk smooth landing. For a skill the girl took for granted, few pilots could match her flying ability. In the cabin, the canoeists made ready to disembark.

Anticipation to launch was high.

Murph the Surf opened the door so that the Mark IIs could be offloaded. Col. Randal and Beverly remained in their seats in the cockpit to be out of the way during disembarkation. Lieutenant Junior Grade Jackson Taylor and his highly disciplined teams were moving with the precision of a well-oiled machine.

The night was pitch-black. From this point on, stealth was all that mattered. Not having the moon up reflecting off the water was fortuitous, though it was pure dumb luck. No one had planned it that way.

The Walrus was rocking gently. The weather in the Aegean was known to be temperamental at times but not tonight. Conditions were almost perfect. Dark, not much wind, and tending toward cool.

Beverly said, "Daddy telexed me back almost immediately. Edo Amphibious Float Gear can be mounted on a Hudson. He's dispatching a plane to the factory to pick up a set. Then he intends to lay on a training mission to fly the floats out to Cairo for us to install."

"That's great."

"I think Daddy just wants an excuse to meet Brandy. We can't let that happen. You're going to have to dream up some reason to send her away before he . . ."

From the back outside the plane came a loud *THUNK*, a groan, and a curse all garbled into one. That was followed by the sound of an animated three-way conversation with no concern for noise discipline.

So much for being silent professionals.

Col. Randal and Beverly turned in their seats to see what was going on. LtJG Taylor came back inside the aircraft. He made his way quickly to the cockpit.

"We have a situation."

 "What happened out there?"

"Freak accident, sir. Jenkins slipped on the float and whacked his arm when he fell."

 Beverly said, "How bad?"

"Broken."

Col. Randal said, "Where does that leave us?"

"It's a two-man job to paddle and attach limpet mines, sir."

"Are you recommending we abort?"

"The RMBPD team had already shoved off, Colonel."

Beverly said, "Can't the Royal Marines carry out a single boat attack without you, Jackson?"

LtJG Taylor said, "The destroyer's our primary target. The reason we're here. Earthworm will be going after the two transports."

Beverly said, "What if we put a splint on Jenkin's arm. You paddle. All he needs to do is place the mines?"

"It's a compound fracture. Bones sticking out. The corporal needs medical attention."

Col. Randal said, "Taylor, you and Murphy haul him back on board the plane. I'll take his place."

"Are you sure, Colonel?"

"I didn't come this far to quit and go home just because things didn't work out the way we wanted, Lieutenant."

"Yes, sir."

LtJG Taylor ducked out of the cockpit. Col. Randal unbuckled his Colt .38 Super and reached around back for the 9mm Browning P-35 he always carried inside the belt in a Mexican slide holster. He handed them to Beverly.

"Take care of these for me."

Beverly said, "This is a really bad idea."

"You have a better one?"

"OK, Jackson told me that ninety percent of the volunteers for the Maritime Unit washed out of the training, it's that tough—have you ever even paddled a canoe before?"

"OJT."

"Seriously, on-the-job training! Have you lost your mind? Lady Jane is going to murder me when I tell her you've gone on a suicide mission."

"I'm not looking forward to that part myself."

Sounding decidedly un-beauty contestant-like, Beverly ordered, "Murph, get up here *now*."

"Ma'am?"

"Any practical experience kayaking or canoeing?"

"Negative. I grew up on a sheep station in New Zealand, with no stream I could not step over

Beverly said, "This is not going to end well."

Col. Randal said, "You're starting to sound like Mandy."

"Maybe she's been right all along—ever think of that?"

"Once or twice."

LtJG Taylor called from outside. "Time to go, sir—if we're going."

Beverly said, "Johnny, you don't always have to be a hero—cowardice is underrated." Col. Randal slipped on his fur-collared bomber jacket and adjusted the .22 High Standard Military Model D in his chest holster underneath it. The silenced weapon and the Remington M- 51 .380 pocket pistol Beverly had given him as a gift would be his only sidearm tonight.

Beverly said, "Wait."

She pulled the tail of her shirt out of her jeans and ripped off a long strip. "You don't have one of those little leather skull caps like the other canoeists. Let me tie this around your forehead for a headband."

"Thanks."

"For what? I'm telling Lady Jane you tried to rip my blouse off. Maybe she'll say good riddance to you or at least not shoot me someplace where it hurts."

"Good plan."

LtJG Taylor was aboard the Mark II, holding the boat against the float to steady it as Col. Randal gingerly climbed down out of the Walrus.

"You're the bow man. That carries with it the honor of placing the limpets. Try hard not to put your boot through the bottom of my boat as you step in, sir."

"Wilco."

The kayak felt like it was made out of papier mâché. It did not seem overly stable. Once Col. Randal was seated, he experienced a stab of vertigo when the folboat wobbled as if it might flip over.

He was careful not to make any sudden moves.

LtJG Taylor passed him a double-headed paddle of the type used by Eskimos. "The idea is to perform synchronized rowing—ever done any of that, sir?"

Col. Randal said, "No, but I saw an Esther Williams movie once."

"We're good then."

The night was dark, bordering on cold, which was good because the paddling was hard work. Col. Randal was struggling to keep up the pace. LtJG Taylor counted cadence softly, a four count, "one, two, three, four," so he knew when to take a stroke. Even numbers to port, odd numbers to starboard.

As he was paddling, Col. Randal was mentally running down a checklist of the situation he was facing like he did in the early stage of every mission. *I'm on board a canvas cockleshell being captained by a playboy/frogman/dentist whose practice is located in Hollywood, California, wearing a Regia Aeronautica bomber jacket given to me by a one-eyed Abyssinian bandit, with a Rolex watch and a Panerai compass strapped to my wrist—both gifts from the married British noblewoman I'm engaged to, and an improvised bandana ripped off the blouse of a University of Texas Tri-Delta Sorority girl is tied around my head. I'm about to enter an enemy harbor ringed by guns with the idea of sticking limpet mines on an Italian destroyer by hand.*

How did it come to this?

"One—two—three—four.   One—two—three—four.   One—two—three . . ."

Behind them, the Walrus cranked up to a roar and took off. After that, the night was dead silent—danger ahead. This mission was now long past the point of no return. It was a lonely feeling. Mixing in a healthy dose of "this is a really bad idea" did not make Col. Randal feel exactly confident.

After what seemed like a lifetime but was about forty-five minutes of semi-synchronized rowing—Col. Randal was not sure if he was helping or hurting with the paddling—a faint dark smudge appeared on the skyline in the distance.

Leros.

A quick glance at his Rolex. Before departing, he had turned on a hooked-nosed flashlight and placed it flat against the watch's face to charge the uranium-based luminous digits. The little circles glowed bright lime green, showing 0135 hours. Only slightly behind the original schedule.

Good.

Next, he checked the Panerai wrist compass he had recharged by employing the same technique. It was glowing as well, confirming that they were skimming across the surface of the Aegean on a bearing of 165 degrees—dead on azimuth.

He wondered what might happen if he dabbed some of the uranium mined in the Belgian Congo on the front post of his pistol sights—would they glow in the dark? He intended to find out. Then a thought occurred to him: luminous digits for watches and compasses could not be the only use for the mineral no one seemed to know much about.

What other uses might there be?

Strange what sometimes came to mind totally unrelated to the execution of the mission at hand—it was nearly always like that.

In between counting cadence, LtJG Taylor briefed Col. Randal about the layout of the kayak. A Mark II Cockle was designed to hold two men and had five storage compartments. The compartment at the left rear of the craft contained a magnetic holdfast, a bailer and sponge, one grenade, a paddle, handgrip, a mine-placing rod, four limpet mines, one spanner, and half of

LtJG Taylor's spare clothes. The compartment at the right rear held matches in a waterproof bag, a small cooker, mine-placing rods, four limpet mines and the rest of the Lieutenant's clothes.

Centered between the two canoeists was a smaller compartment in the middle of the folboat that contained rations and water. In front of Col. Randal was another compartment that contained a camouflage net, a 50-foot line, a repair kit, navigating gear, a paddle handgrip, a sounding reel, flashlight, Benzedrine, and a single fragmentation grenade. At the bow was one last compartment containing spare clothes for the injured Cpl. Jenkins, two fuse boxes, two cups, soap, and four boxes of escape supplies.

Something appeared out of the dark right in front of the kayak—a buoy.

They were at the mouth of the harbor, or possibly already inside it since the sea had gone glassy smooth. While visibility was limited due to the moon being down, fortunately the Italian's blackout discipline was lax. Several lights could be seen aboard ships in the distance, along with other lights dotting the shoreline.

LtJG Taylor said, "We're going to paddle straight up to the destroyer and then go alongside. When we arrive, you will ship your oars, being careful not to bang them against the hull of the ship. Then pick up the placing rod— it will be bundled up like a collapsible fishing pole. Shake it out and the joints will snap into place. OSS uses a slightly shorter pole than the RMBPD . . . ours is four-and-a-half feet long, theirs is six-and-a-half feet."

As if Col. Randal understood the significance of the difference, if any—he did not ask for an explanation.

"Point the tip of the rod back to me and I'll place a limpet mine between the arms of the key on the holder. This part is a little tricky since I also have to lock our canoe against the steel hull of the destroyer utilizing the magnetic holdfast, while being careful to observe noise discipline.

"Once the explosive device is affixed, you'll carefully poke the mine-placing rod down underwater as far as your arm can reach and let the five high-powered magnets on the back of the limpet draw themselves against the side. Once locked on, all you have to do is lift straight up on the placing rod.

The arms on the key will slip off the mine and you're done—mission accomplished.

"It's easier than it sounds, sir."

"How many mines are we going to deploy?"

"We have eight mines on board, sir. We'll try to use them all for maximum effect."

"What's the time on the fuse?"

"Two-hour delay, sir."

"You think that's enough?"

"Our folboat will be averaging about 3 miles per hour in the open sea on the row to Kalymnos. It's approximately twelve miles to our RVP. The plan is to accomplish half of the exfil by the time the first limpet detonates. With any luck, we can reach the rendezvous before full daybreak—not that it matters very much, sir. Extensive sea trials have shown that it's virtually impossible to spot one of these folboats from the air, even if a search plane flies directly overhead during broad daylight."

Col. Randal said, "Good to know, Jackson. I never thought paddling in enemy waters with the sun shining the morning after attacking their shipping sounded like a great idea."

LtJG Taylor said, "Not a problem, sir. By the way, I've been meaning to ask—is Beverly dating anyone in particular?"

"You have any idea how many times I get asked that question, Lieutenant?"

"Afraid that's what you would say, Colonel."

The scheme of maneuver laid out by LtJG Taylor was to paddle straight toward the Italian destroyer. Col. Randal approved of his tactics. Simple plans are best.

That does not mean they always work.

The Mark II Cockle skimmed across the water. Unfortunately, the night was so dark it was impossible to identify their intended target. They did not have a clue where it might be except from the aerial photos, which showed the ship at the back pretty much in the center of the harbor. For all they knew, the destroyer could have been moved.

It is not the best idea to paddle around an enemy port facility looking for a ship to sink.

The darkness posed other consequences. It gave the kayak concealment but made navigation difficult. They almost paddled up onto the bank by accident.

A voice from shore called a challenge.

Col. Randal whispered over his shoulder, "You speak Italian?"

"Negative."

Thinking fast, Col. Randal responded, "Brandenburg Patrola."

"What's that mean, Colonel?"

"German Special Forces."

No other challenge was forthcoming. No Italian soldier in his right mind would want to interfere with Nazi Commandos. Not even if the respondent to their challenge did not sound German. The Brandenburger Regiment was known to recruit foreigners for their language skills.

As they back-paddled as fast as they could, a boat of rowdy drunken sailors returning to their ship from a night on the town loomed out of the dark, almost crashing into the kayak. LtJG Taylor cursed softly under his breath and dug in with his paddle, barely avoiding a catastrophe. The boat slid past inches away and disappeared into the night.

Taking a gamble, LtJG Taylor turned after it. Rowing hard, they managed to catch up enough to follow its wake. A good call. The duty boat went straight to a large ship.

A Folgore-class destroyer.

The good news was, target in sight. The bad news was, enemy sailors visible on deck. There was nothing to do except await developments while hiding in the shadow of a trawler anchored nearby. They paddled up next to the merchant ship to stand by and observe their prey.

Eventually LtJG Taylor decided it was time to chance making their way to the stern of the destroyer. Digging in with their paddles, the kayak glided silently across and pulled in next to the anchor chain under the overhang of the deck. As they were evaluating their prospects, an Italian sailor pulling KP duty came up from the galley and emptied a garbage can overboard, almost swamping the Mark II.

Then he peered over the rail.

Instinctively, Col. Randal drew his silenced .22 High Standard Military Model D and touched the trigger. *WHIIIIIICH*. This was followed by a solid *THUMP* that sounded much like a shopper examining a watermelon at a grocery store. The sailor teetered, leaned forward, and then fell over the rail, landing with a splash right next to the cockle.

Up on deck, a shout rang out that was most likely, "Man overboard!"

LtJG Taylor whispered urgently, "Go."

They slipped around the stern, pulled in tight against the starboard side of the destroyer and waited. LtJG Taylor took out the magnetic holdfast. Being careful to not make a "clang" he attached it to the steel hull of the ship.

Col. Randal reached down for the placing rod. It was folded up. As per instructions, he shook it out. The joints snapped into place with an audible crack. He inspected each one to make sure it was securely locked. Then he pointed the tip back at LtJG Taylor.

The MU officer wedged a limpet on the clamp on the end. "Up."

The whispered command was the signal that the mine was affixed and ready to be placed against the side of the destroyer. Col. Randal pushed the placing rod straight down in the water as far as he could reach, being careful not to let the magnets on the back brush against the steel side of the ship prematurely. They were small in size, but when he did drift the mine against the steel plates of the hull he felt a solid jolt. The magnets were surprisingly powerful.

After a gentle tug, the clamps came off and the first explosive device was in place.

Up on deck at the back of the ship, a state of pandemonium was in progress. Sailors were running and shouting. Flashlights were being shined over the stern down into the water. Orders and counterorders rang out.

LtJG Taylor removed the magnetic holdfast from the side of the ship. Then he paddled a little farther along the side. At this point, the kayak was abreast of the destroyer's engine room. Inside, they could hear the hum of the auxiliary engines, catch brief snatches of conversation, and hear music playing. Col. Randal pointed the placing rod back, and another limpet mine was affixed.

It went into place against the hull as easily as the first one.

Shooting the KP was turning out to be a good diversion. No one on the enemy destroyer was paying attention to anything except the man-overboard drill. However, that could not last forever. Particularly once the sailors had the presence of mind to put a boat in the water to try to find their sailor instead of running around in circles conducting the Regia Marina version of a Chinese fire drill.

A total of four limpets had been emplaced against the hull of the ship when LtJG Taylor whispered, "Time to go. Pressed our luck enough, sir."

"Roger that—let's get the hell out of Dodge."

Throwing caution to the wind, they paddled straight out of the harbor for open water. Maybe not going like a bat out of hell but giving it everything they had. The kayak had almost made it when behind them came a tremendous *BOOOOOM!*

The sound of the massive explosion reverberated across the water. Apparently, one of the limpets the RMBPD team attached to a cargo carrier had gone off prematurely. A monstrous fire ball went up, briefly turning night into day. The supply ship must have been transporting ammunition because the detonation and fireworks display was impressive.

A "Pyro" Percy class explosion.

Every antiaircraft gun on every ship, and all those ashore in the port complex area, opened. The gunners were firing straight up. The result was a spectacular light show of tracers of all calibers.

The Italians mistakenly believed Leros was under an aerial bombing attack. And they were fighting back. Putting their hearts into it.

As a result of mass hysteria, coupled with irrational fear, the firing soon spread from the harbor area to inshore antiaircraft batteries. Then to other guns emplaced across Leros off in the distance. Soon it looked and sounded like every antiaircraft weapon on the island was in action.

Leros was an island with 28.5 square miles of land mass, so the sight was impressive. LtJG Taylor said, "Unbelievable!"

The two were paddling as hard and fast as they could stroke while the Italian antiaircraft gunners behind them seemed intent on depleting every single round of ammunition stockpiled on the island.

Over his shoulder Col. Randal said, "Have you met Karen Montgomery, my chief rigger?"

"No, sir."

"You might like her.

Daylight broke a spectacular scarlet red. The Mark II cockle was approximately five miles off Kalymnos. Col. Randal was physically exhausted. He was not conditioned for long- distance rowing.

Neither the Marines of Earthworm Section Royal Marine Boom Patrol Detachment nor LtJG Jackson were big individuals. But like the Lifeboat Servicemen in Raiding Forces, they had exceptionally broad thick shoulders from all the boat work. Long hard training is required to build those types of muscles and nothing but rowing will do it.

The adrenaline had worn off. Now that they had made it out of the harbor and were no longer trying to save themselves from an immediate threat, the paddling had turned into a long, grueling slog. Five more miles to row is a long way when you are out of steam.

It did not make Col. Randal feel any better when he realized LtJG Taylor was as fresh as a daisy.

The MU officer was not a happy sailor. He studied the sky. "Red sky at morning, sailor take warning."

Col. Randal said, "I don't think the sky can get much redder than it is, Lieutenant."

"Could be a problem, sir. Give it everything you've got. We need to reach the shelter of Kalymnos before the storm catches us."

"I have been giving it everything I've got."

"Keep it up then, Colonel. The Aegean is notorious for tempests that spring up out of nowhere, rage with the force of a hurricane, then dissipate in a poof. This kayak will come apart in a really rough sea."

Shortly after dawn broke, the sky went from red to green. Then it turned black. The sea became choppy, then it broiled as the gusts picked up. Soon the wind was blowing hard, coming straight at their faces. The Mark II cockle was fighting up one side of one monster wave, then racing down the far side, only to find another nightmare wave rolling in behind it.

The forces of nature seemed intent on destroying their canvas canoe. The risk was if the kayak were to broach. LtJG Taylor in the stern had responsibility for keeping the boat pointed straight at the waves. The dentist whose primary practice in civilian life consisted of making movie starlets' smiles sparkle was paddling like an Olympic-class athlete.

Sheets of rain came blowing in so hard the drops caused stinging pain. Kalymnos, which they had been able to see after the sun came up, had now disappeared, obscured by the black storm clouds.

Time seemed to stand still, but a lot had passed by. Waves kept crashing down. They were fighting as hard as they could to keep the folboat upright. The rain went from sheets to a full-on nonstop firehose blast of water blowing almost parallel to the sea, making it virtually impossible for them to keep their eyes open.

The sky was black. The "wine dark sea," as Homer had described the Aegean, was even blacker. Col. Randal remembered Professor Winthrop saying the ancients may have been color- blind. He wished the Greek poet was there right this minute so he could point that fact out to him.

The storm began increasing in intensity.

A wave that looked as tall as the Empire State Building rose in front of them, then came slamming down. There was a loud *CRAAACK*!

Col. Randal was flung from the kayak.

At first, he struggled and choked. Then passed out. It was cold but there was no pain.

Sometime later, was it an hour, a day . . . Col. Randal came to, lying face down on one of the ugliest sea-stained shale beaches, on one of the most desolate stretches of shoreline he had ever seen. No idea where he was. However, the sky was crystal blue, the sea was calm and glassy smooth, though still not the color of wine.

Col. Randal rolled over and saw LtJG Taylor a few feet away — dead.

The folboat was nowhere in sight. All the supplies were on it. He was alone on an enemy- held island.

First thing was to drag LtJG Jackson's body up above the waterline. There was no hope of burying the MU officer. The Italians would find him eventually, and they had a long established record of according military honors to fallen enemy soldiers.

For that reason, Col. Randal left the lieutenant's dog tags on his body for identification, to prevent him from ending up in an unmarked grave.

After securing LtJG Taylor's .22 Colt Woodsman, Fairbairn Fighting Knife, RAF compass and wristwatch, Col. Randal had no option but to egress the immediate area as rapidly as possible. He had no food, no water, and no way home.

In Raiding Forces speak, his situation was officially "not good."

Based on the pre-mission briefing, Col. Randal knew the idea had been to paddle to Kalymnos Island after the raid on Portologo, then break right and keep going down the coast, hugging the shoreline to the rendezvous point (RVP). The problem was, he did not have any idea where on the island he had come ashore. The storm could have blown the canoe a long way off course.

Brandy had strict orders to return home to Castelrozzo at nightfall.

Col. Randal ran through his options. There were only two he could think of: 1) Hide until dark, then try to steal a caique; 2) Continue along the shoreline in hopes of linking up with the MAS boat.

Kalymnos Island was a big island by Aegean standards—over fifty square miles. There were not a lot of towns, so there was not a great chance of locating one in the dark. There was not much hope of linking up with Brandy's boat either.

The idea of doing nothing all day did not hold much appeal. Col. Randal glanced at the fallen MU officer, then moved off along the shore. A lot of tears were going to be shed over LtJG Jackson's death. The Hollywood playboy dentist was very popular with the female set serving in Raiding Forces.

Col. Randal was pretty sure they were going to hold him responsible and maybe he was. There was no way he had been pulling his weight paddling the folboat. It was not something he was proud of.

As he walked, the morning was turning into an idyllic Mediterranean day. Kalymnos was a barren limestone-based island—mostly mountainous—with rugged, rocky terrain just off the shore paralleling the water. Col. Randal quickly discovered the coastline was very irregular, with a lot of sheltered coves. This multiplied his problem of finding the RVP because he could not simply walk along the beach in a straight line.

In military parlance, he was escaping and evading, or "E&E-ing." Walking along the coastline in broad daylight on an island sure to have a contingent of enemy troops stationed on it felt—for lack of a better word—dumb.

Col. Randal reevaluated his situation. He could hide in the rugged terrain and no one would ever find him. Or, he could keep stumbling along on the rocky shoreline, hoping for who knew what. Drinking water was going to be a problem either way.

To keep moving still seemed like the better of two bad options.

Since there was virtually no farming or herding on the island, the population was clustered in villages. The main occupation was fishing or commercial trading with other smaller islands in the Dodecanese chain. The chances of finding a lone farmhouse were slim.

As he was stumbling along making his way around a jagged point, Col. Randal came to a secluded cove. It was a lot like the half-dozen others he had already moved past. Except in this one, a twenty-five foot caique was anchored in the middle of the bay with its sail down.

He instinctively dropped to one knee to take cover behind a pile of white limestone rocks. No one was anywhere in sight. Then a slim, black-haired girl came up on deck from out of the cabin.

She was naked.

The girl dived overboard and disappeared from sight.

Col. Randal did not recall being hit on the head, but it was possible he had suffered a concussion during the storm. Was he hallucinating? This did not seem entirely real.

The girl stayed down for a long time—very long. She surfaced, breathed for a moment or two, then dived again. Came back up and dived again.

Col. Randal had no idea what the girl was doing but he remembered advice Captain "Geronimo" Joe McKoy gave frequently, "Never look a gift horse in the mouth."

The next time she dived, he waded into the water and breaststroked out to the caique, keeping it between them. Climbing out of the water onto the boat on the far side of where the girl was diving was a little tricky. It took a lot of upper body strength to muscle out of the water and then pull himself over the side.

Col. Randal was pretty much spent physically from the night before.

The first thing he noticed was that the sailboat was clean and well-maintained. It did not smell like it had been used for fishing. Someone, probably the girl, had put a lot of work into it.

Col. Randal was reclining on one of the built-in bench seats running along the bulkhead when a bag full of something light sailed over the rail on the far side and plopped on the deck. Right behind it, the girl pulled herself up and swung on board in one supple motion.

She did not seem alarmed to find a strange man on her boat or self-conscious about being naked. That might have been because of the short knife she had strapped to her forearm. The swimmer did not make any effort to cover herself.

Col. Randal said, "Hi."

"Hello."

Unfortunately, that was one of about a dozen English words the girl could speak. Other than *ouzo*, the national drink of Greece, Col. Randal did not know a single word of Greek. It took about thirty seconds for them to establish that communication was going to have to be sign language.

Unknown to Col. Randal, the girl could understand English, having taken the language in school. But she had not used the language since before the war started and was not able to converse.

Col. Randal pointed to himself and said, "USA."

The girl pointed to herself and said, "Greek."

"John."

"Alex."

This was going so well that Col. Randal decided to go for broke, "Castelrozzo." Then he pointed.

The girl's dark eyes sparkled, "Alexandria?"

Col. Randal did not know if Alex was saying her full name or asking to go to Alexandria where there was a large expatriate Greek community, so he nodded and said, "We can sail to Alexandria."

Alex rewarded him with a beautiful smile. "Good." Then she went below to get dressed.

This seemed too easy: naked girl, boat, escape. However, there *was* Captain McKoy's gift horse analogy to consider. Besides, Alex's seeming willingness to cooperate was a lot better than his hastily improvised Plan B, which was to shoot her, dump the body in the sea, and steal the caique.

Then he remembered another one of the Captain's sayings, "Anything that's too good to be true . . . ain't."

If there was ever a case of being too good to be true—this might be it.

On the other hand, if Alex were Greek, there was almost zero chance she would be working with the Italians—the operative word being "almost." When he checked the sack, he found sponges.

Col. Randal had no idea what that meant—if anything.

From the moment Corporal Tom Jenkins broke his arm, there had been a dream-like quality to this mission. And it did not show any signs of changing. Col. Randal decided to go with the "gift horse" advice and take a wait-and-see approach regarding the "too good to be true" warning.

Not that he had much choice.

He took out the Remington M-51 .380 Beverly had gifted him and started to inspect the pocket pistol. His weapons had taken a dunking and then washed up on the shore. Col. Randal needed his pistols to be in reliable working condition and the only way to ensure that was to keep them clean.

While working, he did the math on sailing from Kalymnos to Castelrozzo. It was approximately 170 miles. Lieutenant Commander Adrian Seligman, the officer-in-charge of the Levant Schooner Flotilla, had informed him that a caique under sail could make a speed of 5 mph. That meant it would take thirty to thirty-five hours to reach ABC.

Col. Randal was in the process of reassembling the Remington .380 when Alex came back up on deck wearing a swimsuit bottom and a white shirt tied up at the waist. Without a word, she started unfurling the sail. Clearly his new companion was ready to get their journey started.

He went to the anchor and began pulling it up by hand.

Alex called what sounded like a warning—there was alarm in her voice. A small outboard motorboat with three Italian soldiers on board was entering the bay. The boat headed straight toward the caique.

Col. Randal ducked down and took off his shirt so that he would look nonthreatening like a local fisherman. He slid the .22 High Standard Military Model D in the back of his pants. Then he placed LtJG Taylor's .22 Colt Woodsman under a tasseled pillow on the bench seat.

Having no idea if Alex could understand, Col. Randal said, "You do the talking when they hail us."

Then he did his best to pantomime what he had just said. Charades had never been his game of choice. If the situation was not life or death, he would have felt like a complete idiot.

The motorboat pulled up alongside the caique. The soldiers were ogling Alex and making cat calls. Good-looking Greek girls on Kalymnos were fair game. Rape was the local sport, with bonus points scored if the Greek husband or boyfriend could be made to watch.

The troops of the Italian 33rd Mountain Division could be as depraved as their Nazi counterparts. They were not paying attention to Col. Randal. What was a mere Greek fisherman going to do?

That was a mistake.

The Remington M-51 .380 appeared out of thin air like one of The Great Teddy's magic tricks. The little pocket pistol was advertised as "self-aiming." While that was a stretch, it was a very comfortable weapon in the hand and the range was short.

Col. Randal fired double taps in rapid succession, first shooting the soldier driving the boat. He slumped dead. The other two men panicked. While armed with 6.5mm Carcano M91/38 Carbines, the men had not been expecting trouble. Their weapons were piled out of immediate reach—the rifles falling overboard being more of a concern than easy access.

The shooting was fast. *WHAAAAAP!   WHAAAAAP!   WHAAAP! WHAAAAAP! WHAAAAAAP! WHAAAAAP!*

The little pocket pistol was accurate and easy to control during fast shooting against man- sized targets. The gunfight, if it could be called that, was over in less than three seconds. The enemy patrol never had a chance.

There were only two rounds of .380 ACP ammunition remaining in the Remington's magazine and no spare. It went in a pocket. Col. Randal drew the .22 High Standard Military Model D and, firing carefully with a two-handed hold, shot all three enemy soldiers in the head.

He was in no mood to take chances.

Alex leapt into the motorboat. She secured a line and tossed it to Col. Randal. He tied it off on the stern of the caique.

As he finished hauling in the anchor, Alex jumped back on board, raised the sail, and within minutes they were underway, towing the boat. There was a stiff breeze and the caique made good speed.

When they were out of sight of any land, which was hard to do in the Aegean, little islands being everywhere in all directions, Col. Randal climbed into the motorboat and rolled the three dead enemy soldiers overboard. They sailed for another hour and cut the boat loose.

It was not difficult for a navigator with as much experience as he had to keep the needle of the RAF compass he had recovered from LtJG Taylor's body on the azimuth they needed to follow. The OSS Maritime Unit utilized the same compass as the Levant Schooner Flotilla. All that was necessary was to keep the cursor arrow between the two fixed lines in the direction he wanted to go.

In the best tradition of the LSF's motto to, "Stand Boldly On"—they did.

The caique was pounding for Advanced Base Castelrozzo at tooth-grinding speed.

After having spent so much time with Rita and Lana—who had taken a Zār Cult vow never to speak to him, traveling with a companion who could not or would not carry on a conversation seemed like old times. He manned the tiller while Alex went to the bow to work on her tan—in the nude.

Col. Randal had no idea what was going on in her head. But the pretty, black-haired girl seemed like a free spirit in the Raiding Forces mold. She was beginning to grow on him.

As night fell, Alex got dressed, went below, retrieved Col. Randal's leather bomber jacket and brought out a couple of quilts. The sparkling stars were layered, stacked up high. It was a big sky.

To keep from falling asleep at the tiller, Col. Randal entertained Alex with tales of derring-do from days past she could not understand. They sailed all that night and most of the next day. It was as if they were the last two people on earth. Never a sighting of a ship or an airplane. Islands popped up on the horizon constantly.

Col. Randal was careful to steer clear of them.

As the sun turned into an orange ball and was dipping toward the ocean, a speck appeared in the distance behind the caique. It grew larger by the minute. They were close to Castelrozzo, or at least where Col. Randal thought ABC was supposed to be, but it had not appeared in sight yet. There was no way to speed up, no way to hide, and no way to avoid what was clearly the silhouette of an Italian MAS boat coming toward them traveling at a high rate of speed.

Had the boat been dispatched to intercept them? Did the Regia Marina routinely conduct patrols this close to Castelrozzo? It was the worst possible time to encounter the enemy—almost home free.

Col. Randal had been up for over sixty hours and sleep deprivation was hitting him hard.

Everything seemed to be taking place fast in slow motion. He had zero options.

Hoping Alex could understand him, Col. Randal said, "Claim I kidnapped you."

He knew she was not going to have any idea what "kidnapped" meant but in his groggy condition could not think of a simpler word to use. Pantomiming was a nonstarter. So much for non-verbal communication.

The MAS boat roared up beside the caique. In a showy demonstration of boat handling, the skipper reversed engines and hove to, creating a white-capped wake that rocked the sailboat. A real hotshot.

The MAS boat's loud hailer squealed, "Hello, handsome! Fancy meeting you here."

Brandy Seaborn had disobeyed her orders and stayed over another day at Kalymnos hoping the MU team would make it to the RVP. Now she was on her way back to Castelrozzo with the RMBPD boat team on board.

ABC was dead ahead, just out of sight. "Do you require a tow, John?"

"Hell, no—we're going in under our own power!"

"Follow me."

Alex glanced at him, confused.

Col. Randal said, "We're probably going to need help to explain to you what just happened."

Every member of Raiding Forces, Small Raids Inc., the Levant Schooner Flotilla, the 10th Motor Gunboat Flotilla, and the three intelligence services with personnel stationed on ABC were at the dock to welcome Brandy's MAS boat. Vice Admiral Sir Randolph "Razor" Ransom and Brigadier General William "Wild Bill" Donovan were also present, having flown in from RFHQ when Brandy failed to return per her orders. Captain Billy Jack Jaxx and his SOG patrol were there as well, having arrived back from their own raiding expedition the day before.

Unlike after a civilian sporting event where the spectators cheer as the team is leaving the field, when military personnel gather to welcome soldiers home from a mission, everyone watches silently—sometimes they applaud. The more hazardous the mission, the quieter the crowd.

There was not a sound from the group on the dock.

Things moved fast after the caique glided in. Alex was first off and she said something in her native language. Mandy, who spoke Greek, overheard, and whisked the girl away for an immediate debriefing.

When Col. Randal stepped ashore, Major the Lady Jane Seaborn threw herself on him so violently she nearly knocked him off the dock. She had been crying all day, only stopping moments before when Brandy radioed that he was safe. But now she started again, from relief— laughing and crying at the same time.

So much for being raised from birth never to show any emotion in public except pleasure. Lady Jane said, "First, I am going to murder you, then I am going to kill you, John Randal."

It was not the first time his drop-dead gorgeous fiancée had made that threat.

Beverly, the FANYs, WRENs, and female Royal Marines in the crowd began sobbing when word went around that LtJG Taylor had been killed. The Hollywood playboy dentist had a loyal Raiding Forces fan base.

VAdm. Ransom said, "RAF photo reconnaissance showed a large freighter sunk in Portologo the morning following your raid. A pair of tugboats were spotted attempting to tow the destroyer out of the harbor. Your limpets caused massive structural damage—the ship was sinking by the stern.

"No possible way to save it.

"Nonetheless, a bomber squadron was dispatched to complete the job. When the RAF was done, all that remained was an oil slick. Scratch one Folgore-class destroyer. A major victory for Small Raids Inc.—the equivalent of sinking the Bismarck in our small slice of the war."

Brig. Gen. Donovan said, "Sorry about Jackson, Colonel. He was highly qualified, exhaustively trained and fully aware of the risks involved. You, on the other hand, had no business being aboard his folboat. Ever do anything as irresponsible as that again, and I'll have you court-martialed for stupidity.

"Is that clear?"

Col. Randal said, "Crystal, sir."

ABC had been an emotional pressure cooker after Beverly reported that Col. Randal had replaced the injured Cpl. Jenkins and was last seen paddling off in the dark. Then, Brandy failed to return from Kalymnos as planned. She did not make her final scheduled call, claiming radio trouble.

As they were walking up from the dock, Capt. Jaxx said, "Ain't right, sir. You're a one- man army. Instead of a medal, what happens—you get your ass chewed."

Beverly laughed, "Twice."

Lady Jane said, "Only once—mine was a straight up death threat." She was not laughing.

Capt. Jaxx said, "*Can* you actually be court-martialed for stupidity?"

9

INTER-ALLIED RELATIONS

COLONEL JOHN RANDAL WAS SITTING IN THE ORNATE dining room at the headquarters of Raiding Forces Advanced Base Castelrozzo (ABC) eating a late breakfast of steak and eggs, having slept in after his mission to Leros. The room was fit for a Roman emperor and that was exactly who it had been built for—Il Duce Benito Mussolini. As the story went, Mussolini had never stayed on Castelrozzo. Not even one night. A number of fabulous palaces were said to have been constructed throughout the Mediterranean region over the years in anticipation of a visit from the great one—only to have him never show. The building at ABC was over ten years old and had been sitting vacant from the day it was built.

Raiding Forces personnel were the only people to ever occupy it. Col. Randal had slept in the Emperor's bed last night.

The dining room was empty except for Major the Lady Jane Seaborn, Mandy, and Beverly. They were snacking on pastries crafted by GG, who Lady Jane had decided would run her kitchen. To say that Col. Randal was enjoying himself would have been a fair assessment of the situation.

Mandy said, "Were you aware that Alex is a nun?" Col. Randal said, "Nuns can't be nudists, can they?"

Mandy said, "Apparently, she is a wild child from a wealthy Greek shipping family. Her conservative father eventually tired of the nonstop partying and fast crowd she ran with. He shipped her off to Kalymnos to become a Greek Orthodox nun.

"When you appeared, Alex was in the process of running away from the nunnery."

"She was skinny-dipping for sponges."

Mandy said, "Planning to sell them to raise money to finance her journey to Alexandria."

Lady Jane, who was fluent in Greek, said, "Alex informed me that she tried to tempt you but you conducted yourself as a perfect gentleman."

"Alex said that?"

Beverly laughed, "She told Lady Jane that you said you were faithful to a beautiful princess—you tell Alex that, Johnny?"

"I might have said something to that effect."

What else could he have told the girl under the misguided impression she did not understand English? Late at night, sleep-deprived? Sailing through enemy-infested waters, just the two of them?

He could have said anything.

Lady Jane rewarded him by lighting off one of her most incandescent heart attack smiles ever. "Loved the princess story."

Col. Randal had the distinct impression he had dodged a bullet.

Captain Billy Jack Jaxx stumbled into the dining room. Had Captain "Geronimo" Joe McKoy been present, he would have almost certainly pointed out that the SOG commander "looked like he had been rode hard and put away wet."

And he did.

Mandy said, "Late night of debauchery with one of the local island nymphomaniacs?"

Capt. Jaxx pulled a chair to the table and signaled GG to bring him a cup of coffee. "You know I never kiss and tell."

"Yes, you do, Jack, you tell me everything."

"I leave out the good parts."

Beverly said, "We were explaining to Johnny that his new best girlfriend Alex is a nun."

Capt. Jaxx choked on his coffee, spilling it. "You're making that up."

Col. Randal said, "My thoughts exactly."

"Last night, I was in my room minding my own business, Capt. Jaxx said. "I heard fingernails scratching on the door. When I opened it, Alex marched in, ripped the buttons off my shirt, and it was on."

Mandy said, "You are incorrigible."

"I don't know what that means."

Beverly laughed. "Slept with a fallen angel. A new low, Billy Jack."

"Fallen—Alex arrived on station in my room, smoking in flames, crashed, burned, then blew up. I was collateral damage. How was I supposed to know she was AWOL from a convent?"

Mandy said, "You expect us to take the word of a convicted panty raider?"

Capt. Jaxx said, "I was pardoned for that."

Considering this might be an appropriate time to exercise command guidance, Col. Randal said, "So, Jack, you didn't feel guilty about taking advantage of a displaced refugee— regardless of how great-looking she might be?"

That sounded pretty good.

"No, sir. I was strictly adhering to the Allied Forces Headquarters memorandum issued by General Dwight D. Eisenhower, instructing U.S. Army personnel to foster harmonious inter- allied relations whenever coming in contact with aligned foreigners, in the interest of promoting Allied coalition harmony."

"All right, then—keep up the good work, Captain."

Mandy rolled her eyes. "Jack Cool—Mr. Ambassador of Goodwill."

Col. Randal said, "How did Alex know where to find your sleeping quarters?"

Lady Jane said, "I told her."

Beverly laughed. "Daddy's going to love this story."

COLONEL JOHN RANDAL, MAJOR THE LADY JANE SEABORN, and Happy were doing a walk-through inspection of the waterfront area of Castelrozzo. It was partially in ruins, bombed out and ravaged by fire from an Italian air raid two years previously. The village had no distinct name of its own. Like other towns in the Aegean, it went by the name of the island.

Castelrozzo was a small island—only 3.5 miles across with a 12-mile perimeter, for a total of a little over 4.5 square miles. Most of the population was concentrated in the port village area. Many residents lived in mansions scattered along the sloping cliff face of the mountain behind the town. Before the war, the islanders had been wealthy. Possibly the richest people in the Dodecanese chain—if not all of the Aegean.

Now a majority of the beautiful houses were sitting vacant, abandoned by their owners. An ABC security plan was being developed by Captain Lionel Chatterhorn of the Vulnerable Points Wing. The responsibility for implementing the plan would fall to Major Clive Adair, the officer commanding Phantom, who was the new "Mayor of Castelrozzo." The same post he had held at Oasis X.

Mandy Paige had been tasked to assist Maj. Adair as his counterintelligence officer—a job the pretty brunette had held at Oasis X as well.

The main idea was to relocate all the islanders not currently living in town or in the immediate vicinity to the harbor. The locals needed to be concentrated in one place so the Vulnerable Points Wing security personnel could discreetly keep them under observation. No one wanted Castelrozzoians living out of sight on the far side of the island, where they might come in contact with Italian or German infiltrators.

ABC was a witches' brew from a security perspective. There were a few French and a handful of Italian residents still living there. While the Italians were not being held in confinement, Italy was an enemy combatant nation and its citizens were classified as enemy aliens. The local Greek islanders hated the Italians because they had lorded it over them until the night Raiding Forces parachuted onto the island to liberate it.

The Greeks hated Nazis almost as much, and would not be inclined to willingly aid or abet them—the key word being "willingly." However, with German Forces occupying both France and Greece, the Abwehr had leverage over Castelrozzoians who had family members living on the mainland. The Nazis had the opportunity, means, and disposition to blackmail vulnerable locals into providing intelligence and possibly even shelter Abwehr agents or small teams of Brandenburger Commandos.

An around-the-clock counterintelligence campaign was a must.

However, today all Col. Randal and Lady Jane were interested in was the string of small storefront buildings constructed right along the sea wall of the waterfront. A great many of the commercial structures were sitting empty, damaged by the Italian air raid. The attack had caused most of the population of approximately 15,000 to flee the island.

The majority of people relocated to the large expatriate Greek community in Melbourne, Australia, under the government's welcoming "Populate or Perish" plan. Others moved to Alexandria, Egypt, where the political climate was not welcoming in spite of its large Greek expatriate community. Now there were fewer than 1,300 Castelrozzoians in residence and the place had the feel of being a ghost town—or more accurately, a ghost island.

The locals typically stayed out of sight until evening. Lady Jane said, "What a charming little community."

Col. Randal said, "It was . . . you've got your work cut out."

"Never fear, I shall make the place magical again with bistros, eateries, and a few shops. The village has good bones. As you can see, the architecture is a lovely blend of Spanish Tuscany, Neo-Italian, and Greek Revival with a classical Turkish influence—everything begs to be snow-white.

"Will you help?"

"Bounce ideas off me anytime, but I have no idea what Neo-Italian or Greek Revival means."

"Colleagues, then?"

"Roger that—as long as you're the senior partner."

"Perfect, love it when we work on a project together."

Col. Randal was glad Brigadier Dudley Clarke had asked Lady Jane to take on the restoration. After she had been shot outside the Gezira Club, Cairo no longer seemed like such an inviting place. He felt better knowing she was on the island when he was away. ABC was safer, although there was always the possibility of another enemy air attack.

Lady Jane said, "I am beginning to fall in love with this place."

Curiosity having gotten the better of him, Col. Randal said, "So explain to me about you telling Alex how to get to Billy Jack's room last night."

Lady Jane said, "While you were catching up on your sleep, she and I were in the other room having a conversation. Alex asked how to find the 'beautiful boy with the pistols' who was on the dock talking to you. I told her."

"Pimping for Jack Cool?"

Lady Jane laughed, "I had no idea that was going to happen. Fortunately, he was current on Allied Forces Headquarters policy. Stood boldly on in accordance to orders."

Col. Randal said, "Captain Jaxx has never read an AFHQ directive in his life."

"Exactly."

As they toured the bomb-damaged waterfront, Lady Jane said, "Professor Winthrop has requested permission to come and conduct archeological digs. Are you aware that the island has had at least nine different names? The official title, Megisti, means "largest", but in fact, Castelrozzo is the smallest populated island in the Dodecanese chain. Some believe the Knights who built the fort could not pronounce the word and corrupted it.

"A golden crown was found . . ."

THE WALRUS SPLASHED DOWN AT RAIDING FORCES headquarters. On board were Colonel John Randal, Major the Lady Jane

Seaborn, Captain Billy Jack Jaxx, Lieutenant Chase Starrett, Ensign Theodore Hamilton, aka "The Great Teddy," Master Sergeant Mack Beckwith, Mandy Paige, and the fallen nun, Alex Gataki. Her Greek surname meant "kitten," which had resulted in Jack Cool giving her the nickname "Cat."

He said it was short for wildcat.

The stay on Castelrozzo had been abruptly cut short because of a message from Captain "Geronimo" Joe McKoy requesting their immediate return to RFHQ. Captain Roy Kidd was back from the Congo, as was Waldo Treywick. James "Baldie" Taylor and Captain Cuthbert Bowlby were also recently returned from their visit to Sir Ernest Oppenheimer's private estate in South Africa. But the pressing reason to fly back early was because Major A. W. "Sammy" Sansom of Security Intelligence Middle East had scheduled a meeting that night at the Kit-Kat Club with the Middle Eastern crime lords who would be replacing the recently departed Big Four.

Maj. Sansom described the fresh batch of handpicked underworld mobsters as the new "Criminal Royalty."

Col. Randal's presence was required.

Flanigan was waiting on the dock with transportation when the Walrus landed. Col. Randal rode in the Rolls-Royce with Lady Jane, Capt. Jaxx, and Mandy.

Col. Randal ordered, "Mandy, get with Major Sansom and set up our usual meeting before the meeting tonight."

"Straightaway, John."

"Jack, round up all the CARD GAME players at RFHQ so that we can debrief Roy as soon as we roll in. You're going to be busy, Mandy, but I want you there too.

"Absolutely."

"Jane, what's the drill for Cat?"

"Beverly has taken her under her wing. She is going to outfit Cat with a wardrobe of her things; they are about the same size. We have decided to give Alex time to adjust to being in Egypt before deciding her best course of action going forward."

Col. Randal said, "Beverly can't speak any more Greek than I can."

Capt. Jaxx said, "Language skills not required with that firecracker."

Mandy said, "Shut up, Jack."

Lady Jane said, "Fashion is an international non-verbal language."

Col. Randal said, "When you girls finish playing dress-up, Lady Jane, I'd like you, Mandy, and Beverly standing by this evening to go with me to the Kit-Kat."

"Love to. I enjoy playing gun moll—I shall wear my PPK in my garter."

Mandy said, "We can do the cat-rubbing routine again—you liked it so much last time, John."

Col. Randal said, "Billy Jack, be at the club tonight with as many of our people as you can round up—armed to the teeth."

"Can do, sir."

"I want to put on a show of force to make it clear to the new crew what's going to happen if they cross us like the last bunch did."

"I'll make it happen, sir."

Col. Randal said, "We experienced a failure to communicate . . ."

"Won't happen this time around, Colonel—leave it to me."

Capt. McKoy and Waldo were waiting outside of RFHQ when they pulled up. Capt. Jaxx said, "Hang loose . . . we're getting ready for a CARD GAME."

Capt. McKoy said, "You'll find Roy in the chow hall having coffee with Clint and Cord. They just got back from the States."

Col. Randal said, "Our SOG lieutenants were in the U.S.?"

Capt. Jaxx said, "Beverly's Dad had 'em flown to Big Spring Army Air Field a week ago, sir. Wanted their input on new Pathfinder equipment. Bronc's taken an interest in parachute operations after our Sicily jump."

MSgt. Beckwith stepped out of the jeep that had been following Lady Jane's Rolls- Royce

Capt. Jaxx said, "Up for a hand of cards, Sergeant Major?"

"Affirmative."

"Beverly?"

"Be ready to read 'em and weep, Billy Jack."

Beverly was the best poker player in Raiding Forces—Texas Hold 'Em being her game of choice. If this was going to be a game of chance, she would have been banned from play.

Col. Randal walked inside RFHQ and proceeded to the mess hall, where he found Capt. Kidd sitting at a table with Lieutenant Clint Hays and Captain Cord Granger.

"Captain Kidd, be in my suite in fifteen minutes. Clint, you and Cord keep yourselves available. I'm going to want a debrief on your trip to Texas as soon as we can get to it."

"Yes, sir."

Captain Stephanie Fawcett-Tatum heard Col. Randal's voice and was waiting for him when he came out. "Admiral Ransom would like a word, John. Congratulations on the destroyer. Sorry about Jackson."

"Any idea what the Razor might want? I've already been chewed out about the raid."

"I heard—sorry, not the faintest."

Col. Randal made his way to his old office in the Operations Room, which was now Vice Admiral Sir Randolph "Razor" Ransom's office. The Admiral had seldom used it in the past, but with the center of gravity of operations having shifted from the Great Sand Sea to the Aegean, the Razor was at RFHQ more and more often.

When the commander of Small Raids Inc. saw Col. Randal, he waved him in. "Close the door, Colonel."

Col. Randal clicked on.

VAdm. Ransom said, "No good way to break this to you, Colonel. I shall go straight to the main point, warning you in advance that I was not expecting, nor am I pleased about, a recent development. That all right with you?"

"Yes, sir."

"Lady Jane's husband, Mallory, has been reassigned from the storage depot in the Shetlands of the frozen north, where the Navy has kept him marooned as the supply officer for the Shetland Bus—small civilian craft that run agents and arms into Norway. The new assignment does not mean the man is not still under a cloud—he is."

Col. Randal said, "So what happened, Admiral?"

"Mountbatten has been promoted up and out of Combined Operations. Took long enough to get rid of that poser. The Canadians have been demanding his head ever since the fiasco at Dieppe. Now the silly fool is slated to become Supreme Allied Commander Southeast Asia Command.

"At last a post where the fool can do no harm."

"Sounds like a promotion, sir."

"Way it works when you are second cousin to the King. As I said, up and out. The Southeast Asia Command is as far, far away as you can get from the seat of power and still be on Planet Earth. Lady Mountbatten will be going with him, and she lobbied her husband to give Mallory a position on his staff.

"Whispers of an illicit relationship between the two have swirled for ages. Mallory is a bounder and Edwina a tart. There is a high probability the rumors have merit."

Col. Randal said, "You seem angry, Admiral. What am I missing?"

"The bloody bastard departed for his new duty station without signing Lady Jane's divorce decree."

"Lady Jane know, sir?"

"Negative—how do you want to handle this?"

"I'll tell her, Admiral."

"Hoping you would volunteer. Hate to be the bearer of bad news. Especially to Jane."

"Not a problem, sir."

VAdm. Ransom said, "There is one other item to discuss. We are not having this conversation—you did not hear it from me . . ."

Col. Randal walked out of VAdm. Ransom's office wondering what *else* the day could bring that he never saw coming.

Capt. Fawcett-Tatum breezed past, carrying a clipboard.

"Stephanie, would you book a private room aboard Jane's favorite floating restaurant for 2230 tonight—it'll be a surprise."

"Trying to get back in her good graces after your latest misadventure, hero?"

"Seems like a good idea."

"Jane has always been forgiving of your escapades—eventually."

Col. Randal said, "You're not dating anyone special, are you, Stephanie?"

"Why do you ask?"

"Know Jack Dance?"

"Only by sight. The Major has passed through RFHQ occasionally. We were in the briefing together a few days ago."

Col. Randal said, "I'm not trying to play matchmaker, but how would you feel about being his lunch date at the Gezira one day this week as guests of Lady Jane and myself?"

Capt. Fawcett-Tatum laughed. "You playing Cupid—will wonders never cease?"

Col. Randal said, "I've kept Major Dance in the field pretty much full-time since he's arrived. I'd like a chance to talk to him. Having you and Jane along won't make it seem so much like an interrogation."

Capt. Fawcett-Tatum's eyes flashed. "I would be delighted."

"Jack's not married and he doesn't have a girlfriend."

"For an amateur matchmaker, John, you are doing quite well."

Col. Randal headed upstairs to the third-floor suite. Flanigan was at the desk outside the door. The burly ex-policeman was wearing a glum expression.

"What's the matter, Flanigan? You look like you've lost your best friend."

"I still cannot get over feeling guilty about Lady Seaborn being shot on my watch, sir. Every time I see her, it is a flashback to that 'orrible day. Sometimes I am unable to sleep at night, thinking about it."

Col. Randal said, "Lighten up, Flanigan. I'd have done only one thing differently if I were you that day. Instead of utilizing my own shirt as a compress to stop the bleeding, I'd have ripped off Beverly's."

"Quite right, sir—opportunity squandered."

CARD GAME was assembled when Col. Randal walked in. King and Captain Pamala Plum-Martin were present, which was unexpected. He believed them to still be in Tangier.

Col. Randal said, "I'd like to announce Sergeant Major Beckwith is now an official member of CARD GAME—welcome aboard, Sergeant Major."

"Thank you for having me, sir."

No additional explanation was necessary. MSgt. Beckwith was highly respected. He had arrived with the 575th Parachute Infantry Regiment and made an immediate impact on Raiding Forces. Not an easy accomplishment in a unit so full of talent.

Waldo passed out his custom-rolled cigars to the men, a practice that had become a ritual at CARD GAME meetings. No one fired one up, with Lady Jane having a long-established policy that banned cigar smoking in her suite. The women produced cigarettes, which were permitted.

Col. Randal lit Lady Jane's with his hard service U.S. 26th Cavalry Regiment Zippo.

The mood in the room was wound tight. Everyone was intensely interested in the subject at hand. They were all professionals.

Capt. McKoy took the meeting. "Roy, lead off."

Capt. Kidd said, "The Belgian Congo is seventy-six times the size of Belgium. The topography of the interior of the colony is a nightmare. Rivers are the only means of travel . . . virtually no roads. Once you land ashore, the vegetation's so dense along the waterways that it's almost impenetrable. No one really knows what's behind the deep belts of jungle paralleling the banks. By all reports, there's massive wetlands under triple-canopy jungle no one white man has ever explored. If you fly over it in an airplane, it's so dense you only catch glimpses of the ground, so who knows what's out there?

"All of the Big Five dangerous game animals are to be found. The rivers contain six-foot- long piranhas called Tiger Fish. They're almost as big as a Great White shark.

"Mr. Treywick's not joking about the possibility of dinosaurs. Everywhere I traveled, the Europeans had all heard the stories, though I never talked to any who had actually seen one. The natives say the monsters are to be found living in the maze of interconnected lakes deep in the interior under the equatorial rain forest. They claim the dinosaurs hate hippopotamuses for some reason and can kill one with a single bite.

"The relationship between the Belgian colonists and the African natives is not good. The Europeans treat the natives worse than slaves. Arab slavers are known to still work the region, though that's not a subject anyone wants to admit to. We don't have time to go into the grotesque inhumanity routinely taking place every day in a remote land where total anarchy exists—the horror I witnessed is beyond belief and I served on the Northwest Frontier.

"Here's one example—demand for rubber is so great because of the war that the planters are using unskilled natives with no forestry training to harvest it. The workers are made to tap the rubber tree, then let the liquid squirt all over their body. As the sap dries, it turns into hardened rubber. When a native comes back to the plantation HQ, looking like one of our Frogmen in a wet suit, the rubber is recovered by melting the hardened sap off his body with a blow torch."

Beverly said, "Gruesome!"

Lady Jane said, "Agreed."

"That's stone cold," Capt. McKoy said.

Capt. Kidd said, "The only reason I'm fixating on the state of the civil situation and the geography is because we can turn both to our advantage.

"Here's what you need to know . . . One: The 1,500-mile Kasai River basin is called the 'Diamond Heartland.' Prior to the war, sixty percent of all stones shipped out of the colony to the Brussels diamond centers for cutting were acquired from the potholers working its banks. There's no reason to believe the percentage is any less today.

"Two: Due to the inhospitable terrain, dangerous wildlife, and complete lack of law and order, there's not going to be any diamond trafficking taking place in the interior of the Congo— except along the banks of the Kasai River. Trading posts operated by Europeans are located every hundred miles or so. The diamonds dug up by the potholers are brought to the trading posts to be sold. That's where the majority of the Nazi diamond traffickers do their business, with other buyers cruising the Kasai in boats, looking for potholing areas to purchase diamonds on the spot, saving the natives the trip to a trading post.

"Three: "To accomplish our mission, LEAF EATER needs to seize control of diamond buying at the dozen or so trading posts. Once we accomplish that, the Nazi buyers in the boats are out of business because they will have lost their bases to operate from."

Waldo said, "Just like Joe's correspondence course 'Problem Solving 101' says—'the problem is the solution.'"

Beverly, who had never heard about Capt. McKoy's business administration correspondence course, said, "I don't know what that means."

Waldo said, "When you've got yourself a problem, you say it out loud and the next thing you hear is the answer."

"Seriously?"

"Let's give 'er a try. Say the problem out loud."

Beverly said, "The problem is how to stop Nazis from buying diamonds from the natives along the Kasai River."

Waldo said, "What'd you come up with?"

Beverly said, "Go to where the Nazi buyers are and kill them."

Capt. McKoy said, "Roy's plan down to the ground."

Capt. Jaxx said, "Keep It Short and Simple."

Mandy said, "You expect me to believe that Problem Solving 101 mumbo jumbo always works?"

Waldo said, "Ninety-nine point nine percent effective—battle-proven."

Capt. McKoy said, "Good report, young captain. Now the corrupt government officials blackmailing diamonds from the mine owners and the mine workers stealing 'em from the mines and selling to the Nazis—that's a discussion for another day."

Col. Randal locked eyes with Capt. Kidd and nodded. He had taken what seemed to be an insurmountable problem, reduced it to easy-to-understand terms, and recommended a course of action LEAF EATER was capable of carrying out.

Mission accomplished—at least his on the ground reconnaissance.

Lady Jane blazed away at Capt. Kidd with one of her heart attack smiles and quoted from Raiding Forces Rules, "'Right man, right job'—well done, Roy."

Capt. Kidd said, "One more thing. Frank's planning to station some of his mercenaries on boats to patrol the river, take out the waterborne Nazi diamond traffickers, and replace 'em with his people."

Capt. McKoy said, "That'll work."

Waldo said, "Still talking up the dinosaur deal, huh, Roy?"

"No one I spoke to thought their existence was out of the question," Capt. Kidd said. "I thought you were kidding, Mr. Treywick. Who knows? That place is unbelievable."

Capt. McKoy said, "Waldo, tell us what you know about the new batch a' crooks we'll be meetin' tonight."

Waldo said, "Acting in my capacity as Mr. Big, the diamond buyin' kingpin liaisonin' with the Chicago mob, I've already conducted a preliminary discussion with the new three crime lords Sammy Sansom picked out to replace the late, unmourned Big Four. Look like standard- issue crooks to me—ain't nothin' special.

"Boys is real eager to get started, this deal bein' a big step up for 'em in the world a' crime. We ain't callin' 'em the Big Three—they're just gonna be 'The Three'—no Big to it. No sense givin' 'em the big head.

"Major Sansom's downstairs, so I'll let him fill us in on the details when you're ready for him, Joe."

Capt. McKoy said, "King, what do you and Pam have for us? I wasn't expectin' you back so quick."

King said, "We flew to Tangier, where we initially met with a U.S. Marine, Captain Peter Ortiz of the OSS. He pointed out that the distance from Morocco to Spain is only fourteen klicks by boat, making the coastline impossible to seal off. The strong-arm tactics we use in the Congo and Cairo are not going to work in Morocco.

"A more subtle approach is our only hope of stopping the flow of diamonds."

Capt. Plum-Martin said, "The city of Tangier, aka the "Door of Africa," was formerly a joint French/Spanish Protectorate. When the war started, the neutral Spanish Army moved in unilaterally to secure the city on the pretext that Italy would invade if the French were there in force."

King said, "Logic that makes no sense."

"Now, following TORCH, our Allied Forces control Morocco," Capt. Plum-Martin said. "But for reasons no one we spoke to could explain, the Spanish were allowed to continue policing Tangier. The chief of police, who by all reports is a hardcore pro-Nazi sycophant of Spain's President Franco, had dinner with us—Ortiz arranged it.

King said, "Since I was traveling on a Swiss passport and Pam on one issued by Monaco and Spain being nonaligned, we three neutrals talked freely about the war. As it turns out, the police chief is not the Franco puppet widely believed. His younger brother was killed on the Eastern Front, serving in the Spanish Blue Division."

Capt. Plum-Martin said, "Died fighting for Hitler in Russia and for that the chief of police is bitter."

"We represented ourselves as wealthy diamond dealers willing to offer opportunity to anyone who has gems to sell," King said. "The chief was quick to point out that Tangier is one of the world's diamond hubs. He mentioned being able to steer certain 'merchants' with product to sell our way."

Capt. Plum-Martin said, "For a finder's fee, naturally."

King said, "The police chief has an expensive lifestyle and a weakness for fit, tanned women with hair the color of snow—loves Pamala."

"Man's got taste," Capt. Jaxx said.

"At that point," King said, "having gathered all the information needed, we hopped the next plane back to Cairo. The course of action we recommend is for us to return to Tangier, conclude our negotiations with the chief of police, establish a purchasing office in a public place, and open our doors for business. While we will never be able to stop the flow of diamonds smuggled to Spain, there is a reasonable possibility we can drive the price up so high that the Nazis elect not to compete with us."

Capt. McKoy said, "That's a plan, King."

Col. Randal said, "Yes, it is."

Capt. McKoy said, "What do you need to pull it off?"

"A purchasing agent, a diamond appraiser, and seed money," King said. "The rest should take care of itself."

Capt. Plum-Martin said, "The beauty of our plan is that while we never actually state our firm transships diamonds to the Third Reich, everyone will assume that we do."

Capt. McKoy said, "Yeah, keep the real Nazi buyers off your backs—them thinkin' there's no sense competin' with their own people. Ought to work . . . at least for a while."

"That is the idea," King said.

Col. Randal said, "I like it."

"The profit margin will not be as fantastic as it is in Cairo or the Congo. However, CARD GAME will still make a return on investment," Capt. Plum-Martin said. "Our profit plan will be to ship the stones we purchase in Tangier back here to Egypt, so Mr. Treywick can sell them at an inflated price."

Capt. McKoy said, "Works for me."

King said, "We do not want to stay on in Tangier permanently. Someone will need to be stationed there to act as the LEAF EATER purchasing agent. Once the business is up and running, all that's required of Pamala and me is to make the occasional appearance—consistent with our cover story of being diamond buyers traveling throughout the Middle East.

"Pamala wants to continue flying, and I intend to resume my duties with Raiding Forces."

Capt. McKoy said, "Can do . . . you got it."

Col. Randal said, "Good."

"Pam," Beverly said, "you and King are a great team."

Lady Jane said, "Agreed."

Waldo said, "The setup in Tangier ain't perfect, but you two sure turned a lemon into lemonade."

Capt. McKoy said, "Mandy, go ahead 'n call on down to the Operations Room. Let's get Sansom in here. Wrap this CARD GAME up."

While they were waiting for the Chief of Security Intelligence Middle East to make his way upstairs, Capt. Jaxx said, "Sergeant Major, let's break out Thompson submachine guns for everybody tonight. They're the meanest-looking weapons we've got. When the time comes to make our appearance, we need everybody acting like they want to kill those mobsters—Dog-Roger-Tare."

Beverly said, "DRT . . . I don't know what that means."

"Dead Right There."

Jack Cool.

MAJOR THE LADY JANE SEABORN, BRANDY SEABORN, Mandy Paige and Beverly Blackwell were in the master bedroom of the third-floor suite. They were putting on make-up for the nights' charade at the Kit-Kat Club. The women were having fun. The sound of laughter was coming from the bedroom.

Colonel John Randal was sitting on the couch in the living area reading an Office of Strategic Services copy of a paper prepared for the United States Army War College, Carlisle, Barracks 1943. *SMALL FORCE BIG IMPACT: THE STRATEGIC VALUE OF SMALL-SCALE RAIDING* was written by Lieutenant Colonel David R. Throckmorton, United States Army Air Force.

Col. Randal wondered what a USAAF officer might know about raiding.

"Some of the greatest successes in warfare have come with relatively little bloodshed."

That sounded promising.

"The strategic purpose of a raid is to force a foe to draw away his own strength to protect his threatened rear."

What about the flanks? What about pinprick raids across an enemy's linear front like the escarpment at RAF Habbaniya? The author seemed to have confused raiding with parachute/glider operations.

"Strategy in its highest form is the art of achieving one's goals with the smallest expenditure of blood and treasure."

Not bad, sounded like a line lifted from a Churchill speech. Still, the people on the sharp end would be heartened to know that the staff types planning the war in safety far away from where the blood and treasure were being expended felt that way.

He knew he sure was.

Beverly came out of the master bedroom in full war paint, wearing her standard-issue faded blue jeans and peewee alligator cowgirl boots and looking like she had stepped off the cover of *Glamour* magazine. As soon as the women finished their makeup, they would all be driving to the Mena House Hotel for a private dinner in the suite Lady Jane maintained. Later, the girls would change into evening dresses before going to the Kit-Kat Club.

Beverly plopped down on the couch next to him.

Col. Randal looked up from his reading. "What are you laughing about?"

"Lady Jane—the way she says things, it's stand-up comedy."

"Yeah, like what?"

"It's classified 'Need to Know' and you're not on the 'Eyes Only' list, Johnny—girl stuff."

"I'm cleared for all secrets involving Raiding Forces and attached personnel. I decide who has a 'Need to Know' or not."

"OK, but you can't tell anyone I told you—ever."

"Deal."

"Brandy was teasing Lady Jane about your SOE security clearance—when all those hot undercover agents tried to lure secrets out of you."

Col. Randal said, "I see." Which meant he did not.

"Brandy said SOE, MI-6, and OSS make the combined reports on your bedroom exploits required reading for all agents. What to say and what not to say when having sex with someone who might possibly be a *femme fatale*."

Col. Randal said, "That's not true."

Beverly said, "Then Brandy asked Jane if the thought of you sleeping with so many women ever bothered her."

"Brandy asked that?"

"Know what Lady Jane said?"

"Not sure I want to."

"All that practice is what made you so good in bed."

Col. Randal said, "Never underestimate the value of hands-on physical training— repetition, repetition, repetition."

Flanigan stuck his head in the door. "Mr. Taylor to see you, sir."

"Send him in."

Jim "Baldie" Taylor took a seat in one of the overstuffed chairs. He was not sure whether to start with Beverly present, but when Col. Randal made no effort to send her away, he said, "I shall make this quick since we both have things to do before our meeting tonight.

"As you know, Cuthbert and I met with Sir Ernest Oppenheimer at his estate. He is most unhappy that no one is giving him credit for keeping DeBeers diamond prices at the prewar level. Since the Diamond Company is the beneficiary of a healthy tax write-off for doing so, sympathy for a tax-dodging war profiteer turning a blind eye to backdoor business with Nazi Germany is highly unlikely.

"However, we chose not to explain it to him in quite those terms.

"Then word arrived that the chief of the Léopoldville Police Department had been assassinated for his involvement in supplying black market diamonds to the Third Reich. Sir Ernest became quite alarmed. He may have even suspected Cuthbert and I were there to kill him.

"The upshot of our meeting was a promise for DeBeers to *attempt* to stop the flow of the Diamond Company's stones to Germany through neutral countries. Sir Ernest pledged to make it his top priority. If he follows through, this would be a positive development."

Col. Randal said, "Do you believe him?"

"In a word . . . no."

Beverly said, "Captain McKoy always says 'Greed kills.'"

Taylor said, "Not at the hands of MI-6 or SOE. Oppenheimer is too well-protected by his contacts in the British government. The man is untouchable."

Beverly said, not for the first time, "Don't you hate politics?" It was not really a question—she already knew the answer.

COLONEL JOHN RANDAL, MAJOR THE LADY JANE SEABORN AND Beverly were at the Westley Richards Gun Store in Cairo, having made an unscheduled stop on the way to Mena House. Mandy was going to link up with them later. The reason for the detour was because Lady Jane had a surprise for Col. Randal.

Captain "Geronimo" Joe McKoy was there waiting for them when Flanigan parked the Rolls-Royce.

Col. Randal said, "Buying a shotgun, Jane?"

"Do you remember when I brought you in to have you measured for a 20-gauge over and under?"

"I do."

Lady Jane laughed, "I lied. We were not here for a sporting arm. The Master Gun Fitter was fitting you for a new Beretta M-38 to replace the one you broke on your jump into Sicily. You may be the only officer in the Allied Army with a bespoke submachine gun."

Capt. McKoy, who was present at Lady Jane's request because of his extensive experience with all things weapons-related, said, "Maybe not for long, though. I want to see how this deal works out. If it's good, I'm plannin' to have one built for myself."

The manager escorted them into the fitting room where the Master Gun Fitter was waiting. Lady Jane and Beverly ensconced themselves on a couch to watch the show. Both women had grown up hanging out in their father's gunrooms. The aroma of gun oil and hand- polished dark wood brought back pleasant memories from other times.

The two women were enjoying themselves.

The Master Gun Fitter was holding a 9mm MAB-38 A.

"What we have here is an unfired standard issue Italian Army Beretta SMG, supplied by Lady Seaborn from captured stock. Acting on Captain McKoy's detailed instructions, one of our gunsmiths disassembled the weapon and hand-polished all the moving parts, taking extra care with the two triggers. An 18-karat gold bead was fitted to the front sight blade.

"No other alteration was made to the metal parts.

"I used the measurements of the bespoke shotgun you thought you were being fitted for on this firearm. A stock fits the shooter at five points: the butt against the shoulder, cheekbone ledge mated to the comb, trigger hand gripping the wrist—or pistol grip, as it is called in your country, index finger touching the trigger blade, and the leading hand gripping the forearm. Those were all reworked to your personal body configuration.

"We shortened the butt half an inch, reduced the swell at the wrist slightly, and added a virtually imperceptible thumb groove. It is invisible to the naked eye, but you shall feel it as you mount the weapon. Finally, the stock was given a hand-rubbed oil finish. This SMG should fit you like a glove, sir.

"These subtle adjustments should enable you to get off your first round a split second faster."

Capt. McKoy said, "Important in a dangerous encounter."

Col. Randal brought the Beretta M-38 to his shoulder—perfect fit. Not that he had experience with hand-built custom rifles or shotguns. All of his had been one-size-fits-all military issue or hand-me-down guns when he was growing up.

Standing next to him with a cigar in his teeth, Capt. McKoy was studying the weapon's inspection. He said, "Rack the slide, John, then click it on semi-auto."

Col. Randal reached up and worked the charging handle. The action ran buttery smooth. The semiautomatic trigger broke crisp, with little take-up or noticeable overtravel. He racked the action again and pulled the full auto trigger—same result.

He handed the submachine gun to Capt. McKoy to inspect.

"I like it."

Capt. McKoy studied the SMG and racked the charging handle fast several times. "Beretta is the oldest firearms maker in the world. Amazing what a few tweaks by a skilled smith can do to an already excellent weapon to optimize performance. This is one fine short- to medium-range fighting weapon."

The Master Gun Fitter said, "Not our normal work order, Colonel. However, Westley Richards started out in the 1830s making muskets for the British Army. The staff was delighted to return to our roots and take part in a project for such a distinguished military officer as yourself.

"I shall have your Beretta placed in one of our traveling cases for you, sir."

As the Master Gun Fitter was walking away, Capt. McKoy said, "Georgie Patton got hisself in a little trouble over in Sicily, John."

"Oh, what happened?"

"Ole 'Blood and Guts' shot a Sicilian mule that was balkin' and blockin' a bridge holding up his tank column. Then a little while later. he slapped a couple a' malingerers at a field hospital. Press got wind of it. Now the general's in hot water with the American general public."

"Really?"

"Hard to say what your average reader is maddest about—slappin' the soldiers or shootin' the mule. But they're callin' for General Patton to be relieved a' command."

Col. Randal said, "He's our best general."

Capt. McKoy said, "Heard you got in some hot water yourself. Donovan chewing you out for going on that canoe raid. What a hoot—first thing when he gets back to Washington, Wild Bill's goin' straight to the White House, marchin' into the Oval Office and takin' credit for OSS sinkin' that enemy destroyer, mark my words . . ."

Col. Randal interrupted him, changing the subject, "Now's not the time, this isn't the place—you and I need to talk."

"Sounds a tad ominous."

"You've got a story to tell me, *Captain*."

"Well, maybe I do, and maybe I don't."

10
POLITICIANS PLAYING AT SOLDIERS

COLONEL JOHN RANDAL WAS IN THE LIVING ROOM OF MAJOR the Lady Jane Seaborn's suite at the five-star Mena House Hotel. The place was not really built like a hotel. It was a luxurious detached townhouse with its own private pool. Lady Jane kept it on a permanent basis. In fact, she kept two—one for guests. Prime Minister Winston Churchill stayed in one of them on his trips to Cairo.

King and Captain Pamala Plum-Martin were there having cocktails prior to the night's festivities at the Kit-Kat Club. The Merc was in a tuxedo. Capt. Plum-Martin was wearing a slinky silver evening dress. Col. Randal had decided he needed the beautiful pilot in the room when he met with The Three.

He wanted there to be no question that the women of Raiding Forces were under his protection. The new Criminal Royalty needed to see for themselves who the primary female players were. Brandy Seaborn and Captain Penelope "Legs" Honeycutt Parker, who were in the other bedroom getting ready, would be part of the entourage as well.

Lady Jane came out of the master bedroom in a snakeskin-tight, black evening gown with a high Chinese collar that left her tanned shoulders bare. She slid onto the couch next to Col. Randal. The two of them would be going out to dinner on her favorite floating Nile River restaurant following the business at the Kit-Kat. He had booked a private dining room for just the two of them.

King and Capt. Plum-Martin also had reservations on the boat.

Brigadier General William "Wild Bill" Donovan and Brigadier Dudley Clarke arrived with the ice-blonde Norwegian Rikke "Rocky" Runborg. She had been at A-Force Headquarters transmitting a coded message containing Top Secret intelligence information to Field Marshal Erwin Rommel, the commander of Army Group B in Italy. It gave the exact time and place of the Allied landing at Salerno, and identified the 36th "Texas" Division as the spearheading element of the invasion. The text was encoded, so Rocky had no idea what the message contained. She simply tapped it out so that the Nazi recipient would recognize her keystroke signature.

The purpose of the exercise was a highly sophisticated A-Force deception designed to rehabilitate Miss Runborg's credibility with the Field Marshal. She had provided him false information on two previous occasions that caused Rommel to be out of the country away from his command at the precise moment the British launched major offensives. The hope was if Brig. Clarke played his cards right, he might be able to use Rocky to deceive Rommel again at some later time and place.

Tonight's message was carefully timed to be received prior to the landings but too late for the Germans to evaluate the content, determine validity of the intelligence, and react to it. In any event, Field Marshal Rommel had been called away to Berlin and was not present when Rocky's message arrived at his Army Group B Headquarters. It was not read immediately, which was even better because it would cause a lot of "what if" second-guessing when it was eventually read.

Brig. Clarke hoped that the invasion taking place exactly when and where Rocky predicted, spearheaded by the division she correctly identified, would mean that no one on the German side would ever question her believability in the future. Rocky would be golden.

An asset capable of putting false intelligence on a German Field Marshal's desk—that the recipient would accept as fact—was priceless.

Brig. Gen. Donovan and Brig. Clarke were flying out as soon as the sit-down with The Three was concluded tonight. Wing Commander Tony Dudgeon was standing by with a specially modified, long-range, high-speed Royal Air Force Mosquito to fly them to Sicily. The plane could carry two PAX by not taking along a navigator and having one passenger ride in the bomb bay.

Unknown to Col. Randal, because he did not have a Need to Know, the timing of Wild Bill's visit to Cairo had originally been planned for him to be able to observe OPERATION AVALANCHE, the invasion of Italy at Salerno.

OSS interest in AVALANCHE was in part because it was being covered by an A- Force/OSS deception plan, OPERATION BOARDMAN, designed to mislead the Axis into believing the real invasion would take place on Sardinia. This was the first joint deception operation ever carried out between Great Britain and the United States. For OSS, it was a big development—stepping up to the big league.

Or maybe not. Brig. Clarke did not like to share. He simply gave the impression he was. And that was a deception. With the commander of A-Force, it was never wise to take anything at face value.

When the meeting tonight with The Three came up unexpectedly, it was decided that LEAF EATER took priority over AVALANCHE. The anti-diamond smuggling operation was that important. The generals reluctantly pushed back their time of departure until later that night.

Brig. Gen. Donovan said, "While you were away, Colonel, the Badoglio government overthrew Mussolini. Then last night, the Italians surrendered unconditionally. They are out of the war."

Lady Jane laughed. "Perfect, now I can quit obsessing that Benito will show up for dinner unannounced on Castelrozzo."

Brig. Clarke said, "Il Duce has been arrested and is currently being held in an undisclosed location. You need not worry—the cad shall not be visiting your island getaway anytime soon. Mussolini will be fortunate if he is not publicly executed."

Brig. Gen. Donovan said, "Ever since the dictator was deposed, the Italian Government has been attempting to negotiate an armistice with the Allies. Unfortunately, Roosevelt's impromptu announcement at the Casablanca summit, when he blurted out that the Allies would never accept anything but 'unconditional surrender,' threw a monkey wrench into any negotiations.

"The Italians were backed into an all-or-nothing corner." Brig. Clarke said, "Lucky for us they caved in."

Brig. Gen. Donovan said, "Now the Germans have been put on notice. It's a fight to the death for the Third Reich. No armistice. No negotiated end of hostilities. All because of a slip of the lip."

Brig. Clarke said, "The President became swept up in the moment—carried away by the desire for victory. No one knew the declaration was coming. Possibly not even the great man himself."

"It's been voiced by FDR's critics, of which I'm not one," Brig. Gen. Donovan said, "that his grand strategy for WWII can be written on the inside of a matchbook cover. I brief the President every morning when I'm in Washington and know firsthand that's not true.

"That stipulated, he should never have decided the endgame of the war without first consulting with his allies."

"Typical result when politicians play at soldiers," Brig. Clarke said.

Brig. Gen. Donovan said, "Something else happened while you were trying to win the war single-handed, Colonel. Doug Fairbanks and his Beach Jumpers carried out a simulated landing on the Italian mainland in hopes of causing the Germans to reposition some of their divisions—an A-Force deception idea well worth the attempt.

"Failed to fool the Nazis into taking action, but a few nights later Commander Fairbanks redeemed himself by capturing a radar station on the island of Capri, utilizing his BJ's and the Scout Company of the 509th Parachute Infantry Battalion. Now Doug is ensconced in the villa of Edda Ciano, Countess of Cortellazzo and Buccari.

Brig. Clarke said, "Il Duce's daughter—the Mussolinis are not enjoying much luck with the family real estate portfolio these days."

Lady Jane said, "Hollywood A-list matinee idol of the silver screen turned true action swashbuckler—who would have believed it so?"

Col. Randal said, "Fairbanks is a natural leader."

Brig. Gen. Donovan said, "Since the Beach Jumpers are attached to Raiding Forces and Commander Fairbanks is in charge of a special operations unit suggested to the U.S. Navy by Dudley, it would be fair to say that the three of us are already peripherally involved in the war's next invasion."

This was the first time Col. Randal had been given any indication of what might happen after Sicily. He was not cleared to know about AVALANCHE, even though his Duck Patrol had been conducting pinprick raids along the coast of Sardinia for the last two weeks. Now it was clear those operations were a deception, not the preliminary intel gathering prior to an invasion he had been led to believe it was. The war was marching on.

And getting a lot bigger.

Lieutenant Colonel Sir Terry "Zorro" Stone and his long-time semi-steady girlfriend, Red, arrived. The stunning Clipper Girl was in a dark green evening dress. Green definitely looked good on Red. They, too, had reservations on the exclusive Nile riverboat restaurant later.

Red had flown in after having personally delivered a consignment of King's Swiss watches to Vice Air Marshal Sir Arthur Tedder, commander of Mediterranean Air Command, at his headquarters on the top floor of the St. George Hotel in Algiers. She came bearing a deposit slip to a numbered Swiss bank account belonging to King, confirming a payment made by the Royal Air Force. The Merc was the beneficiary of a big payday, RAF had their precision watches, and Raiding Forces enjoyed the continued goodwill of the senior Allied air officer.

GG, who was serving as Lady Jane's bartender tonight, brought the couple martinis.

Lt. Col. Stone said, "Remember John Rock from the Central Landing School—advocated gliders as the way of the future for airborne operations, old stick?"

Col. Randal said, "I do."

"Promoted to command the Glider Regiment."

"Good for him."

"Actually, not so much. Colonel Rock was killed in a training accident — glider crash."

Captain "Geronimo" Joe McKoy and Waldo Treywick rolled in, with long thin cigars in their teeth, unlit. Capt. McKoy was in full Wild West regalia—to include his favorite pair of .45 Colt Single Action Peacemakers in shoulder holsters. He did not even attempt to conceal them under his yellow buckskin jacket. Both pistols' ivory-stocked handles stuck out for everyone to see.

That was the idea.

Waldo was looking sleek as a seal in a beautifully tailored tux, showing a slight budge under his left shoulder—his custom Smith & Wesson Fitz Special .38–44. The handgun was a gift from Col. Randal. For an ex-ivory poacher, former slave, and almost-famous South African army scout in the Great War who had spent time in Portuguese and Kenyan jail cells awaiting trial for poaching and mass homicide, he wore his money well.

Waldo was acquitted on the murder charge because he was innocent—but he *had* poached that Portuguese ivory.

Tonight, he was taking sex bomb Rikke Runborg—who may or may not have been an agent for the Nazis and the Russians earlier in the war and was now working exclusively, it was hoped, for A-Force—to dinner on the floating palace following the meeting at the Kit-Kat.

Waldo and Rocky had . . . a relationship.

Capt. McKoy was saying, "Clyde Barrow, a' Bonnie and Clyde fame, carried a Fitz Special too, only his was based on a .45 Colt New Service revolver."

Waldo said, "You get it after you and your Texas Ranger sidekick took 'em out?"

"Naw, Frank Hamer did. Nice handgun, though. I'd a' liked to had it."

Major Jack Dance and Captain Stephanie Fawcett-Tatum were next to walk in. Col. Randal had informed the 10th Ranger Battalion commander that Capt. Fawcett-Tatum was to be his lunch companion later in the week, and in typical Ranger take-no-prisoners fashion, Maj. Dance marched straight to the Operations Room and asked her out on a date for that night. Why wait? Since the tall, glamorous brunette was responsible for organizing the other reservations on the floating restaurant, she suggested they dine there too.

The two made an attractive couple.

Col. Randal said, "Stephanie, back room with me at the Kit-Kat. Red, you too. Waldo, have Rocky in there as well."

He wanted—overkill.

James "Baldie" Taylor and Cuthbert Bowlby came next. They were followed shortly by Captain Billy Jack Jaxx. The idea was to have a short strategy session and then stagger everyone's departure for the Kit-Kat. The Three would be kept waiting in club manager Moe's office with Major Sammy Sansom, while Mr. Big and the other attendees arrived in what appeared to be a random fashion but was, in fact, a carefully choreographed sequence planned with military precision.

Nothing tonight would be by chance.

Capt. Jaxx said, "Sergeant Major Beckwith is forming the troops at the club as we speak, sir."

Jack Cool would be escorting Mandy, Beverly, Lieutenant Bentley St. Ledger, and Cat to the floating palace after the meeting. Captain Preston Butterfield III, Captain Roy Kidd, and Captain Cord Granger were planning to link up with them there. Once word had spread that Col. Randal and Lady Jane were dining on the riverboat, everyone made plans to be on board, to include Capt. McKoy, who was bringing one of the Kit-Kat's expatriate Hungarian dancers.

If the Nile Riverboat sank, Raiding Forces was going to be out of business.

Capt. McKoy said, "John, you got a minute?"

The two moved to the far end of the room and leaned against the wall in a corner. Col. Randal said, "You first."

Capt. McKoy said, "Probably better if you did. That way maybe we can cut down on what could be a long-winded story."

Col. Randal said, "The Arizona National Guard, with add-on units from Nevada and New Mexico, is forming a mechanized cavalry division for Federal Service. The governor of Arizona has formally requested the War Department appoint you to command it, *Major General* McKoy."

Capt. McKoy said, "Yeah, well, that's true. But I turned it down. I'm stayin' on in Raiding Forces."

Col. Randal said, "Don't you feel you should have informed me of your true status instead of masquerading as a captain all these years?"

Capt. McKoy said, "The governor and I are ole' quail huntin' buddies. When he got elected, he appointed me to command the State Guard to give us an excuse to travel 'round checking on National Guard armories and huntin' birds. That way our huntin' trips could be subsidized by the state legislature because we was pullin' those inspections."

Col. Randal said, "Any idea how hard to believe that story sounds?"

Capt. McKoy said, "State Guard's different from the National Guard. If the NG's get mobilized for Federal Service, the State Guard moves in to man their armories. They're placeholders—good men, 4-Fs, veterans too old for this one, a few Boy Scouts too young, and some people who never served a day but wanna do their part.

"Point is, they ain't real fightin' soldiers and I ain't a real major general."

Col. Randal said, "So, why are you calling yourself a captain?"

"Showmanship. Major General 'Geronimo' Joe McKoy doesn't have the same snap."

Col. Randal said, "Maybe you would like to explain being a graduate of the Command & General Staff School *and* the Army War College. What else might you be leaving off your resumé, General?"

Capt. McKoy said, "The U.S. Marshal's Service has real generous annual leave. Problem is, you have to use it or lose it. The governor found out I hadn't taken any in a while. Man's serious about our bird huntin' so he shipped me off to military school right then and there. That way, no one could ever question my bona fides. "No big deal. Part a' the classwork's done by correspondence—a moron coulda passed."

Col. Randal said, "You expect me to believe you turned down command of a cavalry division to stay in Raiding Forces?"

"Yeah, John, I do—if you think about it. There's no guarantee an amalgamated National Guard outfit from three different states will ever get deployed overseas. No tellin' how long it'd take to train a lash-up like that. You got your individual training, unit training, and combined arms training. Take at least a year, probably more.

"I might get the division whipped into shape, ready to go, then at the last minute the War Department could bring in a West Point ring tapper to replace me before shippin' out—it happens.

"Besides, and this was the clincher, I talked the deal over with Wild Bill. He informed me in no uncertain terms that the U.S. Army has plenty a' generals standin' in line beggin' to honcho a division. Me runnin' LEAF EATER—and this is a direct quote—'Is a hell of a lot more critical to the big picture.'"

"General Donovan said that?"

"Affirmative."

"Don't you believe that's worth me knowing?"

"Yeah, it is. I've been meanin' for us to have a talk, only you've been pretty busy. And I couldn't figure out how to go about it without you feelin' like I've been tryin' to pull the wool over your eyes."

"You have been."

"Yeah, maybe I have, but I had my reasons. I'd appreciate it if you could see your way clear to keepin' this State Guard major general stuff between the two a' us. Let me stay more or less incognito, serving in the ranks."

Col. Randal said, "Genie's out of the bottle."

Capt. McKoy said, "You're probably right. Even so, if it's OK with you, I'd like to keep goin' by 'Captain.' Zargo uses 'Major,' and he's a full colonel in the Greek Army."

Col. Randal said, "I'll think about it."

Capt. McKoy said, "You know after the war's over, I got me a slot comin' open for a brigadier general—like huntin' birds, don't you, John?"

CAPTAIN "GERONIMO" JOE MCKOY STOOD UP IN FRONT OF the group in the living room. The OIC of OPERATION LEAF EATER did not waste time with toastmaster-type pleasantries. He immediately began issuing orders.

"We're going to roll out to the Kit-Kat at fifteen-minute intervals. Jack, soon as I finish up, you take off.

"Waldo, you're out second. I want you in there with Major Sansom briefing The Three, making real sure they understand exactly how important everybody is as they come in.

"Terry, you and Red can take off after they do.

"Jim, you and Cuthbert are out after them.

"Then General Donovan, you and Brigadier Clarke, you go. I'll follow you two. Colonel, you wait here fifteen more minutes with your entourage before you take off.

"Now remember, the idea tonight is to impress these criminals—maybe scare 'em a little if we can. Ladies, be sunshine and happiness as you arrive, turn it on good—give it everythin' you got. Then when Jack and his boys come stormin' in with their Tommy guns, I want you to look those three baby rapists dead in the eyes, like you'd like to come over the table to cut their hearts out with a knife right there.

"Middle Eastern crime bosses ain't used to women starin' 'em down. In fact, they ain't used to women bein' present in their meetings at all. I'm hopin' havin' you in the room will throw 'em off their game.

"John, as soon as you sit down, make your speech. Blunt and in their faces. King, I want you standing behind the Colonel, cocked and locked, lookin' like the hardcase in a tux you are.

"As soon as John finishes talkin', on signal from Flanigan and Sergeant Major Beckwith, who'll be at the doors front and back a' Moe's office, the cavalry will arrive in force, chargin' in from both ends and makin' what we in law enforcement like to describe as 'a dynamic entry.'

"When everybody's crammed in, we'll do another big time stare down—nobody sayin' a word. Then Colonel, you stand up and exit the room, followed by the women, King, and Flanigan.

"From that point on, we're in business but we ain't friends. The mistake we made last time was bein' sociable with our underworld business associates. This time around, we're the senior partner, and they don't have a vote.

"Any questions?" There were none.

As briefed, departure for the Kit-Kat commenced immediately and went like clockwork. Mena House had limousines standing by for those who needed transportation. Last out was Colonel John Randal, Major the Lady Jane Seaborn, Mandy, and Beverly in the white Rolls- Royce, with Brandy, Major Jack Dance, Captain Penelope Honeycutt-Parker, and Rocky following in one of the limos, and King and Captain Pamala Plum-Martin behind them in another.

Major A. W. "Sammy" Sansom had provided a police escort.

The small convoy raced through the night, with lights flashing, sirens screaming. There was little chance The Three would be able to hear them arrive since they were waiting in Moe's sound-proofed office. However, they could be expected to have people stationed outside the Kit- Kat who would report to their bosses later.

In the car, Beverly said, "OK, you're not going to shoot anybody tonight, are you, Johnny—no need to put cotton in our ears?"

"I might shoot Captain McKoy."

Lady Jane said, "Why would you do that?"

"The old cowboy's been a major general in the Arizona State Guard from the day you brought him to Seaborn House and he's never said a word."

Mandy said, "That is a big secret to keep."

Beverly said, "Seriously, does that mean we call him General McKoy now?"

Col. Randal said, "Negative, wants to be called Captain—claims Major General 'Geronimo' Joe McKoy doesn't have as much 'snap.'"

Lady Jane laughed. "Agreed."

The parking lot of the Kit-Kat Club was packed with staff cars, jeeps, and taxis. Moe was standing outside on the steps waiting for Col. Randal's party to arrive. He waved for Flanigan to pull in and park at the curb by the front door.

Everyone stepped out of their cars, with the women adjusting their evening gowns and the men touch-checking their sidearms. Moe led out, followed by King, then Col. Randal with Lady Jane close behind, almost at his side. The rest of the women followed, with Flanigan bringing up the rear. Maj. Dance peeled off to link up with Captain Billy Jack Jaxx, who was inside enjoying the show along with half of the members of Raiding Forces who were in Cairo at the time and some who had made it in from Alexandria. The other half were around back behind the club, standing by with Sergeant Major Mike "March or Die" Mikkalis.

Loud, raucous music was blaring. It was pitch-black in the main room except for a spotlight playing on Rita and Lana. The girls were performing an act that would have gotten them arrested in Calcutta, where nothing done live onstage in front of a paying audience was illegal. Most of the men and more than a few of the women in the crowd were on their feet catcalling and whistling.

The Kit-Kat was rocking.

Col. Randal's file wound its way through the tables. Moe led them down the long, dimly lit hall to his private office. Capt. Jaxx had gone ahead of them and was standing outside the closed door, waiting.

Moe turned around and made his way back to the main room. King glanced over his shoulder. Lady Jane squeezed Col. Randal's hand.

Col. Randal said, "Let's do this."

Capt. Jaxx opened the door, then stood aside. King led in Col. Randal and the file of women. After Flanigan went by, bringing up the rear, Jack Cool closed the door. The tough ex- London Special Branch Policeman took up position just inside, blocking the exit. He was cradling a .45 Thompson submachine gun.

At the far end of the room, Master Sergeant Mack Beckwith was at the back door leading to the outside of the building. He was also holding a .45 Thompson submachine gun.

In the center of the room was a long table covered with a white tablecloth. The Three and all the dignitaries were seated down the far side with Brigadier General William "Wild Bill" Donovan on one end and Brigadier Dudley Clarke at the other.

On the near side were empty chairs.

Col. Randal took a seat at the center of the table, directly across from the gangsters. Lady Jane sat to his immediate left. She draped her arm over his shoulder with her scarlet nails splayed on his chest, staring across the table at the gangsters like a magnificent leopard studying her prey.

The rest of the women took their places.

Lady Jane turned her head and whispered in Col. Randal's ear, "Game on."

This new batch of criminals were in their mid- to late forties. Thugs in suits. The gangsters were star-struck by the assemblage at the table. At least they had been until Col. Randal showed up with his entourage of females.

Powerful men respect powerful men. Instinctively, The Three knew the officer sitting across from them with the scar on his left cheek was a serious man. Not someone to be taken lightly.

Col. Randal said, "All five of your predecessors are dead. They were foolish, blinded by greed. Only saw what they had to sacrifice in order to do business with our organization—not how much they stood to profit.

"But that was not why I killed them.

"One questioned our business deal, which is not allowed. He was shot right here at this table. The others caused, or knew about beforehand, the harm that came to Lady Seaborn.

"Understand, the women of Raiding Forces are under my protection. Which means they are under *your* protection. Make that known. If anything should happen to any one of them, I will kill you all, then take your money and property for myself, and then turn your families out into the street."

MSgt. Beckwith and Flanigan swung open the doors. A flood of Raiding Forces personnel armed to the teeth with .45 Thompson submachine guns, wearing an assortment of handguns and deadly-looking fighting knives, came storming in. By any definition, making a "dynamic entry."

The Raiders took up position, crowded three-deep all around the walls.

Jack Cool had overachieved, as per usual. Lieutenant Colonel Sir Terry "Zorro" Stone, Maj. Zargo, the two Lovat Scouts, Captain Butch "Headhunter" Hoolihan, Maj. Dance, Major Duke Slater, Major Travis McCloud, Major Taylor Corrigan, Murph the Surf, Captain Roy Kidd, Captain Preston Butterfield III, Captain "Pyro" Percy Stirling, Major Baltimore "Mongo" Farquhar, Captain Roy "Mad Dog" Reupart, Captain "Dynamite" Dick Coogan, all of SOG, the remnants of the old Ranger Patrol, GG . . .

Even Rita and Lana left the dance floor to make an appearance, holding Tommy guns and looking like she-devils.

The Three were dazed and confused. Courtesies have to be observed. Manners are manners. Even in the underworld. What should have been the pinnacle of their criminal careers had turned into a frightening roller coaster ride.

The Three had been promised unprecedented military, police, and intelligence service protection. With that kind of relationship, the gangsters had every reasonable expectation that they would be able to forge a vast racketeering network throughout the Middle East. The possibilities were limitless.

Then, women were brought in to their meeting—a mortal insult. Among top-tier mobsters in the Middle East, the protocol for meetings was strictly "men only." There were no exceptions.

The Three realized Col. Randal was not interested in courtesy or manners. He had no respect for them. The lives of their families had been threatened, which was something else simply not done.

And it was a real threat—The Three knew one when they heard it.

If that was not bad enough, a member of the original Big Five, a man they had long known, respected, and feared, had been shot dead right in this room at this very table for nothing more than asking the wrong question.

What had they gotten themselves into? This was supposed to be the big night when they took over the criminal cartel in Cairo. Now it had come crashing down on their heads.

Col. Randal said, "When our business is concluded, you will be rich or dead—your call." Then he stood up and exited the room. His entourage followed.

FLANIGAN DROVE COLONEL JOHN RANDAL AND MAJOR THE Lady Jane Seaborn to the pier where the floating restaurant docked. So many Raiding Forces personnel had made reservations for the same time this evening that the skipper had made the unusual decision to return and pick everyone up instead of requiring them to take water taxis out to the boat. Even though there was a war on and blackout restrictions were in effect, no one in the Cairo area paid attention to them. The double-decker was lit up like a Christmas tree.

As they were boarding, Col. Randal said, "How do you think it went, Captain?"

Captain "Geronimo" Joe McKoy, who had a date with a spectacular Hungarian expatriate, said, "Just fine, John. When Lady Jane draped her arm over your shoulder and scratched your blouse like she owned you—violated a lot a' protocols."

Waldo said, "I thought those criminals was gonna have a stroke."

Col. Randal said, "It was a nice touch."

Lady Jane said, "I do own you."

Capt. McKoy said, "After you left the building, things kept goin' south for our new associates. Major Sansom showed 'em a movie the Cairo Police Department produced. A real attention-getter."

"What about?"

"The Egyptian Secret Police filmed their interrogations of the Big Four's families. Wasn't somethin' I'd recommend. Even for mature audiences with strong stomachs. The film showed the families all finally being loaded into the back of a cattle trailer stark naked. Then they were driven to Manshiyat Nasser—one-a' the most notorious slums in Cairo, which means the entire world, and kicked out about 0200 hours.

"Your typical crowd a' lowlife scumbag malefactors was millin' around in the public street wall-to-wall like they normally do at that time a' night there in what's known as "Garbage City." The mob swarmed those people like ants the second they hit the ground.

"Crime don't always pay like they say." Beverly said, "Extreme!"

Lady Jane said, "Something out of a horror movie."

Capt. McKoy said, "Yeah, it was, but I think The Three got the message we ain't to be trifled with, and that's a good thing."

Col. Randal said, "Yes, it is."

The group walked up the gangway, laughing and having a good time. While deadly serious, the nights' work was mostly play-acting. Everyone enjoyed having fun at The Three's expense.

Col. Randal and Lady Jane were whisked away to a small private dining room complete with a glittering crystal chandelier and wall of windows looking out at the Nile. It was the same one where he had given her the diamond ear studs. And on another occasion, her Sheba Diamond promise ring.

After they placed their order and drinks arrived, Col. Randal said, "Jane, there's something we have to talk about."

"Is there a problem?"

"There is—Mallory."

"What has he done now?"

"Mountbatten has been made Commander-in-Chief, Southeast Asia Command. Edwina convinced him to take Mallory along as a member of his staff. There are rumors they are having an affair."

"Edwina and Mallory or Louis and Mallory—or is it all three?"

"Edwina."

"Why are you telling me this?"

"Your husband sailed for Ceylon without signing the divorce decree."

"I shall hunt Mallory down to the ends of the earth and make him regret his insolence."

Col. Randal said, "Bold talk for a skinny, green-eyed brunette."

Lady Jane held up her ring so that the stone flared in the light cast by the chandelier, "As long as I have you and the Sheba Diamond—not necessarily in that order, I could care less about who Mallory sleeps with or what he does.

"He shall get his one day. Not signing the documents was no accident."

Col. Randal was relieved to see her sense of humor was intact. Even if he might come in second to a jewel with a sketchy provenance. There was no actual historical evidence that a queen named Sheba ever existed, much less owned the diamond Jack Cool called the "Sheba Rock."

Col. Randal said, "All right, then, we're good."

Lady Jane said, "That why you brought me to my favorite room on my favorite floating restaurant . . . to break unhappy news to me in a lovely setting?"

"Affirmative."

"In that case, we are *really* good."

"All right, then."

"I am not skinny."

"You could be a little skinny . . ."

Someone pounded on the door. There was a divan in each of the private rooms. As often as not, more was going on in them than dining. Discretion was advised before entering.

However, there was nothing discreet about this hammering.

Captain Stephanie Fawcett-Tatum called through the door, "John, a dispatch has been delivered for you marked URGENT EXPEDITE—EYES ONLY."

"Advance and be recognized."

Col. Randal opened the envelope and read:

```
C-47 TROOP TRANSPORTS TO ARRIVE YOUR LOCATION
0600 HOURS STOP HAVE THREE PATHFINDER TEAMS
ON RED ALERT TO BOARD STOP STAND UP THE 575
PIR FOR DEPLOYMENT TIME/DATE TO FOLLOW STOP
SIGNED DONOVAN
```

COLONEL JOHN RANDAL SAID, "STEPHANIE, GO GET TERRY, Travis and Billy Jack. Have them report to me here. Then, instruct the boat captain to return to the dock or call a water taxi for us—whichever is fastest."

"On the way, John."

Captain Billy Jack Jaxx wandered in as Captain Stephanie Fawcett-Tatum was rushing out. From across the dining room, he had observed her being handed an envelope by one of the ship's officers. Then, after reading the contents, she had hurriedly left her table. Curious, he had decided to trail along on the off chance that something interesting might develop.

Capt. Jaxx had the uncanny ability to be in the right place at the right time.

Col. Randal handed him the flimsy, "Put your Pathfinders on STAND-BY READY. Raiding Forces had three phases of alert: STAND-BY, STAND-BY READY, and RED ALERT. Since the unit was a Quick Reaction Force, SOG was always on STAND-BY ALERT. If away, officers and NCOs were required to check in by phone every hour, and at night leave a number and address where they could be reached. Troops checked in every two hours.

STAND-BY-READY meant the mission was a go, only the exact line-of-departure (LD) time had not been issued. All personnel had to be prepared to move out with weapons, ammunition, and equipment, to include parachutes, unless specifically ordered to leave the chutes behind.

RED ALERT meant move to the departure airfield or boat dock, depending on the mission, and board for immediate deployment.

Capt. Jaxx said, "I only have two Pathfinders teams, sir."

"Put together a composite team, utilizing your other SOG people. Or you can pick any man in Raiding Forces. If you need help, get back to me."

"Bronc Blackwell only sent two sets of the new Eureka DZ marking devices, sir." Col. Randal said, "You'll work something out. I've got confidence in you, stud."

"I'll lead the provisional team personally, sir."

Capt. Jaxx departed and proceeded straight to the bridge. Once there, he showed impressive but highly suspect credentials to the skipper, a long retired Royal Navy officer. Access to the riverboat's radio, which he needed to send a coded message to RFHQ, was instantly forthcoming.

When given an order, the young Raiding Forces captain could be counted on to execute it with alacrity. No matter what obstacle stood in the way. That was why he was a young Raiding Forces captain—possibly the youngest officer in his grade in the U.S. Army.

Major Travis McCloud arrived in the private dining room, closely followed by Lieutenant Colonel Sir Terry "Zorro" Stone. Captain Stephanie Fawcett-Tatum slipped back inside and made eye contact with Col. Randal and nodded to let him know arrangements had been made for the riverboat to return to the pier.

Col. Randal ordered, "Stand fast, Stephanie, I want you wired in on this."

He handed the flimsy to Lt. Col. Stone, who scanned the message, then passed it to Maj. McCloud.

Col. Randal said, "Terry, you're responsible for getting the 1/575th and 10th Rangers assembled, organized, armed, and equipped, then transported to the Departure Airfield at the designated time."

Lt. Col. Stone said, "Problematic—some of the men are scattered along the Turkish coastline, living aboard LSF schooners. Others are on one or the other of the six caique patrols we have out raiding islands."

Col. Randal said, "Get with Admiral Ransom and have him arrange return to base transport for as many people as possible."

Lt. Col. Stone said, "Be advised, old stick, the regiment will be substantially understrength at wheels up."

Both officers knew the 575th PIR had been less than one third the size of a TO&E parachute infantry regiment the day it had arrived in Egypt. In addition, it had taken a high percentage of jump casualties on the Sicily drop from the excessive winds, and others had been wounded in action. Many of the WIAs had not been cleared for duty.

Col. Randal said, "Travis, you'll be my XO on this one. I'm flying out with the Pathfinders in the morning. Take charge of the regiment. I want Maj.

Dance, Maj. Corrigan, and Maj. Slater commanding battalions. I'll link back up with you as soon as I can."

Maj. McCloud said, "Any specific instructions, sir?"

"Standardize weapons and ammunition. Let the men carry the weapon of their choice as long as it's .30 caliber for rifles and 9mm for submachine guns—.30 caliber Carbines are authorized as well. Ammo compatibility will be crucial in the event we find it necessary to resupply by air."

"Yes, sir."

Col. Randal said, "808 demolitions and antitank mines the way we did on the Sicily drop."

"Wilco."

"Stephanie, contact Karen Montgomery," Col. Randal said. "I want her riggers traveling with the 575th when it loads out."

"Yes, sir."

Col. Randal said, "Terry, I need you to stay here running things."

Lt. Col. Stone said, "Actually, I would rather prefer to be involved in whatever mission the 575th has laid on."

Col. Randal said, "Negative, you're more valuable coordinating our relocation to ABC and getting our reorganization implemented."

"Under protest, old stick."

"Noted."

After everyone had left the room, Lady Jane said, "So much for our intimate dinner alone."

Col. Randal said, "We'll do it as soon as I get back, promise."

The two made their way down to the main dining room en route to the gangway as the riverboat was sliding alongside the pier. The Big Band orchestra, which normally played mellow mood music as the guests dined before switching to swing later in the evening for dancing, had varied their routine to honor a popular request. A United States Army Air Force B-24 bomber pilot, who tipped big, asked for a boogie-woogie song called *Low Down Dog.*

Cat was on a table, dancing.

11
JAKE THE SNAKE

MAJOR THE LADY JANE SEABORN'S WHITE ROLLS-ROYCE arrived at RFHQ after a high-speed run from the floating restaurant's pier. In the car were Colonel John Randal, Lady Jane, Captain Billy Jack Jaxx, and Captain Cord Granger. King and Captain Pamala Plum- Martin were following in another car. Major Jack Dance and Captain Stephanie Fawcett-Tatum were in a third car behind them. When Col. Randal walked inside RFHQ, Lieutenant Clint Hays and Lieutenant Chase Starrett were waiting in the Operations Room with Master Sergeant Mack Beckwith.

The place was humming with activity.

Lt. Hays reported to Capt. Jaxx, "SOG is assembling, sir. We have most of our people present—reasonably sober—for duty. The remainder are en route at this time."

When they were on pass, SOG had different reporting standards than the rest of Raiding Forces. The men had to notify RFHQ where they were staying. When they went out on the town, they had to leave a number where they could be reached. If they left one location and went to another, they had to call in with an updated number as soon as they arrived at the new place. The operators had to call in every hour on the hour between 0600 hours and 2200 hours and could never be more than an hour's drive away.

In typical Jack Cool style, Capt. Jaxx said, "Listen up, gentlemen, this is a Warning Order.

"Situation: We're in World War II.

"Mission: I have no idea what our mission is. Pathfinders typically precede the main body of paratroops to the designated areas of the initial airborne insertion to mark their Drop Zone. But then, you're Pathfinders and you know that.

"Execution: SOG has been ordered to supply three Pathfinder teams to someone, somewhere, for some reason, currently unknown.

"Concept of the Operation: SOG is to provide three Pathfinder teams to mark a DZ or DZs, at a time and place to be announced. Since we only have two teams, a composite third team will be organized under my command with Lieutenant Starrett acting as my XO.

"Command and Signal: I'll get back to you on that one.

"Administration and Logistics: Pathfinder Team 1 (PFT1), Captain Granger, and Pathfinder Team 2 (PFT2), Lieutenant Hays, should be good to go with their ready loadout gear. Pathfinder Team 3 (PFT3) will have to draw weapons, ammunition, parachutes, rations, etc. as soon as the team members have been designated. Lt. Starrett will get with the Sergeant Major upon conclusion of this briefing to select the PFT3 personnel."

"Questions? No? Take charge of your troops. Expect to go Red Alert around 0430 hours.

"Make it happen."

This was probably not how the originator of the Warning Order had envisioned one being issued. However, it did everything an alert should do. Capt. Jaxx's officers knew what was expected of them and when. They did not know where or what, but that was not his fault.

Col. Randal, standing off to the side observing, with one of Waldo's cigars in his teeth, was well pleased.

Capt. Jaxx said, "Lieutenant Starrett, PFT 3, eight men in the signals section, five men to provide security, plus our command party, fifteen man stick, one chalk. I want to sign off on the team roster prior to you pulling the people in."

SOG's motto was "Dirty Deeds Done Quick." Capt. Jaxx's Small Operations Group had their battle gear pre-positioned at all times in the SOG Ready Room at RFHQ, waiting for the word to go. His operators were untroubled by missions that came out of nowhere and needed to be executed immediately.

That is what they did.

The standing SOG joke was "as soon as possible, if not sooner." It was not a joke, really. Jack Cool's boys, which was what SOG called themselves, were always prepared to deploy by land, sea, or air on short notice.

Capt. Jaxx said, "Wheels up at 0600 hours."

Lt. Hays said, "In that case, Captain, my people have time to hit the rack and catch a few Zs."

Capt. Granger said, "Same here."

Capt. Jaxx said, "Do it."

Lt. Starrett and MSgt. Beckwith went to work selecting the personnel they needed for PFT3. Since SOG consisted of handpicked men from within Raiding Forces—all of whom were already handpicked men— the process consisted of identifying those Raiders who had previous Pathfinder experience, but were not currently assigned Pathfinder duty.

MSgt. Beckwith said, "The Colonel gave me instructions to put Fenwick and Ferguson on the team."

The news came as a surprise to Lt. Starrett. The two Lovat Scouts were Col. Randal's shadows on operations. They were always on standby to accompany him and never attached to teams or patrols or dispatched on missions. However, the two Highland snipers had more experience being first in than any of the SOG Pathfinders, so he was glad to add their names to the list.

The order was no surprise for MSgt. Beckwith . . . he knew exactly what it meant. "Pencil me in too, Lieutenant, I'm the PFT3 team sergeant."

IN THE THIRD-FLOOR SUITE, COLONEL JOHN RANDAL AND King were sitting at a table, field-stripping their personal weapons. Not that they needed cleaning. It was a professional habit of long standing with both men, something they did when they had a moment. Major the Lady Jane Seaborn came out of the bedroom barefoot, having changed into a soft, oversized white shirt and a pair of faded jeans. She took a seat on one of the chairs, with her knees up and arms wrapped around them.

Col. Randal said, "What I'm going to say next stays at this table except for CARD GAME players."

King looked up from the .22 Military Model D High Standard pistol he was dusting with a shaving brush.

Lady Jane's razor-sharp cheekbones tightened an extra couple of notches.

Col. Randal said, "The Arizona National Guard is being mobilized for Federal Service— 4th Cavalry Division. The governor of the state has requested 'Geronimo Joe' be assigned to take command. The old Arizona Ranger has held a major general's commission in the State Guard since before the war. A fact he has failed to mention."

Lady Jane said, "Marvelous—good for him."

"Here's the part we need to keep limited to CARD GAME," Col. Randal said. "When Donovan heard the news, Captain McKoy was informed in no uncertain terms that he's more valuable to the war effort remaining here in charge of LEAF EATER."

Lady Jane said, "Every senior officer dreams of commanding a division."

Col. Randal said, "Cavalry divisions typically contain 6,000 troopers—two brigades with supporting artillery. My question is, how could taking command of one *not* be a more important assignment than trying to stop the flow of diamonds to the Third Reich—something we all know is never going to happen.

King said, "Captain McKoy would make an outstanding division commander."

Lady Jane said, "Agreed."

Col. Randal said, "You're not answering my question."

"LEAF EATER has always been a mystery to me," Lady Jane said. "Some of the tasks we have been asked to accomplish simply do not make sense. The only thought that comes to mind is that the endgame is more important than we are cleared to know."

King said, "If LEAF EATER was only about diamond smuggling, we would have been issued detailed orders specifying how to accomplish our mission. The only specific instruction I personally am aware of is to eliminate the traffickers with extreme prejudice."

Lady Jane said, "Do you suppose the *traffickers* are the target—not the diamonds?"

King said, "Plausible."

Col. Randal said, "You could be right."

"Still, that does not explain why General Donovan attempted to discourage us from operating in Morocco," Lady Jane said. "Lots of traffickers there that we could liquidate to our hearts' content."

"Odds are OSS does not want LEAF EATER ruffling Spain's feathers," King said. "Spanish government officials will take exception to our 'disappearing' the local diamond dealers we suspect of treating with the Nazis. They pay a lot of *soborno* money."

Col. Randal said, "Sounds right."

Lady Jane said, "What if the motive behind OSS's desire to eliminate diamond traffickers is confined to Egypt and the Congo for some reason?"

King said, "You may be on to something, Lady Seaborn."

"So, you two are of the opinion that there's a possibility the smugglers themselves pose a threat to National Security greater than the diamonds reaching Germany? And for reasons unclear, OSS is only interested in eliminating traffickers in certain geographical locations?"

Lady Jane and King glanced at each other.

The Merc said, "Affirmative—it's possible, Chief."

Lady Jane said, "Agreed."

Col. Randal said, "All right, then, let's run it past CARD GAME—get their thoughts."

Lady Jane said, "It might cut through the intrigue if we knew the details of what transpired between General Donovan and General McKoy."

"Doesn't want to be called 'General,'" Col. Randal said.

Lady Jane laughed. "I shall address Joe McKoy by whatever rank I choose and there is nothing he can do about it—as far as I am concerned, he is a general."

Col. Randal said, "Why didn't I think of that?"

CAPTAIN BILLY JACK JAXX HAD GUESSED RIGHT. SMALL Operations Group Pathfinder Teams 1, 2 and 3 went to Red Alert at 0430 hours. That meant they loaded up on "deuce and a halves" with all their equipment and rolled out for the Departure Airfield at that time. Colonel John Randal, Master Sergeant Mack Beckwith, and King would be following them shortly. The Merc had all their gear loaded aboard a jeep out front of RFHQ.

Col. Randal was still in the Operations Room, huddled with Major Travis McCloud, Major Taylor Corrigan, Major Duke Slater, and Major Jack Dance—in his opinion, the most capable field grade unit commanders in the United States Army. They were going over the details of reconstituting the 575th Parachute Infantry Regiment (-) (Separate) (Special), "The Rangers." The regiment was currently scattered all over the Aegean, living aboard schooners or engaged in small-scale amphibious raiding operations.

Mostly, they were discussing a list of problems. Col. Randal had a long-standing policy of assembling his officers, issuing simple orders, then standing aside and letting them get on with planning the mission. The standing aside was the hard part.

Maj. Corrigan said, "We'll be lucky if we can load out with 600 men all up, sir."

TO&E strength of a Parachute Infantry Regiment was in excess of 3,000 jumpers. Not that the 575th had ever had that many people assigned. It had always consisted of only a single battalion, the 1/575th. Now, the regiment had been unofficially reinforced by the 10th Ranger Battalion   (-). One of its companies was detached—guarding Allied Force Headquarters in Algeria—and would most likely never rejoin.

Neither battalion had ever had more than 400 troops assigned, and were down to less than that now, due to casualties—killed, wounded, and men recovering from injuries mostly incurred during the jump on Sicily due to the excessive winds.

Raiding Forces had no ready pool of replacements, which meant there had not been any. Col. Randal said, "Do the best you can."

Maj. McCloud said, "To organize a third battalion, I'll have to cannibalize the other two. That means when formed, the 575th will consist of three battalions the size of standard line infantry rifle companies, sir."

Col. Randal said, "Understood—we'll go with what we have, not what we want."

Maj. Slater said, "Any word on our mission?"

Col. Randal said, "Negative—at this point I'm not even positive there is one."

Beverly walked up. She was straphanging on the flight with Col. Randal and the SOG Pathfinders. Her father, Colonel Sam Houston Blackwell—friends called him "Bronc"—had requested her presence in Sicily for what was described as a "special event."

Col. Blackwell was in theatre to support OPERATION AVALANCHE, the invasion of Italy, with a provisional group of C-47s from his training base in Big Spring, Texas-- the same composite unit that dropped the 575th during OPERATION HUSKY.

It was Bronc's planes arriving this morning to pick up the SOG Pathfinders. King came by, carrying the Texas beauty queen's duffel bag.

Col. Randal said, "Major Corrigan's going to be forming his 2/575th from scratch. That's a serious handicap. When you're deciding which people are to be assigned from the other two battalions, I want him to have the choice of who he wants. Better unit cohesion may result if you transfer platoons, or even companies, instead of individual officers and men."

Maj. McCloud said, "Yes, sir."

Col. Randal said, "I say again, when people are transferred from the 1/575th and 10th Ranger Battalion, Major Corrigan picks who he wants. I need to be absolutely clear about that before I leave."

This time Maj. Slater and Maj. Dance joined into the response, "Clear, sir."

Neither battalion commander was happy. Col. Randal did not blame them. Given the same order under similar circumstances, he would not have been either.

Command is a complex responsibility. Being in charge is not as easy as it sounds. The trick to giving orders is that they have to be the *right* orders.

No two COs approach the job the same way. Some commanders are disciplinarians, others micromanagers, while still others command by force of personality and lead by example. All three styles work.

In Raiding Forces, once Col. Randal issued an Operations Order, his people could not always count on him to be physically present to consult during the organizational phase. His officers and NCOs were often left to their own initiative. For example, this morning he was flying out and leaving them to accomplish a difficult, time-sensitive task, fully confident it would be done.

Loyalty and respect had to flow down from the top as well as up the chain-of-command in a high-speed outfit. His people knew he trusted them. An officer or NCO did not last long in Raiding forces if he did not.

Col. Randal walked over to where Vice Admiral Sir Randolph "Razor" Ransom was in conversation with Lieutenant Colonel Sir Terry "Zorro" Stone. They were strategizing on how best to return all the scattered 1/575th and 10th Ranger personnel to RFHQ. It was not going to be a simple task.

VAdm. Ransom was saying, "I have mobilized every Royal Navy Catalina and Walrus in Egypt. We shall fly as many men to RFHQ as we can. The 10th Motor Gunboat Flotilla has been alerted to stand-by for sailing orders. . . .

Col. Randal said, "I'm moving out to catch my flight. As soon as more information becomes available, I'll be in contact. Terry, I want you ready to arbitrate disputes about the organization of the 575th. There's bound to be disagreements.

"Admiral, back him up, if need be."

Lt. Col. Stone said, "As soon as you go wheels up, I plan to conduct an officer's call. It will be made perfectly clear I am in charge here. And that you have left specific instructions on what you expect to take place while you are away."

Col. Randal said, "Read my mind."

Lt. Col. Stone said, "It would be useful if you would actually issue me a few instructions, old stick."

Col. Randal said, "Make your best effort."

VAdm. Ransom said, "Do not waste one ounce of energy worrying about our being able to assemble your regiment, Colonel."

Col. Randal said, "Won't give it another thought, sir."

Outside, Beverly was behind the wheel of the jeep with King in the back. Col. Randal stepped aboard. They roared off into the dark for the Departure Airfield.

When the jeep pulled up on the tarmac, a lot of activity was taking place. The three C-47s from Big Spring Air Base had flown in and dropped off the floats for the Raiding Forces' Hudson and a team of aircraft mechanics to install them. Fuel trucks were in the process of finishing up topping off the Dakotas. Commands were ringing out. Sticks of Pathfinders were double timing to their plane, or "chalk", as it was called in paratrooper parlance.

The nickname came from the number of the aircraft being marked in chalk on the fuselage. That practice was helpful for easy identification when boarding during periods of limited visibility, high stress, and mass confusion. However, it did not always happen. There were no chalk numerals on the C-47s tonight.

Nevertheless, the planes were still referred to as chalks.

Capt. Jaxx was standing in the middle of the tarmac with Lieutenant Chase Starrett and MSgt. Beckwith, talking to Lieutenant Randy "Hornblower" Seaborn. A lieutenant—wearing a red British Airborne beret from the U.S. 509th Parachute Infantry Battalion—that Col. Randal had never seen before was there as well.

Lt. Seaborn had three Aldis lamps for PFT3, since it did not have the Eureka electronic equipment the other two teams used to guide the main body of troop carrier aircraft to the drop zones. The Aldis lamp, sometimes called a Morse lamp, was a navy optical signaling device designed for ship-to-ship and ship-to-shore communications. Tests had shown the light could be seen by an airplane from a distance of up to twenty-five miles.

It would take a brave band of PFT3 paratroopers to make a jump in the dark of night thirty minutes ahead of the arrival of the main body, then beam a bright light into the sky to guide them in. Sounded crazy. But that was the plan.

Col. Randal said, "So that's your idea? Drop in, and turn on an Aldis lamp that can be seen twenty-five miles away?"

Capt. Jaxx said, "It's Randy's, sir."

"Hornblower's not going to be standing on the DZ when you flip the switch, Jack."

Lt. Seaborn said, "Actually, sir, I shall be jumping in with PFT3 to supervise operation of the signal lamps."

"Not going to happen, Randy. You're the most valuable Sea Squadron officer I've got. Can't let you get killed doing something this crazy."

"You have a better solution, Colonel?"

"Negative, but at the funeral I'm telling Brandy you disobeyed my direct orders, stowed away on the plane, and made the jump without my knowledge."

MSgt. Beckwith said, "I'll back you up, sir."

The Sergeant Major knew a bad idea when he heard one.

Lt. Hornblower said, "If Mother knew of our plan to use Aldis lamps, she would be here right now, demanding I be bumped from the flight so she could be the one who parachuted in to operate them, sir, and you know it."

Col. Randal said, "Where do you want my party, Captain?"

Capt. Jaxx said, "You're with me—Chalk One, sir."

As they were walking across the tarmac to the C-47, Beverly laughed, "That went well. Always a turn-on to watch you take charge, Johnny. Really jacked up your troops."

Col. Randal said, "Glad to be a source of your entertainment."

Beverly said, "OK, seriously, lighting off an Aldis lamp at night a full half-hour before the cavalry arrives is insane."

"Roger that."

They boarded their aircraft. King was already inside, with Lovat Scouts Lionel Fenwick and Munro Ferguson. Beverly went up to the cockpit to visit. She knew a lot of the instructor pilots from her father's air base.

Capt. Jaxx arrived with Lt. Seaborn, Lt. Starrett, MSgt. Beckwith, and the paratroop officer from the 509th. The rest of PFT3 were on board. Beverly came back and took a seat next to Col. Randal. The loadmaster slammed the tail door shut. With no fanfare, the C-47 started rolling down the strip.

No matter how many times Col. Randal had taken off on a mission, this was always a good moment. As the plane was lifting off, he looked across the aisle out the far window. Lady Jane's white Rolls-Royce was parked on the side of the runway.

As soon as the plane reached cruising altitude, Lt. Seaborn and MSgt. Beckwith took five of the SOG Pathfinders to the tail to conduct training on the Aldis lamp. The idea was to rotate groups of five, until everyone on board had been familiarized with the signaling device. Learning how to perform your assignment on board the aircraft en route to a mission was not recommended procedure.

Capt. Jaxx said, "Colonel, this is Lieutenant Novak of the 509th Parachute Infantry Battalion. Jake was at Big Spring Army Airfield with Clint and Cord for the Pathfinder exercise Bronc conducted. He hitched a ride back here. Spent a few days partying with us in Cairo before heading back to the 509[th.]

"We're going to tell his boss he was here observing Raiding Forces small-unit tactics."

Lieutenant Jake Novak aka "Jake the Snake" said, "I was, sir—at the Kit-Kat."

Col. Randal said, "I've been looking forward to a briefing on Pathfinder developments coming out of the Big Spring exercise, but we never got around to it. Why don't you run it down for me, Lieutenant?"

Lt. Novak said, "Colonel Blackwell informed attendees that after his experience dropping your 575th PIR on Sicily, then observing the aftermath of the 82nd Airborne Division's mis-drop of its 505th, which was scattered over 60 square miles, followed by the disastrous shootdown of the 504th by the U.S. Navy on the second night when 24 C-47s were lost to friendly fire, he decided to incorporate airborne operational doctrine into his troop carrier pilot training curriculum.

"Colonel Blackwell discovered that no official doctrine had ever been adopted. For someone like Bronc, finding out a thing like that was like firing off a pistol in a crowded theatre at the same time the fire alarm went off, while the building was hit by a tornado."

Beverly laughed, "That's Daddy when he gets a burr under his saddle."

Lt. Novak said, "Not many senior officers like your father. Everyone calls him Bronc, even to his face. His troops worship him."

Capt. Jaxx said, "Bronc's definitely a stud."

Lt. Novak said, "One day, he loaded up his staff, flew to Ft. Benning, and they went through Jump School. Took the whole course, PT and all. After that, Colonel Blackwell placed observers at the forts hosting the 11th, 13th, 17th and 101st Airborne divisions, to stay current on new developments.

"Then Bronc asked the British 21 Independent Parachute Company to send over a training cadre to Big Spring Army Airfield to demonstrate how they mark DZs because he'd heard the Brits had some fancy new electronic equipment designed to revolutionize Pathfinding. That's when he invited your Raiding Forces Pathfinder Team Leaders and the 509th's Scout Company's Pathfinder platoon leader, meaning me, to participate in joint training. Bronc's smart. . . wanted us to share all our best tricks with each other.

"The problem was the 21st IPC has never actually Pathfindered a combat jump. My boys are all self-taught. And your Raiding Forces Pathfinders—the only people to have performed under actual battle conditions—are using rudimentary improvised locator devices like railroad flares, which the pilots in the main body can only see from a few miles out. Most USAAF pilots can't get close enough to their designated DZ to spot ground flares, sir.

"Bronc says the role of Pathfinders is to make up for poor navigation, so the purpose of the exercise is to give 'em something to see. That's where the 21st Independent Company brought something to the table, sir. They had signals equipment capable of transmitting a ground-to-air electronic signal from the DZ to guide the pilots to the Release Point.

"It works like magic."

Capt. Jaxx said, "Listen to this, Colonel—Jake had his Pathfinder platoon organized *before* the jump on Sicily and the 82nd Airborne refused to let him use it."

Col. Randal said, "That true?"

Lt. Novak said, "Yes, sir."

"Let's hear the story, Lieutenant. We've got a long flight."

Lt. Novak said, "The 82nd is the Army's premier airborne division. Only before Sicily, it had never made a combat jump or spent a single day in combat. The division is commanded by General Matthew B. Ridgway, who for reasons of his own never chose to go to the trouble to become parachute qualified, sir."

Capt. Jaxx said, "You're kidding."

Lt. Novak said, "Negative—for OPERATION HUSKY, General Ridgway ordered the 505th PIR and the 504th PIR to drop on Sicily on consecutive nights because there weren't enough troop transports available to make the jump in a single lift. Then, he landed by sea in an LCI and had to walk inland searching for his men to find out what happened—oh, well."

Col. Randal said, "Walked inland?"

Beverly said, "Seriously?"

Lt. Novak said, "Well, he may have had a jeep. General Ridgway reported to General Patton that he could only locate a little over four hundred out of the six thousand paratroopers dropped. The rest were scattered to the winds."

Col. Randal said, "Ridgway did that?"

Lt. Novak said, "Roger, sir. Most of the paratroopers straggled in later, but Sicily didn't do much for the 82nd's CG's reputation with his troops. Behind his back, the men in his parachute regiments call him the 'Non-Jumping General.'

"But that doesn't stop Ridgway or his straight leg staff from believing they know everything there is to know about airborne operations."

Col. Randal said, "When I toured Fort Benning last year, the 82nd Airborne wasn't interested in my input either."

Lt. Novak said, "The 509th PIB is the world's most experienced bad drop specialists. We made three jumps in North Africa, sir. I was on all of 'em, and not one went according to plan.

"On the initial jump, after flying 1,500 miles from England with the idea of hitting the silk over Tafaraoui Airport in Algeria, my plane was shot out of the sky when it strayed over Spanish territory. Talk about a combat jump. We bailed out as the airplane was going down in flames, then had to E&E across the border to keep from being interned for the duration.

"That's the reason Little Caesar—that's Colonel Raff, sir, our battalion commander— formed my Pathfinder Platoon. To prevent any more screw-ups."

Col. Randal said, "Operational necessity—same reason we organized ours."

Lt. Novak said, "After we'd fought in North Africa for six months, sir, the 82nd arrived fresh from the States and camped near our battalion at Oujda. The 509th was attached to it for administrative purposes.

"That did not end well.

"General Ridgway and Colonel Raff hated each other on sight, awful personality conflict. The 82nd Airborne wasn't interested in the lessons learned from the 509th's combat experience. Refused to even consider Pathfinders. The division G-3 called the idea a 'non-standard Limey concept,' sir.

"They liked to brag there's a right way, a wrong way, and a Ridgway. Relations between the 82nd and the 509th—the most combat experienced paratroop outfit we've got—were so bad the battalion wasn't even allowed to make the jump on Sicily."

Col. Randal said, "Doesn't make sense."

There was no reasonable explanation he could think of why the Commander General (CG) of an airborne division would not attend Jump School—if for no other reason than to make a personal demonstration of leadership. The idea that the CG could land by glider or come in later by sea sounded like an excuse. Or worse—that Maj. Gen. Ridgway was not brave enough to jump out of an airplane. A nickname like "The Non-Jumping General" was going to be hard to live down--- especially since Maj Gen. William Lee the legendary commander of the 101st Airborne Division "Screaming Eagles" was airborne qualified and an enthusiastic paratrooper.

A nickname like "The Non-Jumping General" was going to be hard to live down. Col. Randal said, "How would you rate the 82nd Airborne Division?"

Lt. Novak said, "The men in the parachute regiments are well-trained, highly motivated, hard-chargers, sir."

Col. Randal said, "And the officers?"

"The 505th PIR is commanded by Colonel James "Jumping Jim" Gavin—movie star handsome, lots of personality, leads from the front—on the fast track to General. The 504th's commander, Col. Ruben Tucker, is one of the youngest regimental commanders in the army. He's a tough paratrooper whose troops swear at him and by him, sir.

"Never had much contact with any of the battalion commanders, but the junior officers I worked with are outstanding.

"As for the 325th Glider Infantry Regiment, the 509th never trained with the glider riders, so there's not much I can tell you. Except to say they're not all volunteers, they're not authorized to wear the Airborne flash or jump boots, and they get no hazardous duty pay. There's a serious jumper versus legs pecking order in the division, sir."

Capt. Jaxx said, "I made one training landing in a Waco glider. I know I wouldn't want to repeat the experience. No matter what anybody says, that's hazardous duty, sir."

Lt. Novak said, "Division Artillery is commanded by General Maxwell Taylor. He's not jump qualified, either. Usually right after someone mentions his name, they always say 'he married well.' Not sure what that means, but that's what happens, Colonel."

Capt. Jaxx said, "People said the same thing about General Taylor when I was stationed at Fort Benning."

Lt. Novak said, "Like I said, I don't care for General Ridgway or his know-it-all straight leg staff, but the 82nd Airborne's a red-hot outfit, damn straight, sir."

Col. Randal said, "Beverly?"

"I like him."

"Jack?"

"That's a Rodge, sir."

"King?"

"Affirmative."

"Lieutenant Novak, how would you feel about assisting Captain Jaxx with his Pathfinders—show us how it's done in the Five-O-Nine?"

"You can do that, sir? Place me under Raiding Forces' operational control for a mission?"

"I can."

"My battalion commander's not going to be happy. Don't even want to think about what my company commander's going to say. *Hell, yes*, count me in, Colonel!"

THE THREE C-47 DAKOTAS ARRIVED AT AN UNDISCLOSED airfield on Sicily at 1630 hours. The airfield was crowded with C-47s belonging to the 61st Troop Carrier Group— the same outfit that had dropped the 504th and 505th Parachute Infantry regiments of the 82nd Airborne Division during OPERATION HUSKY.

Trucks were waiting to transport Captain Billy Jack Jaxx's troops to an empty hangar, where they could stage and await developments. Colonel Sam Houston "Bronc" Blackwell was there with a jeep. On his khaki blouse, below his Command Pilot Wings, he was sporting a gleaming pair of silver Jump Wings.

Col. Blackwell walked his talk. However, he was jealous. While Bronc sported two pair of wings, Beverly was wearing a tailored flight suit with *three* sets—Women's Air Force Service Pilot Wings (WASP), U.S. Army Jump Wings and British Parachute Wings (Special Forces).

"Colonel, you, Billy Jack, and Beverly are coming with me. We're running late to a briefing with a bunch of practicing idiots. First, we've got a duty to perform. Won't take a minute.

"OK, Bill, read away."

Captain William Patterson, one of Bronc's aides, produced a folded paper from the pocket of his blouse, and started reciting, "In accordance to orders . . ."

Col. Blackwell said, "Just cut to the last sentence." He tossed Beverly a tiny box that rattled.

" . . . announcement is made of the appointment in the Army of the United States of the following named officer to the grade of . . ."

Beverly opened the box and found a pair of double silver general's stars, "Daddy, they made a mistake!"

"They sure did, baby—pin those on for me. I've been waiting for you to get here to make it official. Air Force jumped me over Brigadier General— no sense fooling with the small change."

Handing him one of Waldo's custom-rolled cigars, which is an army tradition when someone is promoted, Col. Randal said, "Congratulations, sir, how did you manage it?"

Maj. Gen. Blackwell said, "It's all because of you, Johnny. Following the HUSKY fiasco, as it pertained to the airborne phase, the powers that be decided to form Troop Carrier Command. Problem was, nobody wanted to command big, slow, unarmed troop transports and gliders that don't even have engines.

"Ever since the evening before HUSKY, when I watched you disregard orders and we improvised our own, I've been making a study of airborne operations. Didn't take me long to come to the conclusion that you knew the plan Seventh Army laid out wouldn't work the instant you heard it.

"At the time, I thought you were nuts. Only went along with your changes because Beverly had told me you're some kind of a boy wonder tactical genius. She's rarely wrong.

"After Sicily, I wanted to be able to do what you did—read the battlefield. Considering I train the boys who fly the jump aircraft and tow the gliders, I needed to experience what the men my boys are dropping are going through. In the process, I became the closest thing to an expert on airborne operations the Army Air Force has.

"So, that's the reason Troop Carrier Command—a job nobody else wanted—landed in my lap. Now, I've got myself a worldwide command. Go anywhere, do anything, any time. Travel first class."

Beverly laughed, "Something so incredible could only happen to you, Daddy."

Maj. Gen. Blackwell said, "So, here's the deal, Colonel. I'd like you to be my Senior Paratroop Advisor. Travel the globe, see exotic places. Meet new people and kill them."

Col. Randal said, "I'll keep that in mind, Bronc."

Maj. Gen. Blackwell said, "You do that, son. Word is, maybe you've been out on the edge a little too long. Starting to take chances you shouldn't be. Accept my offer—I need you.

"There's a lot to be said for advising men getting ready to jump out of airplanes in the dark of night and do bad things to bad people."

Beverly said, "Sorry, Daddy. Johnny's involved in a classified operation that's probably going to keep him right where he is for the duration."

Maj. Gen. Blackwell said, "Yeah, well, this conversation ain't over—think about it, Colonel."

Stars in place, Maj. Gen. Blackwell climbed in behind the wheel of the jeep, promotion cigar stuck in his teeth. With Col. Randal in the passenger seat and Capt. Jaxx and Beverly in the back, they roared off. Bronc ran through the gears like an Indy 500 race car driver.

Col. Randal said, "Why are we here, General?"

"Friends call me Bronc. You're practically a member of the family, Johnny. That's what I want you to call me too."

"OK, Bronc, why are we here?"

Maj. Gen. Blackwell said, "I'll explain, but you're not going to believe me—don't laugh."

Col. Randal said, "That's not a great way to start a briefing, sir."

Maj. Gen. Blackwell said, "Yeah, well, it goes downhill from here. Fifth Army under some sissy named Mark Clark landed the 36th 'Texas' Division at a place called Salerno three days ago. They're the spearhead of OPERATION AVALANCHE—the invasion of Italy. There was no preliminary naval or air bombardment prior to the assault wave going in.

"Some staff weenie thought it would catch the Germans by surprise."

Col. Randal said, "How did that work out, Bronc?"

"Landed ashore all right, but there was no ground tactical plan, so the Texans just sort of pushed inland. Then, not having been disrupted by an intensive pre-assault naval bombardment, the Germans counterattacked and guess what—no reserve had been established in the beachhead behind the 36th Division.

"This was the 36th's first taste of combat and they were going against seasoned Wehrmacht divisions with long service in Russia. The Nazis came hard and fast. Drove to within a thousand yards of the beach in at least one location.

"Clark panicked and started planning on pulling a MacArthur."

Col. Randal said, "A MacArthur?"

"Ordered his staff to draw up plans to evacuate his HQ by PT boat. Wanted to move up the coast to Montgomery's Eighth Army sector, where the landings are going better, meaning it was safe. Can you imagine what our press would say about an American general tucking his tail between his legs and running away to hide with the British?"

Col. Randal said, "You're right, Bronc, I haven't believed a thing you've said, starting from the point you told me I wasn't going to."

Maj. Gen. Blackwell laughed, "Cooler heads talked Clark down—temporarily. The plans are still in the works. It was pointed out to the General he'd be committing professional suicide."

Capt. Jaxx said, "Unbelievable, sir!"

Maj. Gen. Blackwell said, "Once the troops found out the Italian surrender didn't mean a walkover lthirAike they'd thought when they came ashore, the Texas Division started fighting. Doing a good job of it, too. Those boys don't want another Alamo on their record."

Col. Randal said, "Good for them." Capt. Jaxx said, "Hook 'em."

Maj. Gen. Blackwell said, "There's a young paratroop colonel named Yarborough, the Airborne advisor on Clark's staff, who's put forward an alternate plan. What he's proposed is a night drop of the 82nd Airborne Division's two parachute regiments into the 36th Division's lines as reinforcements."

Col. Randal said, "I've met Yarborough—good man, sir."

Capt. Jaxx said, "He designed the Jump Wings you're wearing, Bronc."

Beverly said, "The tall brown Corcoran paratrooper boots—those too."

Maj. Gen. Blackwell said, "What do you think about Yarborough's proposal?"

Col. Randal said, "A two-regiment drop would result in an immediate infusion of 6,000 paratroopers into the battle area. That would be an impressive show of force, while also raising the morale of the 36th Division. Tactically, sir, Yarborough's plan is one of the purest uses of Airborne—makes sense."

Maj. Gen. Blackwell said, "Sounded crazy to me, after the 504th getting shot out of the sky by our own navy on the second night's lift of OPERATION HUSKY. Going to be a lot a' trigger-happy sailors on those ships offshore Salerno. And a whole bunch more men in the lodgment area, armed and ready, worried about the prospects of getting bombed by the Luftwaffe.

"Why I need you, Johnny—to keep me straight on tactics. My offer's staying on the table. The Paratroop Advisor job's yours anytime you're ready. Beverly, I'm counting on you to keep working on him to take it."

The jeep pulled up in front of the airfield's terminal building. The former Regia Aeronautica HQ was pockmarked with machine gun rounds fired during HUSKY. Compliments of the U.S. 1st Infantry Division, the Big Red One.

Maj. Gen. Blackwell said, "When we walk in, you're going to observe hysteria, fear, panic, arrogance, and stupidity. General Ridgway is dictating terms to the Army, the Air Force, and the Navy. Clark's Fifth Army chief-of-staff is sweating bullets because his boss has declared an emergency, convinced the beachhead is about to be overrun.

"No one's listening to Yarborough because he's junior, and besides, he'd commanded a battalion of the 504th on Sicily, and General Ridgway relieved him—bad blood there. Admiral Hewett isn't being cooperative about standing down the navy's antiaircraft defenses. Tempers are short."

Col. Randal said, "When are you going to get to the part where you say, 'But the good news is . . .', Bronc?"

Maj. Gen. Blackwell said, "Not happening. The problem is the OPERATION AVALANCHE planners misjudged the situation after the Italian surrender. They expected a walkover. Fifth Army got a fight they didn't expect and weren't prepared for from the Germans—what could they have been thinking? Now everyone's pointing fingers and trying to make sure someone else gets the blame for what looks like a major military catastrophe in the making.

"I'm not going to bother introducing you and Billy Jack when we get inside. You two just sort of stand behind me, looking tough or maybe disgusted. No one knows I've been promoted. They're getting ready to find out I command all three Troop Carrier Groups, the 61st, 313th, and the 314th.

"We'll do it my way or I'll pick up my toys and go home."

Beverly laughed, "Daddy never has played well with others."

Maj. Gen. Blackwell said, "It'll be fun."

COLONEL JOHN RANDAL AND BEVERLY WERE STANDING IN the back of the hangar where the Pathfinders were staging, watching Captain Billy Jack Jaxx issue his orders for the night's drop on Salerno. This was a no-nonsense, by the book briefing. Strictly business—no razzle dazzle.

Almost.

Capt. Jaxx covered every one of the five paragraphs and all the sub-paragraphs found in a formal Operations Order. All, that is, except for one small item. The SOG Pathfinders were paying close attention—being the stone-cold professionals they were. The men were assessing their upcoming mission and what it held in store for them and at least one of them took note of the oversight.

What was not apparent, because of his precise military manner and confidence of delivery, was that Capt. Jaxx was basically winging it. His briefing was solely based on the skimpy information he had gathered in the Fifth Army staff meeting concluded minutes prior.

The SOG commander made it sound like his Concept of the Operation had been developed by the Plans Division of the War Department.

"This concludes my briefing. What are your questions?"

Private Norvel "Horn Dog" Hansen said, "Skipped weather—what's the skinny for tonight, sir?"

"Dark—any other questions?" Jack Cool.

While Col. Randal was observing his young captain's highly competent performance, he could not help but reflect on the Fifth Army staff conference. The only useful information he had picked up was the reason for standing up the 575th Parachute Infantry Regiment. It might be needed to be dropped as additional reinforcement to the 82nd Airborne Division's two parachute regiments.

It was announced the 575th PIR would be arriving sometime in the next three days, so it would be available to go in on the third night.

As for the staff conference, until Bronc stepped in, it was the most rattled, disjointed, out- of-control Col. Randal had ever attended—to include the one at RAF Habbaniya when it was announced the base commander had deserted. Fifth Army had lost control of the situation on the ground in Italy. Here in Sicily, the staff was melting down.

No one seemed to know their job. There was no cohesion. No teamwork.

Major General Mark Clark's Fifth Army staff seemed dazed. They were all going to die, be captured, or worse—have their careers ruined. A feeling of impending doom hung over the room.

There was much to be concerned about. After the surrender, German Forces had quickly disarmed the Italian Army. Field Marshal "Smiling" Al Kesselring won a power struggle with Field Marshal Erwin Rommel over who would command in Italy. Hitler preferred the former Luftwaffe general's defensive plan. Privately, the Führer had come to the conclusion that the Desert Fox had turned into a "hypochondriac with defeatist tendencies."

In the Salerno area, Smiling Al had two Panzer Corps: 14th Panzer Corps, consisting of the 15th Panzer Division and the 16th Panzer Division, and 76th Panzer Corps, consisting of the 26th Panzer Division and the 16th Panzer Grenadier Division.

These were tough armored divisions commanded by aggressive veteran officers.

It was not clear who had initially suggested using Raiding Forces, but the idea was to drop SOG Pathfinders to mark three DZs for the main body of the first night's jump, consisting of Colonel Ruben Tucker's 504th Parachute Infantry Regiment staging for the drop at airfields in North Africa. Flying in thirty minutes later, they would arrive following the same flight path as the Pathfinders.

A battalion of paratroopers would be put down on each drop zone.

The plan did not take into account that the 3/504th was detached, assigned to Ranger Force operating with the British Eighth Army. That would reduce the number of paratroopers on the ground the first night by one third. Therefore, there would be no need for three drop zones.

Once again, the 509th Parachute Infantry Battalion was left on the sidelines, not taking part. That made no sense. It would have been logical to use the battalion to make up for the absent 3/504th.

The 505th under Colonel James Gavin would jump in the following night. The regiment had been marshaling to drop as a blocking force on the Volturno River when the new orders arrived. The regiment needed time to reorganize for the change of mission. It was their third change following the canceled OPERATION GIANT I and GIANT II.

In the 82nd Airborne, frustration was running high. Fifth Army had parachute and glider troops standing by ready to go, but it did not seem to have any idea how to use them. Some proposed missions that made it past the preliminary planning phase were suicidal.

One, a drop on Rome, may have been a trap.

Col. Randal was astonished to hear that the direction of flight for the Pathfinders and the 504th PIR was directly over the fleet stationed offshore—a formula for disaster.

There was no getting around it—the AVALANCHE planning staff were clearly not performing well. They may have all been fine peacetime soldiers and sailors, and probably were. But they had much to learn about organizing for combat where the opposition was going to be shooting back with live ammunition.

In one of the most impressive demonstrations of command performance Col. Randal had ever witnessed, Major General Sam Houston Blackwell stepped up and took charge. No one questioned his authority. No one debated the merit of what he proposed. Everyone fell into line.

The attendees at the conference seemed relieved that someone who knew what they were doing had finally stepped forward.

Bronc diagrammed a new flight path. A dog leg from Sicily that angled out to sea, bypassing the Allied invasion fleet stationed offshore and out of range of the ships' antiaircraft guns. Then, when the 313th Troop Carrier Group struck land, all the pilots had to do was bank right and fly down the coastline to the drop zones.

It was a simple plan that reduced the possibility of another friendly fire incident, made up for the Troop Carrier Groups' lack of navigational skills, and made it virtually impossible for the pilots to miss the DZs.

When Maj. Gen. Blackwell concluded his briefing, everyone

immediately rushed from the room to carry out his responsibilities, confidence restored now that there was a clear plan in place. But there was much to do, in a lot of far-flung places, with darkness falling.

And the situation at Salerno was still desperate.

MAJOR GENERAL SAM HOUSTON BLACKWELL WALKED INTO the hanger and stood next to Colonel John Randal in the back as Captain Billy Jack Jaxx was wrapping up his Operations Order.

Bronc said, "The Brits developed a signaling system that's revolutionized the art of marking Drop Zones. Eureka is a ground-based transponder the Pathfinders jump in with and set up on the DZ. It sends out a signal.

"A Rebecca transceiver on board each of the C-47s locks in on the signal. The plane is then guided to the DZ. The pilot green lights the jumpers right on target.

"Works every time."

Col. Randal said, "Captain Jaxx tells me that after the invention of the parachute, the Eureka/Rebecca system is the best thing that's ever happened to the Airborne, sir."

Maj. Gen. Blackwell said, "So you know about the system?"

"Yes, sir."

"No one thought to have Rebecca units installed aboard our Troop Carrier Group's planes, so those two Eurekas your boys brought are useless."

Col. Randal said, "Lovely."

12
"BIGAMY AIN'T EXACTLY LEGAL IN TEXAS"

2100 HOURS SOMEWHERE IN SICILY.

MAJOR GENERAL SAM HOUSTON BLACKWELL TOOK OFF FROM the departure Airfield, leading a flight of three C-47 Dakota aircraft carrying the three SOG Pathfinder Teams. Thirty minutes behind him would come ninety more planes of the 313th Troop Carrier Group with the 1/504 and 2/504 of the 82nd Airborne Division on board. Before the 504th troopers boarded, their regimental commander, Colonel Ruben Tucker, drove around to each plane and shouted, "It's open season on Krauts, boys!"

A last-minute command decision had modified the plan one last time.

After it was learned that tonight would be only a two-battalion jump and that the Rebecca receiving devices had not been installed in the 313th Troop Carrier Group's airplanes, Colonel John Randal suggested they drop everyone on a single DZ. Maj. Gen. Blackwell concurred. Orders went out outlining the change to Lieutenant Colonel William P. Yarborough, who was standing by south of Paestum within the U.S. 36th Division's lines, waiting to receive the Pathfinders on one of the three original drop zones.

Lt. Col. Yarborough suggested constructing a giant Texas "T" out of 55-gallon drums filled with burning fuel oil and oriented with the top on the line of flight. The Pathfinders would all drop on the single DZ and light off the T to guide the main body.

A mad scramble ensued.

While consolidating onto one drop zone simplified things, Lt. Col. Yarborough had to retrieve the barrels positioned at the other two DZs. They would be needed in order to make the one big ground marker. Also, trucks were waiting at the other drop zones to take the paratroopers to the front lines as soon as they assembled after the jump. They all had to be repositioned.

Col. Randal was on board the lead Pathfinder plane. He moved forward to the cockpit in time to hear Maj. Gen. Blackwell say, "You capped a nun?"

Captain Billy Jack Jaxx said, "I didn't know at the time, sir. I don't really believe Cat was a real nun. It was more like she was being held hostage in a convent."

Maj. Gen. Blackwell said, "Wait till I tell this story at the next Longhorns Football Boosters Association meeting. That her picture in your pistol grip, Jack?"

Capt. Jaxx handed over his 1911 Colt .38 Super. There was a nude shot of Alex in the Plexiglas grip panel, with a python strategically wrapped around her, covering up all the parts people wanted to see. Nowadays, Lady Jane was having the photos for his pistol taken by a professional photographer in Cairo—Jack Cool being her favorite.

"Damn, son, what was it like?"

"Canned heat."

The navigator said, "Ten minutes, Bronc."

Maj. Gen. Blackwell flipped the switch that turned on the red light over the rear door in the passenger compartment.

Capt. Jaxx said, "Time for me to go to work, sir."

He moved past Col. Randal and went to the rear of the aircraft to jumpmaster the drop.

Maj. Gen. Blackwell said, "'The Eyes of Texas...'"

Up ahead in the distance, a Lone Star State-sized "T" was burning on the ground. Lt. Col. Yarborough had lighted off the DZ marker early. The improvised signaling device was a half mile long.

No pilot was going to miss the DZ tonight.

Col. Randal said, "Not much use for Pathfinders."

Maj. Gen. Blackwell said, "Still want to drop?"

"Yes, sir."

Maj. Gen. Blackwell said, "I'll be sending a couple of Catalinas over to fly you and the Pathfinders back tonight. Beverly and I will link up with you at the Departure Airfield when you return. The Advanced Party of your 575th Parachute Infantry Regiment should be arriving at Agrigento, Sicily, by then.

"We'll see what develops once all your boys get there."

"Roger."

Capt. Jaxx shouted in a loud, vigorous manner heard all the way to the cockpit. "SIX MINUTES!"

The three Dakotas had been flying in a "V" formation, guiding on Maj. Gen. Blackwell. Now they transitioned into a trail formation, with Bronc leading the way. The big troop transport aircraft were thundering toward the drop zone.

"STAND UP AND HOOK UP!"

From where he was standing, it was hard for Col. Randal to see what was taking place once the heavily loaded SOG Pathfinder personnel struggled to their feet. Up ahead, meaning toward the tail, there was the metallic sound of snap links being hooked to the steel cable running along the roof of the cabin—with the open end of the snap link away from the bulkhead.

There was a reason for doing it that way, but Col. Randal could not remember what it was.

He was the next-to-last jumper in the stick with King, then the two Lovat Scouts immediately in front, and Master Sergeant Mack Beckwith behind him, pushing the stick. Col. Randal did not like jumping this position, it was claustrophobic being crammed in wearing all the gear.

Normally Col. Randal jumpmastered. It gave him a better sense of what was taking place.

Not only on board but outside in the sky around the aircraft and on the ground. "CHECK STATIC LINE!"

All down the cabin, paratroopers rattled their snap links back and forth while grasping a loop of the yellow static line in their right hand to make sure they moved freely along the cable.

"CHECK YOUR EQUIPMENT!"

This was pretty much a formality. The Pathfinders were all going to jump. No matter what they found.

"SOUND OFF FOR EQUIPMENT CHECK!"

Starting with MSgt. Beckwith, a domino effect of "OK, OK, OK . . ." rippled up the stick to Capt. Jaxx. Some units had each man call out his number with the OK. That was the way it was done during jump training.

Raiding Forces had eliminated the number. Calling it out did not accomplish anything and could be a source of confusion. What if the wrong number reached the jumpmaster as he was about to give the next command and the green light was only a little over a minute away? An unnecessary distraction as the plane thundered toward the DZ.

A combat jump is a confluence of talented people with different skill sets, making multiple decisions under extreme stress and performing complex individual tasks that all have to come together at a precise point in time, while screaming through space at a high rate of speed. Pilots flying the plane and finding the drop zone, jumpmasters in charge of overseeing everything happening inside the troop compartment—to include deciding when to go or whether to go or when to go on the green light or not, paratroopers struggling to maintain their balance in a bucking C-47 preparatory to exiting fast in tight formation, and ground personnel calculating when to activate the signal to mark the DZ. A lot of things can go wrong jumping out of an airplane in the dark of night, armed to the teeth, and ready to fight.

And there is not much time to do anything about it when they do.

"CLOSE ON THE DOOR."

The stick of Pathfinders edged forward, each man pressing up tight against the X-type parachute of the paratrooper in front of him. At the door,

Capt. Jaxx had his right arm braced across the opening to keep the first trooper in the stick from exiting too soon. The SOG operators were experienced men, but even they got keyed up on a jump.

"ONE MINUTE."

After mentally counting down the time to green light with five seconds left, Capt. Jaxx removed his arm and swung into position in the door, knees bent, hands slapped outside flat against the skin of the Dakota, eyes on the horizon.

Then he shouted over his shoulder, as he launched out the door, "GO!"

The stick began shuffling toward the door almost double timing. The jumpers were shouting, "Go, Go, Go . . ." Everyone wanted out of the plane now. No one wanted to have the red light catch them before they could hit the silk. Not that it mattered—no one was paying attention to the lights . . . not now.

Col. Randal reached the exit, made a snappy parade ground perfect right face, reached out and slapped both hands flat against the skin of the fuselage outside the door, pushed off hard and leapt out into the prop blast with his head down, chin on his chest, feet and knees together, hands firmly pressing against both ends of the reserve chute on his chest, counting, "one thousand, two thousand, three. . . ." The canopy deployed and he found himself floating down, looking at the giant, burning ground marker.

He was enjoying the ride.

The Pathfinders were dropping from 800 feet. Essentially it was an administrative jump onto a secured drop zone. The DZ was well within the 36th Division's lines. No one was shooting at them.

In the distance inland, Col. Randal could see the flash of artillery. It looked like a thunderstorm. Whatever they were firing at, the Germans were not interfering with the drop.

Why not?

Surely the Nazis had long-range guns capable of reaching the DZ. For some reason, the enemy artillery was not engaging. The Germans *not* putting indirect fire on a DZ that could be seen from miles away did not make sense.

Col. Randal decided his was not to reason why.

He was so relaxed that he had to remind himself to quit having fun and assume the "prepare to land" position. Fists together in front of his face touching the rim of his steel helmet, forearms together, elbows in tight, feet and knees together, knees bent—he rocked them to make sure they were not locked—a momentary sensation of disorientation as things suddenly speeded up, then he was down, coming in backward. Col. Randal instinctively rotated and fell, making what is known as a Parachute Landing Fall (PLF), which is one of the most difficult skills a soldier ever has to master.

Not that it's hard to grade a PLF: they are all PASS/FAIL. Any PLF a paratrooper walks away from is a PASS.

Parachute Landing Falls sound simple enough. All that is required is to let the toes of your boots touch the ground, then swivel left or right and fall, landing on your calf, thigh, buttock, and then the small of your back—the "Five Points of Contact," making certain to keep your elbows in at all times and not bang them on the ground.

The problem is visibility, or more accurately, lack thereof. A jumper almost never comes down facing forward, or even sideways. Most PLFs start out backward.

And they take place really fast.

Except for the fact that Col. Randal was carrying his weapons, this was a Hollywood jump. Tonight he was a combat tourist. When the SOG Pathfinders departed RFHQ, the understanding was that he would merely go along to observe, and he was—observing.

Since there was virtually no wind, Col. Randal came straight down. The landing was soft, which is not the norm with any military parachute jump. He bounded to his feet, hammered the British quick release device (QRD) on his chest, and dropped his harness. A team provided by Lt. Col. Yarborough would police up the chutes later.

Overhead, parachutes were spilling out from the trailing two C-47s as Col. Randal made his way to the assembly point. He passed Lieutenant Randy "Hornblower" Seaborn, who was already organizing the three Aldis lamp teams. King and the Lovat Scouts appeared out of the firelight cast by the burning 55-gallon drums. They had been waiting for him to roll up the stick.

Next, Col. Randal encountered Capt. Jaxx and Lt. Col. Yarborough in conversation next to the top of the burning "T."

Capt. Jaxx said, "Too bad we didn't bring marshmallows, sir." Jack Cool.

MAJOR GENERAL FRED WALKER, THE COMMANDING GENERAL OF the U.S. 36TH Infantry Division, was on the DZ to observe the arrival of the 82nd Airborne Division's 504th Parachute Infantry Regiment (-). The Salerno landing, code named OPERATION AVALANCHE, had been touch and go. The prevailing attitude by the Fifth Army staff prior to the landing was that the Italian surrender guaranteed a walkover. The staff were euphoric, this was what being war managers felt like. What the honor of being tapped to serve as army level staff officers felt like. They were military geniuses.

The giddy attitude of the Fifth Army staff had trickled down to the troops. When they landed, the men of the U.S. 36th Infantry Division were not prepared to find Germans waiting for them, spoiling for a fight. The T-Patchers had the word to expect wine and roses.

There was only one problem. Well, actually two. First: The planning for AVALANCHE had been amateurish military staff work. Second: Fifth Army failed to take into account what the Wehrmacht might have to say about Salerno being invaded.

When the 36th ID landed, the Nazis welcomed the first wave ashore by playing "Deep in the Heart of Texas" over loudspeakers. So much for the element of surprise. Then the Germans counterattacked and things got ugly fast.

Fifth Army Headquarters panicked almost immediately. Institutional hysteria set in, which is not supposed to happen in the U.S. Army. Lieutenant General Mark Clark began planning for a withdrawal, while taking steps to ensure that someone else took the blame for the catastrophe. He pointed an accusing finger at VI Corps commander Major General Ernest Dawley.

Meanwhile, on the beach, the Texas Division went to war. The T-Patchers fought their way inland inch by inch. The beachhead gradually began to expand.

The U.S. Navy finally dispatched additional warships to provide gunfire support for the troops ashore. Naval Fire Direction Control Teams came ashore to find themselves in a target- rich environment and went to work. The ripping silk sound of shells arching overhead to pound the Nazis' positions was continuous and unrelenting.

And it was devastating.

The Navy's big guns were a game changer. The heavy firepower forced German armor to disperse to avoid being destroyed. To be effective, tanks need to be used *en masse*—in penny packets, they become vulnerable.

At the top of the flaming "T", Colonel John Randal encountered Maj. Gen. Walker standing with his aide-de-camp and the Division Operations Officer—both men were his sons. The Walker family was well-represented in the "Texas Army."

Col. Randal was immediately struck by the composure the General was exhibiting. If this were a military disaster in the making and the Salerno beachhead standing by to be overrun, the CG did not seem to have gotten the word. Maj. Gen. Walker was coolly appraising developments on the drop zone, with an ear cocked to the sound of firefights in the distance, fully in command of the situation.

He did not exhibit any signs of being unnerved.

Maj. Gen. Walker said, "Welcome, Colonel. I was not expecting an officer in your grade to be dropping in to mark our drop zone."

Col. Randal said, "I came along to see my Pathfinders in action, sir. Doesn't seem like you needed us. Colonel Yarborough built the mother of all DZ ground markers."

Maj. Gen. Walker said, "When will the 82nd begin to arrive?"

Col. Randal glanced at his Rolex. "They're less than fifteen minutes out, sir."

"Excellent. I'm assigning the paratroopers to a reasonably quiet sector on the right flank of the beachhead. We'll give them a chance to settle in. The two regiments will serve as my reserve."

"Yes, sir."

Col. Randal was not seeing what he expected to find at Salerno. Based on the hysteria in the briefings at the Departure Airfield before Bronc took charge, he had visualized a collapse in the making, along the lines of the British Expeditionary Force at Dunkirk. Maj. Gen. Walker gave the appearance of a senior officer comfortable in command, fighting a battle, with a lot going on—no panic.

"How would you describe the mood at Fifth Army, Rear?"

"Rattled, sir."

"A straightforward answer . . . in short supply on this beachhead."

Col. Randal went in search of Captain Billy Jack Jaxx. He found him with Lieutenant Randy "Hornblower" Seaborn, standing next to one of the Aldis lamps. The light was shining a beam straight up into the sky. In tests, the lamp had demonstrated it was capable of being seen from as far as twenty-five miles away. Having a flight path intentionally designed with simple navigation built in by Major General Sam Houston Blackwell, the giant burning "T", and the three Aldis lamps, the 313th Troop Carrier Group was not going to have any excuse for not finding the DZ tonight.

Maj. Gen. Blackwell was not likely to be understanding if a pilot misdropped for any reason.

Redundancy is a good thing in the military, especially airborne operations, when it pertains to the canopy opening, or finding the drop zone and exiting the aircraft at the exact right time and place to land on target.

Capt. Jaxx said, "Here we go."

The sound of an approaching C-47 could be heard in the distance. The plan called for ninety Dakotas to drop the 504th PIR ( ) one plane load at a time with one minute intervals between aircraft. In an hour and a half, the 1/504 and 2/504 would be on the ground ready to move to the front.

The plane droned straight toward the "T", having reduced speed to 130 mph, the optimum speed to keep the canopies from ripping from excessive opening shock and the airplane from stalling and falling out of the sky. Eight hundred feet overhead, a jumper launched from the tail of the plane with his 28 foot T-4 canopy being pulled from his parachute pack by the static line. There was a *CRAAACK* as it deployed. The T-4 parachute had a vicious opening shock that left nasty burns on a jumper's neck if he did not have his head down, chin tucked on his chest.

Some claimed the paratrooper song "Blood on the Risers" was about riser burn, not bullet holes.

A steady string of jumpers followed the stick leader out the door.

By now the C-47 had flown off, leaving the deployed parachutes alone in the sky, looking a lot like a school of swimming octopuses. Watching paratroopers jump from an aircraft in flight is always an impressive sight. The very best view is standing on the drop zone, looking straight up, having made the jump yourself.

The second plane was over the DZ by the time the jumpers from the first were recovering from their PLFs. It was followed at a sixty-second interval by the next C-47 in the serial. The drop went on and on.

Inserting the 504th PIR (-) into the battle area by parachute was a formidable projection of U.S. military power.

Capt. Jaxx said, "Doesn't make sense, sir."

Col. Randal said, "What doesn't?"

Capt. Jaxx said, "The 504th PIR is a battalion short. They're jumping in to save the 36th Division from being overrun, not sure what they're going to be up against. And they don't bring the 509th Parachute Infantry Battalion with 'em to get the regiment up to full strength."

Col. Randal said, "The 509th is on alert for another mission."

Capt. Jaxx said, "If you were commanding the 82nd Airborne, sir, you'd demand the 509th be released for the operation and you wouldn't take no for an answer."

"Exactly."

"Never realized that naked ambition, petty jealousy, and bruised egos affect some command decisions, sir—ain't right."

As each rifle company assembled, it was guided off the DZ by one of Lt. Col. Yarborough's ground personnel. The troop movement went like a parade ground exercise. Within two hours of the first stick of paratroopers exiting their aircraft over the drop zone, the regiment was on board 2 ½-ton trucks en route to its position on the perimeter of the beachhead.

The SOG Pathfinders were trucked to the beach. They boarded the Catalinas Maj. Gen. Blackwell had dispatched to fly them back to Sicily. Most fell asleep before the planes took off.

It had been a fairly long day.

THE FOLLOWING NIGHT WAS A REPEAT PERFORMANCE with one minor exception—there were no SOG Pathfinders involved because they were not needed. Colonel James Gavin insisted that the 505th Regimental Pathfinder Team jump in prior to the drop anyway. No one cared except Lieutenant Jake Novak, the 509th Parachute Infantry Battalion Pathfinder platoon leader attached to Raiding Forces.

When he heard the word about the 82nd Division Pathfinders, Lt. Novak said, "I knew it—Gavin's been trying to take credit for forming the first U.S. Army Pathfinder Team. Now he's going to claim they're the reason the 505th's drop was so successful. Then I bet he'll claim the 82nd saved the whole Salerno beachhead."

Twenty-one hundred men of the 505th PIR dropped the second night and were whisked away to join their sister regiment. The total number of 82nd Airborne Division men on the ground was slightly less than 4,000—which was less than the 6,000 originally expected. Nevertheless, the reinforcements were much appreciated.

After the first night's drop of the 504th PIR, Colonel John Randal and the SOG Pathfinders were trucked to the beach to board two Catalina PBYs and flown to Agrigento, Sicily. Major General Sam Houston Blackwell and Beverly were waiting when they arrived. They took Col. Randal and Captain

Billy Jack Jaxx to dinner in a restaurant that Bronc had ordered the owner to keep open long after the island's curfew.

The idea was to conduct a quiet debriefing while the operation was fresh in their minds. Maj. Gen. Blackwell may have been a rich Texas cowboy with a penchant for beautiful women and Longhorn football, but he was also a take-charge combat commander who knew how to get things done. Bronc did not see any problem with mixing business with pleasure.

What he was interested in learning was how his pilots had performed from the perspective of the people on the ground—not from reading the fliers' after-action reports.

Following the jump on Sicily, virtually all the C-47 pilots claimed they had dropped their paratroopers on time and on target, when in fact two battalions of the 82nd landed over thirty miles away from their intended drop zone and another battalion missed theirs by fifty-five miles, coming down in the British zone. A Distinguished Unit Citation had been awarded to one of the Troop Carrier Groups for their outstanding performance.

Maj. Gen. Blackwell thought the unit should give it back. Col. Randal said, "Give the General a report, Jack."

Capt. Jaxx said, "Picture-perfect execution, Bronc. Two pilots put their sticks out a mile or so from the DZ. Other than that, the drop was more accurate than most training jumps I've made, sir."

Maj. Gen. Blackwell said, "I'll be having a word with those aircraft commanders."

Beverly said, "Are things really as desperate as everyone is saying?"

Col. Randal said, "There was constant fighting along the perimeter while I was there. However, General Walker seems to have the situation in hand. The 45th ID is landing ashore now. The 34th ID is combat loading aboard U.S. Navy troop ships getting ready to sail. And I've heard the 3rd ID has been alerted to join 6th Corps."

Maj. Gen. Blackwell said, "Signs of panic?"

Col. Randal said, "Only at the briefing before you took charge, Bronc."

Capt. Jaxx said, "People I talked to said it was pretty dicey the first day or two, right. By day three, the Germans had built up a sizable counterattack but by then the 36th ID was holding its own."

Col. Randal said, "Everyone's in agreement on one thing. We didn't come in hard enough. General Clark failed in that regard, sir."

Maj. Gen. Blackwell said, "Clark must have been out of his mind. Only landed one green NG division for starters. No preliminary bombardment— some fool tried to play cute with his tactics. Plus, Fifth Army banked on the Germans rolling over because the Italians surrendered."

Capt. Jaxx said, "What could possibly go wrong?"

Beverly said, "Just about everything—Nazis don't quit."

Col. Randal said, "Roger that."

THE 575TH PARACHUTE INFANTRY REGIMENT (-) (SEPARATE) (Special) "Rangers" began arriving later the next day. It consisted of the 1/575th and the 10th Ranger Battalion (-), or at least parts of the two battalions. The 575th PIR was a regiment in name only; therefore there was no reason to call it one—575th Ranger Force was more accurate since it only had one battalion of its own—the 1/575th with the 10th Ranger Battalion minus one company attached. However, Raiding Forces had been broken down into seagoing patrols that were widely separated all along Turkey's coastline living on LSF schooners, with a number of raiding parties away raiding islands. It had not been possible to assemble all the 1/575th paratroopers or the 10th Rangers in time to load out for the upcoming mission.

Colonel John Randal went into conference with Major Travis McCloud, his dual-purpose Executive/Operations Officer; Major Duke Slater, the 1/575th battalion commander; Major Taylor Corrigan, the ad hoc 2/575th battalion commander; and Major Jack Dance, the 10th Ranger Battalion commander.

Col. Randal said, "Give me a report."

Maj. McCloud said, "Raiding Forces was so scattered, we were only able to pull in 583 men all up, counting you and the SOG Pathfinders. Quite a few of our British troops demanded to be allowed to come with us or we wouldn't have that many. I hope whoever's in charge isn't really counting on a full strength regiment, sir."

Col. Randal said, "I have no idea what Fifth Army's expecting. The most likely scenario is we drop into the 36th ID's lines. If that happens, expect an administrative-type jump, followed by being trucked to our sector.

"Give the men a chance to get a little R&R before they go on alert. Transportation is available to take those who want to go to the beach. Have your company commanders turn their platoons over to their platoon leaders. I want you senior officers and the company commanders to remain on base to be available for immediate consultation once we're alerted for a jump.

"I'm sure you have questions, but I don't have any answers."

Major General Sam Houston Blackwell challenged Col. Randal to an Air Force vs 575th Ranger Force softball game. "Good chance for my crews to get a chance to spend some time with the boys they're going to be dropping."

Col. Randal said, "You're on, sir."

Beverly said, "I want to pitch."

Col. Randal said, "Jack, you manage the team. Put me in at shortstop."

Footballs were provided and several sandlot games started around the airfield by men who did not care to go to the beach or play softball. Nets and volleyballs were broken out. USAAF pilots and crew spent a lot of time waiting around airfields and came equipped for the downtime.

Everyone was having a good time.

It was the bottom of the seventh, with Raiding Forces leading 6–5. Beverly, who always looked like she stepped out of a photo shoot, had just struck out the pilot at bat—a fairly rare event in slow pitch softball. He was complaining to his teammates about it not being fair trying to concentrate on the ball with one of the "Ten Most Beautiful" from UT pitching, when a jeep screeched to a halt behind the batter's box. Bronc was just stepping up to the plate.

His aide hopped out of the vehicle and trotted over to speak to him.

Maj. Gen. Blackwell stuck one finger up in the air and made a circling motion. "Crank it up, boys, we've got a mission."

It was like someone had thrown a hand grenade on the field. Everyone scattered. The USAAF ran in the direction of their planes. Raiding Forces took off for the hangars, where their individual weapons and personal gear were stored.

Maj. Gen. Blackwell, Col. Randal, and Beverly piled in the jeep and roared off to the base Flight Operations Center. Lieutenant Colonel William Yarborough had flown in from the Salerno beachhead to brief. From the oversized map on the wall, it was immediately apparent the 575th Rangers would not be jumping in to reinforce the two 82nd Airborne Division regiments.

Present were the group commander and the three squadron leaders from the 313th Troop Carrier Group and Maj. McCloud, Maj. Slater, Maj. Corrigan, and Maj. Dance. To Col. Randal's surprise, Captain "Geronimo" Joe McKoy was there as well.

Col. Randal said, "What are you doing here?"

Capt. McKoy said, "Had to fly in to link up with Wild Bill tomorrow. We're headed to the States. Need to get this deal straightened out about me takin' command of the Arizona National Guard Division being mobilized.

"Governor's throwin' a blue hissy . . . doesn't like taking no for an answer."

Lt. Col. Yarborough said, "Gentlemen, your target is Benevento, Italy—a road and rail chokepoint located approximately thirty-one miles north of Salerno, in the Campanian Apennines Mountains between the Sabato and Calore rivers. The village has four roads running through it. In addition, it's a major rail communications hub forming the Naples/Foggia railway and serves as the terminus of the secondary rail lines linking Campobasso, Avellino, and Cancello."

Lt. Col. Yarborough tapped the map with a long, red-tipped pointer.

"Your mission is to drop on a meadow along this road one mile southwest of the town— to seize and hold Benevento, located here. In the rugged mountainous terrain, the town—situated as it is in the valley—forms a bottleneck. Your mission is to put a cork in it.

"All road and rail traffic from Rome and northwest Italy must pass through Benevento in order to reach Salerno. The idea is for the 575th Parachute Infantry Regiment to capture the town, hold the chokepoint, and block the 16th Panzer Division inbound from Rome making a road march to the beachhead.

"In the event you have not been relieved after holding the three to five days, the 575th PIR is to make its way south in the direction of Salerno, until linking up with friendly forces— most likely the 36th, 45th, or possibly the 34th Infantry Divisions advancing overland.

"The 509th Parachute Infantry Battalion was dropped eleven miles southwest of Benevento at Avellino last night with the exact same mission as yours."

Under her breath, Beverly said, "Insane!"

Lt. Col. Yarborough said, "Greenlight for your Pathfinders is 2200 hours, with the main body arriving ten minutes later. This concludes my briefing. Good luck, gentlemen."

Maj. Gen. Blackwell said, "What makes you think it's insane, Beverly?"

Beverly said, "The beachhead was about to be overrun, with General Clark planning to run away yesterday. Now those same troops who were about to be driven into the sea are suddenly expected to break out, attack over thirty miles through mountainous terrain, and fight off a Panzer Division to relieve Johnny—seriously?"

Maj. Gen. Blackwell said, "Put that way, you ain't wrong, baby." The briefing broke up.

Maj. Gen. Blackwell huddled with his fliers to discuss the air route they were to take. Col. Randal pulled his XO and battalion commanders together and began issuing short staccato instructions. Lt. Col. Yarborough walked over to listen in on the Raiding Forces senior officers getting their marching orders.

Col. Randal said, "You responsible for planning this mission that you won't be coming along on?"

Lt. Col. Yarborough looked like he had been slapped, "As the Airborne Advisor to General Clark, my job was to suggest alternate plans for airborne operations, designed to interdict the 16th Panzer Division during its movement south to Salerno. The General desires all available parachute assets to be utilized. Risks have to be taken. Sacrifices made—mission over men.

"Fifth Army is fighting for its life, *sir*."

Col. Randal said, "Not in my outfit, Yarborough—get the hell out of my area and stay out.

As the Fifth Army Airborne Advisor stalked away fuming, Capt. McKoy said, "No prior plannin', maybe *no* plannin', practically zero intelligence, no tactical scheme-of-maneuver, no Plan B, an Operations Order that didn't cover nothin' and sounded sorta like somethin' a Cub Scout mighta issued at a den meetin' about the weekend weenie roast—what could you have to be cranky about, John?"

Col. Randal said, "Not Yarborough's fault. Man has his job to do. I just needed to get him out of the way so that he doesn't hear what I say to the Rangers."

Beverly had been standing quietly, observing everything taking place. "This mission would be slapstick comedy if it weren't so crazy stupid."

Capt. McKoy said, "How does Yarborough expect lightly armed paratroopers to capture a communications center, which by definition has multiple high-speed avenues of approach, and stop hardcore Nazi German tankers, who outnumber 'em twenty to one, from blowin' right through 'em with all that practice those bad boys got under their belts fightin' in Russia?"

Col. Randal said, "I was hoping you'd tell me."

Capt. McKoy said, "A yellowjacket can outrun 'a John Deere tractor."

WHAT HAD BEEN A LAZY AFTERNOON IMMEDIATELY KICKED into high gear. On a normal jump, there was a well-rehearsed assembly line, complete with a manifest being typed up at a portable table right on the side of the runway at the Departure Airfield to account for every paratrooper and piece of equipment. The idea was to end up with the jumpers seated in the right stick, aboard the right aircraft, in the right serial, ready for take-off.

That process was not going to take place tonight. It did not matter who was where as long as everyone in the 575th Ranger Force was on board *some* aircraft with the right gear, ready to jump. Nevertheless, a multitude of tasks would have to be accomplished. And some people would have less than an hour to get ready before wheels up.

Captain Karen Montgomery and her riggers were going to be extremely busy.

Major Duke Slater, Major Taylor Corrigan, and Major Jack Dance issued Warning Orders to their company commanders. The company commanders issued the identical order to their platoon leaders. Then the platoons were assembled and each platoon leader issued the same order to his platoon. In this way, the word filtered down from top to bottom—everyone knew what everyone else knew.

The important thing was that the officers and men of the 575th Ranger Force all had the same information—that built confidence, resolve, and unity of mission.

Under normal circumstances—which this was not—at this point, preparations for the mission would commence: rehearsals begun; weapons test fired; additional ammo, grenades, or explosives drawn; parachutes inspected, etc. Everything had to be concluded in time for the troops to be issued the Operations Order.

The Warning Order was supposed to contain the time and place of the Operations Order—that had intentionally been left out today.

What *did* happen was that starting with the 10th Ranger Battalion, all the officers and men of the three battalions were called into a hangar one battalion at a time and the doors closed. Guards were posted outside with instructions not to let anyone not associated with Raiding Forces inside.

Colonel John Randal was standing on a platform in front of a giant map as the Rangers filed in.

"Stand at ease . . . you men gather around close."

The battalion crowded the stand—183 men strong—twenty-five percent strength of a TO&E parachute battalion.

Col. Randal said, "Everything I say from this point on is classified. Do not discuss it with anyone not in this hangar. Is that clear?"

"CLEAR, SIR!"

"Tonight, 575th Ranger Force will drop in the vicinity of Benevento, Italy. The town's a high-speed road and rail communications hub. The 16th Panzer Division is, or will be, making its way through the town en route to the Salerno beachhead. Our mission is to delay them for three to five days. Fifth Army wants us to drop in, seize, and hold the town. Then, in the event the U.S. 6th Corps has not arrived to relieve us, at that point we're to escape and evade the thirty-odd miles back to Salerno.

"That's not going to happen, men. We're not seizing and holding anything."

The hangar was dead still. The troops were hanging on every word Col. Randal said. In the back, Major General Sam Houston Blackwell had slipped in and was standing with Captain "Geronimo" Joe McKoy and Beverly.

Col. Randal said, "Here's what we're going to do. The 575th Ranger Force will conduct its jump as ordered. It will not be a concentrated drop as laid out by Fifth Army—that's not doable. The Campanian Apennines Mountain Range has peaks up to 4,000 feet.

"We'll have to exit our aircraft at 3,000 feet, with some of the mountains higher than our troop carriers."

A gasp came from the Rangers. They were expecting a typical 500 foot low-altitude combat jump. Not one person in the hangar had ever dropped from 3,000 feet.

There had never been any reason to.

Col. Randal said, "No matter how accurate the navigation from 3,000 feet, we're going to come down widely dispersed. Do not, I say again, DO NOT attempt to assemble.

"Gather in parties of no more than six men. If more people turn up, break the group down and go your separate ways. I want small teams scattered all over the countryside, knocking down telephone lines, placing mines on the road and rail line, dropping trees across the roads, and shooting up thin-skinned vehicles.

"Your mission is to wage a hit-and-run guerrilla war—strike and be gone. Do not get drawn into firefights. Stay out of the valleys during the day. Panzers are roadbound—the valleys are where the roads are and where the Nazis will deploy their Panzergrenadiers to conduct searches for you. Do not go into Benevento or any other village except to conduct a quick raid against a point type target—pull out immediately.

"Operate at night, utilizing the element of surprise under cover of darkness and then before daylight, travel high into the mountains or deep in the forest to hide. If you're in the mountains, take up a position with good observation of the valley below. Lay up during the day. Observe—plan your targets for the next night.

"Then do it all over again.

"If the Germans pursue, ambush 'em. Inflict casualties from as long range as possible.

Then slip away to a new hide position.

"I say again, do not allow yourself to be drawn into an extended firefight. Do not allow the enemy to pin you down. If you lose your freedom of movement, the Germans will call for indirect fire, reinforce, then maneuver on you with superior numbers—don't let that happen.

"Start leapfrogging back south toward the beachhead overland on the second night. Cover three to five miles, then turn and strike. Plan your moves. Use your explosives to block the roads, blow the rail lines, knock down phone lines.

"Do what we do best. Hit hard and fast, leaving a wake of destruction as we disappear into the night.

"Good luck and happy hunting."

Col. Randal's order had an electric effect on the men of the 10th Ranger Battalion. Spontaneous cheering erupted, then the chanting started, "Go, Go,

Go. . . ." The troops were fired up and ready. This was a mission the Rangers could understand, explained in clear, concise terms. And they had a commander who was going to jump #1 on Chalk 1—first man in.

As the battalion was filing out of the hangar, Maj. Gen. Blackwell walked up to speak with Col. Randal.

"So, I can quit worrying about my boys trying to locate the primary drop zone?"

"Yes, sir."

"That's good, because those mountains would interfere with my pilots' line of sight to ground markers and they would reflect any ground radio directional signals your Pathfinders might set up. This drop never stood a Chinaman's chance from the start. Just like Sicily, when we put you down in those excessive winds."

Col. Randal said, "If my 575th Ranger Force jumped onto a single DZ, assembled, and attacked Benevento as ordered by Fifth Army, the 16th Panzer Division would wipe us out before noon tomorrow, Bronc."

Maj. Gen. Blackwell said, "You realized that the minute you looked at the map?"

"I did."

Maj. Gen. Blackwell said, "Just like old times—watching you improvise, adapt, and disregard. Can't say you're not predictable, Johnny— some mission statement you just gave.

"There's going to be small bands of highly trained teenage paratroopers armed to the teeth, who'll lack serious adult supervision, roaming the Italian countryside and trying to collectively remember your orders to march to the sound of the guns, blow up everything in their path, and kill anyone not wearing a uniform same as theirs or *something like that.*

"Damn, son, you've unleashed the 'Dogs of War.'"

2120 HOURS

CHALK 1 OF A SERIAL OF 39 C-47 DAKOTAS, PILOTED BY MAJOR General Sam Houston Blackwell, the Air Mission Commander of a serial of 38 planes, was preparing for takeoff when somebody outside started pounding on the C-47's door. The USAAF loadmaster opened it and leaned out. He engaged in a brief conversation with someone on the tarmac who could not be heard inside the cabin over the airplane engines.

The loadmaster said, "Colonel Randal, you need to step out of the aircraft, sir."

Colonel John Randal was sitting next to the door. He was the jumpmaster on Chalk 1. No more being crammed in at the tail end of the stick. Jumper #1.

He was going to lead the way—first out the door.

When Col. Randal climbed out of the plane, he found Lieutenant General George S. Patton and Captain—or was it Major General— "Geronimo" Joe McKoy standing by the aircraft.

Lt. Gen. Patton said, "Heard you were here on Sicily, Colonel. I drove over to personally wish you Godspeed on your mission tonight. Joe's briefed me on some of the details. Doesn't Fifth Army understand that paratroopers need to be relieved by ground troops attacking overland within seventy-two hours or less?"

Col. Randal said, "Always that ten percent that don't get the word, sir."

Lt. Gen. Patton said, "The 509th dropped on Avellino last night. Photo reconnaissance at first light this morning showed parachutes on the ground scattered for forty-five miles. The jump was a debacle. Sounds like Fifth Army is ordering you to repeat it."

Capt. McKoy said, "Experience is the ability to recognize a mistake the *second* time you make it—ain't happenin' around here. When I get back from Washington, John, we're gonna make us a rule to never work for Fifth Army again. Our boys deserve better."

Lt. Gen. Patton said, "Joe tells me you've crafted an alternate plan that allows you to accomplish your mission *and* bring your troops out."

Col. Randal said, "Best I could come up with, sir, considering…"

Capt. McKoy said, "John didn't have much to work with, but I sure wouldn't want to be a Nazi German anywhere near Benevento once the Rangers get on the ground."

Lt. Gen. Patton said, "Salute, continue to march, do your duty, don't complain—that's the spirit, Colonel. Get back in one piece. If I ever get out of the doghouse for shooting those two mules, I'm going to need you to help me win this damn war."

Capt. McKoy said, "I'll see you when I see you."

Col. Randal climbed back in the Dakota. The loadmaster slammed the door shut. Maj. Gen. Blackwell immediately began taxiing for takeoff and Chalk 1 was on the way. There was no false bravado from the paratroopers. Everyone was sitting quietly, clutching their weapons and thinking their own thoughts while the airplane's powerful engines hummed.

Tonight was a serious mission. The Rangers had all volunteered for hazardous duty. This was hazardous duty.

Normally, the first men in were Pathfinders. Not for this drop. There was no reason to mark the drop zone. C-47s did not carry navigators and the 313 Troop Carrier Group pilots were not capable of making the flight to Benevento and locating a small pinpoint DZ on their own.

The pilots had been ordered to fly to the vicinity of Benevento and put their paratroopers out over the first flat piece of ground they came to. The idea was to try to drop into meadows along the road in the narrow river valley winding its way south out of the town to Avellino where the 509th was fighting. No one actually believed that was going to work either. The problem was there were a lot of roads and meadows and from the air they would all look alike.

Nothing could be done about it.

The results were a given—the pilots would become disoriented and the formation would fall apart. Jumpers would be exiting from aircraft flying alone or in clusters of twos and threes instead of the thirty-eight plane follow-on serial to Maj. Gen. Blackwell's lead aircraft. The 575th Ranger Force could count on being dumped out along some road in some valley scattered all over the Italian countryside. Who knew where?

But then that was the plan—Col. Randal's revised, unofficial, unauthorized version.

The loadout on Chalk 1 was an unusual mix. Captain Billy Jack Jaxx was aboard but this was not SOG stick. Captain "Dynamite" Dick Coogan was there, with four of his demolition men. His mission was to attempt to blow the road bridge spanning the Sabato River out of Benevento leading to Avellino where the 509th PIB had dropped last night.

He was initially slated to be a company commander in the composite 2/575th. However, since there were not going to be any company tasks, he reverted to being a demolitions expert. An assignment for which the Georgia native was a true professional.

Raiding Forces' other demolitions expert, Captain "Pyro" Percy Stirling, had also come along with the 575th Ranger Force when it departed RFHQ. He was farther back in the serial on Chalk 14, with a team of his demolitions men from the former Railroad Wrecking Crew. The word on Pyro was that when he blew something up, it stayed blown up. In his highly colorful career, he had struck fear into many a heart—more often than not, hearts belonging to his own troops.

His mission was to blow the rail bridge spanning the Sabato River.

The two bridges were key targets in the 575th Ranger Force's plan to disrupt the 16th Panzer Division from reaching the bridgehead in time to influence the landing.

Also on board Chalk 1 were Lieutenant Chase Starrett, Lieutenant Clint Hays, Lieutenant Dan Bonham, and Lieutenant Jake "The Snake" Novak. The 509th Pathfinder Platoon Leader had volunteered to make the jump since he had not been able to return to his battalion in time for their drop on Avellino. He was considering requesting a transfer to Raiding Forces permanently.

Master Sergeant Mack Beckwith and King were on the plane as well.

The reason for having so many leaders stacked in the fifteen-man stick was to get them on the ground first, where they would each be in position to grab a few men from the follow-on planes, form an ad hoc team, then explode out from the DZ to begin a guerrilla campaign.

Col. Randal had dozed off when the USAAF loadmaster came over to talk to him. "Sir, the General would like to speak to you."

He got up, moving clumsily in his parachute with his 9mm Beretta MAB-38 submachine gun, pair of Colt 1911 .38 Super pistols, 9mm Browning P-35, .22 High Standard pistol with silencer, .380 Remington Model 51 pocket pistol, Fairbairn knife, grenades, and as many magazines of 9mm ammunition as he could strap on. Col. Randal was not carrying much in the way of rations. He was planning to live off the land, which is only marginally better than having no plan at all.

In the cockpit, he found Maj. Gen. Blackwell in the command pilot's seat with his daughter, Beverly, as his co-pilot. This was probably the first father-daughter combat mission in the history of the United States Army Air Force. Women were not authorized to fly combat in the USAAF—but who was going to tell Bronc no?

Maj. Gen. Blackwell said, "We're approaching the Salerno beachhead. Benevento's about fifteen minutes out. Red light in ten."

Off in the distance Mt. Vesuvius was erupting, which added an additional sense of unreality to the night.

Down on the ground, teardrop-shaped lights were winking. German antiaircraft guns zeroing in on the C-47. Flack began exploding and the Dakota side slipped, bucking and yawning.

Unruffled, Maj. Gen. Blackwell said, "I've done things in my life I regretted. Pretty sure tonight's going to be pretty close to the top of the list, when it's all said and done.

"You be sure to follow your own orders. Shoot and scoot. Don't try to win the war single-handed."

Col. Randal said, "Wilco."

Maj. Gen. Blackwell said, "I've got me an idea you just might go for, on how we can work the Airborne Advisor deal. Now's not the time to end up dead or behind barbed wire in a POW camp. We've got work to do."

Col. Randal said, "Understood, sir—we'll talk when I get back."

Beverly said, "OK, just so you know, Johnny. I'm staying in Sicily until you get back.

Lady Jane will have to find out about this mission from somebody else. "I'm not breaking the news to her."

Col. Randal said, "Good plan."

Maj. Gen. Blackwell said, "We're probably gonna have a bigger problem that makes fighting panzers with handheld weapons seem like a walk in the park."

Col. Randal said, "What might that be, Bronc?"

Maj. Gen. Blackwell said, "Word is you and that drop dead gorgeous Lady Jane woman I've heard so much about are so tight, you're like Siamese twins—tease each other all the time, finish each other's sentences. And Beverly, I don't know if you're aware of it or not, but she's got a big time crush on you, Johnny. She hasn't paid any attention to any man less 'an about sixty years old since going off to UT until you . . ."

Beverly laughed. "Daddy, will you stop."

Maj. Gen. Blackwell said, "I'm just saying—bigamy ain't exactly legal in Texas."

13
JUMPING FROM AN AIRCRAFT IN FLIGHT

"TEN MINUTES!"

Colonel John Randal held up both hands with his fingers splayed when he gave the first in the series of jump commands. Tonight he was going to be using a much abbreviated set. Everyone was jumping, so there was no sense performing useless checks.

King would be exiting right after him, then Master Sergeant Mack Beckwith, the two Lovat Scouts, then Captain Billy Jack Jaxx, followed by the rest of the stick. Col. Randal did not know if his plan to put so many leaders on the ground first was a good idea or not. Major General Sam Houston Blackwell had informed him that the photo reconnaissance mission to Avellino showed the drop had been scattered over a 45-square mile area, so maybe he had overthought things. There might not be any follow-on serials dropping on his DZ for the leaders to link up with to form raiding parties.

Col. Randal stamped his boot on the deck of the C-47, arms outstretched, holding up six fingers, "SIX MINUTES! STAND UP AND HOOK UP!"

The Rangers struggled to their feet. There was the metal-on-metal clicking of static lines being snapped on the steel anchor cable. The aisle was cluttered with life preservers the men had pulled off and discarded as soon as the Dakota was over land. The troops were all weighted down with weapons, ammunition, and equipment, plus their main and reserve parachutes, so they were happy to get rid of anything they could before the jump.

Too late to do anything about it, Col. Randal realized he had made a mistake. The life preservers should have been thrown out the door. The last thing he wanted was the stick tripping over them on the green light—the longer it took the Rangers to exit the aircraft, the wider the dispersion.

Col. Randal grabbed the sides of the door and arched himself outside to make a jumpmaster check. The wind was howling. Since Maj. Gen. Blackwell was flying the lead aircraft, there should have been at least one other C-47 flying formation off the left wing and another off the wing on the far side that would have dropped into a trail formation at the ten- minute warning. Nothing—the only thing he could see were the small lavender lights on the tip of the Dakota's wing.

The formation had become separated.

Down below in the valley was the road that led, presumably, to Benevento. Steep mountains jutted up on both sides of the hardball. Nothing was moving on it. In the distance, approaching fast, was the DZ in the meadow a mile from town.

Col. Randal swung back inside.

"ONE MINUTE! CLOSE ON THE DOOR!"

King shuffled up close. Col. Randal made eye contact with the Merc, then turned and took up his position in the door. Almost immediately the red light flashed green.

"LET'S GO!"

It was a beautiful, clear night. Big moon with stars twinkling. From the time he exited the door, things started going in slow motion as his static line pulled his X-type parachute's canopy from its pack and it began to deploy. Col. Randal was silently counting, "One thousand, two thousand, three thousand . . ."

There was a soft tug—the British X-type parachute was known for gentle openings. And then he transitioned from falling into sitting easy in the canvas saddle, drifting through the midnight sky—backward. There was no way to see where he was going, but he could observe Bronc and Beverly winging out of sight, still in slow motion, in the now-vacated C-47 Dakota troop transport.

He saw the moon. He saw the mountains. He saw fields terraced down the side of the mountains. He saw the road.

What Col. Randal could not see were any other parachutes.

Then he looked down between his boots and saw rooftops flashing past below. That was not part of the plan. Col. Randal realized he had drifted over a mile. Only now had he finally reached normal jump altitude, which meant there was still a way to go to the ground.

A lot of things could go wrong with this parachute landing fall—fast, and there was not much Col. Randal could do about it. He assumed the "prepare to land" position early. Coming down in a built-up area was not exactly conducive to making a textbook PLF. There was no school solution on how to perform a parachute landing fall in the middle of a town.

What had been a lovely, slow, long hang time descent under a beautiful star-studded sky suddenly switched to fast forward—like going over Niagara Falls in a canoe. Although his chin was tucked down tight on his chest, he could see buildings whizzing past out of his peripheral vision. Col. Randal did a quick check to make sure his elbows were pulled in tight against his sides and his knees were loose—*not* locked. Then the toes of his boots touched down on white Tuscan tile—he knew that because of Lady Jane's remodeling project.

Then extremely fast, he hit all five points of contact in perfect sequence with beautiful form.

The only problem was, Col. Randal was on a two-story sharply sloped roof. The momentum of his PLF carried him over the edge. He fell to the ground into someone's freshly tilled flower bed.

All in all, one of his better landings.

Col. Randal hit the quick release, dropped his parachute, then took his 9mm Beretta MAB-38 submachine gun out of his leg bag and assembled it.

He had carried it broken down. There was no way he was going to risk damaging the weapon like he had done on the Sicily jump.

A quick assessment of his situation told him absolutely nothing. Only one thought came to mind. He had violated his own orders to stay out of Benevento.

Nothing was moving. The town was blacked out. It had been heavily bombed by the USAAF in recent days, and the population was staying inside with lights out—not taking any chances.

In the distance, airplanes could be heard passing over—the 313th Troop Carrier Group bringing in the rest of the 575th Ranger Force. Quite possibly the citizenry mistook them for bombers.

From aerial photos, Col. Randal knew Benevento was a long and narrow town, strung out down the valley along the river with a population of some 30,000 people. What could Fifth Army have been thinking to task an understrength Ranger battalion of less than 600 men with seizing and holding a place that big for three to five days? And with no heavy weapons—the Rangers had not brought mortars or crew-served machine guns, preferring mobility over firepower.

Besides, there was zero chance of finding bundle-dropped weapons after a 3,000-foot release.

The best thing to do, Col. Randal concluded, was to exfiltrate the metropolitan area as rapidly as possible. It was a spooky feeling moving alone down narrow streets in a blacked-out town, thinking there could be a 16th Panzer Division Panzergrenadier with a burp gun lurking in every shadow. He had a map, but it was a 1:25000 topographical that was little help, showing only the shaded outline of the town. He did not even bother to take it out.

After sliding down the side of a building with his back to the wall, a quick head check around the corner revealed a German weapons carrier backed up to a blacked-out storefront. Panzergrenadiers were looting the place. Inside, beams of flashlights played around as they searched for more items to steal.

Col. Randal was weighing his options when he spotted a figure stroll out into the middle of the street not more than ten yards from the weapons carrier, then kneel down on one knee in the wide open. The Nazis were so absorbed in their larceny that they failed to take notice. The silhouette cast by his cut-down Australian bush hat gave him away—Jack Cool.

What could his SOG commander be up to?

Only one way to find out—Col. Randal stepped around the corner and out into the street, feeling exposed, as he was. His rubber-soled, canvas-topped raiding boots did not make a sound. He walked up behind Capt. Jaxx.

"What's going on, Jack?"

Seemingly unruffled by his commanding officer appearing out of nowhere, Capt. Jaxx said, "Trying to figure out how to load this Bazooka, sir."

"Where did you get a rocket launcher?"

"Found it lying on the ground a couple of streets over, with a container of three antitank rounds—somebody must have dropped it, sir."

A small number of M1A1 Rocket Launchers, known as Bazookas or Stovepipes, were issued to the 575th Ranger Force prior to boarding their aircraft. A new weapon—not one single person in the unit had ever fired one. A U.S. Army demonstration team had arrived at RFHQ unannounced a few weeks prior and put on a demonstration for everyone who happened to be on the premises at the time. About the only thing Col. Randal remembered was the advisory not to be standing behind the bazooka when the gunner fired.

The back blast, which was what made it recoilless, was said to be deadly. Col. Randal said, "I'll load."

The HEAT (High Explosive Anti-Tank) round went in the back end until the fins disappeared, and he heard an audible click. Next, he flipped the little ball-headed lever on top of the tube at the back to the upright position. He hoped that was all there was to it.

"Good to go." Which was probably not the approved Anti-Tank school solution command, but then Col. Randal had no idea what that was supposed to be.

Capt. Jaxx said, "Don't try this at home."

BOOOOOM!

The bazooka launched its 2.36-inch rocket out the front end, while simultaneously belching smoke and flame out the back. The back blast was deafening and the flash signature blinding. The HEAT round, which was a shape charge, zipped down range. It was possible to watch it in flight as the rocket sailed past the weapons carrier, shattered the plate glass window, and detonated inside the building with an even bigger explosion.

The blast was accompanied by a brilliant white flash and a hurricane of dust, followed by a sudden shockwave. Smoke was billowing out of the store. The results were highly satisfactory.

Col. Randal had been expecting Capt. Jaxx to aim at the weapons carrier, and maybe he had been. Nevertheless, the effect on the enemy soldiers could not have been greater. All the Nazis inside the store were either down, killed, or stunned by the blast.

The Panzergrenadiers outside loading the vehicle were shredded by a blizzard of razor- sharp glass shards. Col. Randal and Capt. Jaxx immediately advanced on the weapons carrier, firing as they came. The rounds from the .30 caliber Baby BAR and 9mm Beretta MAB-38 converged on the Germans toward the back of the vehicle—most of whom were already down or staggering around horribly mutilated by the cloud of microscopic glass particles.

One second the Nazis had been happily stealing electronic equipment—the next the world exploded in their face.

Capt. Jaxx moved down the side of the weapons carrier, then around the back with his Baby BAR at the ready. He shot the two Panzergrenadiers who were still on their feet despite horrific wounds. Then the four on the ground.

Col. Randal stepped through the broken plate glass window and put a short burst into each of the five forms crumpled on the floor of the store.

"Clear."

Capt. Jaxx said, "Crime doesn't pay—not for these Nazis." Col. Randal said, "Let's get the hell out of Dodge."

LIEUTENANT DAN BONHAM HAD BEEN IN THE MIDDLE OF THE stick aboard Chalk 1. He was the most recent 10th Ranger Battalion officer attached to the Small Operations Group. Captain Billy Jack Jaxx was grooming him to become a member of SOG.

That meant Lt. Bonham had seen a substantial amount of action recently.

The flight to the DZ had been uneventful, except for the ack-ack when the Dakota flew over the beachhead. He spent most of the trip dozing—not really asleep. Hard to get comfortable with all the gear he was strapped into.

Lt. Bonham was armed with a .30 caliber M1 Carbine. The .30 caliber round that the carbine fired was not to be confused with the .30 caliber round the M1 Garand Rifle fired. The carbine round was basically an expanded pistol cartridge, whereas the rifle round was the military's Geneva Convention-compliant version of the 30–06 cartridge loved by deer hunters everywhere.

The advantages of the carbine were that it was smaller, lighter, had a magazine capacity of fifteen rounds versus eight for the rifle, and it was possible to carry nearly three times as many M1 Carbine rounds as M1 Garand rounds.

The disadvantages were that the M1 Carbine did not have the range or knock-down power of the M1 Rifle. However, the M1 Carbine's pluses were important considerations, especially for those times when fighting behind enemy lines for days, with no means of resupply—like tonight. It came down to a matter of personal choice.

The majority of the Rangers were armed with the .30 caliber M1 Garand Rifle.

All Lt. Bonham wanted was for the jump to be over with. He was ready to get on the ground and round up a handful of paratroopers—then start his guerrilla campaign.

When Colonel John Randal shouted, "STAND UP AND HOOK UP!," Lt. Bonham struggled to his feet, tripping over all the discarded life preservers on the floor.

"ONE MINUTE! CLOSE ON THE DOOR!"

The men in the stick surged forward until they were crammed into the jumper in front of them. Tension was thick in the air. Chalk 1 may have consisted of highly experienced professionals, but to a man they all wanted out of the plane.

"LET'S GO!"

The stick started shuffling forward, almost running, shouting, "GO, GO, GO . . .", all the heavily loaded Rangers charging the door. Up ahead, he could see jumpers exiting. Then Lt. Bonham was out, caught in the prop blast of the C-47's powerful engines and being tumbled over and over.

The chute cracked open and he was pleasantly surprised, as he always was, that it had. Lt. Bonham looked down. He was way high. The moon cast a silvery glow on the landscape. There were other parachutes in the sky but they were all widely separated.

The Rangers were being taken for a ride by the swirling air terminals.

Floating down, Lt. Bonham spotted a small, round, black spot on the ground that looked suspiciously like a water well. As he was coming in, the hole seemed to chase him. That was officially not good.

In a desperate attempt to slip away from the evil-looking black spot, he started pulling down on his right riser, hand over hand, spilling air out of the canopy until the lines came down and were between his fingers. No joy. Coming in, the landscape seemed to spin, giving him the brief flash of vertigo not uncommon to parachute landings.

His X-type parachute's canopy tangled in an olive tree.

But that did not keep Lt. Bonham from going into the hole like he had been sucked down by some supernatural force. It was a water well all right, but luckily it was under construction. The odds against landing in the hole after all his rigorous efforts to miss it had to be astronomical.

While he was trying to extricate himself—and thanking his lucky stars the well was only about five feet deep and not twenty or thirty feet of water— a white-haired Italian ran up to help him climb out.

Speaking in heavily accented English, the man said, "How are you? I live in New Jersey three years. Welcome to sunny Italy."

It was 2415 hours.

Lorenzo—his new friend claimed that was his name—kissed the American invasion flag on Lt. Bonham's sleeve. Then he pointed in the direction of where he claimed there was a 16th Panzer Division "car park with 100 vehicles located a mile up the road."

In typical Ranger fashion, Lt. Bonham said, "Show me."

PRIVATE FIRST CLASS WALLY MALINOWSKI WAS JUMPING Chalk 2. The pilot had become separated from Major General Sam Houston Blackwell's lead aircraft when the ack- ack started as they passed over the beachhead. Then the flier became disoriented. Now he was flying low, below the mountain tops, trying to find a recognizable terrain feature.

Naturally, he got it wrong.

Major Duke Slater was jumpmastering. The red light was on. He gave the Ten Minute Warning, then leaned out and saw the drop zone up ahead. When he swung back inside, the red light went off. Maj. Slater expected it to come back on. It never did, and the next time he checked, they were passing over the DZ.

Maj. Slater unhooked his static line and ran up to the cockpit. "You've overflown our drop zone."

"Negative, that was a premature red light. My watch says we have four more minutes flying time. The Ten Minute Warning will . . ."

Maj. Slater ordered, "Turn this crate around and take us back—NOW!"

The pilot, who was in over his head on this mission and possibly scared, shouted, "You can't give me orders on board my own airplane—I'm the aircraft commander."

Maj. Slater placed the barrel of his Colt 1911 .38 Super against the pilot's right ear and cocked the hammer. It made two distinctive clicks.

They were unmistakable.

"I'm wearing a parachute. Your co-pilot knows how to fly this plane. Nobody's going to miss you much if I pull the trigger."

In a panic, the pilot banked hard, coming around until the plane was traveling back in the direction from which it had been traveling. Now they were flying straight at the oncoming sky train of troop transports. Trying to avoid a head-on collision, C-47s started dodging all over the sky, which was not much of a problem since they were no longer flying in any semblance of a formation anyway.

Maj. Slater said, "That wasn't so hard."

Ten minutes later, the Rangers jumped. On the long ride down, PFC Malinowski spotted one of his buddies, Private Zeke Swearington, riding easy in his chute, being carried along by the air thermals. He tried to slip his direction so that they could land close to each other and hook up for the upcoming fight.

PFC Malinowski was dropping faster than Pvt. Swearington, but not by much. It was a long ride down. He began to have concerns that jumpers from the other aircraft would land on top of his canopy and cause it to collapse. There are a magnitude of things for a paratrooper to worry about— an active imagination being a drawback.

Below, he heard people on the ground calling, *"Viva Americani."*

It took a minute to realize the cries were meant for him. Then he saw the terrain his parachute was dropping into. Trees, farmhouses, barns, a river, fences, cows, big rocks—not good. PFC Malinowski tried to slip to avoid a barn and ended up in a tree, dangling down about a foot off the ground. The welcoming locals rushed over to help him get untangled.

Tonight's was the first jump he had ever made that did not end with a PLF.

Pvt. Swearington was coming in hot, trying to miss the farmhouse, but he made a bad job of it. He hit the roof dead center and disappeared. People in their night clothes started flying out of the door, windows, and places where there did not seem to be any sign of an exit.

After a few minutes, Pvt. Swearington staggered out the front door minus his parachute, with his M1 Garand at port arms. He and PFC Malinowski hugged each other. They were both down on the ground alive, which was always cause for celebration after a night combat jump.

In accordance to orders, the two Rangers set out in search of bad guys to kill.

LIEUTENANT CHASE STARRETT OF THE SMALL OPERATIONS Group was the jumpmaster on Chalk 19. His plane drew fire over Pompeii, which was not the flight path it was supposed to be taking, and turned up the wrong valley toward Benevento—the pilot was very lost. The red light came on.

Lt. Starrett began issuing his jump commands.

After giving his stick the six-minute warning, he arched out the exit door to make his safety inspections—no planes too close that might interfere with his stick. Not a problem. Everything looked copacetic, which is paratrooper-speak for good. Then he tried to spot the DZ. There was a meadow up ahead with a road running past.

It looked exactly like the one in the aerial photos.

Chalk 19 began taking ground fire. The left engine started burning. Lt. Starrett shouted, "CLOSE ON THE DOOR—FOLLOW ME!"

When Lt. Starrett exited, he could see his stick was right over the meadow. He also saw that Chalk 19 was the only aircraft in the sky. That did not seem right.

What could not be seen was the rest of his stick because they were behind him as he floated down. Lt. Starrett did observe the C-47 wing over, crash, and explode. As far as he could determine, none of the crew made it out.

Like in all combat jumps, a lot was going on—all compressed into a short period of time and at an accelerated speed. In one of those freak unexplainable coincidences that happen occasionally when jumping from an aircraft in flight, Sergeant Fred Waltmier, who had been the last jumper, landed right next to him. The rest of the Rangers were coming down in the meadow in a neat pattern that could not have been more perfect if this were a training jump made from 500 feet with Pathfinders marking the DZ.

As he was getting out of his parachute harness, Sgt. Waltmier came over and said, "This ain't the right place, El Tee. We missed the drop zone by a Kentucky mile."

What neither man knew was that they had missed it by slightly over 100 miles—worst drop of the night.

Lt. Starrett, a 10th Battalion Ranger who had been on board the *Dallas* with Colonel John Randal during TORCH before being tapped for SOG, was not easily discouraged. He said, "No big deal, Sergeant. Round up our stick and break it down into three teams. You and Corporal Lanier each take one and I'll take one. We'll start our war from here."

"Yes, sir, Lieutenant—sir!"

Lt. Starrett said, "A German's a German."

CAPTAIN ROY KIDD HAD INITIALLY BEEN SLATED TO BE A company commander in the ad hoc 2/575th. With the Benevento mission, that had changed. Like every other officer, he was now going to be a high-paid rifleman and maybe a team leader—if he could locate enough men to form a team.

Capt. Kidd was the jumpmaster on Chalk 23. This should have been a simple jump. The pilots were flying the same route as they had flown on the Pathfinder drop into the beachhead. It had been designed for simplicity by Major General Sam Houston Blackwell—only extended for an additional thirty miles to Benevento. The key word being *should*. All the pilot had to do was follow the plane in front of him all the way to the drop zone, turn on the green light, fly home, have a drink, and put himself in for a medal.

All of those things happened except the part about "follow the plane in front of him to the drop zone."

The pilot of Chalk 23 was disoriented almost from the time his C-47 took off from Sicily. The antiaircraft fire over the beachhead sealed any chance of the plane regaining its position in the formation. That said, he got close.

Capt. Kidd led his stick out the door approximately a mile short of the DZ. In the distance was the railroad line running along the river between Benevento and Avellino. He landed on a plowed terrace on the side of a mountain. Two of his men dropped nearby. There was no telling where the rest of the stick came down. So he decided to commence operations with the troops at hand.

Gathering the two Rangers for a brief Frag Order, he said, "We're going to march straight to the rail line and blow it. Barnhardt, you take point. I'll be your slack man, and Doyle, you pull rear security.

"When we reach the tracks, I'll place the explosives. You two men provide security, Barnhardt east, Doyle west of where I'll be working. We're traveling now, move out smartly— let's go."

Here and there in the distance, the sound of firing broke out from all directions, reverberated intensely, and then died out. Explosives boomed, echoing in the night. The 575th Ranger Force was on the ground fighting, albeit sporadically.

The team patrolled down the side of the mountain across two more plowed terraces and picked up another Ranger, Private First Class David Marko, who was looking for someone to link up with and was very happy to be found. Then the patrol crossed a paved road one at a time, and dropped off the far side into a narrow, flat belt of ground where they came upon the railroad tracks. Over a steep precipice on the far side of the rails, the river could be heard down below.

Capt. Kidd posted security, "Put your ear to the track to listen for a train. That's what they do in Western movies. If you hear anything, let me know."

He had no idea if the trick worked or not.

Then with PFC Marko as his assistant, Capt. Kidd started placing demolitions along the far rail that ran next to the drop-off above the river.

Prior to departure, acting on Colonel John Randal's request, every man in the 575th Ranger Force had been issued an M-37 Demolition Kit. Each contained eight prepared explosive charges of C2 that could be ignited with a fuse lighter, singly or all at once. This was without a doubt the smartest move Fifth Army staff made to support the Benevento drop—putting out the effort to requisition the excessive amount of demolitions asked for.

Col. Randal had made it known he wanted his men to bring their M37 Demolition Kits home empty, guaranteeing that all manner of enemy transport, equipment, and material was going to be blown up. The math was simple. Eight charges times nearly 600 Rangers came to a big number of bangs.

Everyone in Raiding Forces was trained in the use of explosives. With well over 150 Ranger teams on the prowl tonight, the environs of Benevento Province were about to become a very noisy place.

Capt. Kidd was placing a sixth charge in a daisy chain, to be detonated simultaneously, when Pvt. Doyle rushed up, "Sir, the tracks are vibrating — train's coming."

Not really a surprise. At the prejump briefing, it had been pointed out that the Nazis were being forced to utilize rail transportation at night because of the increased Allied air attacks, particularly by the deadly USAAF fighter bombers the Germans called "Jabos."

Quickly cutting the fuse short (Capt. Kidd had no idea how short—he was improvising), the Rangers climbed back up to the road and lay in wait to see what happened. The idea had originally been to simply blow the rail so it would have to be repaired. Now the hope was they might get a little more than that.

The demolitions went off with a loud ringing explosion. Then—nothing. Total silence, except for the ringing in their ears. Not a rewarding experience. Capt. Kidd's team experienced a letdown, but then they were blowing a section of track, not doing a "Pyro" Percy end-of-the-world type spectacular.

In the distance, from the direction of Benevento, a train was approaching. Had the engineer seen or heard the demolitions? Apparently not . . . it continued to huff and puff.

An ancient steam engine, with smoke belching from its stack, chugged into view out of the dark. It was pulling a coal car and two box cars. Not much in the way of trains, but then so far, the whole night had been like that.

On came the locomotive into the turn, but it kept going straight, out and over the edge of the cliff, until it crashed on the rocks far down below before tumbling into the river—then it exploded. The detonation would have made Captain "Pyro" Percy Sterling proud. The sound and fury shocked the Rangers. Most likely, the train had been transporting ammunition to the Kampfgruppen of 16th Panzer Division headquartered in Avellino.

It must have had a high concentration of tank rounds on board.

The fireworks lit up the night, and after the initial blast, rounds continued cooking off. Capt. Kidd's team was jubilant. This was more like it. Hoping to find an opportunity to do something like it again, the team moved off.

The Rangers had a lot of charges left.

PRIVATE NORVEL HANSEN, AKA "HORN DOG," A SOG OPERATOR and confirmed wise-ass but natural leader of men—most often into one scrape or another in Cairo, which was why he was a private, not a private first class, a corporal, or maybe even a sergeant— came drifting down in his parachute and landed somewhere . . . he knew not where. Nothing looked anything like the DZ in the aerial photo passed around at the SOG prejump Mission Order. Four other chutes were already on the ground when he came in. The Rangers banded together in an olive grove. With no officers or non-coms present, Pvt. Hansen decided to go into business for himself.

"Let's go kill some bad guys. That's what we're here for."

"Yeah!"

Since nobody knew where they were, the only thing Pvt. Hansen could think of was to move to the road he had spotted on his ride to the ground. After traveling only a short distance, a middle-aged Italian appeared out of the dark. The word had gone 'round that American parachutists were dropping and he wanted to come see for himself.

The Italian local introduced himself as Rodger and said, "I drove a cab in Chicago for four years—love those White Sox."

Pvt. Hansen said, "Well, Rodger from Chicago, do you know where we might find Nazis this fine night?"

Rodger said, "Everywhere."

"Can you be a little more specific?"

"The *Tedeschi* travel up and down the roads both day and night, stealing from every place they come to. On any road, you will eventually see them passing by. I will show you."

The five-man team shook themselves out into a loose column formation balanced heavy right and, following Rodger, moved off in the direction of the road. The moon was up. Visibility was good.

There were no officers or NCOs around. There were enemy soldiers to shoot up. They had a guide. Militarily, it did not get any better than this for Horn Dog Hansen.

Rodger led the team to a road. A long, straight stretch offered possibilities as a good place to set up a linear ambush. Pvt. Hansen posted security, then he and the other four Rangers placed charges from their M37 Demolition Kits on four of the tall trees that grew along the sides of the road.

Rodger watched the proceedings with interest.

When the trees were wired in, Pvt. Hansen pulled the ring on the fuse lighter that was attached to the det cord running to the charges. Everyone took cover. The smell of burning could be detected but not much else happened. Then the C2 went off.

The trees seemed to lean over in slow motion, then they fell to the ground like a string of dominoes, blocking the roadway. Pvt. Hansen had selected this ambush site because there was not any easy way to drive around the fallen trees. It was a good roadblock and would be difficult for the Germans to clear—meaning they could, but it would take time.

Pvt. Hansen's team had been waiting in the ambush site for a half hour when they heard a motorcycle approaching. The troops perked up—soft target. Every man was armed with a semi- automatic .30 caliber M1 Garand, which was the best infantry rifle fielded by any army anywhere.

The Rangers were itching to engage something.

A BMW R-75 motorcycle, with a sidecar affixed, occupied by a very large Panzergrenadier who looked stuffed in the little passenger seat, roared up to the first fallen tree and screeched to a halt.

Pvt. Hansen ordered, "Let 'em have it."

Not the jargon typically used to initiate an ambush, but it worked.

The Rangers engaged as one, shooting as fast as they could pull the trigger. A cone of fire vectored in on the Nazi cyclists. The two Panzergrenadiers never knew what hit them. They went down, riddled by an angry swarm of big .30 caliber steel-jacketed rounds.

It was over fast.

The Rangers immediately reloaded, cramming 8-round clips into their M1s, their hands moving automatically. None of the men even glanced down at their weapon as they worked, preferring to keep their eyes up, scanning for possible new targets.

Out of the dark, an Sd. Kfz.234 armored car roared up, firing its 20mm automatic cannon as it came. The tracers looked like the size of glowing softballs cracking overhead. This was more than the lightly armed Rangers had signed on for.

Pvt. Hansen shouted, "Break contact!" Then he threw a hand grenade.

The team ran through the woods up the side of the mountain for a half mile, laughing with adrenaline-fueled relief at their close call. They set up a rally point near a vineyard in sight of a blacked-out farmhouse. Their hide position overlooked the road down below. The Rangers were fired up. This was the way to fight a war—light 'em up, hit and run.

As per the Colonel's orders.

When Pvt. Hansen conducted a head count, Rodger had apparently decided his services were required elsewhere. No problem. The Rangers did not require a guide any longer. They knew what to do.

Besides, Horn Dog was a Cubs fan.

14
CHAOS

WHEN KING HIT THE SILK, HE WAS IMMEDIATELY CAUGHT by an updraft. Instead of going down, his X-type parachute went up. While this was not a common occurrence, it did happen from time to time, even on jumps that were not in mountainous terrain. The good news was he would not go up forever. The bad news was, dangling under a parachute over enemy-occupied territory for any more time than absolutely necessary was not a great idea.

King could see the other jumpers in his stick floating down. His plan had been to land, link up with Colonel John Randal, and start the fight. That was not going to happen now.

When the Merc finally drifted in for a landing, his canopy caught in the top of a fifty-foot tall tree, leaving him dangling thirty feet off the ground. No problem. King pulled the handle on the reserve parachute strapped on his chest. It came off in his hand like it was supposed to—only during a high speed, midair parachute malfunction, when that happened, it would likely not make a paratrooper feel overly confident.

King tossed the handle away and began feeding out the reserve chute. Unlike the canopy, which was pulled out of the main deployment bag automatically by the static line, the jumper has to deploy his reserve parachute by hand. Once it was out and dangling to the ground, the Merc hit the quick release on his chest, slid out of the harness, and then hand over handed it the rest of the way down.

Being all alone behind enemy lines did not bother King. In fact, he liked it. No witnesses. King assembled his 9mm Beretta MAB-38 submachine gun, touch-checked his Colt 1911

38 Super, .22 High Standard with silencer, and his Fairbairn knife, which was strapped to his left forearm, as was his Rolex watch—being a highly paid soldier of fortune, King had only the best gear—and wrist compass. The fact that the Merc was armed identically to Col. Randal was no accident. He wanted weapons and ammunition compatibility with his boss.

Then King moved downhill in the direction of the road. Panzergrenadiers were vehicle mounted, road-bound soldiers only dismounting to conduct sweeps or set up ambushes. The best place to find them was along a hardball.

The slope of the mountain came straight down to the right of way. There was no traffic when he slid into position. King lay observing for a while, getting a feel for his environment— taking his time, absorbing the situation.

Then he ghosted to one of the telephone poles that ran along the road and started climbing. It would have been easier to blow down the pole with one of his demolitions charges, but saving them for a better opportunity later seemed like the better plan.

As King was cutting the last line with his Fairbairn Fighting Knife, he heard a motorcycle approaching. No unit in any army utilized motorcycles in greater numbers than a Panzer Division. Dispatch riders could be expected to constantly be moving between 16th Panzer Division's eight battalion-sized kampfgruppen night and day.

King shinnied down the telephone pole. Then he picked up one of the phone lines and tied it to the trunk of the pole, crossed the road, dropped off the shoulder into a ditch and waited, leaving the line laying in the right-of-way. He did not have to wait long.

The BMW R-75 came roaring down the center of the road. The

messenger was either in a big hurry or a thrill seeker to be traveling that fast at night with only his cat's eye light on. It did not cast that much of a beam.

The Nazi never saw the phone cable laying in his path.

King jerked it taut. The line caught the rider on the Adams Apple and the Nazi was lifted off his seat. He landed flat on his back and never moved, staring straight up—dead. The BMW performed an unmanned wheelie, running down the road for about ten yards on its rear wheel before crashing.

The Merc quickly searched the German, taking his 9mm Walther P-38 pistol, and sticking it in his belt around back. He dragged the man to the edge of the road and pushed his body into the ditch. Then he rolled the BMW off the shoulder down behind him.

Once off the high-speed avenue of approach, the Merc searched the motorcycle's saddlebags. In addition to a shaving kit and the cyclist's dispatches, there was a mess tin containing sauerkraut and wieners—still warm. That was good.

King had worked up an appetite.

MASTER SERGEANT MACK BECKWITH WAS THE LAST MAN OUT of Chalk 1. His idea was to land, roll up the stick, and then link up with Colonel John Randal. That plan did not make it to the exit. The man in front of him stumbled on one of the discarded life vests as they came to the door.

He went down.

The Sergeant Major—as Col. Randal called him, the troops called him "Top,"—reached down, grabbed the Ranger with one hand, dragged him to the door, and shoved him out. Then he jumped, afraid he would be caught by the red light—headfirst.

You are not supposed to exit an aircraft in flight headfirst. The wind of the prop blast grabbed MSgt. Beckwith like a giant hand. Except he was upside down. And he seemed to be frozen in place.

When the parachute cracked open, MSgt. Beckwith was jerked upright. It was a pretty big jolt. He was thinking this was not going well.

Then he looked up and saw that things had gotten worse.

One of the lines had somehow ended up over the top of the canopy, causing a malfunction affectionately known to paratroopers as a "Mae West" because of the two large humps made in the inflated parachute. Immediate action was required. MSgt. Beckwith went back into the tuck position, feet and knees together.

He ripped the handle off his reserve as hard as he could possibly pull. It tore across the top and came off in his hand as designed. MSgt. Beckwith threw the handle away and immediately started pulling the reserve out by hand.

It blew back in his face. He grabbed it and threw it away from his body as hard as he could. MSgt. Beckwith was a longtime experienced paratrooper, having been an original member of the Test Platoon at Ft. Benning. He knew that if he did not get the reserve canopy to deploy, it would likely blow back again and tangle in the risers over his head and that would be game over as far as the reserve went.

Still in the tuck position, he leaned backward hard.

On the second try throwing it out, the reserve canopy caught the wind and popped open. Once the reserve deployed, the line over the top of the main chute corrected itself and it was freed to blossom open. Now MSgt. Beckwith was coming down under two parachutes.

The problem with that was the fully deployed reserve's lines and risers were a lot shorter than those on the main parachutes. Its canopy stole the wind. The main collapsed and fell down past MSgt. Beckwith, which was not a sight to instill joy in the heart of any airborne trooper.

Shortly the main's canopy refilled with air. But because it was now underneath the reserve, the main stole the wind out of the reserve's canopy. It collapsed. And fell. And refilled itself.

MSgt. Beckwith was in free fall in between the two canopies refilling with air. This was not a problem as high as he had jumped. Unless it happened as he was coming in to land.

Then he was going to crash and burn—in paratrooper speak.

Tonight had turned out to be one of his worst jumps ever. Fortunately, his main was fully deployed as he came in, after a ride that seemed to last a lifetime. When he landed, MSgt. Beckwith made a classic PLF.

After he popped his quick release and recovered his M1 Garand, three Rangers appeared—Corporal Joe Henderson, Private Mark Loewenberg, and Private Dave Rickles. Since no one else was around, MSgt. Beckwith decided not to waste time searching for additional men. "Saddle up, look sharp," he ordered. "We're heading down to the road. We'll set up an ambush—maybe blow the railroad tracks if we can find 'em."

The three Rangers were mighty pleased to find themselves under the command of Raiding Forces' Sergeant Major this night.

Cpl. Henderson said, "Lead the way, Top."

The four patrolled down the side of the mountain. They did not encounter any other jumpers as they moved. Planes could be heard overhead in all directions.

MSgt. Beckwith did not need anyone to tell him this was "one screwed-up operation."

The sound of firing began to break out in the distance all around. There were demolitions going off. Gunfire. And still, C-47s flying overhead to drop their jumpers anywhere but where they were supposed to.

Two miles from where he had landed, MSgt. Beckwith arrived at the road along the Sabato River. He halted his patrol. Everything in their immediate area was dead still.

An Opel Blitz truck came around a turn in the road. A squad of German Panzergrenadiers was riding in the bed. Probably racing to a firefight. The vehicle was far enough off that the Rangers had time to move up on line to set up a hasty ambush and toss Hawkins mines out onto the right-of-way.

The left front tire of the Opel hit one of the No. 75 Hawkins mines. At the same, MSgt. Beckwith ordered, "COMMENCE FIRE!" Everyone opened at point-blank range.

The truck swerved, ran off the road, and crashed down the slope through the woods on the far side. The ambush was over fast. There was no way to know how many of the Germans had been shot or injured in the crash.

MSgt. Beckwith did not have any intention of hanging around to find out. "Saddle up. We're moving. Stay frosty, boys."

CAPTAIN "PYRO" PERCY STIRLING AND CAPTAIN "DYNAMITE" Dick Coogan jumped different chalks with four demolition men each. Their planes had been widely separated in the serial. There was no good explanation for how they had come down so close together. Except that the pilot of Chalk 7, the C-47 Capt. Coogan was on, had somehow managed to find the DZ where Major General Sam Houston Blackwell had put his jumpers out.

Capt. Stirling was the only British officer that Lieutenant Colonel Sir Terry "Zorro" Stone had allowed to make the drop. British Army officers were in critically short supply in Raiding Forces these days. There was no pipeline of replacements due to a serious manpower shortage in the UK because of full mobilization this late in the war, and commanders of line regiments were increasingly reluctant to allow their officers to volunteer out for special service.

The only reason Capt. Stirling was cleared for the operation was because no one had more experience blowing railroads than he did. His railroad-destroying days dated as far back as far as the early days of pinprick raiding on the coast of France out of Seaborn House, and Force N in Abyssinia.

Two of the rail lines in the Benevento area led south to Salerno. They needed to be interdicted to impede the 16th Panzer Division's drive on the Salerno beachhead. Capt. Stirling was "Right Man, Right Job." His gun jeep patrol had not been called the Railroad Wrecking Crew without cause.

For his part, Capt. Coogan's father owned a demolition company based out of Atlanta, Georgia, that specialized in taking down buildings. Dynamite Dick had grown up traveling all over the United States with his father, demolishing functionally obsolete structures that needed to come down without falling on the adjoining properties—precision demolition. He was a master in the art of knocking down big things and making the pieces end up exactly where he wanted them.

In addition to their demolition skills, both officers were topnotch combat commanders. Tonight, their mission was to take down both the road and the rail viaducts over the Sabato River. The two bridges were a quarter of a mile apart. Capt. Stirling would be responsible for the rail bridge. Capt. Coogan would be responsible for the road bridge.

Capt. Stirling had managed to assemble three members of his team. Capt. Coogan had all four of his. They spread out to conduct a search and found three of their door bundles, which was about as close to a miracle as it gets under the circumstances.

First off, they opened the bundles and redistributed the demolitions.

Since blowing a brick-and-mortar bridge was a technically more difficult task than bringing down a wooden rail bridge, Dynamite Dick's people took the lion's share of the explosives. The two demo teams knew where they were and where their targets were. Following orders to operate in groups of no more than six men, the two teams split up and proceeded independently to their objectives.

The moon was out and there were a million stars. Both demolition parties made good time. The river was not all that big, but the drop from the bridges was approximately seventy- five feet.

The two teams arrived at their objectives and performed a reconnaissance in order to make an estimate of the situation. There were no structural surprises at either bridge. There was a small guardhouse visible on the far side of the road bridge—no way to tell if it was manned.

Capt. Coogan chose to ignore it. He did not have enough explosives to bring down the entire bridge. The best he could do was render it impassable and weaken the structure enough that it would not support tank traffic. That meant blowing the embankment on the near unmanned side with most of the demolitions being placed under the bridge.

The hope was the Nazis would not see them going about placing the charges in the dark.

It would take hours to complete the task. Time was short.

Both teams needed to be away and gone up in the mountains before daylight.

COLONEL JOHN RANDAL AND CAPTAIN BILLY JACK JAXX began exfiltrating Benevento. Occasionally, a truck or weapons carrier would race by. They were careful to stick to the shadows or take cover when a vehicle was approaching. There was no sense in getting pinned down in a firefight. German Panzergrenadiers had a reputation as tough, aggressive soldiers. In the built-up area, the chances of shooting it out and escaping every time were slim. Being channelized to streets and alleys in a strange town was a recipe for disaster.

They needed to get out into the countryside where there was freedom to maneuver.

In the distance, short, vicious bursts of firing and a growing number of explosions could be heard. It was easy to distinguish between the Rangers and Panzergrenadiers from the sound signature of the weapons. Col. Randal was satisfied that his people were initiating the majority of the firefights, obtaining fire superiority, and then breaking contact.

Years of experience sizing up a battlefield he could not see, going back to his antiguerrilla days in the jungles of the Philippines, allowed him to visualize with a reasonable degree of accuracy what was taking place by the sounds of the action. His troops were engaging in a fluid hit-and-run campaign as per his orders, using their demolitions liberally. Col. Randal was confident his Rangers were taking it to the Nazis.

Exactly as they were expected to do.

Troops fight how they train. The men making up 575th Ranger Force had been trained by battle-experienced professionals. They had all spent time behind the lines, so the experience was nothing new to them.

As Col. Randal and Capt. Jaxx moved closer to the outskirts of Benevento, they passed the occasional parachute draped off a roof or from a telephone pole. Bits of equipment were strewn on the ground. Jumping out of an aircraft traveling 120 mph is tough on personal gear no matter how tightly it's strapped down.

A dead paratrooper still in his chute was dangling from a lamp post.

After recovering the trooper's M1 Garand, ammunition, M37 Demolitions Bag, and the lightweight No. 75 Hawkins grenade/antitank mine that every man had strapped to his leg for the jump, they had no choice but to move on.

Working their way through the streets for what seemed a long time but probably was only about twenty minutes, they made it out of town and hit the road that ran along the river southwest to Avellino. They had not traveled far before coming to a series of trees that were down blocking the roadway.

Rangers had been here.

Carefully, they worked their way on foot through the woods instead of climbing over the trees. Rangers sometimes liked to booby-trap obstructions to give the Germans something to think about when they cleared them. Why take a chance?

Troops on foot could negotiate the obstacle. Vehicles were blocked. It would require effort to move the trees and that could take days.

Just for this one roadblock.

They skirted along the edge of the forest on the side of the road, sticking to the shadows. They believed they were a short distance from the bridge Capt. Coogan was assigned to knock down, when a challenge suddenly came from out of the dark.

"Drop dead."

Col. Randal responded with the countersign. "Gorgeous."

Lady Jane was going to laugh when she found out the 575th Ranger Force's Friend or Foe authenticator.

King stepped out of the shadows.

Knowing full well who was there, Capt. Jaxx ordered, "Advance and be recognized— how's it going, King?"

The Merc said, "Good, Jack, everything appears to be working to plan. Except our people may be thinner on the ground than anticipated. The drop is badly dispersed."

Col. Randal said, "You block the road back there?"

"Negative—heard the explosions."

"Anyone else pass by?"

"You and Jack are the only people I've seen all night, Chief, except for a motorcycle dispatch rider—he's laying over there in the ditch."

Col. Randal said, "Good work, let's go check on what's happening at the bridges."

For miles in every direction, short violent bursts of gunfire flared to a crescendo, then died out, sounding like sudden downpours of rain on a tin roof. Explosions—some loud, some muffled by the distance—were thundering, and an occasional flash lit up the sky, adding to the storm effect.

575th Ranger Force was in action all over Benevento Province.

Capt. Jaxx said, "Most scattered drop ever—we've made Airborne history." Jack Cool.

LIEUTENANT DAN BONHAM, HIS ITALIAN GUIDE, AND TWO Rangers he had picked up as they traveled, Private Samuel Isles and Private Norm Wojinski, were on the side of a steep slope, looking down on the German car park a hundred yards or so below. The Italian had not exaggerated. Parked with Teutonic precision in neat rows were nearly as many thin-skinned vehicles as he claimed.

German guards patrolled the perimeter.

Not that it mattered. Infiltrating the motor pool was not an option. It would not accomplish much. The three Rangers did not have enough explosives to blow all the vehicles even if they could slip in undetected. Lt. Bonham's orders were to strike, then run away to fight again at another time and place. Getting captured was not part of the plan.

There was a POL (petroleum, oil, and lubricants) station where the vehicles could refuel. It offered possibilities. Between the three Rangers, they had one M1 Carbine and two M1 Rifles. Not much firepower for an area-type target this large. However, Pvt. Wojinski had an M7 grenade launcher device attached to his M1 Rifle.

The grenade it fired was the standard MK2 fragmentation grenade mounted on a 22mm tube with stabilizer fins. It had a maximum range of 220 yards. This was good, as the fuel storage tanks were within easy range.

Lt. Bonham said, "How many rifle grenades have you got, Wojinski?"

"Forty, sir."

"Carrying a heavy load."

"Wouldn't mind unloading some of it, Lieutenant."

"Now's the time. Isles and I'll spray the trucks. You light up the fuel storage tanks."

Pvt. Wojinski laid out ten of his grenades. They looked like little rockets. He might not be able to fire them all. Reloading was a multistep process. The M1 could only be fired single shot utilizing a blank round when employing the M7 device. The blank cartridge would have to be reloaded by hand between shots because it was not powerful enough to recycle the rifle's action.

Care had to be exercised—loading a live round by accident was a flunk.

Prior to firing, the M1 Rifle grenadier—meaning Wojinski—had to pull the pin on the grenade. Forgetting that step would be like throwing a rock at the bad guys. The safety handle of the grenade was held in place by the M7 device. When fired, it sprang open once in flight.

As a further complication, firing from the shoulder was prohibitively brutal. The M1 with grenade affixed had to be fired with the butt of the rifle placed on the ground and the barrel elevated up or down, left or right, exactly like employing a 60mm mortar without its bipod.

All of this was a lot to have to remember in the heat of battle. While handy weapons for paratroopers to take with them on a combat jump, rifle grenades were not very popular with the troopers who had to carry them. However, like all Raiding Forces personnel, Pvt. Wojinski was an expert with his individual weapon. When not in the field on an operation, he was required to train with it every day, firing inert grenades for practice.

At this range, the Ranger could drop a grenade in a 55-gallon drum. Lt. Bonham said, "We'll follow your lead, Wojinski."

The M1 fired. The blank made a flat bang, and the grenade was away. Lt. Bonham and Pvt. Isles immediately started blazing away at the trucks as fast as they could pull their weapon's triggers. The plan was to fire one round into the hood of each truck. It was questionable if they were going to do much damage, but since their orders were to start leap-frogging back to the Salerno beachhead the next night, any damage was good damage if it slowed down an element of the 16th Panzer Division's pursuit—even for a few hours.

The grenade flew through the air. Since it was not contact detonated, if it hit one of the fuel tanks it would bounce off and fall to the ground, where it would hopefully have enough explosive power to penetrate the metal once the four-second fuse cooked off. By the time the first grenade exploded, Pvt. Wojinski had a second on the way.

After Lt. Bonham had run through three 15-round magazines firing his M1 Carbine, nothing much was happening in the area of the fuel tanks other than a continuous string of thundering grenades. Except that now the Germans were beginning to return fire.

Lt. Bonham was being evaluated to see if he had the right stuff to become a full-fledged SOG officer to replace Captain Cord Granger— transferred out because of his promotion. Every SOG officer carried at least one magazine loaded all tracers—good for signaling targets during a firefight or starting fires from a distance. He inserted his.

Then Lt. Bonham began firing at the base of the nearest fuel storage tank. That was where there could be damage caused by Wojinski's grenades creating a leak. Almost instantly, he was rewarded by a flicker of flame. The fire ran up a river of fuel to the tank.

It exploded.

Lt. Bonham ordered, "Break contact—rally!"

He had already decided to go up and over the ridge, then down into the next valley, and cut back to the road to blow more trees.

His war was just getting started.

COLONEL JOHN RANDAL, CAPTAIN BILLY JACK JAXX, AND King patrolled up to the road bridge. One of Captain "Dynamite" Dick Coogan's men assigned to pull security challenged, "Drop Dead."

King on point responded, "Gorgeous."

The Ranger was not taking any chances. Nazis were known to be tricky. "Advance and be recognized."

Capt. Coogan appeared out of the dark to investigate the commotion. Col. Randal said, "Give me a report, Dick."

"We don't have enough C2 to bring down the bridge or even any large portion of it, sir. What we *can* do is make it impassable. We can also weaken the integrity of the piles so it won't be stable enough to handle tank traffic.

"The Nazis can bridge the gap if their engineers bring up heavy earth movers and bridging equipment. But they'll have to shore up the support structure if they want to move armored elements of the 16th Panzer Division across. That takes time, sir."

Col. Randal said, "How long?"

"A day. Maybe two, Colonel."

Col. Randal said, "Make it happen. The two bridges are our primary objectives. Meet me tomorrow morning at the highest elevation on the mountain due south of your position here."

"Yes, sir."

"Carry on, Captain."

At that moment, headlights appeared on the far side of the bridge.

Everyone took cover. Firing on the vehicle was not an option for fear of alerting the German guards. The vehicle, a Dodge command car captured from the British Eighth Army in Africa, still painted in tan colored desert camouflage, continued across—clearly unaware enemy paratroopers were hiding and watching.

It rolled on, turned right, and drove in the direction of Avellino. The car was only out of sight for a few minutes when a violent full-on rifle ambush was executed. Seconds later, three hand grenades exploded.

Then silence.

Col. Randal, Capt. Jaxx, and King began moving in the direction of the firing. It did not take long to come to the Dodge sitting stalled, blocked by trees felled across the road. The car was riddled with bullet holes. All three occupants—a lieutenant colonel, a captain, and the driver—were dead.

No sign of the ambushers. Long gone. Operating independently— whoever they were. Exactly as Major General Sam Houston Blackwell had predicted, "teenage paratroopers armed to the teeth without serious adult supervision roaming the Italian countryside."

Col. Randal liked the way the situation was developing. His men were adhering to orders. If these type actions were taking place all over Benevento Province, the 16th Panzer Division was about to be temporarily paralyzed.

Tiger tanks are not effective against guerrillas in the night.

MAJOR GENERAL SAM HOUSTON BLACKWELL ORDERED A photo reconnaissance mission be flown over Benevento Province at dawn. When it returned, he stood by at the base photo analysis dark room until the photographs were developed. The results were shocking. Parachutes could be seen on the ground spread out over a 250-square-mile area. One cluster of chutes was over 100 miles from the initial DZ where Bronc had put out Chalk1.

Maj. Gen. Blackwell had the 313th Troop Carrier Group Commanding

Officer and his three squadron commanders waiting in the Base Commander's office to review the photos. Bronc walked in, tossed them on the desk, and relieved all four officers on the spot.

No explanation needed. The pictures spoke for themselves.

FIELD REPORT FROM GENERAL MAJOR RUDOLF SIECKENIUS, Commanding, 16TH Panzer Division to Generaloberst Heinrich von Vietinghoff, Commanding, Tenth Army: "Large bands of American Paratroopers are marauding Benevento Province and the surrounding area, ambushing our motorcycle couriers, patrols, and truck convoys, planting road mines, blowing up bridges, cutting the rail line, and attacking outposts . . ."

With additional reports pouring in, Gen. von Vietinghoff quickly came to the conclusion, which he forwarded to Field Marshal Albert Kesselring aka "Smiling Al" at Tenth Army Headquarters, "At *least* one airborne division has landed in Benevento Province."

The Tenth Army Commander reacted with alacrity to this serious threat in the rear of his army. Tanks, Panzergrenadiers, artillery, armored cars, etc., en route to attack the U.S. Fifth Army at the Salerno bridgehead were turned around and ordered to perform anti-parachutist duty. Before the day had fully begun, heavily armed German battlegroups who should have been slamming into the beachhead were instead racing about the countryside searching fruitlessly for will-of-the wisp paratroopers who were nowhere to be found.

The Rangers were hiding in the mountains.

MAJOR GENERAL FRED WALKER, THE COMMANDING OFFICER of the U.S. 36TH Infantry "Texas" Division, made an entry in his private journal as he was having an early breakfast at his CP. It was a practice he performed periodically throughout the day. The notations reflected his personal views and were not intended for public consumption.

"Last night, an American Ranger Force of less than battalion strength was dropped around Benevento located 31 miles northwest of Salerno City. Since both ourselves and the British are on the defensive, I don't think the Rangers will be in action very long.

"They are strictly on their own."

COLONEL JOHN RANDAL WAS AT THE 4,000-FOOT PEAK OF an unnamed mountain, looking down at the Sabato River Valley. He was studying the terrain through his Zeiss binoculars captured at Calais. The railroad bridge had collapsed when a train attempted to cross it after Captain "Pyro" Percy Stirling had blown out a pair of support pilings. The train and approximately thirty cars were lying down below in the river.

Traffic was backed up at the road bridge, which was still standing. However, a large segment had been blown out on the south abutment, making it impassable.

For miles up and down the road, trees had been felled in clumps of six or eight—a lot of trees. The 16th Panzer Division was not going to be traveling this route anytime soon. With luck, the handful of secondary tracks in the province had received equal treatment overnight at the hands of roving bands of Rangers.

Single shots could be heard periodically, though exactly where they were coming from was hard to determine. Ranger riflemen at work. The AO was a target-rich environment. Col. Randal's troops were not willing to pass up the chance to take out a Nazi when the opportunity presented itself. Sniping during daylight hours was not strictly in accordance to his orders to hide during the day, but he was pleased with his mens' enterprise.

King walked up with three people. He and Captain Billy Jack Jaxx had been out on the ridge, looking for Rangers following orders to go high in the mountains to hide out before first light. When they found a team, they brought the leader to Col. Randal.

Orders had been not to form into groups of more than six men. The teams arriving were all smaller than that. The high altitude of the drop and winds aloft had really scattered the parachutes, making linking up difficult.

The three team leaders, Sergeant Willard Jones, Corporal Tommy Franklin and Corporal Gary Lazuli, were in good spirits. Col. Randal had each of them provide a brief description about their activities during the night.

All three had good stories.

Col. Randal listened intently, attempting to formulate an estimate of the situation. Tacticians never have all the information. The best are able to make the right decisions based on what limited intelligence they do possess. Military professionals call it "seeing over the hill."

His ability to see over the hill was one of the things that set him apart.

When the NCOs finished their reports, Col. Randal picked up a stick and started scratching out a diagram in the dirt. "I want you to spread your teams out like this. Tie in with the others that have already arrived—at a distance—barely in sight.

"Set up on the military crest of the ridge where you can observe two other teams. That way, the three teams will be mutually supporting but not close enough for you all to come under attack at the same time. In the event a German patrol comes up the mountain, it'll be taken under fire at maximum effective range by the first team that spots it.

"They'll engage, break contact, and pull back. As they're moving, when the enemy comes into sight, you fire, then fall back. While you're executing your retrograde movement, one of the other teams will open to cover you.

"Imagine a checkerboard. Your team is one checker. As the leader, you make your moves like you're playing the game—only making your moves backward. Engage, withdraw, set up, and be ready to engage again.

"Whatever happens, don't allow yourself to get committed to a firefight. In the event a major attack should develop, we'll all break contact and make a run for it over the ridge, remaining in our individual teams. We will stay to the forest and travel as far away from here as we can, always moving to the next high ground during daylight.

"Questions? If not, King will escort you to your position. Rest up—be ready. We'll all go our own way at dark—search and destroy, hit and run."

As the three NCOs and King were departing, Captain Billy Jack Jaxx walked up, having found no other groups of Rangers.

He said, "You used this checkerboard tactic against the Huks in the jungles, sir?"

Col. Randal said, "I did."

Capt. Jaxx said, "Hope you won't be offended by me pointing out that we're not in the jungle and those bad guys down there in the valley ain't Huks, sir—you sure your board game's going to work?"

Col. Randal said, "You have a better idea, Jack? There's only twenty-seven of us spread out for approximately two miles along the military crest of this mountain. And I have no idea where anyone else is we could bring in to boost our strength."

Capt. Jaxx said, "Don't worry—the boys are out there, sir. Laying up, making plans.

Hell-raising is on for tonight." Jack Cool.

15

ROLL TIDE

THE 16TH PANZER DIVISION HAD SEEN HEAVY COMBAT ON THE Eastern Front.

Essentially destroyed by nonstop combat against the Red Army, it had to be reconstituted with its surviving veteran troops as the cadre. This made for a dangerous combination—battle-wise old vets and bold young replacements.

It was a New Model division, meaning it was a combined arms team with tanks, artillery, mobile anti-aircraft guns, and mechanized infantry. Prewar German armored doctrine called for tanks to support. Under the New Model, tanks were supported.

The idea was maximum mobility, with all arms fully mechanized. This made for an agile, hard-hitting, armor-tipped fighting force. The combination proved extraordinarily successful. A German Panzer Division was virtually unstoppable, provided that mobility was retained. Take away their ability to maneuver, and tanks become nothing more than pillboxes. Mechanized infantry are reduced to straight leg infantry, and stationary self-propelled artillery become sitting targets that can be outranged by bigger, conventional guns.

Under normal conditions, lightly armed paratroopers did not stand a chance against panzers. However, in restrictive terrain as found in parts of Benevento Province, the 16th Panzer Division was channelized onto roads cutting through deep valleys encased in thickly wooded forests running up the sides of mountains. With the hardball blocked, the result was the same as if the panzers had run out of gas.

Until the roadblocks were cleared, 16th Panzer Division was not going anywhere.

As for the vaunted Panzergrenadiers, they were basically curb-to-curb fighting men— asphalt soldiers. Arguably, Panzergrenadiers were the toughest heavy infantry in the world. But being in a tank outfit, they were trained to ride into battle, dismount, and assault point-type targets from close range. Panzergrenadiers were not particularly skilled at patrolling or other light infantry tactics. They were not taught counterinsurgency and they preferred not to fight under cover of darkness, except in the attack against hard targets with direct support from the division's organic heavy weapons.

On the second night, improvised Molotov cocktails started to become the weapon of choice of 575th Ranger Force. Tanks, trucks, command cars, self-propelled guns, flak wagons, and anything on tracks or wheels stalled at a roadblock could expect a bottle of gasoline with a flaming rag stuffed in its neck to come flying out of the dark and smash into flames against their steel sides. There was nothing the Germans could do about it. Vast amounts of ammunition were expended, fired off in the night, but seldom was there anything to aim at.

The Rangers were gone.

No big targets were attacked. No major firefights developed. What was taking place were deadly pinprick strikes by little bands of paratroopers who had gone into business for themselves. The result for 16th Panzer Division was what the Chinese call "death by a thousand cuts."

It was working.

Colonel John Randal chose not to go down into the valley to the road as night fell. The hardball was so thoroughly blocked at this point that knocking down a few more trees would not significantly contribute to the course of the action. His plan was to stay where he was and observe developments from the mountain for a while, then move five miles south before daylight and set up near another high vantage point.

Benevento was a target-rich environment. By 2100 hours, fires were visible as far as he could see in a 180-degree arc. Explosions were cooking off like fireworks on the Fourth of July. Tracers zipped back and forth—red were Rangers, green/white were Nazis. Some of the fires, out of hearing distance, could be seen to silently explode, presumably when a gas tank or cargo of fuel or ammunition blew up.

Occasionally a German vehicle, identifiable by the slits of its cat's eye running lights, was visible racing down a road. Inevitably, it would come to a halt or be engulfed in an explosion. The Rangers deployed their lightweight No. 75 Hawkins mines, which were sometimes called grenades, everywhere they went. The mines were only capable of blowing the track off of a tank, but they were death on thin-skinned vehicles.

It was possible to watch the fires, strings of tracers glancing off hard objects ricocheting into the sky, and listen to distant explosions as they marched south. Rangers were leapfrogging back toward Salerno, leaving a trail of death and destruction in their wake. At the rate they were moving, if elements of Fifth Army did not advance and relieve them, it was going to take 575th Ranger Force at least a week from the time they dropped to reach friendly lines.

Col. Randal hoped his men were conserving their demolitions but had doubts. A lot of trees were down—maybe into the thousands on the primary roads. He wanted to be able to keep felling them for the next couple of nights. Then back off.

Blocking the roads between Benevento and the bridgehead was a double-edged sword. 575th Ranger Force needed to impede 16th Panzer Division's ability to pursue, while not preventing Fifth Army from advancing to relieve them.

U.S. Army commanders were not going to be thrilled when they hit those wall-to-wall obstacles created by the fallen trees.

Captain Billy Jack Jaxx said, "Sir, if you were the local German commander, what would you do to counter all these attacks?"

Col. Randal said, "I have no idea."

King said, "Nothing the Axis general can do except scream to his higher for reinforcements."

Col. Randal said, "That was the plan."

COLONEL JOHN RANDAL, CAPTAIN BILLY JACK JAXX, AND King moved off the mountain. Their intent was to travel a little over five miles to the highest peak on the next range. The distance was calculated as the crow flies. In the mountains, that is not how to get from point A to point B.

The march was a hard slog with a stiff climb at the end.

They avoided farmhouses and stayed off roads or trails. The idea was to slip unobserved to another place where they would have good observation of the Benevento AO. The only sign of life they encountered was a couple of dogs that barked as they made their way across a field.

The sound of distant gunfire and demolitions could still be heard as they traveled, however most of it was northwest, toward their rear. The Rangers were not slacking off one bit. While the actual number of casualties they were inflicting on the 16th Panzer Division was likely minimal, and the damage done to the road/rail infrastructure and landline communications was not catastrophic, it would have to be repaired.

That was going to cost the Germans time.

Beginning their climb through a thick forest on the far side of the valley, they came to a winding snakeback dirt track approximately a third of the way up the mountain. It was not indicated on the map, but there was nothing unusual about that. A lot of terrain features on the ground were not shown on the charts. That's what makes map reading as much of an art as it is a science—with a little crystal ball psychic ability being a plus.

King, on point, stopped and knelt to observe. From the left, the sound of an approaching vehicle was unmistakable. Col. Randal and Capt. Jaxx moved up on either side of the Merc. With no conscious thought or orders given, they silently established a linear ambush and stood by.

There was not long to wait. The cat's-eye blackout lights on a Volkswagen Kubelwagen rolled into view as it wheeled around the turn, driving toward the ambush site—entering the kill zone.

Four Panzergrenadiers were riding in the convertible. Col. Randal ordered, "Now!"

They stood, took dead aim, and opened with Col. Randal's and King's 9mm Beretta MAB-38 submachine guns and Capt. Jaxx's Baby BAR. It was point-blank range. The automatic weapons roared in the enclosed space created by the dense trees, sounding like a lot more than merely three shooters. Hit multiple times, the driver swerved hard and lost control and the car flipped, rolling.

King approached cautiously—no sense taking a chance and put a burst into each of the Nazis laying on the ground. Then he collected their weapons. Col. Randal searched the bodies for anything of intelligence value.

Capt. Jaxx began placing prepared charges from his M37 Demolition Kit on the trunks of four tall trees beside the road. As he worked, Col. Randal and King took up positions fifty yards out in each direction to provide security.

The road still being drivable when they reached it indicated they had traveled out in front of the scattered teams of Rangers working their way south toward friendly lines. It was a piece of information Col. Randal had not possessed previously. In addition to other things, it meant this track needed to be blocked even if it was not indicated on the map.

King heard movement. "Drop dead."

"Gorgeous."

"Move out in the open where I can see you."

Lieutenant Jake Novak, aka Jake the Snake, stepped out into the road. "Man, am I glad to see you, King."

"Anyone with you?"

"I've been chasing firefights ever since we jumped. You're the first Americans I've seen.

Ran into a few Nazis."

That was obvious. In addition to his .30 M1 Carbine, Lt. Novak had a pair of 9mm MP40 machine pistols hanging off his shoulders, a 9mm Walther P-38 stuck in the front of his pistol belt which contained his .45 Colt 1911, and German stick grenades protruding out of the leg pockets on the pants of his khaki jump suit. Plus, there was a jump knife strapped to his left boot.

Jake the Snake was dressed for success.

King said, "The Colonel is down the road. Stand by here with me. Capt. Jaxx is preparing to blow trees to set up a block."

From down the track came, "Fire in the hole."

Under normal conditions, that announcement would be repeated three times in a loud command voice, with the demolitions man turning in different directions each time he did. However, being behind enemy lines, Capt. Jaxx gave a single warning. The warning was barely louder than a whisper. Not that it mattered, with all the firing that had taken place.

A daisy chain of sharp explosions rippled like a string of dominoes. The tall trees swayed. Then in slow motion, they began falling across the road.

Jake the Snake, being an Alabama native, said, "Roll Tide."

No one would be driving this track anytime soon without a lot of effort to clear the block first.

The four of them were moving up the mountain again within minutes of the last tree hitting the ground. Not much time was spent on greeting Lt. Novak. That's how it worked at night following a combat jump. People appeared and disappeared without explanation.

The line of march was tough going, but the trees thinned out somewhat at the crest. In the distance, the Rangers were still setting demolitions. Tracers streaked lazily as if searching, until they blinked out.

From a distance, the phosphorous rounds looked beautiful, not dangerous.

King and Capt. Jaxx spread out in different directions to be on the lookout for Ranger teams that might be moving to high ground. Col. Randal took a position and debriefed Lt. Novak.

The 509th PIB Pathfinder Platoon Leader did not have much of intelligence value to report. He had dropped, found himself all alone, started moving south, heard firefights that were over by the time he could reach them, and had shot five Panzergrenadiers in three different encounters. During the day, he had moved deep into the forest to hide out.

Lt. Novak had seen six months of close combat in North Africa. He had raised and trained the specialist Pathfinder Platoon made up of triple volunteers—for the army, for the paratroops, for Pathfinders. While his actions so far on the Benevento jump were nothing more than expected of every man in 575th Ranger Force, he was exactly the type of officer Col. Randal was looking for—judgment, initiative, and the desire to accomplish the mission even when all alone.

Nothing seemed to rattle him.

Rangers began drifting up the mountain. By dawn, eight teams had reported in, averaging four men per team. They were spread out along the ridge line in the two-tier checkerboard pattern, with half the teams down the slope below the military crest of the mountain and the other half along the ridgeline.

When Captain Roy Kidd arrived, he brought in two stragglers from the 509th PIB. The paratroopers walked over to report to Col. Randal. One of them shouted, "It's Jake the Snake!"

Lt. Novak said, "What are you gents doing in this part of the world?"

Pvt. Willie Johannsen said, "We're ex-POWs, sir. Me and Don are Headquarters Company boys. We was on the plane with Colonel Yardley. Before the battalion took off, the Colonel called a formation—told everybody, "Don't get captured and don't get shot in the ass."

Pvt. Don Watkins said, "Trying to make a pre-jump joke, sir."

Pvt. Johannsen said, "Some joke! Within thirty minutes after we dropped, he'd been shot in the ass *and* captured."

Pvt. Watkins said, "Yeah, us *with* him too."

"The Nazis loaded the three of us on a truck and boogied out of there,"

Pvt. Johannsen said. "We was in the back with no guard. The Colonel ordered us to bail out, so we did."

Pvt. Watkins said, "Truck never slowed down. Didn't know we was gone. We've been MIA—escaping and evading ever since."

Lt. Novak said, "Yardley hit bad?"

"He was in a lot of pain, Lieutenant—couldn't come with us," Pvt. Johannsen said.

Col. Randal asked, "How did Colonel Yardley get shot?"

Pvt. Watkins said, "About thirty of us men landed on the DZ at Avellino next to the Pathfinders about a mile from town—the Colonel with us."

"Our orders was to capture Avellino and hold it for four or five days—something like that," Pvt. Johannsen said. "Colonel Yardley said to follow him. We marched straight there.

"And that was that."

COLONEL JOHN RANDAL CALLED A LEADERS' CONFERENCE. Lieutenant Jake Novak, aka Jake the Snake, was given the two 509th paratroopers to form a team, so he was in attendance. That meant now there were twelve raiding parties on the mountain, averaging four men per. By this point, the Rangers were running low on just about everything.

Col. Randal made the decision to continue operations one more night; then acting independently, the raiding parties would begin to E&E (Escape & Evade) back to friendly lines. There were three reasons he made the call. One, going to high ground was a pattern he wanted to break. The Germans were good at spotting tendencies and could be expected to react to it. Two, he was ready to bring his men out after their having inflicted as much damage as they had. Three, he felt like Ranger Force had pressed its luck—it was time to go.

Col. Randal wished there was some way to communicate his desire with the other parties scattered across the countryside, but that was impossible.

Reentering the lines was going to be tricky. No one knew where the friendly lines were. They did not know what division's lines they would be reentering. And they did not have the password.

Frontline troops tend to shoot first and ask questions later. It was not unknown for spooked soldiers to fire a round, then call out, "Halt, who goes there?" Any U.S. Army soldier who had spent time in the Salerno beachhead had a right to be a little edgy.

As Captain "Geronimo" Joe McKoy liked to say, "Friendly fire ain't friendly."

Returning to the Fifth Army lines following the Benevento operation was one of those things that had not been adequately thought through in the mad rush to get the mission underway.

Meaning it had not been thought through at all.

Col. Randal issued a frag order to the team leaders, who ranged in grade from Private First Class to Captain. He had a lot to cover, but because of the disparity in ranks he followed the Raiding Forces Rule to "Keep it Short and Simple."

"Situation: We're on a mountain in Benevento Province. We're behind enemy lines . . . or maybe not—that's not exactly clear. We don't know where the friendly lines are. It's possible we're approaching Fifth Army elements pushing out from the beachhead. For all we know, our people may be over the next ridge or around the next bend in the road.

"We could have passed through friendly lines and not realized it.

"Mission: Stay in your positions throughout the day. Tonight, team leaders will take charge of their teams and conduct a final night of raiding targets of opportunity. Then, instead of moving high in the mountains to a Rally Point, sticking to the forest, you're to travel southeast independently and keep going until you reach friendly lines.

"Execution: For the rest of the day, be prepared to execute a checkerboard type ambush in the event our position here should come under ground attack.

"Concept of the Operation: The first patrol to spot an enemy force approaching will take it under fire at the maximum effective range. Fire, fall back, and take up another position. Adjoining patrols will engage the Germans as soon as they come into view. Then they too will disengage, leapfrog back, and set up again.

"The idea is to inflict casualties on the Panzergrenadiers so they will have to evacuate and to exhaust them by making them continue the attack uphill once they have reached their initial objective. Then be forced to attack over and over and over, nonstop, as we continue to conduct a fighting withdrawal.

"If no attack develops, tonight as briefed you will take your teams, move over the ridge, go down into the next valley, and travel southwest toward our friendly lines, engaging targets of opportunity as you go.

"Command and Signal: In the event we come under attack here—if I fire a full magazine of tracers straight up in the air, that's the signal to break contact immediately. Take your teams, move out, drop down the far side of the mountain, and keep going. Do not regroup.

"What are your questions?"

.

THE PANZERGRENADIERS CAME FOR THEM AT 1715 HOURS. THE first indication was a single rifle shot from a .30 caliber M1 Garand fired by one of the teams near the center of the position. A fusillade of German submachine guns the Rangers called "burp guns" returned fire. This was the Panzergrenadiers' favorite tactic—spray any opposition with automatic weapons fire, then immediately follow up with an assault.

Exactly what Colonel John Randal had been counting on them to do.

Unfortunately for the Panzergrenadiers, they had to attack uphill and they had to expose themselves when they launched what they expected to be their "final assault" on a lone unit of *Amis* numbering a handful of men. When the Nazis stood up, not only were they fired on by the first team that spotted them, but they were observed by a second team 200 yards to left who also engaged.

The Rangers were exceptional marksmen. Most were armed with the excellent .30 caliber M1 Garand rifle. Any Nazi who showed himself at under 400 yards was dead.

Captain Billy Jack Jaxx was resting his Baby BAR over a rock, hoping for a target. "Where did those Nazis come from?"

Col. Randal said, "Probably found the Kubelwagen we shot up. Tracked us up the mountain. My guess is the local commander would not have sent more than a platoon to deal with what he'd expect to be five or six parachutists."

The firing died out almost as soon as it had started. The first team immediately moved back past the second echelon of teams and took up another firing position. The second team that had engaged remained in place, awaiting developments.

Panzergrenadiers are aggressive fighters. These were well-trained and well-led. They went to ground and pulled back out of sight in good order, taking their casualties with them.

Then all was quiet.

Thirty minutes later, having regrouped and reorganized, the Germans tried again. They slid to the left for 400 yards, moving closer to where Col. Randal, Capt. Jaxx, and King were located. Thinking they had flanked the Rangers that had fired on them, the Panzergrenadiers stood up and assaulted behind a blazing barrage of submachine gun fire, which—while noisy— was ineffective.

There were three problems with this maneuver. The Germans had not flanked anything. In fact, they had unknowingly moved closer into the center of the Rangers' position. Their 9mm burp guns were out of range. And they had unwittingly exposed *their* flank to a third Ranger team that immediately took them under enfilading fire, knocking down Nazis like bowling pins.

The Panzergrenadiers went to the ground again.

Both Ranger teams used the opportunity to leapfrog back. Now, unknown to the Germans, they faced a concave formation of small teams spread out on a line for nearly two miles. No platoon can attack over open ground uphill near the crest of a mountain with scant tree cover and not suffer severe losses.

While the numbers were roughly equal on both sides, the Panzergrenadiers were ensnared by superior tactics. Any move they made subjected them to accurate fire. It was not possible for the German commander to estimate the size of the force he was up against.

From his perspective on the side of a mountain, with no reinforcements or indirect fire support, it seemed like he was up against the entire U.S. Army.

More time went by as the Panzergrenadiers contemplated their next move. The sun was beginning to set. Suddenly, right in front of Col. Randal's position, the Germans stood up. Firing as they came, they assaulted straight up the mountain, thinking once again they had outflanked the Rangers.

They were shooting at an angle back toward the location of the last team that had fired on them. That team was no longer there, but the Nazis had no way of knowing that. That was the beauty of the orders to fire and fall back.

The assault line was out of range for Col. Randal and King's 9mm Beretta MAB-38 submachine guns. Capt. Jaxx, however, was in a perfect firing position. He opened with his Baby BAR on semi-automatic calling his shots.

The team to the left and the team to the right joined in. It was not the heavy fire. But it was accurate.

No unit can suffer the percentage of casualties the Panzergrenadiers took in a matter of seconds and still be combat effective. With nightfall looming, dead and wounded piling up and needing to be evacuated, the German platoon commander, a seasoned veteran of three years fighting on the Eastern Front, made a tactical decision. He concluded discretion was the better part of valor, considering his troops had attempted three attacks and never made it out of their start position on any of them.

The tough veteran of the vicious fighting in Russia knew he was outclassed—this was not his day.

Col. Randal pointed his 9mm Beretta SMG straight up and let off a 30-round magazine of red tracers.

"Let's get the hell out of Dodge."

COLONEL JOHN RANDAL, CAPTAIN BILLY JACK JAXX, AND King went over the crest of the mountain. Then straight downhill. According to the map, from this point on, they could expect heavy forest and less mountainous terrain moving toward the coastal plains.

They traveled all night.

As dawn pinkened the sky, they stumbled onto a dirt track. Moving along a road is a good way to run into people you do not want to meet if you are behind enemy lines or think you are. So, staying to the woods, they paralleled it.

Coming around a bend, parked in the road the three saw a U.S. Army Jeep. It had a .30 caliber Browning M1919 air-cooled machine gun mounted on a pedestal, pointed in their general direction. Where there was a vehicle in plain view, it was to be expected that there were other soldiers in concealment covering it.

Col. Randal called, "575th Ranger Force."

"Step out in the road, Ranger."

Since he was armed with a U.S. Army-issue weapon and Col. Randal and King were carrying Italian submachine guns, Capt. Jaxx walked out into the open with his hands in the air.

"Don't shoot. There's three of us. We don't have the password."

"Come on in, but keep it slow, Mac."

Col. Randal and King stepped out of the woods, making sure their weapons were slung across their backs out of sight. This would not be the time for confusion. Why take a chance? "Friendly fire ain't friendly" was not a Raiding Forces Rule, but it might as well have been.

"Identify yourself."

"I'm Colonel Randal. This is Captain Jaxx. And King here is my bodyguard."

"You're Colonel Randal?"

"Roger that."

"Come on in, Colonel, we've been looking for you, sir."

"Who might you be?"

"Major Odell Rankin, sir, S-2 of the 180th Regiment, 45th Division—the Thunderbirds. Welcome back. My orders are to scoop you up and escort you to Division immediately, if you came through this checkpoint. We've got people out looking for you all along the Forward Edge of the Battle Area."

Col. Randal said, "What's this about?"

"There's a general at GHQ raising hell for us to locate you, Colonel. He's got the best- looking blonde with him I've ever seen in my life—looks like a movie star. You have something going with her, sir?"

"Not exactly."

"That's too bad, Colonel."

They climbed in the jeep and went tearing down the road. A trail of red dust followed them. Not a good thing on the forward edge of the battle area (FEBA).

A German forward observer spotted the dust cloud. He called for a fire mission. A barrage of 150mm rounds from a six barreled Nebelwerfer-41 screamed in, leaving no doubt as to why the weapon was called a "Moaning Minnie." They exploded in the road behind them.

All that did was motivate the driver to put the hammer down and go faster.

When the jeep pulled up at T-Bird Forward, the 45th Division HQ, Col. Randal was rushed inside. Major General Sam Houston Blackwell and his daughter were in the Tactical Operations Center. Beverly hugged him around the neck—he could feel her heart pounding.

"What took you so long?"

"Well, we . . ."

Maj. Gen. Blackwell said, "Brandenburger Commandos landed on

Castelrozzo last night, Colonel."

Beverly said, "Lady Jane's Missing in Action."

TO BE CONTINUED IN THE WAR THAT NEVER WAS
~ BOOK XV IN THE RAIDING FORCES SERIES ~

~ ~

The Raiding Forces Series continues . . . all the way to VE Day.
To be on our notification list for the next book, contact <u>phil@philward.com</u>.

ABBREVIATIONS
ORDERS & AWARDS

Bt   Baronet
CB   Companion of the Bath
CMG   Companion of the Order of St. Michael & St. George
DCM   Distinguished Conduct Medal: Awarded to noncommissioned
            officers for distinguished conduct in action in the field.
DFC   Distinguished Flying Cross (Royal Air Force)
DSC   Distinguished Service Cross (Royal Navy)
DSM   Distinguished Service Medal: Awarded to ranks up to and
            including Chief Petty
DSO   Distinguished Service Order
GC   George Cross
GCB   Grand Cross in the Order of the Bath
GM   George Medal
KBE   Knight Commander of the Most Excellent Order of the British
            Empire
KCVO   Knight Commander of the Royal Victorian Order
LG   Lady Companion of the Order of the Garter
MC   Military Cross
MM   Military Medal
MVO   Member of the Royal Victorian Order
OBE   Order of the British Empire
SS   Silver Star Medal
VC   Victoria Cross

ACRONYMS

ABC	RFHQ Advanced Base Castelrozzo
AMPC	auxiliary military pioneer Corps
AO	Area of Operation
BAR	Browning Automatic Rifle
BDU	Battle Dress Uniform
BJ	Beach Jumper
BMNT	Beginning Morning Nautical Twilight
CBTC	Commando Basic Training Center
CG	Commander General
DCO	Director of Combined Operations
DRT	Dog–Roger–Tare – Dead Right There
DZ	Drop Zone
E&E	Evasion and Escape
GHQ	General Headquarters
GSS	Greek Sacred Squadron
HDML	Harbor Defense Motor Launch
HEAT	High Explosive Anti-Tank
HQ	Headquarters
IPC	Independent Parachute Company
ISLD	Inner Services Liaison Department
KP	Kitchen Police
LCI	Landing Craft Infantry
LD	Line of Departure
LFP	Levant Fishing Patrol
LMG	Light Machine Gun
LRDG	Long Range Desert Group
LSF	Levant Schooner Flotilla
MAS boat	*Motoscafo armato silurante* (torpedo armed motorboat)
MGB	Motor Gun Boat
MEHQ	LMiddle East Command Headquarters
MI	Military Intelligence
MIA	Missing in Action

MU	Martine Unit
NAF	Naval Aircraft Factory
NG	National Guard
NID	Naval Intelligence Division
NOIC	Naval Officer in Command Cyprus
OG	Operational Group
OIC	Officer in Charge
OJT	On–the–Job–Training
OP	Observation Post
OSS	Office of Strategic Services (The Outfit)
PAX	passengers10
PBY	Patrol Bomber
PFT	Pathfinder Team
PIB	Pathfinder Infantry Battalion
PIR	Parachute Infantry Regiment
PLF	Parachute Landing Fall
PM	Prime Minister
POL	Petroleum, Oil, and Lubricants
PSTO	Principal Sea Transport Officer
PT	Patrol Torpedo (boat)
PWE	Political Warfare Executive
RAF	Royal Air Force
RFHQ	Raiding Forces Headquarters
RMBPD	Royal Marine Boom Patrol Detachment
RVP	rendezvous point
SAS	Special Air Service
SBS	Special Boat Section
SD	Security Police
SDB	Seaward Defense Boat
SI	Secret Intelligence
SIME	Security Intelligence Middle East
SIS	Secret Intelligence Service
SMG	Small Machine Gun
SO	Secret Operations
SO	Special Operations
SOE	Special Operations Executive

SOG	Small Operations Group 1
SRI	Small Raids Incorporated front
SS	Protective Service
STEAL	Strategic Taking and Extracting to an Alternate Location
TO&E	table of organization and equipment
WIA	Wounded in Action
XO	Executive Officer

LIST OF CHARACTERS

AB Damian Smith Alex "Cat" Gataki

Alexandra (Mandy) Paige, OBE, RM

Beverly Blackwell, SS

Brandy Seaborn, GC

Brig. Dudley Clarke

Brig. Raymond J. "R. J." Maunsell

Brig. Stewart Menzies, DSO

Brig. Gen. Maxwell Taylor

Brig. Gen. William "Wild Bill" Donovan

Buck Meredith

Capt. Billy Jack Jaxx, MC, SSM

Capt. Butch "Headhunter" Hoolihan, DSO, MC, MM, RM

Capt. Cord Granger

Capt. Cuthbert Bowlby aka Curly, RN

Capt. "Dynamite" Dick Coogan

Capt. "Geronimo" Joe McKoy

Capt. Hawthorne Merryweather

Capt. Karen Montgomery

Capt. M. H. S. McDonald aka Snow White

Capt. Lionel Chatterhorn

Capt. Pamala Plum-Martin, DSO, OBE, DFC, RM

Capt. Penelope "Legs" Honeycutt-Parker, OBE, GM, RM

Capt. Preston Butterfield III

Capt. "Pyro" Percy Stirling, DSO, MC

Capt. Roy Kidd, MC

Capt. Roy "Mad Dog" Reupart

Capt. Stephanie Fawcett-Tatum, RM

Capt. William Patterson

Cdr. Gen. Frank Polanski

Col. Douglas Turnbull

Col. James M. "Jumping Jim" Gavin

Col. John Randal, DSO, OBE, DSC, MC

Col. Ruben Tucker

Corp. Gary Lazuli Corp.

Joe Henderson

Corp. Leslie Cooper

Corp. Matt Jefferson

Corp. Ralph Jenkins

Corp. Tom Murphy aka Murph the Surf

Corp. Tommy Franklin

CWO Hank W. Rawlston

Dr. Layton Winthrop

Ens. Theodore "The Great Teddy" Hamilton, OBE

Fg. Off. Peter Sturgis

Fg. Off. William Lansdale Flanigan

Guido "GG" Grazinni, MC

Happy

King

Lana Turner

Lt. Bentley St. Ledger, RM

Lt. Chase Starrett

Lt. Clint Hays

Lt. Dan Bonham

Lt. Douglas Fairbanks, Jr., USNR

Lt. Jake Novak aka Jake the Snake

Lt. Paul Duncan

Lt. Randy "Hornblower" Seaborn, DSO, OBE, DSC, RN

Lt. Tremaine Burnet

Lt. Cdr. Adrian Seligman

Lt. Col. David "Big Sloth" Stirling

Lt. Col. Guy Prendergast

Lt. Col. H. J. "Kid" Cator

Lt. Col. Sir Terry "Zorro" Stone, KBE, DSO, MC

Lt. Col. William P. Yarborough

Lt. Gen. George S. Patton

LtJG Jackson Taylor, USNR

Maj. Zargo

Maj. A. W. "Sammy" Sansom

Maj. Baltimore "Mongo" Farquhar, MC

Maj. Clive Adair

Maj. Duke Slater

Maj. Jack Dance

Maj. Jeb Pelham-Davies, DSO, MC

Maj. Odell Rankin

Maj. Taylor Corrigan, DSO, MC

Maj. Travis McCloud

Major General Ernest Dawley

Maj. Gen. Fred Walker

Maj. Gen. Mark Clark

Maj. Gen. Matthew B. Ridgway

Maj. Gen. Sam Houston "Bronc" Blackwell

Major the Earl George Jellicoe, DSO, MC

Major the Lady Jane Seaborn, LG, OBE, RM

Moe

Mr. Valerian Lada Mocarski

MSgt. Mack Beckwith

PFC Bronson

PFC David Marko

PFC Hale

PFC Wally Malinowski

Pvt. Dave Rickles

Pvt. Don Watkins

Pvt. Doyle

Pvt. Mark Loewenberg

Pvt. Martagree

Pvt. Norm Wojinski

Pvt. Norvel Hansen aka Horn Dog

Pvt. Samuel Isles
Pvt. Willie Johannsen
Pvt. Zeke Swearington
Red the Clipper Girl
Rikke (Rocky) Runborg
Rita Hayworth
Rodger from Chicago
Scout Lionel Fenwick
Scout Munro Ferguson
Sgt. Frank Hawkins, MM
Sgt. Roy Dunlop
Sgt. Tim Authury, MM
Sgt. Willard Jones
Sgt. Maj. Mike "March or Die" Mikkalis, MC, DCM, MM
Sgt. Fred Waltmier
T/Sgt. Ronnie Allred
VAdm. Sir Randolph "Razor" Ransom, VC, KCB, DSO, OBE, DSC, RN
Veronica Paige, OBE
Waldo Treywick
Wg. Cdr. Paddy Wilcox, DSO, OBE, MC, DFC
Wg. Cdr. Tony Dudgeon

ABOUT THE AUTHOR

Phil Ward is a decorated combat veteran commissioned at nineteen. A former instructor at the Army Ranger School, he has had a lifelong interest in small unit tactics and special operations. He lives in Texas on a mountain overlooking Lake Austin.

~~

OTHER BOOKS IN THE RAIDING FORCES SERIES:

Those Who Dare

Dead Eagles

Blood Wings

Roman Candle

Guerrilla Command

Necessary Force

Desert Patrol

Private Army

Africa 1941

The Sharp End

Raiding Rommel

Strategic Services

Tip of the Sword